LINDEN HIGH SCHOOL LIBRARY

"I JUST WANT YOU TO KNOW THAT THE IMPORTANCE OF THIS ASSIGNMENT HAS BEEN NOTED AT THE HIGHEST LEVEL OF GOVERNMENT. THE *HIGHEST*."

Jude's temper reached its breaking point. "Man, oh, man, this is too much!" he exploded. "First, you people kick me out. Then, after several years of pretending I don't exist, you suddenly show up and want me to do something like this! Not only that, but you don't *ASK* me to volunteer, you twist my arm! What makes you so certain I won't screw it up just to get back at you?"

Armstead stared at Jude for several seconds before answering. "Reasonable question," he said finally. "But we've thought of that, too. First, the warrant against Molly Silva can be resurrected. Second, you're still too much of a pro to deliberately screw it up—your professional instincts wouldn't let you. And third—" Armstead smiled broadly "—even if you managed to botch the job, the Russians wouldn't let you out alive. Now that's the kind of incentive a man responds to, don't you think?"

BURIAL IN MOSCOW

P9-DMO-302

By the same author:
Blood of the Eagle

DISCARD

FRED DICKEY

BURIAL IN MOSCOW

Linden High School Library
7201 Silver Lake Road
Linden, Michigan 48451

WORLDWIDE.

TORONTO • NEW YORK • LONDON • PARIS
AMSTERDAM • STOCKHOLM • HAMBURG
ATHENS • MILAN • TOKYO • SYDNEY

BURIAL IN MOSCOW

A Worldwide Library Book/January 1988

ISBN 0-373-97053-6

Copyright © 1988 by Fred Dickey. All rights reserved.
Philippine copyright 1988. Australian copyright 1988.
Except for use in any review, the reproduction or utilization of
this work in whole or in part in any form by any electronic,
mechanical or other means, now known or hereafter invented,
including xerography, photocopying and recording, or in any
information storage or retrieval system, is forbidden without
the permission of the publisher, Worldwide Library,
225 Duncan Mill Road, Don Mills, Ontario, Canada M3B 3K9.

All the characters in this book have no existence outside the
imagination of the author and have no relation whatsoever to
anyone bearing the same name or names. They are not even
distantly inspired by any individual known or unknown to the
author, and all incidents are pure invention.

® are Trademarks registered in the United States Patent and
Trademark Office and in other countries.

Printed in U.S.A.

BURIAL
IN
MOSCOW

CHAPTER ONE

THE SHADOWS OF EVENING closed over the stadium like a strangler's hand, the long fingers clutching in a tightening grip of gray.

While the screams of thousands of sports fans in the stands made the concrete supports far below seem to vibrate with echoes, Jude Miller huddled in a hidden corner and watched as two men faced each other among the dark recesses of the pillars. Both seemed typical of the crowd: ordinary people dressed casually, in search of weekend diversion at a sporting event. Jude couldn't see their faces, but he could tell from their bearing that one was short and middle-aged, the other tall, probably in his late twenties, with one hand in a jacket pocket. Nothing was unusual except their presence in the otherwise deserted bowels of the stadium, strangers meeting as though in a private room.

The older man handed his companion a small package, which was immediately pocketed, then turned and started to walk away. He had gone just a few steps when the other quickly slipped a plastic surgical mask over his own nose and mouth and pulled his hand from its pocket hiding place to reveal it encased in a rubber glove and holding a tiny aerosol bottle. He moved toward the back of the other man with the purposeful speed of the practiced stalker. He clamped a long arm around the neck of his surprised prey with a pitiless force that jerked the shorter man's feet off the ground. In the same motion, he swept the bottle around and jammed it into the helpless man's mouth, holding it there for long seconds. The victim tugged with fluttering fingers at the iron vise that held his throat, and his feet jerked as if in a gallow's dance.

The faint odor of bitter almond told Jude what was happening—hydrocyanic acid—and he sadly watched the inevitable unfold. The poison hit the man's system with the force of a concrete fist, and immediately shut off air supply to his body's cells. In the first few seconds, he began gasping desperately as his body fought for air that it could no longer use. His arms waved weakly and aimlessly and his legs turned to rubber. Unconsciousness followed quickly, accompanied by desperate spastic convulsions as his muscles and nerves protested with their last strength at the trauma they had been forced to endure. The cardiac arrest that occurred within sixty seconds was merciful as the tortured body became the loser in a hopeless fight.

The assailant lowered the dead body to the ground with an ironic gentleness. With the speed that comes with knowing an exact routine, he removed a whiskey bottle from his jacket, poured some down the dead man's throat and smashed the bottle directly beside the man's face. Jude realized he was using the liquor to disguise the faint odor of cyanide. He felt himself nodding involuntarily in acknowledgement of the assassin's skill, because he knew the highly professional job would fool the average medical examiner into believing this was a routine heart attack—just another crazy fan getting carried away.

Jude looked on with bitter sadness as the lifeless form lay crumpled on the concrete, deprived of the spark, the essence of life that, when so cruelly ripped out of him, left only a puppet with broken strings. He shuddered at the indignity and offered belated sympathy to the man. Had he been a kind father? A fellow with whom you would like to share a beer? A guy always ready with a new joke? Jude felt anger at what humans do to humans, and a deep sorrow that it needn't be.

The assassin matter-of-factly put the utensils of his murder into a plastic bag, pocketed it and started to saunter toward the exit in Jude's direction. As the man neared the light, Jude recoiled in fright that he might be seen, and with mounting panic he looked in vain toward the surrounding girders that teased with their thinness and offered no protection. Jude went limp with the knowledge he was about to come face-to-face with the killer, and threw up a desperate prayer that the man would pass him by and disappear forever into the fogbank of a bad memory. But, slowly, the killer's body moved out of the shadows. Starting with his feet, the light gradually moved up his long, slim frame until he stood revealed in the dim light of dusk. Jude then knew his identity.

It was himself.

THE RAW WIND ROARED off the Pacific like a river in flood, defying anything to withstand it. It swept up the Big Sur mountain slopes, through the cedars and pines that groaned in patient protest at the whistling intrusion, through the small clearing in the forest, and slammed against the side of Jude's cabin. The wind hammered the weathered, rough siding of the simple little house and invaded through the numerous cracks where it spent itself by flaring the fireplace coals with a final weak draft.

Jude's tense, sweaty body jerked awake to escape his nightmare and he looked wildly around him, still alert to the danger his mind had just encountered. He relaxed as he became aware of the familiarity of his own home. Gratefully, he pushed the contrails of the familiar bad dream from his mind, and stretched out in the old-fashioned double bed. He pressed closely against the sleeping body of Molly, and enjoyed his cozy refuge under the heavy quilt.

Jude opened his senses to the rustic cabin for reassurance. He inhaled deeply to absorb the pungent pine fragrance coming from the stone fireplace across the room and blending with the smell of baked bread that had come out of the ancient oven the evening before.

His eyes swept the large room dimly lit by the softly glowing fire and the moonlight streaming through the windows. The simple place he had come to love as an anchor of his second life passed under his gaze. He thought to himself that the most lavish room he had entered in his previous life was not nearly so loved as this plain room and its simple utensils. His look of affection caressed the old-style water faucet silhouetted in the corner atop the sink, which brought cold, clear water from the deep well behind the cabin through pipes that knocked like a bass drum; the hand loom that Molly operated like a harpsichord on quiet evenings; the rough but comfortable furniture, either picked up at swap meets or crudely but painstakingly built by his own hands out of redwood burls. Jude and Molly talked of adding a dishwasher and color TV whenever his small salary as a Russian instructor at a nearby college and smaller-yet CIA pension, and her wages earned aboard a fishing boat might allow. But they also recognized that a color TV might lead to a VCR, and to other gadgets, and they really weren't willing for the tendrils of materialism to curl around even their ankles.

The lulling howl of the wind was to Jude a voice of reassurance that the dangers and fears of the world of people would not invade this secure place, and as he looked upward out of the window above the bed, he yearned to believe that the stars of the winter night would cover him and Molly with the protection of their tranquillity and keep evil away.

Despite the comfort in his surroundings, Jude's mind kept returning to the letter.

His apprehensions caused him to thrash in frustration, and he twisted his head and found himself looking into Molly's face. She was no longer sleeping. Her large brown eyes were staring intently but with understanding and sympathy at his discomfort.

She reached out and gently ran her work-coarsened hand down his rough cheek. "You're bothered by the letter, aren't you?" she asked, sympathy coating her voice with love and support. "Want to talk about it?"

"Not now, not tonight. No point in both of us worrying," Jude said and reached out and placed his hand on her round, tanned face. He stroked the braided black hair bestowed by her Portuguese genes, then reached over and hugged her.

"Loving someone earns you the right to worry with them," she said, adjusting her position in the bed to accommodate his embrace. She wiggled nearer. "Meantime, I know how to get your mind off it."

He reached up and took her warm face in his hands and slowly pulled her closer to him. Suddenly, magically, her body, which had grown strong and hard from the grueling rigors of the fishing boat, turned into warm, yielding softness. He lifted the bottom of the nightgown and she arched her hips as he slipped it up her body. He pushed down his own underwear and they were lying together, warmth to warmth, softness to hardness. He caressed her breasts; they were full but also firm, in the way of a hardy young woman who has never borne children.

Slowly he slid his lips down her body until they rested atop the mound of soft black hair, and the scent of her musk filled his nostrils like some sweet, primordial perfume. He gently touched her thighs; she recognized the signal and parted them, shuddering in anticipation of what was about to happen. He placed his lips over the milky softness and massaged her with his tongue. Somewhere above him she was moaning, and he felt her hips begin to gyrate as the feverish feeling reached her, and the excitement touched him as well. When her moans turned to quick, hard gasps, he raised up and entered her as she spread her legs wide apart. It was quick but very sweet; they were lovers who had nothing to prove to each other. After several hard thrusts, Jude felt the familiar—but always new—rush of passion spread through his lower body and propel him toward that moment when all other consciousness would be lost in his heat. She sensed what was coming and the thought of him receiving pleasure from her body, in turn set off a reaction in her. Together, they surrendered to the moment, and the moment repaid their desire.

THE FIRST LIGHT OF MORNING was filtering into the cold cabin as Jude climbed over the sleeping Molly and quickly put on threadbare jeans and a patched wool shirt. He greeted himself by pausing in front of a small mirror hung near the sink. He ran his fingers over a three-day growth of blue-black beard and thought perhaps he might shave within the next few days. He surveyed his sharp features with the satisfaction of having been told by many women that he was a handsome man. Although he could ordinarily walk down a street unnoticed, a closer scrutiny, perhaps under candlelight, gave his deep-set dark eyes, thin lips, bushy eyebrows, curly black hair and aquiline nose a classical Greek look. Given the proper romantic setting, he generated a brooding aura that seemed to excite women, a tendency he was too polite to discourage.

Jude dropped more wood on the glowing embers of the fire in the fireplace, blew patiently until a flame sprang to life, then walked over to the propane stove and broke several eggs for scrambling. He stirred the food and pushed other thoughts aside. Morning was his favorite time, when the cold of the cabin made it a sweet pain to climb from a warm bed, and the awakened sun penetrated the cabin like golden beams from a lighthouse of the gods. He was at home in his refuge from the pain and bad memories that prowled impatiently just beyond the edge of the forest.

He turned at the sound of Molly restlessly tossing in her sleep, on the verge of awakening. He studied the form hud-

dled under the blankets and smiled to himself. She had been
his reminder of how nice life could be ever since she entered
his with a giggle.

Jude's thoughts drifted back to the day about a year ago
when Molly approached him in the seedy little neighborhood bar in Santa Cruz where he had gone for a quiet beer.
She was playing shuffleboard with some barstool cowboy who
was working hard at trying to pick her up. Jude was absently
listening to the marshmallow lyrics of a country song on the
jukebox and politely ignoring the regulars seated along the bar
who were eager to talk about baseball, politics, ex-wives and
other trivia of interest to them. Jude had lowered the blinds
of his consciousness and blocked it all out and contentedly
submerged his mind into that tank of quietude from which
no bubbles escape. He was deep into his favorite haunt—his
own memories—when laughter that sounded like wind
chimes compelled him to turn around on the stool and look
at a woman leaning against the far wall holding a beer. She
appeared a little on the light side of thirty and was dressed in
jeans, plaid shirt, cowboy boots and hat. Her shimmering hair
was braided and her slightly plump figure testified to more
beer and peanuts than she probably needed.

Jude turned back to his beer, but soon felt the presence of
someone directly behind him. He swiveled around and found
himself face-to-face with the woman, except now she was
scowling at him. She snapped angrily, ''How dare you do that
to me!''

Jude's mouth dropped open, but before he could protest
his innocence, her scowl dissolved into a wide toothy smile
that crinkled her face like cellophane. She repeated herself,
but laughingly this time. ''How dare you turn your back on
me when I'm flirting with you from across the room.''

Jude could think of nothing to do except pat the adjoining
stool in invitation while the cowboy threw hateful glances at

him and juggled the shuffleboard puck from hand to hand, not knowing whether to throw it down the board or at Jude.

The woman glanced over her shoulder at the spurned man, and said to Jude, "Don't worry about him, he fights like he plays shuffleboard."

The two sat in the bar drinking Coors while the hours stole the afternoon, and then the evening. As the empties lined up on the burn-scarred, beer-ringed mahogany, their steps to the jukebox to trade quarters for songs about pickup trucks, jailhouses and faithless lovers became more weave than walk. He asked her name. She said Molly Silva. He asked what she did. She said, "I use my gift."

"What is that?" he asked.

"I see the humor of life," she said.

Molly Silva was the only child of an IBM vice president and his socially ambitious wife in quite acceptable Scarsdale, New York. Her adolescence had been swept up in her parents' headlong rush toward success and away from the stigma of the family "embarrassment," her Portuguese grandfather who dirtied his hands on a fishing boat out of San Francisco's North Beach. The smell of dead fish was to Molly's father a memory to flee, but one that in his mind pursued him into every paneled boardroom.

Molly played the game and followed her parents' wishes all the way through an Ivy League MBA and into the marketing department of a large tobacco company. Her career went according to plan, until one day she was sitting in a meeting called to decide how best to market a new cigarette on college campuses. As the conference wore on, she became increasingly restless. The questions about how she was spending her life and why she was working for a company that made products that killed their users kept writing themselves on her memo pad. They had been interrupting her sleep and popping up before her in the kitchen, on the television screen and in other places where she was irritated to find them, and now they had invaded the sanctuary of the corporate conference room. The questions wouldn't quit. Finally, in surrender to the thoughts that had finally conquered her head, she interrupted the speaker, who happened to be her boss, and said, "Herb, why don't we tell these kids that it's socially responsible to use our product."

"Huh?"

"Think about it, Herb. We can have billboards near campuses saying, 'Smoke Eagles and fight the population explosion. Help lung cancer and heart disease do their part.' Maybe we can start a campaign to induce more smoking in Third World countries: 'Genocide Tastes Better.' 'Come to Cancer Country.' Our answer to famine, Herb."

Molly looked down the long polished table, past the gaping mouths and into the tight-lipped glare on her boss's face. She smiled brightly and said, "Looks like an adjournment for one." She gathered up her papers and walked out.

Molly visited a physician friend and talked him into letting her have a chest X-ray film from a patient who had died of lung cancer. She mailed the film of the ruined lungs to her boss with a note that said, "Herb, you didn't know him, but he smoked Eagles. We mourn the loss of a good customer." At the bottom, she included two quotations.

Oh God! that bread should be so dear,
and flesh and blood so cheap!—Thomas Hood

Fuck the Eagle Tobacco Company!—Molly Silva

Within a week, Molly sublet her apartment, gave her tailored business suits to friends, closed out her bank account, traded her BMW for a Volkswagen bus and headed west. She hit California with five hundred dollars and a big smile. The money she soon spent; the smile grew. She looked for work and she looked for herself. She found both. She was a waitress, she read Jack Kerouac; she picked fruit, she made friends; she ladled soup in a welfare kitchen, she created smiles and passed around the abundance.

No one, family or friends, could figure out what had compelled Molly to throw away the promising future in big-time business she had worked so hard to attain. They sat around and puzzled over it. She certainly didn't get these notions from her parents; the extent of their social concern was an occasional charity ball. Her friends wore the conservative uniform like a Costa Rican general. Their idea of radical was Teddy Kennedy. No leftist professor had inflamed her mind with grandiose ideas of human equality. There was no history of erratic behavior in her family.

So what happened to Molly? All they could do was sigh and shake their heads. They couldn't know that the voice she heard spoke too softly for them to hear; its volume was meant only for those with an inner ear, those created by nature, by genetics or by God to attune to the sounds of the muse. All they knew was that she was different, and they lamented the sadness of it.

Molly, however, didn't look back. Propelled by the childhood memory of a strong Portuguese immigrant with leathery face and thick mustache beneath defiant black eyes, who smelled of mackerel and lye soap, she talked her way onto the crew of a small fishing boat operating out of Monterey. At first, she did the dirty jobs her suspicious crew mates thought beneath them—hosing fish guts and heaving garbage. Slowly, though, she proved herself to her mates, to herself and to that stern old fisherman who smiled in her memory, the most worthwhile man she had ever known.

At two in the morning, the bartender had pulled the jukebox plug, then turned up the lights and looked expectantly down the bar at the laughing couple.

"You actually said that to your boss?" Jude asked. "He must have been ready to strangle you."

"Fuck 'em if they can't take a joke," she said with a tipsy giggle.

"That's all, folks. That's all she wrote," the bartender announced.

Jude and Molly looked at each other. "Time to go home," Jude said.

Neither spoke any further, but with the understanding that comes when the eyes reach agreement, she picked up her purse and waited while Jude paid the bartender.

JUDE PLAYFULLY STALKED THE BED, then with a clamorous rush, yanked the blankets off Molly, roaring with delight as she, still nude from their lovemaking, shrieked and grabbed for a robe in defense against the chill.

The morning horseplay ritual completed, though less gleefully than usual, they sat and ate quietly, each thinking again of the letter that waited on the table before them. Molly glanced at it, then asked, "What are you going to do?"

Jude shook his head. "I don't know." He stared without appetite at the half-eaten eggs as they grew cold. "I need to think." He abruptly pushed back from the table, picked up the letter and left the cabin.

Outside, he walked to the broad clearing between house and forest. He took a seat on a stump and leaned forward, elbows on knees, watching dew glisten beneath redwoods and listening to mourning doves. Scattered in the distance were dwellings with wood smoke meandering out of chimneys. Their occupants, with lives as varied as mountain flowers, were preparing, like people everywhere, to go forth to survive the day.

People live on the edge of the forest for all the reasons they live in the middle of the city: they're hiding; they're trying to catch their breath; they want to be near nature and far from man; they landed there one day and don't know how to leave. In their shacks and rusted house trailers, they scatter among the trees, usually near enough to a highway that Nebraska vacationers whizzing by in their air-conditioned Volvos can point to a rough cabin and say to each other, "Isn't that neat? Wouldn't you love to live like that?" But people—Volvoites and cabin dwellers alike—never seem to learn that life isn't so easily fooled. No pine has grown big enough to hide a man from himself—or from those wanting badly enough to find him.

Jude heard the screen door slam and the crunch of shoes approaching. He said nothing as Molly sat down on a cushion of pine needles with her back to a big tree close by. They sat silently for a few moments, then Molly reached over. "Let me see the letter again."

Jude handed her the envelope. "You've read the damned thing twenty times in the past two days. It's going to say the same thing: we have thirty days to clear off this land or the government will kick us off because we don't have a lease."

Molly again scanned the letter from an Interior Department lawyer and shook her head. "Why us? None of the neighbors got a letter. Everyone in these mountains is a squatter and no one's been bothered before. This isn't fair."

Jude snorted. "Don't be naive."

Molly flared. "Damn it, I've got a stake in this, too."

"I'm sorry," Jude said, "but communicating with the government is like dealing with a snake: it either bites you or hides from you."

Molly returned the letter to the tattered envelope. "We'll fight. We're not defenseless."

"Oh, yeah? What're we going to do when a big bulldozer comes down that road, write our congressman?"

"Haven't you ever heard of a court injunction?"

"Molly," Jude said, trying to remain patient, "do you have any idea what it costs to sue the government? The money you've saved for your own boat would just about buy us a cup of coffee with the type of lawyer we'd need. I'm not ready to surrender, but let's be realistic.''

Molly struck the ground with the flat of her fist. ''I can't believe the United States government would push citizens around like this. One day, we have a home; then a letter comes in the mail, and—nothing.'' She looked forlornly at the small house. ''This place was just a run-down dump when we came here. All the work . . .''

Molly's lament trailed away at the sound of an automobile coming slowly down the narrow, winding road. Apprehensive, they watched the car, each wondering what additional bad news it might bear.

The car pulled off the road about a hundred yards distant, and both Jude and Molly strained their eyes to examine the rare visitors. Only Jude, however, tensed with recognition as the driver stepped from the car and singled him out with a level, unsmiling gaze.

As though answering an unspoken summons, Jude motioned for Molly to stay put and slowly walked toward the car, hesitating only a moment when he saw a woman get out from the passenger side and join her companion in watching his approach. As Jude neared the car, the only sound was the crunch of gravel underfoot; the apprehensive stares the three exchanged were silent.

Jude glanced from one to the other. The man, he knew. Richard Danton still displayed a face that looked like the moon—round, and covered by pits and shadows. A look from him was a vague accusation that hinted he knew the contents of one's psychic closet. Danton's thinning brown hair was combed straight back and the rest of his six-two, 240-pound body—both clothes and carriage—said this was a man who cared little for what others thought because he knew he was always right, and probably was enough of the time to be unnerving. Richard hadn't changed.

The woman was unfamiliar, but someone who could be that only once. Her short hair was jet-black with streaks of obviously premature gray running through it; it told Jude she was secure enough in her self-image not to be threatened by the appearance of gray hairs. She was of medium height, and the severe blue business suit she wore gave her a boxy look that Jude sensed would be transformed into soft curves in different attire—say a negligee. Her face was round and softly sculpted with a small thin mouth and dark eyes accented by prominent cheekbones. She was the type of woman who would be called pretty by people who would then wonder why. Jude had no idea who she was, but the unmistakable way she carried herself left him no doubt what she was.

Jude stopped a few feet short of the big man and waited, his hands clenching and unclenching with tension. Danton and Jude stared at each other, neither knowing how to break the impasse. Finally, without taking his eyes from Jude, Danton said, "This is Lana Martin, she's working with me."

Jude looked at the woman and gave a short nod, then returned his eyes to Danton. "What do you want, Richard?"

The pained expression that Danton couldn't quite conceal revealed his distaste for the mission. "I've been assigned to ask you to return for one more job."

Jude stared at him, incredulous. "Return? I've been retired for four years. Why would I want to do that? The answer is no."

"Retired?" Danton gave a short, nasty laugh. "I guess you could call it that."

"I'm sorry you wasted your time," Jude muttered, and turned his back and started to walk away when Danton's words stopped him in midstride.

"I understand you're having a little real estate problem. Uncle Sam can be a rough landlord. Yes sir, real hard to deal with."

Jude wheeled in anger. "I should have known you assholes would be behind something like that. What right do you have to screw around with people's lives?" Jude hesitated, then said in a growl, "Did *he* order the squeeze put on?"

Danton lowered his voice as though sharing a great confidence. "The director knows what's going on."

Jude moaned softly and shook his head in futile protest.

Danton gave a snicker so subtle it was sensed rather than observed. "You know the service always makes it tough to say no."

Jude glanced at Danton's feet. "You're trampling wild mushrooms. I don't think you know how to conduct yourself up here. This isn't a natural habitat for thugs."

Eyes blazing, Danton made a move forward, so slight that only Jude's trained eye picked it up.

Jude knew better than to insult a man like Danton without being ready. He had been watching Danton's huge hands, which by reputation could kill a man as if breaking a matchstick. When he saw the fingers twitch, he recoiled into a defensive position, then laughed when the threat didn't materialize. "Wise decision, Richard. I don't think your masters would like seeing you come back carrying your patriotic balls in a basket."

The woman suddenly thrust herself between them and started talking like a reproving schoolteacher lecturing two squabbling boys. "Okay, enough. If I'd wanted to see bad comedy, I'd have stayed home and watched television. Grow up, voth—both—of you." She corrected herself and glanced quickly at Jude, who was looking at her with a curious expression.

Lana used a nervous laugh to break her eye lock with Jude. She ignored Danton. "I've only been with the service a little more than a year, so you're only a dusty dossier to me, but from reading it, I can see why you're needed, and badly. And don't pretend such shocked outrage that the government would hold your little hippie pad for ransom. The stakes are a hell of a lot more important than some refugee from reality hiding out in the woods.''

"How dare—"

Her strong voice overrode his objection. "The book on you is that after getting into that trouble, you quit and became a burnout. You probably think you became sensitized to the good things of life. Whatever. The important thing is, we need you." She took an official-looking envelope from her purse and extended it toward Jude. "This is for you." She pulled the envelope back slightly. "But first you must understand that this is all in strict confidence."

Jude grimaced. "And above all, I've got to hear *that*."

She held up a hand by way of apology. "I understand, but you know I had to say that."

Curious, he opened the envelope and scanned the few lines typed above a scrawled signature. He handed it back to her. Lana removed a cigarette lighter from her purse and all three watched as the letter curled into a black ash. "Convinced?" she asked. "Not many of our recruits get a personal appeal from the director of the Central Intelligence Agency."

He shook his head resolutely. "Sorry, I don't work for the man anymore. He'll just have to write someone else a letter."

"Well, then, how about this?" Danton said. "Play ball and help us, and you can forget the order to move from here."

"Until you want the next thing from me, then the blackmail starts again."

Danton shook his head. "No, you have *his* word on that. You can trust the director."

"We can't say anything more," Lana added, "but I can tell you the job wouldn't take more then a few weeks, and you'd be paid generously."

"I don't want your money anymore. Besides, you'd probably want me to do some of the dirty work you specialize in. Could you promise me you wouldn't?"

She shook her head. "You know we can't."

Jude leaned forward and bit off the words. "Then I guess you can tell your director to kiss my ass. We'll just find someplace else to live." He threw them a curt wave of dismissal and started to walk away.

Danton shouted at his retreating back. "Okay, hotshot, let's raise the ante. I'll tell you where that little Portugee you've been shacked up with will be living—in a federal prison!"

Jude wanted to laugh and tell them to go to hell, but he knew Danton. He turned and waited.

Danton grinned. "She's got a warrant on her a couple of years old for planting pot up the coast. She and her boyfriend were regular farmers. The had sinsemilla growing like Iowa corn in August. If that crop was foreign aid, Ethiopia could have gotten high." Danton shook his head in mock sympathy. "Very serious charges, my friend. We're talking several years, and you better believe it."

Jude's voice became a hiss. "Why, you dirty bastards. She told me about that stupid charge. The case was against the guy she was living with. They never wanted her. That warrant is dead."

Danton's lips twisted. "Well, maybe it's a Lazarus warrant. Maybe it'll rise from the dead." The grin left his face. "You know we have the power to do it, Miller. Don't think I'm bluffing. If you turn your back on us, you'll be turning it on her, too. She'll serve time—plenty of it—that's a promise."

Jude felt sick to his stomach. "Fuck you," he managed in a weak voice and walked rapidly away, not wanting to show his shakiness.

"We'll be back tomorrow," Danton said quietly, but the words carried well on the morning air and swirled around Jude's head as he retreated.

MOLLY WAS WASHING DISHES and slammed down a skillet in frustration. "This isn't Russia. The government has laws to keep people like that off your back. Besides, you're retired from the stupid CIA," she protested, almost in a whine.

"Molly, they *are* the government. There's more to it than you learned in high school civics. Understand, this country isn't run by a bunch of kindly old uncles."

"I understand we have to fight. I understand that much," she said in a cold rage.

"Fight what? It's not like calling city hall about the neighbor's dog."

"Damn it, Jude, don't patronize me. When people try to screw you, you fight back."

Jude walked over and stood behind Molly and enveloped her shoulders in an affectionate hug. "When you're mad, you can be tough as a pit bull, but I don't want to see you land in jail."

She whirled, unintentionally twisting free of his arms. "Jail? I didn't do anything. It's just a silly marijuana charge that any lawyer could beat. That type of rap went out in the sixties."

Jude spoke slowly for effect. "Distribution of a dangerous drug . . . conspiracy to violate narcotics laws . . . they'd crucify you."

Tears welled in Molly's eyes and she brushed them away, angry that they made her seem less strong, less determined. "If you told them to go to hell, and they knew you meant it, then they'd be wasting their time persecuting us. They're bluffing, Jude, I know it." She was pleading. "Let them have this broken-down old shack; we'll never look back. It's the jail threat that's scary, and since it's against me, it should be my decision." She took a deep breath and her chest puffed up. "I say we tell them to go fuck themselves."

Jude said nothing and looked away.

"Well?" she said.

"I've dealt with these people, Molly. Trust my judgment."

"I trust my feelings," she said. "And they say to me that if we give in, things will never be the same. I happen to like our lives the way they are, don't you?"

"Shouldn't I at least find out what they want? Maybe it's not a big deal."

Molly threw her dish towel onto a chair. "That's not what this is all about. The issue is *us*. You told me you were through with all that. You said you wanted nothing more than what we have right here. If you do this thing—whatever it is they want you to do—you'll be turning your back on all we've built together."

"For Christ's sake, Molly, I try to discuss things with you rationally, and you make these hysterical statements. I'm the one they're putting the heat on."

"How can you even consider trusting these people? They're the ones who ended up with your balls as a souvenir in a personnel filing cabinet. Why would they even want you?"

Jude's lips compressed in anger and he pointed a finger at her. "In case you hadn't noticed, my balls are quite intact. Goddammit, I was a good agent, and don't you say I wasn't."

"I only—"

"Don't judge things you don't understand."

Molly was crying now. "You never talked about your time in the CIA, and I never asked. Now I'm glad, because at this moment I can feel something in this room. It's standing between us and I can't get around it; something inside you that you never showed before. Maybe you're not even aware it's there. I'm scared to death that you want to go with them. Maybe it's something you have to prove. Maybe you're bored with me. . . ."

"Molly!" Jude said, shocked. "This is my home."

"A person can love one thing and still want—need—something else."

Jude slammed the flat of his hand against the table. "Goddammit, you don't know them! I'm not going to see the woman I love torn apart by jackals and not try to save her. One more quick job and it'll be over for good."

"What'll be over, Jude? Would *you* be over, would *we* be over? For sure, *they* wouldn't be over, and they'd be back the next time they wanted you. People who twist your arm one time will break it the next. I don't know anything about the CIA, but I do know me, and I thought I knew you."

Jude shook his head in exasperation. "So, after a ten-minute conversation, you decide what's in my mind."

"No, dear, not a ten-minute conversation. I know you. I'm the woman you sleep with, remember?"

Jude took her hands in his. "Molly, I love you. Trust me to do what I have to do."

"Have to do, or want to do?"

"If I go, will you still be here?" Jude whispered.

"If you stay, you'll be doing it for us. If you go, it'll be for yourself, and I'll owe you no promises."

DANTON MEASURED JUDE with his eyes as though he were guessing his weight. Finally, he said with triumphant condescension, "So the answer is yes? I never doubted it."

"As long as you keep your promises."

With a superior smile, Danton reached inside his jacket and removed a thick envelope. "Here's a ninety-nine-year lease on this property, and a letter from the Justice Department promising not to prosecute Molly Silva. Your worries are over."

Jude fingered the envelope. "Or just beginning. Don't expect me to be grateful. Now, what am I supposed to do for this?"

Danton looked at Lana Martin and shrugged to make his ignorance seem unimportant. "The director will have to tell you that. My job was to convince you to take the assignment.''

Jude scoffed. ''Convince? You couldn't talk a horny rabbit into a hard-on. Blackmail is more your style, and I'm sure your talents are much appreciated by the director.''

Danton glared at Jude with a look that promised another day.

Jude ignored the silent threat. ''Just give me the plane ticket,'' he said wearily.

CHAPTER TWO

HERBERT FARLEIGH ARMSTEAD LOOKED OUT the bullet-proof, tinted window at the rolling Virginia countryside, but the pastoral setting did nothing to calm the deep fears that roiled inside him. By all appearances, he was a man who, through fifty-seven years of ruthless guile and vast accumulated power, had become immune to the threats and dangers that beset ordinary mortals. He had lived to win, and he had won: wealth and power. Others feared him, and he feared no man. Yet on this day he awaited the confirmation of the foreshadowing of doom as surely as though he could hear the hangman's steps approaching.

The discreet knock and entry of the secretary interrupted his commiserating. "Dr. Hapson is here to see you, sir," she said.

Dr. Fred Hapson was a world-renowned neurologist who left his office at the summons of few men, but one of them was the director of the Central Intelligence Agency.

"Have a seat, Doctor," was followed by a perfunctory handshake, and Armstead sat on a couch a few feet away, tense with anticipation.

The doctor cleared his throat nervously. "Mr. Armstead, we've completed the brain biopsy, and I'm afraid the news is not encouraging." Hapson paused and looked expectantly at Armstead, but his patient's intent stare encouraged him to continue. "Mr. Armstead, I don't know how acquainted you are with Alzheimer's disease, but . . ."

Armstead thrust forward on the couch, his fists clenched in tension. "Are you saying . . . ?"

Hapson shook his head with regret. "I'm sorry. I didn't mean to back into this. Yes, I'm afraid the diagnosis is as near definite as it can be. I'm truly sorry..." His voice trailed off as though he had just pronounced his patient dead.

"How can you be sure, Doctor? Maybe another opinion..." A look at Hapson's face pulled him up short and restored the grim determination to his face. "Give it to me—the whole thing."

"Mr. Armstead," the doctor resumed. Confidence steadily crept into his voice as the psychological edge shifted to his expertise, and the intimidating director of the CIA became just another scared patient. "Let me explain what the disease is and what it does. It's actually a form of senile dementia, characterized by progressive debilitation. It usually starts in older people with gradual memory loss, then difficulty performing simple calculations, then depression, then loss of motor function—meaning you lose control of your body, including bowels and bladder. Eventually, the patient loses all awareness." Hapson looked sympathetically at the powerful figure opposite who had suddenly become an old man, and said, "And then the patient dies."

"Isn't there any chance... maybe you're wrong?"

The doctor shook his head firmly. "The biopsy is the most certain means of diagnosis we have. The presence of neurofibrillary tangles indicates with virtual certainty the presence of the disease. Also, your performance on the workup indicates a definite slippage on language skills, memory and spatial ability. No, Mr. Armstead, the diagnosis is solid."

Armstead's face maintained its thin-lipped grimness, but his shoulders slumped perceptibly. "Is there any place to go for treatment, any place where I can get help?"

"Unfortunately, there is no cure, but help is available to ease the development of the symptoms. A place such as St. Catherine's Convalescent Hospital in Washington, D.C.

specializes in making life comfortable for Alzheimer's patients."

"Is there any hope of finding a cure—soon?"

Hapson shook his head ruefully. "Progress is being made, but it takes time—too much time, I'm afraid."

Armstead rose from the couch and wandered to the window, where he gazed silently over the landscape, his back to the doctor, who took that as his cue and excused himself, stammering his regrets as he moved toward the door.

Armstead stared out the window a while longer, then went to the intercom and pushed the button. When a secretary answered, he said, "Have my car brought around immediately."

"Yes, sir."

"Oh, another thing. Find out where St. Catherine's Convalescent Hospital is in D.C., then call and let them know I'm coming for a visit."

ST. CATHERINE'S DIRECTOR OF NURSING nervously awaited her prominent guest, mystified as to why such an important man would be visiting upon an hour's notice. When the limousine pulled up to the door, a wiry, athletic man exuding an air of great importance got out of the car and strode directly up to where she stood.

"Welcome to St. Catherine's, Mr. Armstead. To what do we owe the honor of your visit?"

"I'm sorry to bother you on such short notice, Mrs.— Madam, but one of my principal assistants may shortly be in need of a facility such as yours, and since he has no family, I wanted to personally inspect what you offer here. Could I be shown around?"

"Certainly, sir."

The tour wound its way through the pharmacy, kitchen and chapel, the virtues of which were proudly extolled by the nurse, to which her distinguished guest nodded with bored courtesy. It was only when they reached the dayroom that his darting glances slowed and the look of impatience was replaced by one of troubled fascination as he watched the old people sitting in groups or wandering aimlessly around the large, sun-lit room. The nurse stood beside Armstead and beamed happily at her charges, like a Scouts' den mother.

One woman was sitting in a wheelchair staring at them with unblinking, vacant eyes and with an idiotic smile creasing her wrinkled face. Armstead glanced at her lap and saw she was tied to the chair. Another woman was shuffling around the room in a continuous circle, the slippers on her feet flopping rhythmically, the shapeless flowered housedress hanging on her skinny body like the dustcover on a chair. As she wandered, the woman chanted over and over, "Please, God, forgive me; I'll never do it again. Please, God, forgive me; I'll never do it again. Please, God . . ."

Armstead turned to the nurse. "What's she so remorseful about?"

The nurse shrugged. "Who knows? Perhaps she forgot to pack her husband's lunch one day. Maybe she neglected to sew a button on her daughter's dress. It's symbolic of this disease that the patients lose all sense of proportion. A mere oversight years ago can seem like a heinous crime to them. Their torment is brutal, but there's nothing we can do to ease their guilt."

An old man padded up to the visitors and headed straight for Armstead. When he was within touching distance, he held out his hand to give something to Armstead. The CIA director automatically held out his hand and looked down, but instantly gave a sharp cry and recoiled angrily. What the man had tried to hand him, loosely wrapped in a white paper napkin, was a small, cylindrical lump of human feces. The old man ignored Armstead's angry glare and asked softly, "Would you please give this to the police?"

The nurse stepped between them and took the napkin from the old man. "Thank you, Edward. I'll see they get it." Then, turning to Armstead, "I trust you realize he meant no offense," she said without embarrassment. "Edward once was police chief of New Orleans, so I guess he's still on the job. He believes his body waste is important evidence for some crime. We're really quite used to it."

Suddenly, a startling shriek erupted from the far side of the room. The nurse rushed over to a shaking old woman and gently put an arm around her bony shoulders. "Now, Nora," she cooed, "everything's all right. We've got company, and we don't want to disturb him, do we?" She comforted the woman for a few moments and then returned to Armstead.

"What frightened her?" he asked.

"I have no idea. Neither has she."

Armstead shook his head sadly. "I can't believe adults can degenerate to this."

"These patients are in the early stages of the disease," the nursing director said.

"Show me the worst," Armstead demanded.

She hesitated, then said, "Come with me."

They walked down a dimly-lit corridor until the nurse came to a closed door with only the number 36 distinguishing it from any other. She opened the door and invited Armstead to follow. Inside, the room was almost empty except for a criblike bed in a corner with a form huddled in it. Armstead started to walk toward it, but the nurse stopped him with a hand gently held against his arm. "Remember, those you saw in the dayroom were still ambulatory. This is how they end up—all of them."

Together they approached the crib, and what Armstead saw made him jerk back in horror. Lying on the bed, curled into a fetal position as though encased in an invisible womb, was an old man, shriveled to almost a skeleton. He lay in a coma with a thin tube running into his nose and completely unaware of their presence. When Armstead dropped his eyes below the man's face, he wrinkled his nose in involuntary disgust: the man wore a diaper.

Noticing Armstead's chagrin, the nurse said, "It's so sad. All we can do is try to make them comfortable."

Armstead looked around the empty room and spotted a solitary framed certificate on the wall. He walked over and read it.

This is to certify that Samuel B. Winston achieved a hole in one on the 178-yard third hole at Mountain View Country Club, August 6, 1958.

"I've seen that name someplace," Armstead said.

"Probably in the newspaper. This is Samuel B. Winston. He headed one of the largest steel companies in America." She shook her head. "Six months ago, he was one of those in the dayroom; two years ago, he dined at the White House. Now he's fed through a tube."

Armstead looked around the room and at the walls again. Nothing else. He turned to the nurse. "Is this piece of paper what his life has come down to? Does he have any family? Does anyone visit him?"

"At first they came, but after a while . . . well, it's difficult to visit with someone who doesn't know you're there." Her glance joined his in looking at the empty walls. "And no point in hanging pictures that don't mean anything."

The nurse walked to the limousine with Armstead, and as the chauffeur held the car door for one of America's most powerful men, she said, "Well, sir, I hope we've answered your questions."

He turned and looked at her with the veiled expression he had perfected over a career of practiced inscrutability. "Yes, you answered my questions. All of them."

LINDEN HIGH SCHOOL LIBRARY

ARMSTEAD LEANED BACK in his chair and stared toward the ceiling, but he didn't see the ornate tiles and gleaming crystal chandelier. All he saw was death. "Please, God," he implored, "I don't deserve this. It's not fair. I'm doing your work. No one else can do it as well. I'm needed here. If this nation is to resist godlessness, it needs men who understand the threat, and there are so few of us. Please, God, let me live—just for a few more years, until my work is done." He clasped his hands together tightly. "Lord, if you will spare me from this, I promise I will deliver this man Khrushchev. I will prove I serve you well." His voice cracked. "Not yet. Please, not yet."

The intercom's buzzing interrupted Armstead, and he automatically pushed the button and cleared his throat before he spoke. "Yes?"

"Mr. Miller is here, sir."

"I'll see him in five minutes."

Armstead went into his private bathroom, splashed cold water on his face and washed his hands. He looked closely at the image in the mirror as he dried his hands, and saw something he had never seen before. He saw the lines of age in his tanned, lean face. He also saw the shadow of fear. He stared at the mirror for a couple of minutes, then took a deep breath and willed it all to go away.

Armstead returned to his desk and picked up a stack of papers. He was officiously shuffling them as Jude walked through the heavy oak door and stepped onto the plush carpet as though entering an executioner's chamber. Jude fidgeted nervously and looked around at the familiar, luxurious surroundings he had hoped never to see again. And then he saw the office's occupant sitting exactly where he knew he would be, behind the same huge desk with photos of luminaries lined up behind him, looking just as he had the day he crucified Jude.

"Hello, Jude. Welcome home."

"Hello, Mr. Armstead." He didn't add, glad to be back.

The director, smiling and with a spring in his step, moved from behind the desk and took his hand. "Your country needs you, son. I'm pleased you saw fit to come."

Jude nodded glumly. He felt like saying: You gave me no choice, not if I wanted to save my home and friends. But why me? You were the one who threatened me with prison if I didn't resign. For the good of the service, was the way I believe you delicately put it.

Instead, he said nothing.

Armstead guided him by the elbow to facing easy chairs in a corner of the office, where they sat under the intimidating gaze of former CIA directors staring down from the wall.

Armstead patted him on the knee, and said, "I know what you're thinking, my boy, why should we want you back after the way you left the service? Well, why don't we consider that ancient history? We all make mistakes."

Jude shook his head doggedly several times. "It's not that easy. After what I was put through . . ."

Armstead's voice toughened slightly. "As I said, that's in the past. If you accomplish this mission, that unhappy affair will be removed from your files; it'll vanish forever and you'll be restored to your old job."

"I don't want my job back. I just want to be left alone. But I guess you know how I feel. Anyway, what is it you want me to do?"

"Understand, Jude, that this is top secret with clearance at only the highest levels."

Jude nodded impatiently.

"Your job is to bring Khrushchev out of the Soviet Union."

Jude looked at him blankly. "I guess I don't understand you. What Khrushchev?"

"Nikita Sergeyevich Khrushchev, former premier and head of the Soviet Communist Party. The one who challenged

Kennedy on the Cuban missiles, the one who pounded his shoe on the table at the United Nations.''

"I know my Russian history. In a way, I helped write a little of it. But any newspaper reader knows that Khrushchev died in '71. This is damned silly.'' Then, remembering who he was talking to, Jude lowered his voice contritely. "I mean, that's not possible, sir.''

Armstead laughed loudly. "See, isn't this worth coming back for, Jude? Khrushchev didn't die. He's living in Moscow with a fake ID, just as alive as either of us. He even walks the streets on occasion.''

Jude slowly waved his hands in front of him as though to ward off an hallucination. "Hey, wait a minute. Time-out. The man is dead. I was in Moscow when it happened. He was out of favor, living in disgrace. The Russians would have no reason to lie. He's buried in a small cemetery in Moscow. I even know where it is.''

"No, Jude, *they* didn't lie, *he* lied, Khrushchev and his friends. They faked his death, and as far as we know, the Soviets are as much in the dark as we were.''

"How do we know all this?''

Armstead looked at Jude as if he were a schoolboy who had neglected his homework. "The way we always know these things—informants tell us. In this case, we've got a reliable one. He's convinced us.'' He fumbled with a small tape-recorder and inserted a cassette. "This first tape is of a speech Khrushchev gave at the United Nations back in the early sixties.'' He pressed the Play key and a thunderous, belligerent voice boomed out of the machine. Armstead let the tape play for a couple of minutes then stopped it in midsentence. He switched cassettes and played the second without comment. It was of a voice speaking the same Russian dialect but sounding much older and more subdued, like a man who had lost his audience. Armstead switched off the machine. "What you're hearing here is the same man. The only difference is years of aging. We know the second tape is current because he was reading headlines from an issue of *Pravda* printed last month. Also, the tape it's recorded on is of recent Russian manufacture, and our experts assure us there's no chance it could have been copied from an earlier tape." Armstead paused for effect. "There is no doubt the two voices you just heard are the same man."

Jude whistled soft and low. "There's always the chance of a fake, but . . . wow! But why does he want to come out, and why now? He must be in his nineties."

"Born in 1894. He's certainly no youngster, but he's a tough old bugger. As to why he wants to come out, part of the answer is that his wife died a short time ago, so there's nothing to keep him in a place that treated him like a criminal. But the complete answer will have to come from him, and getting him here in one piece so we can ask him is your job. Your first stop is with our key contact, the man we can thank for these tapes."

"Who and where?"

"You begin by going in the opposite direction, so to speak. Your first stop is Mexico."

"Mexico?"

Behind his masking smile, Armstead noticed Jude's suspicion. "I can understand your concern. This is a tough assignment. I wouldn't try to fool you, you've been around too much for that. I just want you to know that the importance of this assignment has been noted at the highest level of government. The *highest*. If we can get the old boy back here alive and in good shape, imagine what a propaganda coup it will be for us, not to mention how Khrushchev could fill in a lot of holes in our intelligence picture, even after all these years. The possibilities for this nation are enormous. If you can get him out."

Jude rolled his eyes heavenward. "Man, oh man, this is too much. First you people kick me out, then after several years of pretending I don't exist, you suddenly show up and want me to do something like this. Not only that, but you don't ask me to volunteer, you twist my arm. What makes you so certain I won't screw it up just to get back at you?''

"Reasonable question," Armstead said. "But we've thought of that, too. First, that warrant against Molly Silva can be resurrected; second, you're still too much of a pro to deliberately screw it up, your professional instincts wouldn't let you; third, even if you managed to botch the job, the Russians wouldn't let you out alive. That's the kind of incentive a man responds to, don't you think?''

Without waiting for Jude's response, Armstead went on, "Okay you obviously have a thousand questions, and the boys downstairs will brief you. The routine hasn't changed. But just to give you an idea, you'll get into Russia as a common seaman serving on a fishing boat. How's that for a start, eh?''

"Sir, how am I supposed to get aboard a Russian fishing boat?"

"We've made arrangements through a friendly and suddenly more prosperous Russian captain who's a member of the secret Ukrainian Freedom Movement. You remember those boys, a nasty bunch of fanatics. He'll add you to his crew when his ship puts into Anchorage, Alaska for supplies in a few weeks. You'll have all the identity papers you need to pass as . . . let me see here—" Armstead shuffled through some papers on the edge of his desk "—yes, you'll be Petr Markov, a sailor from Moscow who was left behind by a previous boat because of acute appendicitis. Now you're recovered and ready to catch a berth back home.''

"Why the roundabout route? Hell, Russia has the longest border in the world. It seems to me there'd be easier ways to slip into the country. Spending my nights with a bunch of dead fish in the Arctic doesn't have much appeal.''

Armstead laughed. "They say you get used to the smell. But to answer your question, there are two reasons. One, it may be slow and circuitous, but it's safe—"

"Relatively safe," Jude interrupted.

Armstead forced a smile. He wasn't used to being interrupted. "That's understood. As I was saying, the other reason is the biggest one: the fishing boat is the way the Ukrainians want to do it. And since they control the person of Nikita Khrushchev, they get what they want."

"Can you tell me my contact inside Russia?"

"You'll be given that information in Anchorage by one of our people there." Armstead waved away further questions. "But you'll be briefed on all that. What I want to do is welcome you back and wish you Godspeed." Armstead casually got up and headed for the door, applying subtle pressure on Jude's shoulder for him to follow. "And I especially want you to know how grateful I am, personally, that you returned to help us." At the door he took Jude's hand and firmly pumped it. "Now, my boy, do you have any final questions for me?"

Jude felt the pressure on his shoulder and looked into the cold, alert eyes of the man he feared and admired, loathed and respected, and he wanted to say: You could be a great man, so why do you cheapen what this country should stand for by your dishonesty, your killings, your thuggery, your twisted values? Why do you force me to return to a life I have come to despise?

"No, sir, no questions."

After Jude left, Armstead returned to his desk and, disregarding the three telephones of different colors on the surface, removed a small black phone from a locked drawer. He dialed a coded number and said into the receiver, "I'd like to speak to the President." A wait of several minutes was followed by Armstead saying, "Hello, sir. I'm calling to let you know that the Khrushchev rescue operation we discussed is underway. We got the man we wanted for the job."

"Well, that's just great, Herbert. I tell you, it's easier being president knowing I have men like you to rely on."

"The respect is mutual, Mr. President, as you know." It cost Armstead dearly in ego pain to pander to anyone, even the President, but he had long ago resigned himself to being obsequious to politicians if it achieved for him the power necessary to defend his country against the evil from the East. Armstead was one of those men who would be deeply chagrined for anyone to know how deeply he cared, how deeply he hated the things he felt threatened the way of life that had rewarded him so handsomely. Armstead considered himself a patriot, though he seldom spoke of it.

The President's voice became concerned. "This agent fellow, the one you persuaded to return to duty, are you sure he's the man for the job?"

Armstead gave a relaxed chuckle. This was his ground. "I'd bet on him before my golf game. This is the man who went in and got the proof on the Russian poison gas production in Siberia. When that KGB agent, Sherenkov, wanted to defect, he's the one who brought him out. Disguised Sherenkov as a Bulgarian chess master and walked him right through Checkpoint Charlie. Speaks Russian like Moscow was his hometown. He's tough, resourceful, and will finish what he starts. And because of what he went through, he's questioning himself, which makes him all the more dependent upon us. He's the perfect man for this job."

"What if his heart isn't in it anymore?" the President asked.

"No concern there, Mr. President. His feelings are hurt over what we did to him, but I can tell he's thrilled to be back in the business. He doesn't realize it himself, but he's like a bird dog who's been turned loose in a cornfield in pheasant season. You can see him sniffing the ground already. Don't worry, sir, I know my man. I can control him."

"What did you say the man's name was again?" the President asked.

"What man, Mr. President?"

"You know, the agent."

Armstead was silent as the horror gathered thick and tightened in his chest. "I—I don't remember at the moment, Mr. President."

The President laughed. "Better watch it, Herbert. Sounds like you're slipping."

"No, sir. I won't let that happen."

CHAPTER THREE

THE BIG RENTAL BUICK was a cocoon of comfort as it thumped over the pockmarked Mexican road. Jude leaned back in the passenger seat, uncomfortable with the constricting strangeness of the suit and tie he wore, even though the car's coolness protected him from the dusty heat. He had seen poverty in every part of the world, and had considered himself inured to the depression its presence can cause to the mind, but there was something especially unnerving and sad about such poverty so close to the border. The contrast between the glittering sunbelt riches of San Diego just to the north, and the Third-World stink of Tijuana stuck in the throats of the brown-skinned men who watched vigilantly while they stood idly on street corners. As Jude and Lana Martin drove by in their air-conditioned sanctuary, the glances seemed to say: Just wait, our time will come. Even the sun seemed to be a conspirator: across the border it tanned; here, it baked.

"Where do we meet this guy?" Jude asked.

"At the vull-bullfights."

Jude was silent momentarily, then said, "Sounds strange."

Lana shrugged. "It makes sense. No way is he going to invite us to his house just so the neighbors can wonder who the strange gringos are. He wants it in a busy, public place, and he happens to like bullfights." As she spoke, Lana swung the car onto a rock-strewn dirt road that led to the Downtown Bullring, if the signs could be believed, which in Mexico sometimes took a considerable act of faith. The garish stucco shacks of pink, lime-green and purple with roofs of rusted corrugated metal seemed to edge nearer one another as the road narrowed and the poverty crowded closer, like an unwelcome embrace. Each shack appeared to double as a junkyard. The bare patches of dirt that passed for yards for the hovels were littered with old refrigerators, bald tires and assorted junk of all kinds. It was as though the owners somehow hoped the market for broken stoves and engine parts for '67 Chevys would somehow turn upward. And everywhere were the universal signs of poverty: no grass, no flowers.

Lana slowed as she approached an octagonal red sign that said Alto. As she braked to a stop, Jude glanced out the window and saw a girl of about ten standing at the edge of the road selling brightly-painted plaster figures of the Virgin. The two locked eyes—Jude, relaxed in climate-controlled comfort and lounging on velour plushness; the girl standing shoeless in the dust and broken concrete, squinting into the midday sun. She revealed nothing in her dark face, but something about her touched Jude, who motioned suddenly for Lana to hold the car, then got out and approached the girl. *"¿Cómo se llama?"* he managed in tourist Spanish.

"Theresa," came the shy reply, big brown eyes sweeping over him like radar.

"How much…eh, *mucho peso?*" he asked, pointing to the cheap figurine.

"*Un* dollar," the girl replied shyly, using the only English word her parents had taught her before stationing her at the corner several hours before.

Jude took out his wallet and searched for a dollar bill. But on impulse he reached for a twenty and exchanged it with the girl for the statuette. "Adios, Theresa," he said, smiling as he got back into the car. The girl said nothing, merely looked at him and held the bill. She had heard that Americans, though such loud, cruel people, could sometimes do crazy things. And giving her such a fortune and asking nothing in return confirmed that to be true. Theresa didn't think of it as charity, because in her pinched world that was a quality she had not been introduced to.

As the car spun gravel and Theresa faded in Jude's side mirror, he turned to Lana. "You still haven't told me anything about our contact."

"His name is Antonio Bustamonte. He's a Soviet emigré living in Mexico and he's the head of the Ukrainian Freedom Movement in this hemisphere. His name in the old country was Giorgi Harbuziak. He's very cooperative with us because the U.S. supports him in a capitalist style he's come to appreciate."

"Pretty cynical," Jude teased.

"It doesn't take long to get that way. Sainthood will elude most of those we work with in this business," Lana said.

"Why is it I never heard of this guy when I was active?" Jude asked, trying to keep suspicion out of his voice.

"He only surfaced a couple of years ago. He's been very helpful. His information has always panned out. He's considered very valuable by the service."

As they neared the Tijuana Plaza de Toros, a festive atmosphere started like a subtle hum and mounted until the street spilled into the broad plaza that contained the tall, circular bullring where it became an allegretto of Latin excitement. Small children ran from person to person hawking pennants, trinkets and cushions—"Is okay to throw at the bullfighters, *señor*. Only two dollar." Old men stood next to tubs of iced beer shouting, *"¡Cerveza, cerveza!"*

Trying to politely ignore the young peddlers who managed to get in their way like playful terriers, Lana and Jude passed through the turnstile with tickets Lana took from her purse. Instead of heading for the grandstand, she led the way to the lower boxes, small enclosed rooms on the level of the bullring itself, and reserved exclusively for the well-to-do and influential. Lana went directly to one of the boxes and rapped on the closed door. Instantly, the door was opened and they were facing the suspicious glare of a florid-faced man in his sixties, his heavy black mustache twitching as he looked at Jude. *"¿Hola?"* he asked in heavily accented Spanish, but then his small black eyes lit up and his weathered face crinkled like parchment as he recognized Lana. *"Allo, lyubovnik,"* he said in perfect Russian, "hello, honey." Then, checking himself because they weren't alone, he switched to broken English. "Welcome. Come in, please."

Once inside, Lana introduced Jude to Giorgi Harbuziak, exiled leader of the Ukrainian Freedom Movement, bullfight aficionado and retainer of the CIA. "It's okay to speak Russian, Giorgi. Jude understands it perfectly."

There were only two other occupants of the eight-seat box. A dumpy Indian woman was cooking chicken over a small charcoal grill. While being introduced as Inez Gonzales, their host's housekeeper, she didn't take her eyes off her work. Sitting off to the side was a man who appeared to be in his fifties but had the brittle, stooped bearing of an old man. He stared silently ahead as spittle seeped from the corners of his mouth. Harbuziak gave a slight wave in his direction. "This is my old friend, Basil. He's had a stroke. Poor bastard's about paralyzed—can't even speak." He turned to Jude and spoke in a whisper. "I'm afraid his mind is gone. We have to cart him around like a baby." Then, just in case he was wrong, he turned back to the sick man and raised his voice. "We used to kick some ass together, eh, Basil?"

Jude nodded to the silent man as Harbuziak waved him to a chair at the edge of the wide opening facing the sandy bullring, which was just a few feet away on the other side of a narrow runway. He then approached Jude, pressed his hand in a drawn-out shake and stared intently into his face. *"Señor,"* he said softly, mixing languages freely and sounding like a Voice of America broadcast, "you have been given a grave responsibility, one that can advance the cause of freedom and democracy the world over. I hope you are equal to the task."

Jude smiled awkwardly and discreetly tugged his hand free. "Well, it's not like I'm an amateur, but why don't you start by giving me what details you have on the situation." Jude didn't like the look in Harbuziak's eyes. There was something that didn't match the smile. It was as though Harbuziak's face was made of plastic overlays, the bottom half that of a friendly, outgoing good fellow, the top half that of a ruthless schemer. He reminded Jude of a man who would tease a mouse before killing it. Jude felt vulnerable, in a place where vulnerability was traded upon.

At that moment, the lonely sound of a single bugle signaled the release into the arena of the first bull of the afternoon. Twelve thousand spectators held their breath in collective anticipation, then screamed their excitement as the twelve-hundred-pound black brute rushed in fury to the center of the ring. Once there, and finding it empty, he stood on the smooth sand, his tiny brain trying to understand where he was and searching for the enemy—any enemy—to satisfy the genetic craving to smash and destroy that had been bred into his kind for hundreds of years. He was a killer, but one without malice. His bloodlust was in response to a drive that could not be sated, and one that would soon lead him to death.

Harbuziak pulled Jude away from the others and asked quietly, "Do you know anything about Nikita S. Khrushchev?"

Jude shrugged in slight irritation. "I've done my homework. Premier of the Soviet Union from the mid-fifties until the mid-sixties when he was booted out for not being able to make the trains run on time. He was a short, fat peasant type who liked ladies who were a hell of a lot better looking than he. Supposedly died in '71, or I and the rest of the world thought he did. How much more do you want? I can tell you the middle names of his grandchildren, whether he snored in his sleep and a lot of other trivia that you should give me credit for being professional enough to have learned."

Harbuziak laughed loudly. "Touchy, touchy. I like that, Lana. Shows your young man has professional pride."

ALONG WITH THE CROWD, Manuel Molina watched silently as the bull rushed menacingly into the arena, but he had a different reason. He was the one the bull had come to kill. He was the matador. Manuel studied the animal as his assistants worked it with capes, hoping to learn some little thing that might prevent a painful, perhaps fatal, goring. Did the bull hook to the right or left? Did it seem more intelligent than normal, perhaps enough to unravel the deception of the cape too quickly? As he observed the furious animal charge the teasing, dancing capes, racing from one end of the arena to the other, each sprint adding to the heaving of its sweaty flanks and reducing its racehorse speed, Manuel noted with satisfaction that it was a brave bull. Like all matadors, Manuel dreaded a cowardly bull, one that would paw the earth in indecision and look for a way out, one with a lack of spirit that might quiet his natural rage and lead him to study the matador instead of blindly rushing ahead with murderous intent.

As he watched the animal that would in a few minutes seek to drive those sharp horns into his groin and squash him into the ground behind the pile-driver force of that massive body, the churning feeling in Manuel's stomach threatened to rise to his throat and send him retching in terror away from this death. To fight down the urge to run, Manuel glanced at the crowd, the rows of heads and faces that waved like a wind-swept cornfield in the festive excitement.

Manuel knew that for thousands of wisecracking American tourists and boozy Mexicans sitting just above him, their anticipation was not for the time-honored art of the ring, nor for the symbolism and ritual of manhood that so revealed Latin culture. They had come to witness death; no, to celebrate it with drunkenness and shouted obscenity. They wanted a spectacle of blood at bargain prices. And perhaps, if they were really fortunate, they could say years later: I was there the afternoon the matador Molina's luck ran out.

Well, he would give them their show, and hope not to give them his blood. Though, like any sane man, he wanted to turn and run from what lay before him, he was steadfast out of pride and the ever-fresh scars of desperate childhood poverty, of living in a scrap-wood and corrugated-metal shack with a dirt floor and remembering the hurting emptiness of hunger. His poverty was long ago, but Manuel knew it was as close as one disgraceful performance.

Using small nervous tugs, he straightened the waist of his lime-green, embroidered pants of his *traje de luces*, and put one slipper behind the opposite leg and scratched an imaginary itch beneath his white silk knee stocking. He reached for his cape, the heavy rose-and-yellow-colored *capote*, and stepped from behind the barricade. As he did, the bull across the arena turned in response to the crowd's roar and faced his tormentor.

HARBUZIAK CHUCKLED. "No matter how you study, you still know Chairman Khrushchev in the way of a schoolboy." He shrugged when he noticed Jude stiffening. "No offense. There's no other way you could know him, even though, as I am told, you have an excellent knowledge of Russian and have been in the country many times."

Harbuziak turned his attention to the bullring and gestured to Jude to follow the action. They sat facing the unfolding drama before them, but hardly noticed what was happening. Harbuziak gave Jude's shoulder a friendly squeeze. "Ah, you had to understand the chairman. I worked for him when he was party chairman in the Ukraine." He smiled at the memory. "Those were good, good days. The chairman was an earthy man, a simple man. A peasant, if you like. But he cared for his people, and they knew it, and loved him in return. That's all that can be asked of a leader—that he care.''

MANUEL GRIPPED THE COLLAR of his *capote* with sweating hands and held it low to the side of his body. He watched the bull pounding toward him with the speed of a fast horse; nearer, nearer the beast bore down until it seemed the vast black bulk filled his vision and he feared the small red eyes behind the sharp horns were looking into his soul. Don't move the feet. Manuel's subconscious cautioned him. He smelled the pungent odor of the animal as it swept past, and felt the vibration of the earth as the hooves came within inches of his unmoving legs. Manuel's cape guided the bull's head low and into the enticing fabric, and then the animal was past and Manuel completed a veronica with a flick of the wrist, and the heavy cloth fluttered gracefully. The crowd shouted "olé" in unison and Manuel watched as the bull turned.

Again the animal thundered down, again the cloth waved and again the crowd roared. Fear was forgotten momentarily as the cheers, the grace of his art, his feeling of mastery over his enemy, *el toro*, took control of Manuel's senses. Graceful pass followed graceful pass, the cape swirling elegantly like a flashing skirt. Manuel finished by gathering the cape at his hip and shortening the swing of the cloth, which lured the bull into trying to turn in a space shorter than its own length, and brought it to a skidding halt. Manuel turned his back to the bewildered animal and strutted away, waving to the crowd. He knew that the bull, having come to a stop, would almost certainly not follow immediately, but he knew the gringo tourists did not know that, and their enthusiastic cheers were savored, nonetheless. But Manuel also knew the dangerous part must now be faced....

JUDE WAITED FOR THE CHEERS to subside and then asked Harbuziak, "How could it be that a man who was believed dead by the whole world, was *seen* dead by the very leaders who replaced him, could suddenly be alive? Even though I heard the evidence for myself, you almost ask me to believe too much."

Harbuziak snorted at the thought of the Soviet rulers. "Men are made blind by complacency. Those in the Kremlin were deceived by their feelings of total power. When people get cocky, they get careless."

"You may be right about human nature," Jude said, "but human nature doesn't bring the dead back to life."

The Mexican woman handed each of them a piece of greasy barbecued chicken, and Harbuziak took a bite and wiped his mustache before answering. "It was the simplest thing in the world. Like many men of great power and a lot of public demands on them, Khrushchev had a double, a man who looked so much like him that only their families could tell the difference. It was almost spooky that such an identical double would exist, but I suppose that out of 250 million people, the odds aren't that great. Anyway, this double—Tarkonian his name was, an Armenian—was the exact image of Comrade Khrushchev. You probably saw his picture more than once at some official event, and thought he was the real thing.

"But back to Khrushchev. After he was booted out of office like a horny leper out of a whorehouse, he lived quietly for a few years, becoming more and more forgotten. No one in power thought of him anymore, until word came out that he had died. That's all, just died. So they shrugged, buried him and went back to their business of being important."

"But it was really Tarkonian, the double, is that what you're saying?"

"Poor Tarkonian, even in death he had to pretend to be another man. Some of my group—the Ukrainian Freedom Movement—learned that Tarkonian was dying of heart disease. They also knew that in his later years, Khrushchev had grown to hate the bastards who ran the Kremlin. And it was no secret that his life wouldn't be worth a beggar's dream if he spoke out against the regime. So, seeing an alive and hidden Khrushchev as a possible embarrassment to the people they hated, my compatriots switched Tarkonian into Khrushchev's house and bed. The smug bureaucrats came and certified Khrushchev dead, and that was that. Plop! into the ground he goes. It was easy for my friends to arrange a disguise and hiding place for the old man, which is where he is today, just waiting to reveal himself and embarrass the hell out of those bastards.''

''Why now?'' Jude asked.

''Because his wife, Nina Petrovna, recently died. He wouldn't do it while she was still alive and could be a reprisal target. Even though they could only see each other a few times, and then very secretly, he was loyal to the end.''

''If he's such a loyal guy,'' Jude asked, ''why's he doing this? Unless my dictionary is wrong, what Khrushchev wants to do is called treason. Does he want to be called a traitor by millions of his countrymen?''

Harbuziak wagged his finger in front of Jude. ''But the chairman has no intention of being a traitor. He is the most patriotic of Russians. All he wants to prove to the world is that the present masters of the Kremlin have betrayed the revolution, have tried to corrupt Communism to serve their own greed. He would never reveal anything of strategic value to the West. Never.''

Jude didn't say it, but he knew skillful CIA interrogators would trick the old man into revealing everything he knew within days, if not hours. ''It'll be nice to meet a ninety-year-old idealist,'' he said. ''Most of the ones I've known lost their idealism by thirty.''

MANUEL WATCHED IMPASSIVELY as the banderilleros danced their teasing pirouettes around the bull, turning on a circumference too tight for the animal to follow, and implanting the nasty barbed sticks into its shoulders until the blood coursed down the black flanks. Gradually, the thick muscles surrendered to the pain and the massive head began to droop ever so slightly.

An inexperienced assistant, too frightened to get close to the animal, almost threw his banderillas over the bull's horns and then ran for cover. The barbs failed to catch and were shrugged off by the bull. Behind him, Manuel heard some spectators loudly guffawing. He turned and saw four blacks sitting in the first row, drinking beer and exchanging jokes as if they were at a baseball game. "Sheeet," one man said in a loud, drunken voice, stretching out his e's like a string of paper dolls, "let that bull walk down Sixty-third Street in Chicago and one of the brothers do a better job with a razor. That ol' bull be barbecued inside two blocks...."

As soon as the bugle called away the tormentors and four gaily beribboned barbs were flopping against the bull's back, Manuel reached across the wooden barrier for his *estoque*, a rapier, and his muleta, a matador's red flag.

Manuel appeared cocky and nonchalant as he strolled toward the center of the arena; the bull turned slowly and watched every step of its enemy's progress. It was deathly tired and confused by the feeling, because its monster body had never known fatigue before. But the breeders had done their work well: the urge to kill still raged inside and the sight of the teasing cloth once again sent it on a maddened charge. Manuel extended the muleta and willed his heart and *cojones* to control his feet, to plant them unmoving in the soft sand, not only for his safety but for his art, which required steadfastness in taking the bull's charge.

The bull was upon him again, slower, weaker but more wary. Its dim brain was beginning to separate the fantasy of the cape from the real enemy standing alongside. Then the bull was by, throwing his head in frustration at again missing the elusive target. Manuel knew time was his real foe now: he needed time to further tire the bull for the kill, but each pass the animal made gave his dull brain one more shrewd bit of evidence that his pursuit was misdirected—a realization that could kill Manuel.

Pass after pass, the laboring bull strained for the cape, only to vent its rage at unresisting air. Manuel watched the beast cautiously, waiting for that moment when the tired bull would reach the point of exhaustion that would lead to death.

After three more passes, culminating with Manuel holding the cape outstretched behind his back and leading the charging bull under his arm like a dancing partner to the delight of the crowd, he faced his opponent from a distance of ten feet. Man and beast stared across the short distance at each other, taking measure for the final confrontation. The bull, having hurled its half-ton mass at full speed against one hundred illusory targets under the hot Mexico sun, stood with heaving, blood-soaked sides and slobber pouring from his open mouth. But the dense black eyes began to focus on the man staring back at it with the red cloth now held limply at his side. The bull now knew the truth, that it was the man he had to kill, the man in whom he could sense fear rising like mist from the earth.

Manuel saw with relief that the bull's front feet were close together, a certain sign that fatigue had conquered and that the shoulder blades would be at their farthest span to allow the sword thrust to reach vital organs. It was the moment of truth, when he had to go directly over the wicked horns to plant the sword. It was a moment Manuel hated because it exposed not only his guts, but his fragile nerve as well. Manuel looked at the eyes again and saw recognition—recognition that seemed to tell him through their impenetrable blackness: I now know you and I will kill you before this is done.

"*Vaca*," Manuel shouted at the bull in the traditional insult, "cow." He gripped the sword handle more tightly in his sweaty hand and slowly sighted the curved blade toward a spot in the withers just behind the neck. His quick movement forward caught the bull momentarily unaware, and a quick flick of the muleta in his left hand distracted the animal and drew its horns involuntarily toward the cloth for the instant required to reach the vulnerable spot, the spot that would end this misery for both of them.

With a flash of alarm, Manuel felt the sword point strike bone and the shock of it jarred numbness into his arm. He felt the horns brush past his leg at the same instant the sword bounced off the bone and slid easily into the bull's lungs. Manuel released the sword and moved numbly along the bull's flank, which was heaving now like a bellows. The blood from the animal's sides stained Manuel's silk costume with a streak of dirt-smeared crimson. Because he had missed the aorta, Manuel knew the bull would not collapse immediately. He only hoped the wound was sufficient to fell the animal and he would be spared the messy and embarrassing job of retrieving his sword and going over those terrible horns again.

He studied the bull impassively and waited for its lungs to fill with blood and slowly force those mighty knees to buckle and surrender to the steel. The bull no longer glared at him, but chose to ignore the existence of its tormentor. It now faced a more dreaded foe, something in its chest that was beyond goring or trampling, a searing hot weight that pulled it toward earth with increasing strength.

After three minutes of tottering on unsteady legs, the great fighting heart meekly surrendered and the bull sank to earth, resting on curled-up legs, but with head held high, and awaiting that which it could not combat.

With the bull on the ground, a matador's assistant slipped behind him with a long dagger and administered the *descabello*, a well-aimed jab that severed the spinal cord directly behind the head. After a stiff-legged shudder, the bull's battle ended.

The rules-makers had placed the greater value on the man and had made the rules lopsided against the bull. The rules won.

Manuel raised his arms to receive the cheers as a team of jittery mules dragged the dead bull from the arena, leaving a red smear along the sand that was hastily raked over in preparation for the next smear. As the bouquets and sombreros floated down from the adoring, half-drunk crowd, Manuel smiled and took deep breaths to quiet the fear that still pounded in his head and made his legs weak. His smile widened; tonight he would again have the women and the wine.

HARBUZIAK GLANCED TOWARD THE ARENA when the crowd roared. "Well, that's over. Molina makes another kill. They say that man is absolutely fearless."

While Harbuziak was admiring the matador's work, Jude glanced at Basil, who was being fed by the Mexican woman. She held a chicken leg and he awkwardly took bites from it. The sick man, his face ravaged, ate chicken like a small child, with grease streaming down his chin. Jude saw the noncommittal black eyes of a man who could only be seen and not heard. What Jude could not see were the images in Basil's mind....

The youth lay on the cold barn floor. The winter wind pierced the cracks in the walls like a knife, bloodlessly cutting his flesh with the cruelty of a sadistic attacker. He tried to remove his mind from that hard floor, from the stink of the guards in the room, from the German patrols that sought them all, from the memory of blood and fire that burdened his senses like a disease that wouldn't heal.

The youth's attention was diverted from his own misery and fear by the sudden cold blast from a door thrown open and heavy boots stomping into the room. He pushed himself to a sitting position, half out of curiosity, half out of respect for the authority he had learned stomping boots usually represented.

"On your feet, prisoner," the guard commanded gruffly. In immediate response, as though zeal to obey would rescind the death penalty against him, the youth jumped to his feet. He pressed himself against the cold wall and looked into a face familiar to him through numerous newspaper photographs and wall posters. He stiffened at the importance of the occasion. The man facing him was short and pudgy with a round white face that looked like a potato, except for the two buttonlike eyes that blinked several times as he scrutinized the hapless boy. It was the face of a peasant, and despite the desperation of his situation, the prisoner felt slightly comforted.

"This man is condemned, Comrade General Khrushchev. He abandoned his post—ran away—during a raid on a German munitions train. He'll be shot Saturday."

The important stranger stopped blinking and stared steadily at the trapped boy. "What is your name?" he asked in a hoarse, matter-of-fact voice.

"Basil, Comrade."

"Did you do the thing you're accused of, Basil?"

The youth swallowed painfully and nodded his head sadly.

"If you weren't here waiting execution, where would you like to be?"

Basil answered hesitantly. "Back with my comrades, fighting Germans, making up for what I did."

"A brave answer, or a clever one." The man nodded approvingly. "Both qualities are useful to us right now." His thoughts ranged for an instant to the recent purges of the Red Army conducted by the paranoiac Stalin, in which thousands of high-ranking officers had been shot for trifling or for no reason at all. On impulse, he turned to the officer accompanying him. "Comrade Colonel, I suggest you return this boy to his unit. Let's not be so hasty to shoot our fellow Soviets. It's not as though there are too few Germans to go around."

The colonel gaped in astonishment. "But—but Comrade General Khrushchev! This soldier has been court-martialed and found guilty. The paperwork is all completed. The records—"

His superior waved his hand in dismissal. "Throw the records away. You made them, you tear them up."

Turning to the youth, who was tearful in gratitude, he said, "I **give** you back your life. Use it to kill Germans." Then, followed by a mumbling colonel, he turned and walked back into the snow. . . .

Jude waited until Harbuziak turned away from the action in the bullring, then asked, "Where is Khrushchev being held? What is his health? There are a thousand things I need to know."

Harbuziak smiled and shook his head. "My dear compatriot, there's an old Ukrainian saying that you can't bait a fox trap with haste. There's only so much I can tell you. The rest you'll learn—or you won't learn, depending on you."

As they prepared to leave, Jude glanced briefly at Basil and met the same stolid stare. In the instant their eyes locked, Basil tried to will his thoughts through to the man who could save the one who had once saved him. But he could only cry out in his silence: You are betrayed! Death is at your elbow!

Jude turned away from the man who could not speak.

THE SUN WAS TEETERING on the western horizon when they left the Plaza de Toros just as the last bull of the afternoon was dragged from the ring. As they pulled away in the Buick ahead of the crowd, Lana said, "Look at that sun! I know a place not far from here that offers the best sunset on the Pacific, and the best lobster this side of Maine. How about it?"

"I'm with you," Jude said. "Sounds better than that greasy chicken."

The Buick immediately nosed into a side street that led into the depths of the poorest section of Tijuana. As they drove carefully through narrow, winding streets, the hovels grew seedier and the streets more potholed. People thronged along the narrow sidewalks to the accompaniment of tinny mariachi music coming from cheap radios perched on windowsills, and the greasy smell of frying food seemed like fumes in the air. Jude glanced curiously at Lana a couple of times, but she seemed to know exactly where she was headed.

As though guessing his doubts, she said reassuringly, "We're almost at the place. It's terrific. I've eaten there a couple of times." Earlier they had driven for an hour from the San Diego airport and not said ten sentences to each other, but now Lana began to chatter about the bullfights, about the preparation of lobster, about shopping in Tijuana. She kept Jude so occupied he didn't notice a beat-up old Chevy about two blocks back that made every turn the Buick made.

After another twenty minutes of snaking the big car through the slum, she pulled up close and parallel to a pink stucco building set next to the broken sidewalk, obviously a restaurant by the garish neon that bedecked it. She shut off the engine and turned to Jude. "Well, here we are. It doesn't look like much, but you're about to taste the best lobster in Baja California."

Inside, a silent bartender absently massaged a glass with a gray-stained towel and watched them walk across the bare linoleum floor. A television in the corner above the bar prattled on with a game show in English, a pickup from a San Diego station. A bedraggled band of two guitarists and a violinist picked and sawed away at some Mexican ballad, more for their own pleasure than that of the handful of customers seated at unmatching tables. Lana and Jude took a table near a dirty window that overlooked a bottle-littered beach and the glorious Pacific crashing against the rusted hulks of several abandoned autos.

A fat woman with stringy hair and wearing bedroom slippers shuffled over and stood passively by their table. Lana ordered lobster for both of them, but the woman cocked her head apologetically and said, *"Siento, señora*, sorry, no lobster today."* She handed them two food-stained menus instead.

Jude wasn't about to entrust his intestines to the mercies of this kitchen. Bottled beer, at least, was safe. *"Cerveza, por favor."*

Lana agreed. *"Dos. Carta Blanca."*

They sat and watched the sunset for a while, each the prisoner of personal thoughts. Finally, Lana turned to Jude with a funny little smile and studied him while slowly running a finger along the rim of her beer glass.

"Whatever amuses you, share. I'm ready for a laugh," he said.

"I was just thinking about you and the little girl you gave the money to. Know what that tells me about you?"

"That I like little girls?"

"And probably big girls. But my theory is that you come from a big family, and probably a poor one."

"Just because I gave a few bucks to a cute kid? Lady, you should be reading palms." Jude laughed, but with a touch of sarcasm.

"Tell me I'm wrong."

"Okay. You're wrong.

Lana shrugged. "Well, it seemed like a good theory. If I'm not more intuitive than that, I might as well be a spy. Tell me, how wrong was I?"

"Only child and comfortably middle-class."

"Come on, now," she teased. "No one's just 'middle-class.' That's being evasive. I want to know who this Jude Miller really is."

"You mean beyond the briefing you had about me before taking on this assignment? My, the CIA isn't very thorough these days. Okay. First, I'm not really Jude Miller." He waited for the flash of surprise to pass from her face. "Don't worry, it was nothing subversive. I was born Judah Moskowitz. If I seem to have long arms, it's because they were stretched from being in a tug-of-war between a born-again Baptist mother and an Orthodox Jewish father."

"That's quite a combination," she said. "How did that come about?"

"They met in the South during the Second World War. He was stationed down there. It was about the first time he'd met anyone not from Brooklyn, and the first time she'd met anyone not from Alabama. I'd call it fascination at first sight. They got married, as horny, enthralled twenty-year-olds are inclined to do, and moved back to New York where they are still living, unhappily ever after."

"So what religion are you?"

He shrugged. "I dunno. Pick one. As a kid I was shuttled back and forth between the haftarah and the Sermon on the Mount. I've been bar mitzvahed and I've been baptized."

Lana almost choked on her beer, and couldn't suppress a laugh. "How, for God's sake?"

"When I was a kid, I'd spend Christmas with my mother's folks in Alabama, and then visit my dad's family every summer. Talk about being raised schizoid ... Being a good kid, eager to please, I became whatever each family wanted. Hell, I was just a passenger, they were doing the driving. The only thing both families agreed on about me was circumcision, and then for different reasons. Between my mother's side and my dad's, I had two views of America, different as night and day, except for one thing—both were fanatic patriots. But it was kind of funny, the two families couldn't even agree on that. Grandpa Moskowitz worshiped Roosevelt. He was an old-line socialist and believed FDR could do no wrong—except when he didn't go far enough to suit grandpa's radical tastes.

"Grandpa Johnson, on the other hand, thought Roosevelt was the devil incarnate. Called him a traitor to his class, which is funny when you consider Grandpa Johnson probably never had a thousand dollars in his pocket at one time in his whole life. But he sure protected those rich folks back East." Jude chuckled at the irony. "He was a hardscrabble farmer, but he read all the time and kept the faith. Yes sir, no one ever accused him of being un-American.

"Grandpa Moskowitz believed the government should be into everything—including nationalizing General Motors. Grandpa Johnson thought the only purpose of government was to stay the hell out of his life. He wouldn't even describe schools as public schools—he always called them 'tax-supported schools.'

"They hated each other, even though they'd never met. Communist and Fascist, that's what they called each other. You can imagine how a small boy who loved them both enjoyed hearing that crap."

"Which one did you agree with?" Lana asked.

"Both, depending on which one I was with at the moment. I loved them and wanted desperately for them to like each other. But I guess neither was able to open his mind that far. What I probably wanted was for them, by their actions, to tell me that the two sides of me were compatible, that I wasn't a dichotomous freak, half-Baptist, half-Jew. I wanted my world pulled together.

"The only thing both sides could give me without an argument was an unshakable belief in the ol' U.S. of A. That's one thing I could believe without starting an argument with one or the other. So that was our common ground, that this country was the greatest place on earth. My dad even changed his name to Miller so it sounded more 'American.'"

"That's kind of sad," she said.

He shrugged. "Didn't do any harm. What's in a name? He just wanted his son to be mainstream. He meant well. He was a Shriner—you know the guys with the silly fez hats—American Legion, Little League umpire, you name it. He believed in it, so he wanted the same for his only son.''

Lana nodded. "And what better way for a wholesome, mainstream American boy to please everyone than by joining the CIA right out of college? Almost like being a preacher, or a rabbi. Jude finally found a religion that pleased everyone.''

He started to back off, "Well, it was satisfying for a while.''

She poured the last of her third beer into his glass. "I once read that no one's so lonely as a priest who's lost the faith. I guess it soured for you after... after the...''

Jude suddenly concentrated on the check and tossed a bill on the table. "Don't believe everything you read in personnel files.'' He looked around the room as a means of breaking off the conversation. "This beer is starting to overflow. I'm going to the men's room; be out in a minute.''

"I'll wait for you in the car,'' she said, and started toward the door.

JUDE FINISHED and looked for a place to wash his hands, saw the dirty towel above a dripping, rust-stained sink, thought better of it and walked out of the room marked Hombres and through the front door.

As he emerged from the restaurant into the ocean mists of late evening, Lana was not in sight. The sidewalks that had been teeming with Sunday strollers when they arrived an hour ago were now deserted. The restaurant's neon was suddenly switched off, making him a stranger on a dark street. Mystified and a little apprehensive, Jude began walking toward the car. In the corner of his eye he caught movement coming at him from the shadows. His training returned, and he whirled to meet whatever was trying to creep up on him.

Suddenly standing directly in front of him where they had emerged from a dark doorway were two Mexican men, and the tense glares they directed at Jude made it obvious this was not a friendly visit. They exuded all the charm of dyspeptic rattlesnakes. The two men were in their early twenties and looked like the punks seen on street corners in bad neighborhoods in any big city. They were dressed in tight, shiny black pants, flowered polyester shirts open down the front exposing hairless, bony chests, and cheap, high-heeled patent-leather shoes, one with a green pair, the other with red. Their arms were tattooed with the type of amateur design recognized in every police station as "jailhouse tattoos," done in prison yards by artists with more time than talent. Both men were small and skinny, but Jude knew from experience that, even with his six feet one inch, and 180 pounds, stature bore no relationship to deadliness.

He instantly recognized three mistakes on their part: they were wearing leather-soled shoes, thus giving him a big advantage in traction; they hadn't sprung at him instantly, thereby losing the advantage of surprise; and they had positioned themselves so the building wall was close behind them, which gave them little room to maneuver.

Jude's heart began flopping like a carp in a boat and his nerves zoomed to maximum RPMs, but he silently held his ground and watched as one of the men made a switchblade appear from his pocket as though part of a magic act. The other man was not quite so quick and Jude saw him start to pull from his pocket what emerged as the butt of a small, cheap pistol. Jude knew if he didn't act quickly it would be all over, and he wouldn't like the result.

After giving a shoulder fake to the assailant with the knife, which momentarily put him on the defensive, Jude pivoted on his left foot and swung his right in the direction of the man who had just managed to pull out his pistol. Jude's toe buried itself in his adversary's groin like a soccer ball, and sounded as if he had stomped on a mud bank. The man screamed and slumped to the ground holding his crotch, whimpering like a child whose favorite toy had just been broken, and letting the forgotten pistol clatter to the ground.

Jude whirled around just as the knifer slashed the air right in front of his eyes. Before the man could recover to swing again, Jude slugged him in the face—just a glancing blow without his shoulder behind it, but enough to stun him and give Jude the second he needed to desperately scan the dark ground for the pistol. Just as the knife-wielder bunched himself for a second attack, Jude spotted the gun a few feet to his right, about equidistant from himself and the knifer. The other man followed Jude's gaze and also spotted the gun. They both went for it at the same time, but Jude's rubber soles took firm hold on the concrete while his adversary's leather ones slipped and he fell to one knee. It took him only an instant to recover, but by the time he was ready to strike again with the knife, he suddenly found himself staring into the unblinking black eye of a pistol pointed directly at his face. The assailant's look changed from rage to concern to fright as he slowly backed away from his prey, who had suddenly become the predator. The man turned sideways to Jude, trying to flee but afraid to remove his eyes from the threatening gun. He was joined by his companion, still nursing his savaged groin. Jude, suddenly in command, balanced the pistol judiciously as the pair retreated down the broken sidewalk, the knife man glancing back apprehensively, and his comrade hobbling along crablike and holding his testicles as if they were thin-shelled eggs filled with nitroglycerin.

As Jude watched the pair scamper down the street, he heard movement behind him and whirled to face Lana, who had suddenly appeared. "What in the world is happening here?" she demanded.

Jude's legs were shaking and his breathing came in labored rasps. He leaned against the building and wiped the sweat from his face. He took deep, gulping breaths until the aftershock of two men trying to kill him subsided enough for him to talk without a trembling voice. "I was jumped by a couple of thugs. They seemed to be waiting for me." He looked closely at Lana, then peered suspiciously in the direction the two men had disappeared into the dark, then checked the other way. "I thought you were going to be at the car."

"Oh, I decided to go to the bathroom, too. God, I can't believe this happened right on the street." If Lana had caught his look, she ignored it. "Are you going to call the police?"

He looked again at the pistol he still held. "The last thing we need is a messy encounter with Mexican cops. Whenever Americans get mugged down here, the local cops seem to think the gringos are guilty of picking on poor Mexican criminals just trying to make a living. Plus, I'd rather not have to explain how I came to be holding this." He bounced the gun lightly in his hand. "So—" Jude opened the revolver, removed the cylinder and threw it far into the weeds, and the rest of the gun into the ocean surf. "Okay, let's get out of here."

The drive back to San Diego was quiet. Jude tried to compose his jangled nerves by gazing longingly—and, he hoped, discreetly—at the round dimpled knees and soft thighs that showed beneath the edge of Lana's skirt as she worked the pedals. Lana seemed sympathetic to his ordeal and expressed her concern in a velvet voice with the therapeutic value of soft warm water.

After she returned the car to Hertz and they prepared to go their separate ways, Jude said goodbye. *"Proschaite, Russkii."*

The words jerked her head back like a slap. "How—how did you know that?"

"It wasn't that tough. Bustamonte spoke Russian to you until he saw me, but anybody can speak the language—me, for instance. It was the way you spoke that tipped me off. Your diction is almost flawless, but I picked up on little things; Russians tend to confuse *v* and *b* in the same way Japanese trip over *l* and *r*. Your English is excellent—it could fool almost anybody. But perhaps you forgot that I'm not just anybody.'' Jude frowned. ''Why wasn't I told you were from Russia? What's the damned secret? Being kept in the dark on something like this really pisses me off.''

A smile barely creased her lips. ''Maybe we wanted to find out if you've slipped.''

She smiled, then cocked her head to listen as the public address called her flight. ''Look, I've got to run, but I'll explain it to you when we meet again.''

''Again? When's that? Will you please—'' But Jude was talking to an empty corridor. Lana had disappeared in the direction of her boarding gate. He was suddenly alone, staring at the disappearing backside of a very mysterious woman he found immensely attractive. He loved the view, but the unanswered questions lingered like a bad odor.

CHAPTER FOUR

JUDE LEANED AGAINST THE PILLOWS of the cranked-up hospital bed and stared out the window at the stunted far-north fir trees and gathering gloom of the Alaska winter. It was only two in the afternoon, but the Arctic darkness was already extending the shadows until they neared the point of merging into early night. The treeless, rocky peaks of the Chugach Mountains formed a perimeter around the Anchorage basin and combined with the dark waters of Cook Inlet to hold the city in a prison of brittle, crystalline cold.

Jude mused over the happenings of the past month. First, he had been tested for resistance to seasickness, then given a crash course in the speech mannerisms of the ordinary Russian seaman, and next, a frustrating and sometimes painfully hot education in the duties of galley cook on a fishing vessel. Fortunately, his life in the California woods had given him the requisite rough, weathered skin on his hands and face to pass for a sailor. Finally, and by far the least enjoyable, his CIA overlords had felt it necessary to reopen his old appendicitis scar, just in case he had to prove the reason for his layover in Anchorage to suspicious new shipmates. He gingerly touched the almost healed incision and shook his head at the thoroughness of his playmates.

The nurse on duty opened the door and silently ushered in his first visitor. Early on the hospital staff had given up in frustration in their efforts to communicate with the patient who spoke only Russian. Especially since he had been brought into the hospital by ambulance with a fresh incision and no explanation of what it was for and where he had received it.

Into the room now marched a small man of about fifty, dressed in a wool suit that appeared to have been bought off a rack at the Salvation Army and that hung on him like a Halloween costume. His face was rough and chapped and weathered to a burned rust color, and his manner reflected either his discomfort at the bright, sterile environment of the hospital, or the danger of the role he was playing.

"Good afternoon, Comrade Markov. I'm Captain Mitrovich. I'm told your recovery is very satisfactory. I'm pleased for you," he said in rapid-fire Russian. He was jumpy and obviously wishing he were in a Siberian mine rather than in that room.

Jude studied the master of the *Novi Mir*—New World—the ship that would be his means of slipping into the Soviet Union. The man was risking certain execution for being a party to such a treasonous enterprise, and Jude wondered what compelled him to do it.

"Thank you, Comrade Captain. I'm about to be released, and looking forward to serving under you," he said in flawless Russian.

Mitrovich edged closer to the bed and looked at the ceiling and around the room as though for eavesdroppers. He lowered his voice and said, "Goddamn, man, I have to be crazy to do this. The very idea, smuggling a CIA agent into the country—and as a galley cook!" He shakily lit a cigarette and then extinguished it and threw it away in disgust. "Jesus, don't you realize they'll kill us both if you're found out?" The captain started muttering to himself and looking as if he had just bitten into a wormy apple.

Jude was alarmed at the man's lack of self-control, recognizing it as a gun pointed at his own head. "Why don't you try to relax? You look like you're halfway down the last mile.

Edginess like yours is like walking around carrying a flashing red light.''

The captain forced a smile and valiantly took several deep breaths. After a moment he gained control of himself. ''Let's get back to the ship. The crew is waiting to get ashore like a bunch of horny bulls in a dairy barn. They don't get many chances at shore leave, and they have a preference for the 'capitalist' women you have here.''

''What's a 'capitalist' woman?''

The captain, now over his jumpiness, grinned lewdly. ''It's where the price you pay to get the clap is competitive. My men don't have much money, but they sure are eager bidders.''

Jude slipped into faded but clean Russian work pants, threadbare flannel shirt, heavy work shoes, and then put on a heavy parka and black stocking cap. He picked up the battered canvas bag that held the rest of his belongings, and led the captain to the door. ''Let's go meet my new shipmates.''

The two men took a taxi to the dock where the *Novi Mir* was berthed. Jude stood for several moments on the pier as the blowing snow swirled about his feet like crystallized mist, and examined the vessel that would be his home for the next several weeks. It was a modern trawler of medium size, painted white with red and black stripes running along the hull. As well as having cranelike net davits, it looked like a floating radar station, making it obvious that the ship also served for electronic surveillance.

As they walked up the gangplank, which was suspended shakily high above the ice-clogged water, several curious members of the crew ambled over to greet them. Captain Mitrovich suddenly turned brusque and beckoned for the second mate. ''Here, Andrey, this is the new cook I told you about. His name's Petr Markov. Take him below to a bunk, then see if you can get some work out of him. Let's hope he can improve on the slop we've been forced to eat.'' Then, turning to Jude, Mitrovich said in a loud voice, ''Okay, sailor, just do your work and keep your nose clean and you'll get along fine. But I warn you, get out of line and you'll see what a tough bastard I can be."

"Yes, sir."

The mate eyed Jude with interest as they descended to the crew's quarters. "So you've been vacationing in the U.S.A., eh? How was it? Did you get laid?"

Jude gave a short laugh. "In a hospital bed with my belly sliced open? I'll tell you, I didn't think much about pussy. Even when the nurses gave me a bath."

"Pretty nurses?"

Jude shrugged. "They were female—ordinarily, that's all you need."

"Hah!" the mate snorted. "Wait'll you see some of the oinkers aboard this ship. Female weight lifters with bad breath is what they are. Man, just thinking about them makes my pecker shrivel."

Two flights down the iron stairs they came to a large room filled with triple-tiered bunks. The room contained lounging sailors engaged in a variety of time-filling activities, waiting for their one evening of shore leave. Some were writing letters, some reading, some just surrendering to temporary inactivity; others were clustered in small groups, laughing at jokes they had heard before, playing cards. The air was filled with the blue-gray billows of a dozen cigarettes. The Russian folk music blaring over the loudspeaker was tinnily sniped at by several transistors playing American rock.

The mate gestured to an empty bunk and Jude arranged his possessions in the footlocker next to it, then flopped down and tried to relax by staring at the wire cross-hatching of the mattress just inches above his head. He took deep breaths and tried to calm himself, knowing that the first test was only moments away. Would he be convincing to these uncomplicated men who, in some respects, could be more difficult to fool than a KGB expert?

It wasn't long before one of his shipmates wandered over and extended his hand. "I guess you're the new man, the one from the hospital." He was a tall, lanky man with shaggy prematurely gray hair and a greasy black turtleneck sweater above dirty work pants. "Name's Kruglov, from Minsk. Machinist, just off shift."

Jude reached for the hand. "Markov, Moscow. Yeah, I got left behind when the old gut kicked up a fuss. Thought I was gonna bust. The Americans took pretty good care of me, I gotta give them that."

Kruglov sat on the edge of the bunk across from Jude. "Mikhail," he said simply.

"Petr," Jude answered.

"What part of Moscow?" Kruglov asked.

"I was raised on Novoslobodskaya Street, between the Soviet Army Theater and the Savyolovo railway station. They tore our little house down to put up some big ugly building." Jude adopted a sour expression to mark the memory.

"The mate said you were a cook. Damn, I hope you're better than Derevenko. The old bastard is drunk most of the time, fucks up everything he does when he's not. He's got this one little creation we call maggot stew. Need to hear more?"

Jude laughed. "I get the picture." Nonchalantly, he opened a small duffel bag and let the contents spill out on the bunk. The dozen cartons of Marlboros, four pairs of blue jeans and two quarts of American vodka lay on his blankets sending out a message like neon.

"Where'd you get the goods?" a voice from the back asked.

"One of the nurses in the hospital took pity on a poor seaman," Jude said.

"Were you fucking her?" the voice asked hopefully.

"Does a gentleman tell tales on a lady?" Jude teased.

An excited buzz filled the room and a group of sailors crowded around, eager to trade for Jude's goods. In minutes, he had gained a fur hat, a new down-filled vest, promises to take several of his late deck watches, and a quart of Jack Daniel's.

The sailor who had surrendered the Jack Daniel's for the two bottles of Smirnoff vodka eyed the unfamiliar bottle with the Russian name. He opened it and took an experimental sip, then grimaced and wiped his lips. "Bah! This is cow piss. Half water. They should call it Pantywaist vodka, not a good Russian name like Smirnoff." He reached for the Jack Daniel's. "Trade's off," he said, glaring at Jude.

Kruglov grabbed the man's wrist and held it a few inches short of the Jack Daniel's bottle. "Kruglov's second law of the sea: a deal's a deal," he said quietly to the man, who grumbled and walked away carrying his vodka bottles.

"Thanks, but I could have handled that," Jude said.

"The bastard knows the rules. When someone tries to cheat, it's everyone's business."

"By the way," Jude asked, "what's Kruglov's first rule of the sea?"

"That every sailor eventually takes an unwanted bath." Kruglov slapped Jude on the back. "We're going ashore tonight to check out some pussy. Want to come?"

Jude almost begged off, but realized such an act would impress his new shipmates as strange behavior, so he said, "I'll try for as long as I can." He patted his stomach gingerly. "As long as the old belly holds up."

Kruglov became increasingly animated as he anticipated shore leave. "They say those Alaska Eskimo women in the bars will give you a blow job for just buying them a drink. And they've got fuck movies you can go see right out in public, like you were buying a ticket to the Bolshoi." He laughed with delight. "Personally, I think the capitalists have the right idea about sex. The whorehouses don't even have queues in front of them." Kruglov looked around at the lounging men. "Which reminds me of a story."

At the hint of a new off-color story, the men stopped what they were doing and looked expectantly at Kruglov.

"There's this young girl who goes to her professor and asks what her grade is going to be. The professor tells her she's going to fail. 'Oh, professor,' she begs, 'I'd do anything for a good grade.' 'Okay,' the professor says, 'I want you for tonight.' Well this is a very proper girl, a virgin, but she'll have to go to work in a factory if she fails school, so she says as sexy as she can, 'What do you want me to do?' The professor says, 'Go to the bakery at 6:00 p.m. and stand in line. My wife will relieve you in the morning.' "

The men hooted and groaned at the punch line, but the noise dried up like a Sahara rain as they glanced up and saw a familiar shadow approaching slowly down the narrow aisle. Silence flooded the area like a tidal wave and snuffed out the festive mood with its oppressive weight. The man approaching them exuded all the charm of a piranha that had just had a root canal. He was tall and bald with a pocked face and sallow cheeks that made his head resemble a skull covered only by a mask of skin. He was dressed in work clothes, but they were clean and neatly pressed. His hands looked soft and he didn't have the wind- and sun-burned face of the other men. He glanced around the area, taking stock of those present like a judge in a courtroom. He smiled no greeting and received none.

"Have any of you comrades seen Gurko?" he asked.

"No, Comrade Florinsky," Kruglov answered deferentially. "Have you tried the engine room?"

Florinsky's face reddened as he glared at Kruglov, who was innocent but handy. "When I send word I want to see him, I don't expect to hunt him. When you see the little idiot, tell him to report to my cabin immediately." He turned to leave, but noticed Jude, who could feel his cold gaze boring into the top of his head. Slowly, Jude raised his eyes in a way he hoped was nonchalant, and waited with a forced smile.

"You're the new man, the one from the American hospital." It was a statement, not a question.

"Petr Markov," Jude responded and started to extend his hand, but saw it wouldn't be welcome, and lamely diverted it to smoothing his hair.

"Well, Comrade Markov, we'll have to become acquainted. I'm curious about someone who's spent time around Americans, curious to see what ideas he's picked up." He turned abruptly and left.

Seeing the quizzical look on Jude's face, Kruglov volunteered the answer. "That's Kyril Florinsky, the ship's political officer. He's a real prick, but don't tell him I said it. Don't cross the bastard at all. He can have you thrown in the brig if he wakes up with a stomachache and thinks that'll cure it. Even the captain doesn't cross him. Funny thing, most political officers try to be nice guys so they can develop stoolies, but that asshole must think he's Stalin's ghost or something."

Jude smiled engagingly. "I get along by going along. He won't even know I exist."

"Fuck, don't bet on it," Kruglov said, drawing the oath out like a sigh. "His own mother probably disowned him when he sent her to a labor camp. Anyway, what's to be done about it? Just tell him what he wants to hear—Comrade."

Jude looked quickly at Kruglov to see what he meant by the sarcastic "comrade" reference, but decided it was just a typical sailor's cynical comment on the shopworn form of address.

They were interrupted by a commotion headed their way down the aisle. Both turned at the noise and saw a small man approaching, poking one sailor and then playfully shaking the bunk of another.

"Here comes Gurko," Kruglov said. "Wait'll I tell him he's in Florinsky's shit can.... Hey, Gurko! Florinsky wants to see you in his cabin. Better hurry, he's pissed."

The racket stopped as Gurko evaluated the news. Then, with great deliberation, he pronounced his judgment. "Fuck him." He plopped down next to Jude and began to study the newcomer by staring into his face from a distance of about one foot.

Jude couldn't help but return the stare. Before him sat a gnome of a man not much more than five feet tall, and nearly as broad. His nose was long and crooked, as though he had tried to tuck his head into a box and the lid wouldn't close without bending the nose. It was given an extra centimeter of unneeded length by a mole crested by several hairs that waved when he wrinkled the nose. His tuft of black hair was as tangled as a can of angry worms. His eyes resembled those of a basset hound with insomnia bags. He might as well have been one-handed because he kept his right hand steadily employed picking his nose. First one nostril would get a swabbing, then the other, then back to the first. He looked ageless in the way of people who don't fit standard appearance patterns. He could have been thirty or forty.

"What's your name, you ugly asshole?" he said to Jude in an inquisitive, but not unfriendly way.

"Markov. Petr Markov. Who the hell are you?"

The man removed his finger from his nose long enough to smirk, and Kruglov answered for him. "This is Boris Gurko. He's a liar, a thief, a coarse goddamn nose-picker, but the best ship's mechanic from Vladivostok to Arkhangel'sk. Don't loan him any money, stay away from any women he screws until they've been in quarantine about a month. He attracts clap like garbage attracts flies."

Gurko shrugged. "He's just jealous 'cause I'm the only one on this ship gets laid regular." He looked at Jude appraisingly. "What tragedy in your life brought you aboard the *Novi Mir*?"

"Appendicitis. I was on *Zvezda* out of Odessa when my gut turned into a cement mixer here in Anchorage. Had to stay over. That put me on this ship."

"Let me see your scar," Gurko demanded bluntly.

Jude hesitated, but then realized there was no reason not to show his scar, so he loosened his belt and dropped his pants enough for the ugly red slash to show.

"Yob!" Gurko swore, impressed. "I've cut myself worse than that with a razor. A Russian doctor would have carved you like a holiday goose. Remind me to find myself an American doctor next time I'm sick.

"What're American hospitals like?" Gurko asked as Jude refastened his belt. "I bet the biggest difference between them and Russian hospitals is the Americans put their bathrooms indoors." He laughed loudly at his own joke, sounding like a parrot mimicking a donkey.

"About the same. Nurses are ugly and everyone snores."

"What's your job?" Gurko seemed the self-appointed in-quisitor of the crew.

"I'm a cook."

Gurko let out a whoop and leaped to his feet, almost jamming his finger in a nostril. "Hey, Derevenko, come here!" he shouted in the direction of the adjoining galley. While he waited for the man to appear, he rubbed his hands together and chuckled. "I love it. I fucking love it."

Soon a fat man in a dirty apron waddled into the bunk area and growled something unintelligible at Gurko that Jude took to be a greeting, perhaps friendly, perhaps not. He appeared to be about sixty, with tufts of white hair sticking up from the sides of his otherwise bald head and with a heavily veined boozer's nose that looked like a river delta from an airplane. It seemed clear he found little in life to smile about.

Gurko put an arm on the cook's shoulder and theatrically extended the other in the direction of Jude. "I wanted you to be the first to know of our deliverance, Derevenko. We now have in our midst, a *real* cook. Meet Comrade Markov, a graduate chef of the finest schools of Paris and New York, and celebrated throughout all the land for the perfection of his dishes. In another day, he would have prepared table for czars, but under our glorious socialism, his talents are devoted to us, poor workingmen. Rejoice, for we are saved from the slop you spill on our plates, Derevenko. This is just one more bit of proof that Communism works. Either that, or there truly is a just god."

Jude fidgeted uncomfortably under Gurko's bombast, and Derevenko's glare. "Hey, look, I'm not a chef. I'm not even a good cook. Would I be here if I was?" Then, casting a conciliatory glance at the staring and silent Derevenko, "I don't want to take anyone else's job."

Derevenko muttered something and waddled back to the galley. Jude looked crossly at Gurko. "Now, he'll probably make life miserable for me. A workingman never needs extra enemies."

Gurko picked his nose, then examined what he speared with a sharp, dirty fingernail. "Derevenko will drink anything that'll run downhill. Buy him a bottle of vodka and scrub the pots and he'll proclaim you the prince of the kitchen; buy him two bottles and he'll even make you chief cook, 'cause he'll be too drunk to care. If you call Derevenko a drunk, you'd also call the North Pole cold. I shipped with him for five years and didn't know he drank until I accidently bumped into him sober one day."

Gurko suddenly clapped his hands and shouted. "Hey! Shore leave tonight. We're gonna drink this town dry and screw all the women." The men standing around picked up the excitement and headed for the showers, singing, hitting each other playfully on the arms and hoping that soap and water would remove the embedded engine grease and odor of fish from their lean, work-toughened bodies.

"Any idea where to go?" Kruglov asked no one in particular as he picked up a towel and soap.

Gurko conspiratorially motioned Kruglov and Jude close to him. "I have it on excellent authority that a place called the Cherry Pit is where to find cheap booze, and good-looking broads with a desire to ease international tensions."

Kruglov grinned. "I've got a tension that could stand some easing."

Gurko removed a finger from his nose and placed it to his lips. "Then be quiet. What we do not need tagging along is the entire Soviet fishing fleet."

JUDE, GURKO, KRUGLOV and Derevenko stood hunched together on the dock in the bitter cold like old men protective of fragile bones. Like most who live and work year-round in freezing temperatures, they had no relish for the cold, and the idea that exposure made them somehow immune from its effects would have earned a groan of disbelief, and probably a thoughtful insult or two.

After a few minutes of cursing and slapping gloved hands together, Gurko spotted a cruising taxi in the distance. He shouted and ran down the street waving his arms until the brake lights went on and Gurko signaled for the others to hurry. Although each of the four spoke a little English, as would be expected of world-traveled sailors, nothing Derevenko said in any language was understandable. Gurko, who had the best English, became the spokesman by default because Jude allowed himself only a few words, which he used haltingly.

The cabbie, a bored, tobacco-chewing man in his fifties wearing a three-day growth of beard and a dark red Washington Redskins cap boasting a bold R on the front, assessed his passengers in the rearview mirror and saw four workingmen, probably sailors, excitedly talking a strange language. "Where to?" he interrupted.

"Cheery Peet," Gurko responded.

The men leaned back in the warmth of the cab and savored the idea they were just minutes away from a prime fleshpot of the decadent West. Kruglov dug his elbow into Derevenko's fleshy waist. "Ready to dip the wick, old-timer?" Derevenko grunted something, then Gurko butted in to translate the grunts. "He just said he's had the same girlfriends for years and he won't be unfaithful. He's getting it from Madame Palm and her five daughters."

"Where you boys from?" The driver turned down a side street and prepared to boost his fare by driving his unknowing passengers double the distance to the nightclub.

Gurko leaned across the front seat, and said, "Soviet trawler *Novi Mir.*"

The driver took a harder look in the mirror and was quiet for a few moments as he balanced the conflicting values of a nice fare against certain ideals. Deciding, he slammed the brakes into a sliding stop. His passengers looked perplexed because there was no nightclub in sight. The driver swiveled to face them, and said, "I fought in Korea and Vietnam—damn near got my ass shot off. I ain't got no use for Communists, man or boy. I reckon I don't need money so bad I gotta haul Commies down to some whorehouse to get their ashes hauled. So I'd be obliged if you boys'd jist get your asses outta my decent, God-fearin' American cab. I mean pronto."

After a rough and hurried translation by Gurko, the sailors reluctantly piled out of the cab and onto the freezing, deserted pavement. Before he slammed the door, Gurko turned to the driver and shouted, "Too bad they shot your balls off in Vietnam, you capitalist asshole."

The door was jerked from his grasp as the driver pulled away in a shower of snow and ice from beneath the spinning wheels. About fifty feet down the road, he stopped, rolled

down the window and shouted back, "Fuck commies." As
he accelerated hard again, a sudden gust of wind ripped the
cap from his head and it rolled back to the feet of his ex-
passengers. He instinctively braked and looked back but
thought better of it, then gunned the car down the street.

"*Rasproet tvoyu mat!* Fuck your mother all to hell!" Gurko
shouted some profanity about the cabbie's mother as he drove
off, then walked over and picked up the cap, examined it
briefly and put it on his head. With an air of resignation, the
four, walking in a cluster for warmth, started moving toward
the glow of neon in the distance.

After being directed and misdirected several times, they finally arrived at the door of a nondescript bar with a huge neon
sign depicting a nearly naked dancing girl, topped by a
twenty-foot cocktail glass and the blinking letters of the words
Cherry Pit running vertically down the length of the sign with
No Cover Charge directly below. The inside of the place was
shrouded in darkness except for serving lights at the bar and
a dimly lit stage on which a fat, bleached blonde with a heavy
bruise on one thigh and tattoos of butterflies on both breasts
strode up and down, laboriously removing clothing while a
scratchy tape played selections from *Flower Drum Song*. The
woman ignored the rhythm of the music and moved like a
blacksmith with a limp. She carefully piled the shed articles
of clothing on a straight-backed chair instead of letting them
flutter to the floor in the traditional way, as though she considered a wrinkled or dusty garment was too high a price for
sensuality. She was a businesswoman with a product to sell,
and didn't try to conceal that she thought the price too small
and the customers contemptible.

The atmosphere of the Cherry Pit was that of a cave occupied by shadowy figures most of whom neither spoke nor
looked at one another, but each of whom seemed transfixed
by the bored woman on the stage, as though witnessing a
primitive rite.

The four sailors took seats just below and facing the stage, the lip of which served as a barlike table for those seated directly below the dancer. A waitress immediately appeared and asked for their orders. After quickly glancing at the others, Gurko said, "Vodka."

"Four screwdrivers?" the waitress asked, writing on a napkin.

"No, vodka," Gurko responded. Jude immediately picked up the communication problem, but couldn't intervene.

"White Russian?" the woman countered.

"We all Red," Gurko answered defensively, not wanting to be linked with the anti-Communist movement of Russian history.

"Look, honey." The waitress retreated a step and placed a hand on her hip in exasperation. "It's been a long shift. If you want to order a drink, fine, if not, you can't sit here. Now what's it gonna be?"

Jude leaned between Gurko and the woman. "Beer," he said.

"What kind?" the waitress asked, then quickly said, "Never mind. Four beers."

The men turned their attention to the stage where the blonde had finished undressing and was doing a few desultory bumps and grinds. The twin butterflies fluttered lazily on her flopping breasts and her patch of black pubic hair oscillated directly in front of the upturned, rapt faces at the edge of the stage. Abruptly, the music stopped and she grabbed her clothes from the chair and departed stage left with no acknowledgment to her audience. No offense was taken by those of the craning necks. The ritual dance to cut-rate eroticism had run its course. Derevenko turned to Gurko and grunted something. "Our friend here wants the one who just finished. She reminds him of the women aboard ship," Gurko said to Jude and Kruglov.

"Fat as she is, how'd he know where to put it in?" Kruglov asked.

"For our friend Derevenko, the master chef, that would be no problem," Gurko said. "He'd just roll her in flour and look for the wet spot."

The music started again and another woman slinked from behind the curtain and onto the stage dressed in a thin negligee that Jude guessed had once hung on a K-Mart rack and had been intended for the siren allures of some bank teller's wife in Ohio. Derevenko recognized the dancer as their waitress and grunted pleasantly but loudly at the coincidence, a noise that drove the dancer toward the far end of the stage with a wary look.

"God, Derevenko, you creep," Gurko said. "One grunt from you can even drive whores away."

A large red-faced man wearing a baseball cap advertising Snap-On Tools was sitting next to Derevenko and turned in surprise at the sound of the foreign language. He gave a friendly nod past Derevenko to Gurko, and said, "How ya doin'?" With the encouragement of Gurko's answering smile, and between glances at the dancer, he extended his hand past Derevenko's stomach and said, "Name's Thompson—Ray Bob, from Tulsa. Work on the North Slope. Oil's my game." He pronounced oil like "all." "Where you boys from?"

Gurko tugged the taxi driver's cap more securely onto his head, took a long swig of beer, then looked at the man with a big smile. "Russia," he said.

"Yeah?" Ray Bob's small eyes narrowed in his fleshy face and his smile disappeared. Then, as though remembering his manners, he smiled again and said, "Well, guess you all didn't come to the Cherry Pit to start World War Three." As he savored his joke, Ray Bob's belly started to jiggle beneath his bright red Boomer Sooner T-shirt, making the football printed on the shirt bounce like a fumble and his heavy shoulders lurch up and down as though he were astride a galloping horse. He turned to a younger man with a heavy black beard and said, "Hey, Eddie, I told these boys from Russia here that I didn't reckon they came to the Cherry Pit to start World War Three. Get it?"

Eddie Faletto turned toward his partner without glancing at the Russians, but spoke loud enough for all to hear. "Never knew you was a Commie-lover, Ray Bob. Far as I'm concerned, they can try and start any war they want right here." "Right here" sounded like "rat chere."

Ray Bob pointed to Gurko's cap. "What's the *R* for, Russia?" He wheezed out a long chuckle and looked around for anyone who might have overheard his humor.

Gurko took off the cap and studied it. "It stands for Reds. That's the name of my karate team in Moscow."

Ray Bob's brow furrowed like an elephant's skin. "Karate, you say. Hmm."

Jude watched in silent trepidation, because the last thing he wanted was a fight that might land them all in jail. His fretting was interrupted by a slight tapping on his shoulder. When he turned he was looking into the face of a woman standing expectantly at his shoulder. She was tiny and dark with narrow Oriental eyes, a broad nose and high cheekbones. Her straight raven-black hair hung almost to her waist. She was dressed in a blouse cut low enough to reveal that there was almost nothing to reveal, and a black skirt with a slit up the side that showed a thin leg in heavy mesh stocking all the way to her hip. She reflexively pushed her hair over her shoulder, and said softly, "Hi, sailor, buy me a drink?"

Jude shook his head and turned back to his beer, but she tugged sharply at his elbow. "Come on, let's see some balls."

Jude hesitated, but Gurko shouted, "Coward! Show her what a Soviet sailor can do. All of Russia is counting on you. Go on."

Reluctantly, he allowed her to lead him by the hand away from the others, much to their leering approval and guffaws.

She weaved in and out among tables toward a far corner of the large room where light penetrated the least and where a few customers were huddled close to bar women as if they were sharing a secret. A few couples were grappling in heavy embraces, uncaring about prying eyes nearby.

Jude and the woman sat in the darkest corner in a booth with seats covered with Naugahyde. She immediately threw one arm over his shoulder and caressed his face with her other hand. Almost as a reflex action, his hand slid around her slim waist and he felt her even breathing beneath his fingers. "My name's Candy," she whispered in his ear. "What's yours?"

"What? Name?" He was careful to sound awkward with English. "Name Petr."

"I think you're cute, Peter. Will you buy me a drink?"

The instant Jude reached for his wallet, a waitress appeared out of the shadows. "What'll it be, Candy?"

"I'll have champagne. You'll buy me champagne, won't you, Peter, baby?" She was nibbling his ear and slowly rubbing his inner thigh.

Before he could answer, the waitress had produced a split of cheap champagne and plopped the tiny bottle in front of Candy. "That'll be twenty dollars," she said almost defiantly to Jude, who reluctantly counted out the money.

"Thanks, love." Candy saluted him with the glass and took a tiny sip.

"Who—are—you?" he asked, careful to take pains with the words.

"I'm an Eskimo chick working my way through medical school, what's it look like?" Then she laughed. "At least I'm Eskimo." She continued to gently knead his thigh, moving her hand higher and higher with maddening slowness. She breathed heavily into his ear. "God, what a hunk. Do you want to play games, you big Russian hunk? Oh! What's this I feel?" Her hand had finally gone high enough. "Oh, God, I want it!"

Before he could answer, the waitress reappeared and served another bottle of cheap champagne, and again collected twenty dollars from a mildly protesting but very distracted Jude.

Through the dimness of the club Jude's three mates watched the couple in the booth with open envy. "Jesus, do you think he's going to fuck her right there?" Kruglov asked excitedly.

Also watching was Eddie, who had interrupted his glaring at the three to inspect what was happening in the booth. "Shit," he said loudly to Ray Bob. "Isn't it just like those fucking squint-eyed, ugly Eskimos to swap spit with a lousy godless Red instead of good Americans?" He glared at the Russians. "We oughta teach the smirkin' bastards a lesson."

Kruglov, who was already half-drunk, mainly on the excitement of being in such an exotic place, started to stand up, but Gurko pushed him back into his chair. Then, trying to defuse the situation, he massaged the buttocks of an uncomplaining waitress nearby and grinned at Eddie while also trying to quiet Kruglov, who was speaking Russian in an angry voice.

Candy gathered up the champagne bottles and glasses and took Jude's hand. "Come on. Two bottles earn you a few minutes in a room." He tagged along like a little boy as she led him to the backstage area and into a tiny curtained room with a soft red light and worn couch. Gently she pushed him down on the couch in a half-reclining position and snuggled into his lap. She began kissing him passionately and moaning with desire while massaging his penis through the heavy fabric of his work pants.

Candy moved her lips to his earlobe and began nibbling. She continued to sigh deeply, but between her moans, she spoke in a whisper to him. "We can talk, but it must be like this. There's a peephole in the ceiling for the manager to observe, to make sure the girls aren't being abused. If we talk low enough, he'll just assume I'm talking dirty to you. I have a message for you, Jude Miller.''

At hearing his real name, Jude tensed and began to rise, but she firmly pushed him back down. "For chrissake, stay there," she whispered. "I'm your contact here. I'm instructed to tell you that there's been a leak. The KGB knows you're coming, but they don't know your cover or your mission. You'll be contacted in Moscow. Check into the Kirovskaya Hotel when you get there."

Jude's voice started to rise in astonishment, but he was cut off when she roughly kissed him on the lips and whispered, "For God's sake, keep it down."

"I need to know more," he whispered harshly. "Where was the leak? How do they know this cover's safe? Is the mission aborted?"

Jude knew the answer to the last question as soon as it left his lips. Leaks were a common hazard to the profession on both sides, and missions were not aborted merely because the other side knew something was going on. So far as the Russians knew, he was only one of about five million men spread over eight and one-half square miles who would fit his description. Of all the CIA operatives in the Soviet Union, he was just one more, and for all the KGB knew, perhaps merely a very minor one. He was still only a needle in their haystack. But a leak, in spying as in a dam, always had the potential to widen. The danger light was blinking red.

"That's all I know," she whispered. "Now, give me fifty dollars, and make it very obvious. If you don't give me money, the manager will call me out."

Jude reached into his pocket and counted out the money in the clumsy way of someone handling strange currency. He handed it to her, and whispered, "Who are you?"

"I'm who I appear to be," she whispered back. "I'm an Eskimo from a miserable bush village—the asshole of the universe—who makes her living dancing naked and giving hand jobs to drunks and horny sailors. I also work on the side for the CIA.''

"But why?" he asked. But upon seeing her quizzical look, he said, "I don't mean why the CIA, I mean why this joint? You seem pretty sharp.''

He could feel her silent laugh in his hands. "What should I do? In my village, everyone drinks all night, watches television all day and eats whale blubber. Winter days are dark for twenty hours, and the summers are owned by the mosquitoes. If I tried to get a job here in Anchorage, the whites would smirk, make me some kind of minimum-wage clerk and feel they had done justice to the white man's burden. Here, I can make forty thousand and afford good dope.''

"But what kind of future—"

"I have an Eskimo's future," she interrupted. "Which means damn little. We're a people robbed of our culture. Our values come from daytime soap operas and our pride from a bottle. We're amusing toys of the white man." She started to unzip his fly. "We came in here for a purpose; we better get to it." She opened his pants and his stiff penis sprang out like an oiled switchblade.

"You don't have to do this," he protested in an insincere whisper.

"It's expected. Why do you think you gave me fifty bucks? Besides—" she shrugged "—it's what I do.''

He sighed as she poured warm oil into her hands and reached for him. He leaned back and closed his eyes and allowed the sensation of her nimble fingers to take control. His body became a coiled spring gradually tightened by desire, inexorably nearing the moment of release and—

Suddenly, a crash of furniture and a stream of angry oaths in Russian interrupted them. She jumped to her feet and said, "Come on." Together, they rushed for the main room, fumbling with their clothing as they went.

GURKO THOUGHT he had soothed all the ruffled feathers when a man approached from another table. He was a professional type with large wire-rimmed glasses, a three-piece suit with vest unbuttoned and tie askew. He stumbled against their table, upsetting a beer bottle and then spilling most of the beer by fumbling for it all over the table. "'Scuse me," he slurred. "I—I have something to say." He tried to straighten his tie to achieve a bit more dignity, but only managed to smear it with beer.

"What is it, my friend?" Gurko asked, grateful for the diversion.

"My name is Davis, and I am a Russian interpreter for the United States Army." His brow furrowed as he pondered what he had said. "I mean I interpret Russians . . . I mean I interpret the language. Anyway, I overheard your friend a minute ago—" he pointed a waving finger at Kruglov "—and I don't think he should have called this fine gentleman a *dolboyob*." This time he pointed the finger at Eddie. "That's not nice talk for a visitor to this country. Your friend should be ashamed of himself," he said with exaggerated self-righteousness.

Eddie stood, tall and menacing. "Tell me, buddy, what does that mean, dol-boy-ob?"

The drunk turned with a grave air toward Eddie. "It means stupid ass."

"Watch it, Eddie, they know karate," Ray Bob shouted.

The music stopped and the house lights went on as bouncers rushed to separate Eddie and Kruglov, and also to get in a few punitive blows of their own. Ray Bob had grabbed Gurko by the ears and was shaking him while screaming, "I tried to be nice to you, Commie, but no, you had to rile Eddie." Derevenko was grunting furiously and lying on his back under a table like an overturned turtle.

Jude tried to protect his incision with one hand and to separate the combatants with the other. He heard Candy behind him say angrily, "Shit! Cops, that's all we need."

Jude watched her disappear behind the stage curtains as the police surrounded the scene. His erection was gone.

THE LAWYER, HASTILY HIRED by telephone by the Soviet consul in Seattle, led the four seamen into the brightly lit courtroom where they sat as directed on a front-row bench like repentant children. Ray Bob and Eddie were across the narrow aisle, Eddie glaring through bloodshot eyes at Kruglov. Jail hadn't been so bad. Most of them had seen the insides of far worse before. What spooked the four was the arrival of political officer Florinsky to obtain their release. And it was he who now stood at the rear of the court and glared at their backs as they waited for their case to be called.

The judge was an old man with tousled white hair and bifocals that seemed to be resting on his chin. In a raspy voice he was talking to a man in jailhouse denims standing contritely before him. "Hello, Mr. Johnson. What brings you back here? As I recall, I gave you ninety days just a couple of weeks ago."

The prisoner, a meek-appearing man of about twenty-five, told the judge in halting, ungrammatical English about the miraculous religious conversion he had experienced in jail three days ago. And now that the Lord was by his side, this time to stay, he believed he could be trusted to write no more bad checks, to fight no more and to get drunk no more. Would the judge please commute his sentence to time served so he could get on with serving Jesus?

The judge looked hard at Johnson over his glasses. "Mr. Johnson, I have sat on this bench for almost twenty years. During that time I have witnessed many miracles the Lord has wrought in the Anchorage city jail. Bountiful have been the blessings poured down upon those temporarily residing therein. Unfortunately, the anointing seems to stop the moment they walk out the door. I have been forced to conclude that Satan lurks at those gates, and that God is displeased

CHAPTER FIVE

THE PRISONER GROGGILY OPENED his swollen eyes and waited as the fuzzy images swam slowly into shape. Through rivulets of blood that ran into his eyes like a spring rain, he made out the flushed, angry face of his inquisitor, a devil of a man with silky white hair and a hideous blind eye that seemed a window to hell through the smoke curling up from the cigarette between his lips. He had heard the man called Papirosa (the cigarette).

Though for six hours Papirosa had exhausted his inventory of torture on the prisoner, he was not the one most feared. Standing fifteen feet behind Papirosa, seemingly removed from the proceedings, was Ivan Kolchak, the KGB's scourge of dissidents, casually chewing gum as though waiting for a bus. The sight of his ice-blue eyes, long nose and slicked-back thinning sandy hair made the prisoner's heart race with renewed fear.

He knew his predicament was caused by Kolchak alone.

The prisoner was sitting in a hard-backed chair—actually tied in with rope to keep him from falling—in a soundproof room in the deep cellar of an innocuous office building in the middle of Moscow. It was one of many places used by the KGB to interrogate its suspects. Passersby looking at the plain shabby exterior could not hear the screams inside.

"Pay attention, you Zionist asshole," Papirosa shouted at the prisoner and slapped him hard across the face. The blow showered the room with drops of blood from the tangle of rose branches which had been tightly wrapped around the prisoner's forehead, the thorns biting deeply into the flesh.

"Again, what do you know about the Defenders of Zion? Who was behind contacting them in the U.S.? Who's in charge of the Jewish conspiracy here?"

"I've told you, and told you, and told you, I don't know anything about it," the prisoner answered in a grinding whisper. "For God's sake, don't hurt me any more." His head sank to his chest as he went limp. Only the roses kept him in the chair.

Kolchak threw away his chewing gum, and said, "He's a tough one, Papirosa, but he'd tell if he knew. They always do. You can try again when he revives, but it won't do any good. Kill him when you're convinced of that."

Frustrated, Papirosa grabbed the prisoner by the hair and shook him roughly. "Tell me, you bastard!"

The prisoner's eyes opened to slits. "Kiss my ass," he managed to get past his swollen tongue.

Papirosa's face twisted with rage and he began hitting the prisoner in the face with his fists and screaming at him.

Kolchak spoke sharply. "Stop that! It's unprofessional. Don't ever let a prisoner get your goat. I taught you better than that. Our job is to provoke, not to be provoked."

Papirosa backed away. "Sorry, Comrade Kolchak."

Kolchak went over to the barely conscious prisoner. "Better pray to your god, Jew, while you have time." He snickered. "He'll be glad to see you when you get to heaven. Maybe you can have a reunion with your pals. We can give you a list of the ones we've already sent." Kolchak turned to Papirosa. "I'm going home to dinner. We'll try again with another one soon. Unfortunately, there's no shortage of Jews in Russia."

As Kolchak reached the door, Papirosa spoke deferentially. "By the way, Comrade Kolchak, the men got a big laugh out of the crown of thorns. Very creative."

Kolchak tipped his head and modestly smiled his thanks.

VIEWED WALKING BRISKLY down the Moscow street en route to the metro station, Ivan Kolchak would pass for a midlevel bureaucrat, engineer or educator about halfway through a modestly satisfying career. His suit was inexpensive but well fitted, his manner was confident but not arrogant. He blended well, which was his purpose.

As Kolchak entered the train, his fellow commuters' glances bounced off him like rain off a rock. They looked briefly and then looked beyond. But had they known his identity, their eyes would have riveted to him in fear.

Ivan Kolchak was born forty-two years before in the city of Agata in the Central Siberian Plateau. It was a dreary, cold place filled with internal exiles, political criminals, including his parents. Ivan was a boy who defied nature's rule that children should laugh and be innocently happy. He hated Agata and hated his parents for having defied the Stalin regime enough to have been sent there at the end of World War II. Ivan didn't know their offense—indeed, they themselves claimed not to know—but his teachers and leaders in Young Pioneers had convinced him that no one was sentenced for no reason, and as the years passed, his gratitude grew that he had not been punished for his parents' crimes. Watchful eyes soon picked him out for his leadership qualities. His family became nothing, the party everything. He learned to despise weakness. Deviationism was betrayal. The state gave life and could take it away. Morality was meeting a quota. Right was Communism, wrong was anything else. Obedience was his god, and the *Internationale* was his hymn.

Kolchak selected an aisle seat next to an elderly woman in work clothes carrying a shovel and so weary she hardly seemed to know he was there. He looked her over sourly and opened his copy of *Izvestia* to the sports page. He tried to relax by concentrating on the results of a weight-lifting match, but noise from the front of the car distracted him.

He glanced up and saw two young men of about twenty enter the car. They were dressed in American blue jeans and athletic jerseys with huge numbers front and back. Their hair was long and stringy, and one loudly sang an American rock song while the other imitated a guitar. Every few moments they would laugh at some invisible thing they found humorous and slap their palms together, saying in Russian, "Give me five, bro!"

Kolchak looked around to see how his fellow passengers reacted to the pair, and felt disgust at their indifference. The old woman next to him looked vacantly at the two and wearily closed her eyes. Other commuters ignored them in favor of books or magazines or even laughed at their antics.

Kolchak was not amused. These youths represented a part of Soviet society he had pledged his life to eradicate—the aping of Western degeneracy and capitalist excess. He hated the bloated softness, the greed and the gutless disregard for discipline that characterized America. Kolchak silently went to the front of the car and sat directly opposite the two youths. He said not a word to either, but fixed a steady, fierce stare on them.

The singing youth was the one to notice the tight-lipped glare of the man across the aisle. He was used to societal disapproval, in fact, he courted it, but this was different. This was danger. The song died on his lips as if a plug had been pulled, and he nervously tugged at the human guitar's arms and pulled him off the train even though they were one stop short of their destination.

Kolchak watched the departing pair and silently said to them: It is war between us. I swear to keep trash like you from contaminating my country. I will squash you like the American vermin you wish to become.

As if to some silent ultrasonic signal, the rest of the car became aware of Kolchak's malevolence, and a nervous pall settled over the other passengers and didn't lift until Kolchak reached his stop.

Kolchak had much for which to thank the Communist Party. Even despite his criminal parents, he had been allowed to attend the university in Moscow to study engineering. Afterward he was honored with an army commission and a tour of duty during the Vietnam War as an adviser to the North Vietnamese army. It was there that he had first seen the sickening weakness of American character. Despite their overwhelming superiority in weaponry and support, the Americans lacked the resolve and toughness to win. It was a joke among the ragtag, puny North Vietnamese soldiers that you could recognize an American troop column because a platoon of soldiers would always be followed by a truck caravan bearing drugs, candy bars and beer.

When it was suggested an opening might be available to him in the KGB, he applied gladly, hoping that he could protect Mother Russia and her revolution against the evils that would destroy her. To arm himself for that battle, he had learned to hate, to kill, to be pitiless. He had done everything correctly, except one thing—he had married Xenia.

Xenia Vyrubova had come into Kolchak's life at a time when he was vulnerable. He was fresh from the rustic hinterlands of Siberia, older than his peers, but terribly ignorant about this frightening new world of university and big city, and painfully aware of it. She was the smiling, shy student who sat next to him in class and never sniggered at his backwardness. She was his beau ideal of the Russian woman: stout, but not fat; dark blond hair braided across a wide forehead; a natural flush across the high Slavic cheekbones; a family of solid Communist respectability.

When they married, Xenia's friends grumbled that she had reached below her station. Xenia herself was well aware of it, but reassured Ivan that their love transcended such things.

He wasn't comfortable at their social imbalance, but considered himself too lucky to resent it.

But time changes things, and in this case, time overdosed on irony. Xenia's father fell from favor. No one knew why, but one Tuesday he was sent to a penal camp and the family was stripped of all the privileges they had come to think life owed them. Ivan, Xenia and their two children were forced to move from the spacious five-room apartment they shared with her parents into their own airless three rooms in the middle of a cramped housing project. Kolchak couldn't even learn the crime his father-in-law had committed. He had been arrested by the GRU, the intelligence branch of the Red Army, and all they would tell an agent from the competitive KGB was some vague story concerning "undermining of public morale."

Kolchak renounced Xenia's father at every opportunity, and had no indication that any connection had been made between them by his bosses. Still, he felt he wore the association like an odor in his clothes, and try as he might, he couldn't wash it out. Every time he thought of his father-in-law, Kolchak resented Xenia.

But that wasn't the worst. A short time ago, about six months after her father's arrest, Xenia had put a burden on Kolchak almost beyond bearing: she had acquired religion. Not just a mild case of Easter and Christmas nostalgia, but a full dose of Jesus Saves. Several times each week, whenever Ivan was not around to stop her, Xenia would recover the tattered Bible from where she had hidden it, and walk to the rundown old Baptist Church that the state allowed to exist for appearances' sake, past the police observers taking notes and names at the entrance, and into the shabby sanctuary. There, she joined a few dozen old men and women and a handful of captive children in seeking a higher solution than the politburo to the cares of life. The Communist Manifesto gave way to the Gospels. At first, the embarrassed Kolchak dismissed his wife's faith as an aberration resulting from the shock of learning that her father was an enemy of the state. But as time passed and her fervor was unabated, his embarrassment turned to anger and bordered on fear.

For a man as ambitious and dedicated to the party as Kolchak, having a religious wife was akin to liking rock and roll and the New York Yankees. It was perceived as an American corruption that marked the household as one deficient in Soviet values. As the knowledge of his wife's peculiarity spread among his colleagues, he thought he detected a growing number of disapproving glances and a few sniggers. If a man couldn't run his own home, they seemed to say, how could he be trusted to serve the state? Kolchak had considered divorce, but even that would mark him as a failure, and leave two growing children in his care, a prospect for which he had little zeal.

He approached the housing complex and gritted his teeth in anger. The smells of cooked cabbage and squalling babies assaulted him from all eight stories as soon as he turned into the walk. The bare dirt he walked across was the result of five hundred noisy brats whose shiftless parents allowed them to ruin grass and waste time playing instead of studying mathematics or Marx. A man of his value to the party deserved much better. He had lived down the shame of his own parents; now it was his in-laws and wife who threatened him. As Ivan walked through the dark hallway which smelled of vomit and urine, he vowed that his service to the state would not go unrewarded because of a dumb bitch and her superstitious mumbo jumbo.

He turned the key quietly in the lock by habit and entered his home. The two children, Andrey and Mathilde, looked up in alarm and quickly started picking up the books they had scattered across the parlor floor as they studied. Ivan ignored the kids and looked angrily at an old record player in a corner softly playing a scratchy recording of a Christian hymn. Ivan crossed quickly and jerked the record off the turntable as the music turned into a shriek. He smashed the record against the wall and turned to glare at Xenia who had come from the kitchen in a panic when she heard him enter, and now stood cowering against the doorway.

Kolchak's face turned beet-red and he shook his fist at her. "Goddammit, I've told you over and over that I will not allow that crap to be played in this house. You stupid bitch, are you trying to get me run out of the party like your traitorous old man?" He crossed to Xenia and slapped at her face but hit her forearms, which she had hidden behind as he approached. She fell into a chair and peered at him from behind protective fingers.

"I'm sorry, dear," she whimpered. "I don't play it loud, and I enjoy it so much. It doesn't seem wrong. . . ."

"I'll decide what's wrong around here," he thundered, turning to glare at the children, so that they would know the message encompassed them, too. "If you ever do anything like that again, I'll throw you out of the goddamn house. And you better stay away from that fucking church, too. Do you hear me?"

Xenia straightened up and smoothed out her plain dress, which hung straight on her round figure. "I'm sorry, Ivan, I can't do that. My faith tells me I have to disobey you on that. I must—"

With a roar, Kolchak sprang at her and aimed punishing blows at her covering arms, which already were splotched with brown bruises. Over his curses, she sobbed and prayed, "Dear Lord, forgive him, he knows not what he does. . . ."

Twelve-year-old Andrey rushed up to his father and grabbed his arm to protect his mother. When Kolchak turned on him with arm raised, the boy hurriedly said, "Father, Comrade Nesterov called a few minutes ago. He wants you to go to the office right after dinner. He said it's important."

At the mention of his superior's orders, Kolchak released his wife and said calmly, "What's for dinner? I've got to be going soon."

DMITRY NESTEROV, Hero of the Soviet Union, Order of Lenin, was a specialist, a specialist in survival. He had lived through the Nazi invasion, the Stalin purges, the shake-up after the dictator's death, and the deadly infighting of the KGB power struggles. He exuded the confidence of one who outwitted every danger, and the wariness of one who realized that danger, like an amoeba, regenerates itself. He was a hard old man who had resisted the biological process of softening. He grew tougher and meaner with time, and he grew more dangerous, because he also grew more crafty. This was the man who impatiently awaited the arrival of his subordinate, Ivan Kolchak. No pressing business demanded such an evening session, but Nesterov worked late because he had nowhere else to go and saw no reason why his key assistants should not work also. In Kolchak he saw himself thirty years earlier. He had hopes for him, possibly as successor in his Division of Foreign Sensitivity. But time would tell, and Nesterov relied upon what time would reveal to him. . . .

"Sorry, Chief," Kolchak called out as he entered the large paneled office and hung up his coat. "I was spending a quiet evening with the family when I got your message. I came immediately."

"How is the family, Ivan?" Nesterov asked blandly, glancing up from a stack of papers.

"The kids are great. Both are near the top of their classes. Xenia is . . . well, Xenia is still struggling with the delusions she adopted after her father's arrest. I'm hopeful she'll start to come around."

Nesterov cleared his throat. "Well, I hope so, too." He stood and started pacing the rare Oriental carpet that covered the middle of his office. "What'd you get out of that

Jew?'' he asked without lifting his eyes from the papers in his hands.

Kolchak shook his head. "Not a damned thing. They're making them tougher these days. It took us six hours of hard work to find out he knew nothing. Four hours was our previous top."

"And what did you do with our new record holder?"

Kolchak smiled mysteriously. "He's resting on his laurels."

"Are the Defenders of Zion operating in this country?"

"Probably not as an organization, but our New York sources say there's been contact between them and agents of Russian Jews. We've detected stirrings among Jews here; I just don't know if there's a tie-in to worldwide Zionism. But something's up, and I plan to keep working on the known agitators."

"I wish you would," Nesterov said. "Those Jew bastards are fanatics. The last thing we need is a bunch of crazy Zids running around making trouble. That would not reflect well on us, and that would displease me very much." Nesterov didn't harden his voice as he gave the implied threat. He didn't have to.

Nesterov shuffled the papers in his hands and gave one to Kolchak. "Here's one that might interest you. Remember an American CIA operative named Miller, Jude Miller?"

Kolchak studied the report for a moment. "Vaguely. Wasn't he kicked out because of some scandal a few years back?"

"That's the one. We have a report from an agent in Mexico that he's been reactivated and is infiltrating this country on a mission for our old friend Herbert Farleigh Armstead."

Kolchak thought and slowly shook his head. "Doesn't sound likely. How reliable is the agent?"

Nesterov laughed. "How reliable is any agent? Answer that question and every intelligence organization in the world will be renamed in your honor."

"How much do we have to go on, Chief?"

"Just that he's headed this way. Nothing about his cover or the particular type of mischief he's up to."

"You mean the agent doesn't know?" Kolchak asked.

"I mean the agent isn't saying. You know these damned thieves, there isn't one of them you can trust. Either this one doesn't know or is holding out for more money. We'll keep working that end. In the meantime, get Jude Miller's dossier from inactive files and brush up on him. It may amount to nothing, so don't let it interfere with the Jew thing."

"Got it, Chief." Kolchak rose, smiling. "That do it for tonight?"

"That's all, Ivan. Thanks for coming back this late." He watched Kolchak head for the door, then spoke again. "You know, Ivan, you really should do something about that wife of yours."

Kolchak turned back to his superior, but he was no longer smiling. "I'll take care of it."

KOLCHAK LEANED BACK in his upholstered chair and looked thoughtfully at the microphone in his hand. He depressed the On switch and began dictating. "Memo to file number 14950. The Defenders of Zion is a group of fanatics that originated in the United States for the purpose of advancing the conspiratorial goals of international Zionism. They have branched out to Israel, where they have caused trouble for the civil authorities by harassing innocent Arabs. Their membership is estimated by our intelligence sources in the U.S. and Israel at about 2,500, mostly hangers-on. They're generally young and either students or blue-collar. As yet, they haven't received substantial backing from the Jewish intellectual community, which tends to think of them as troublesome riffraff.

"There are clear indications that this group has had contact with Jewish traitors in this country. Obviously, the intent of these Russian Jews is to learn the tricks of terrorism in order to stir civil dissatisfaction among Jews here. See earlier memo.

"Thanks to diligent work by our people in the U.S., we're fortunate to have early knowledge of these meetings, and we should capitalize on it by vigorous action to locate and eliminate the Jews responsible as soon as possible. As agent in charge, I am relying primarily on the standard methods of informants, infiltration and interrogation to accomplish that.

"Judging from the history of the Defenders of Zion, and the criminal element in this country that might try to emulate them, we should be prepared for a campaign of terrorism and propaganda. Their object will obviously be to pressure the Soviet Union into bowing to demands concerning emigration to Israel and freedom to work religious mischief within our borders.

"The Soviet Union, due to diligent police work and a patriotic population, has through the years avoided any substantial amount of dissident lawlessness within our borders. Only the Ukrainian fanatics have persisted in trying to destroy our society, and we now have them on the run. I cannot stress too strongly the importance of ruthlessly stamping out this militant Zionist movement before it gets a foothold in this country. Though Russians are intensely loyal, this type of thing can spread like a virus if not contained early—especially among people as unstable as Jews. We can hear the drums beating in the distance, and we must act before they get louder.

"More to follow in later memos."

Kolchak put the cassette in an envelope for his secretary to transcribe, then poured a cup of thick black coffee and removed from his briefcase a manila file marked Miller, Jude. USA—CIA. Inactive. He leaned back in his swivel chair and turned to the first page.

CHAPTER SIX

HE WAS VERY OLD, and when he slowly opened and blinked his eyes, he had to wait as they came into focus like an old, dust-clogged camera. He looked once at the shabby, small room to make sure it was still there. It had been his hiding place for years, but he was certain of nothing anymore.

His world intact, he concentrated on getting out of bed. After a night of restless sleep, his body was like rusty machinery that creaked in resentment at every slight request made of it. But he didn't mind anymore. It seemed he had been old forever, and the suppleness of youth was no longer even one of the memories he called upon.

He inched one leg at a time over the edge of the bed and pushed with his hands to help his brittle knees raise him to his feet. He stood for a moment to make certain his legs would not betray him, then shuffled slowly to the small stove to heat water for tea. That accomplished, he faced the problem of filling another day. His eyes tired too quickly to read for any length of time, and there was usually no one present he desired to talk with. His life consisted of hate, of memories and of what he could see through a small dirty window that overlooked the backside of a steel mill in a grimy industrial area of Moscow.

Despite all this, he was not depressed. Although he had once been a mighty leader whose voice was heeded throughout the world, he was at heart still a common man. In his great years his gluttony had been prodigious—power, liquor, women, adoration—but he never forgot he was just a peasant. They had laughed at that self-image, but the old man had known that, to survive, he would eventually need the poor man's hardiness of spirit and grim understanding that life is ultimately cruel.

And despite what they all believed, he had survived. He had lived to see his own funeral.

He relaxed in the rough chair he sat upon; he felt the coarse clothing on his back; he admired the plain food sitting on the plank table. He chuckled to think of how the poseurs and prancers he had consorted with on the world stage would manage such a humble condition. But commonness was the sinew of his spirit. He was a child of the revolution; the higher his rise, the deeper his commitment to the idea that he had been called from the plow to lead his people. The calluses would never leave his palms and the dirt would permanently stain his fingernails. He was what his critics accused him of being; he was what the jokers laughed about; he was what he believed he was—a peasant. That was why he didn't die when they stripped him of power. Peasants don't die, they burrow in.

The old man's smile dissolved from his wrinkled face as the thoughts that caused it wandered out of his mind. He felt hungry, so he reached for a pickle jar on the table and started to unscrew the cap. His brain was tired and worn and operated like a light bulb with an electrical short, at times strong and surging, but always on the verge of blinking out. He was mercifully spared such knowledge, because when his mind would sputter, he had no awareness of the fact.

With a lost, mystified look, he leaned back heavily in his chair and dark mists began closing in on his world. . . .

The old man heard a scraping sound and swiveled his body awkwardly to look. Standing near the window was a stranger. The weak light illuminated only half of the man, but the bushy white mustache and wrinkled red skin told the old man that the stranger was himself very old. The man stood strong, though, with his foot resting on the seat of a kitchen chair.

The high boots with trousers securely tucked in, the home-spun smock tightly belted at his waist and the visored cap pushed far back on his head in a relaxed pose told the old man that this was a peasant from the Ukraine. He prided himself on recognizing such things.

"Who are you?" he demanded. "Have you no manners? You damn well don't just barge in on a man like myself."

The visitor threw back his head and laughed heartily. "Don't you recognize me, Nikita Sergeyevich Khrushchev? There was a time when a man from the village of Yuzovka would welcome a neighbor. It's *your* manners that should be questioned. But I'll forgive you, provided your vodka bottle isn't empty."

The old man shuffled to a cupboard and poured a generous portion of vodka into a water glass. He gave it to the visitor, who towered over the old man, but then, most men did. "I'd join you," he said, "except I no longer drink. The stuff goes through my guts like steel wool. But there was a day when I'd empty glasses with any man alive. I'd—"

"Women, rubles and wine," the visitor saluted the old man. "And may flowers grow in Yuzovka."

"May they be red roses," the old man answered automatically. He held the bottle up for a refill and squinted closely at his visitor. "You say you're from Yuzovka. Why don't I know you?"

"You left and became a great man," the visitor answered. "How would you remember a simple blacksmith, a man who never even traveled to Kiev, a man who has accomplished nothing in life except dodge bullets?"

The old man nodded his respect. "A lot of good men had no luck at all with bullets. What is your name?"

"Fedor Yakovlev, at your service."

The old man studied his visitor and squinted at the effort to remember. The curtain of time parted in his mind and revealed a small village on the Ukrainian plain. In the distance, the Carpathian Mountains rose through the smoky veil of the coal mines on the outskirts of Yuzovka. The old man's memory escorted him down the muddy street deeply creased by wagon-wheel rims and pockmarked by countless horses' hooves. Along the edge of the road, dwindling dirty snowbanks faded into the warmth of spring. He gingerly picked his way through the puddles and sucking mud. On either side of the road were small log huts with smoke curling from dried-mud chimneys, stove wood piled against outside walls, dilapidated privies, and each with either a goat or old milk cow staked nearby. In the distance, he could see the small Jewish shtetl off by itself, characterized by the extra crowded poverty that separated it from the other dwellings as effectively as a high wall.

The constant clamor and shouting from the mines and the small foundries overwhelmed the normal sounds of village life. No baby's cry, no dog's bark, no mother's scolding, no peddler's hoarse urgings could lessen the clang-clang-clang of the mines. Night and day it was an iron carillon that pounded into the villagers' ears the fact that all within its hearing belonged to the cold, wet pits, which gave them bread but in return took their youth, their hope and the sun. Down the street he picked his way past the deep puddles, recognizing ancient babushkas hiding beneath their kerchiefs while rocking babies in grassless yards; old men staring into the distance or aimlessly exchanging familiar stories with one another, trying to forget the pain of arthritis or black lung that the mines had carved into their bodies and for which no help, no relief existed except death. He saw maidens happily skipping through their chores, not aware that their song of youth would be cruelly short and with no refrain.

It was a village of no past, no future, no consequence. Multiplied a thousand-fold, it was Russia.

As he neared the mines, he saw a young blacksmith hammering on a long rod of glowing iron. The darting flames of the forge in the darkened shed accented the gleaming sweat and grime on the smith's thick arms and bare chest behind the leather apron. He looked up and his blackened face broke into a familiar friendly smile....

The old man grinned in triumph at the recaptured recollection. "Now I have you, Fedor Yakovlev. You were the one who lived in the small yellow house with the shop in the rear. Down by the Frenchman's mine, right? Yes...yes..."

"That was me, Nikita Sergeyevich. I used to watch you go by on your way to work before sunup every morning. Everyone used to say what a feisty little runt you always were—"

"They didn't say it to my face," the old man groused.

"Not unless they wanted a bloody nose." Yakovlev laughed. "Man, but you were a pisser. It's a wonder the czar's police didn't shoot you and have done with it before it was too late."

The old man chuckled. "Those were some days, all right.... Ah, the time I organized the strike at the Rutchenkovo mine in '15. I tell you, those damned capitalists were tearing out their hair. They'd never had to look workers in the eye before. Well, we taught them how to do it. Were you there?"

"I had a fight of my own back in '15. The German army. You should have been *there*, Nikita Sergeyevich, but the war didn't interest you, did it?"

The old man scoffed. "Damned if I was going to get my ass shot off to protect a sissy czar and the property of a bunch of grasping capitalist bastards. That war was nothing but a quarrel between exploiters fighting to see who would be the greediest, who could suck the most blood. I tell you, I learned young that you can't fill a duck's crop and you can't fill a rich man's pockets.

"The people hated the war. I remember the mothers used to go about their chores singing a popular ditty." The old man started humming. "Let's see, it went like this:

We are sick of it, we are sick of it,
The German war.
Maidens, pray to God
That it may end in peace."

Yakovlev listened, then said, "I never heard that one, but I remember a song we used to sing at night in camp to Czar Nicholas. Even the officers, after a while, picked it up. It was a slow tune:

What have you done, you white czar?
Out of time you have made war,
Out of time and out of season,
They have led us off to war.
What have you done, Nikolasha?
Our Russia is perishing."

The old man shook his head at the memory. "Sad songs for a sad time. But they helped wake people to the truth that the war was a chess game with workers as the pawns. The blood of that war made our revolution. It served a purpose."

"We were fighting for Mother Russia," Yakovlev reminded him.

The old man snorted loudly. "While you were marching back and forth for your puppet masters in the czar's army, I was fighting the real enemies—the landowners. I remember one day I had to escape through a mine shaft. It was this close." He held up two fingers and laughed. "The police were behind me like terriers after a rat. I didn't know whether to crap or cry. But I got away, and then I came right back."

Yakovlev nodded. "Yes, you came back and you won your war, that can't be denied."

"Damned right we did," the old man huffed. "You should have been there that day in '17 when we got word from some railway workers that the czar had been booted out on his ass.

We elected workers' soviets that day and went straight down and arrested the police and the mine bosses. You should have seen their fat faces when Nikita S. Khrushchev walked up and pointed a rifle at their guts.''

"Some good men were also caught in your snare," Yakovlev said. "I knew some of them. Just ordinary policemen trying to do an honest job. They were lined up and shot while their families watched.''

"Good men, you say?" the old man returned. "They weren't so damned good when they were arresting workers for just trying to find a little bread for their families and justice for themselves. No, Yakovlev, don't waste your sympathy on them.'' He waved a hand in dismissal. "Anyway, we were in a hurry.''

The old man's eyes narrowed toward his visitor. "By the way you talk, I wonder if you were one of those capitalist lapdogs who jumped around for the bosses' amusement and who'd bite workers when sicced on them?" The old man thought for a moment, then frowned. "You opposed the revolution, didn't you?''

Yakovlev walked to the far side of the room and sat in a chair facing the old man. "Opposed? Could I have lived so long if I opposed? Wouldn't you and your friends have had me shot? Not everyone had your strong voice and your guts, Nikita Sergeyevich. Some of us, when we saw our neighbors and friends point guns at one another, all we knew was to be quiet and stay out of the way. A revolutionary can't be timid, but most men are. That's why there are so few revolutions. Opposed? I was a simple man who knew nothing but how to hammer a horseshoe. I only wanted the winner not to be angry with me and to let me repair plows in peace.''

The old man shook his head. "It wasn't possible in those days. You had to be on one side or the other.''

Yakovlev's voice became harder. "Is that the big favor you did for the workers, made them take sides? What did you do

for those who just wanted to be left alone to raise their children and work their land?"

"We made them free."

"Free of what?" Yakovlev demanded. "Free of the mid-
night pounding on the door? Free of fear? Free of poverty?
Free of ignorance? What exactly did you free the peasants of,
Nikita Sergeyevich?"

"We knocked the capitalists' boots off their necks."

Yakovlev stood and walked with a heavy clumping to the
window and looked out at the steel mill. After a moment, he
turned back to the old man. "You were born poor and lived
among common folk, but despite what you like to think, you
weren't one of them. Your ambition made you different. You
became a man to fear because of your religion."

The old man laughed incredulously. "Religion? Me? Why,
I'm about as religious as the Pope is a Communist. That's a
laugh. The church oppressed the people, and got me as an
enemy in return."

"Your religion, Nikita Sergeyevich, was your revolution,
and you were a true believer. And do you know what the
peasant has learned to fear most? The true believer. Because
the true believer won't allow him the only thing he really
wants, and that is to be left alone."

"Do you think the bosses and the police left him alone?"
The old man's face was splotched red with anger and he
shouted hoarsely, "Was he being left alone when taxes left
him with no food before a long winter? Was he being left alone
when his children grew up ignorant and with no chance to be
anything more than he had been? Was he being left alone
when he had to walk two miles home from a mine in winter
in filthy wet clothes because the bosses were too damned
cheap to give him a changing room? That actually happened
to me, Yakovlev, so don't laugh."

Yakovlev nodded. "Yes, there were wrongs, but common
folk have always known how to survive. They knew their kind

would go on, outlive whoever happened to be oppressing them at the moment. Remember, only a half-century before, they'd all been serfs—slaves, in all but name. And they had seen serfdom disappear. All they needed to make it through the bad days was God, and you people took God away from them."

The old man looked aghast. "God? God? Do you know what God did for them? He played them right into the hands of their oppressors. God make them like the sheep I used to watch as a youngster, wide-eyed and stupid, doing nothing more than a little polite bleating when the bosses robbed them of their wool. I can just hear those damned priests now." The old man struck an effeminate pose and raised his voice to a soprano level. " 'Oh, my son, don't worry about the sickness in your family, or your confiscatory taxes, or the hopeless future of your children. God will provide. Just trust and obey your bosses.' " He deepened his voice to normal, and thundered, "Don't mention God to me, fool. God is a trick, just like the shell game that cheats the farmers out of their crop money when they go to the city. Before we stopped them, the capitalists were running the game and calling it religion. After we threw them in jail, we looked under the shells of their God game, and guess what? There was no pea there!" The old man chuckled at the image. "It was a curse upon mankind the day God was created by the plutocrats to huckster poor people."

"If God is only a trick, then why have people the world over and through all ages found him such a comfort?" Yakovlev asked.

"There are a lot of plutocrats, my friend."

Yakovlev removed a pouch of rough-cut tobacco from his smock and carefully tamped it into a large pipe. "The future of an old man is ill served by mocking God, I'm thinking." He held a match to the pipe and watched as the blue, pungent smoke rose to the low ceiling before billowing outward.

"In your haste to overturn things, to cause revolution, you destroyed the cycle of the common people's lives. You tore their anchor loose and let them drift. The peasant is a man of nature, a man of the seasons. He spends his life watching a patient world: he plants in the spring, waits for rain in the summer, then harvests in the fall. Waiting and hoping is his life. He knows that patience will get him more than guns. Patience is his only real weapon."

The old man shouted angrily, "But we gave him a real weapon, and it wasn't patience. It was a rifle."

"Yes, Nikita Sergeyevich, but at whom was it pointed?..."

The old man rubbed his eyes, looked around, then continued unscrewing the pickle jar cap.

CHAPTER SEVEN

THE HEAVY THUMP-THUMP of the twin 1500-horsepower diesels was to Jude a heartbeat, the heartbeat of the animal his fear had become. Each day aboard the *Novi Mir* was a tightrope he was forced to walk across a deep chasm of discovery. His shipboard confinement was a constant nagging reminder of a basic undercover agent's survival rule: safety lies in movement. The more the same people are exposed to you, the greater the chances of a major mistake—or even a tiny inconsistency—that can lead to exposure. The minute-by-minute caution Jude was forced to practice wearied him like manual labor.

The ship made an abrupt roll in the choppy swells of the Bering Sea and he grabbed frantically to save a bowl of sauerkraut as he lurched against the galley bulkhead. He cradled the sauerkraut to protect it from harm, like a mother with her baby. To his surprise, he found he took great pride in his cooking, and it gave him the added advantage of isolation in the galley since Derevenko was drunk most of the time.

At the moment, Jude was preoccupied with *shchi*, a sauerkraut soup with three kinds of meat in the Ukrainian style. He calculated the recipe for the crew of sixty, silently moving his lips as he converted measurements: twelve pounds of pork shoulder, eight pounds of lamb shank, sixteen pounds of beef chuck, two gallons of water, a handful of peppercorns, four heads of cabbage, eight pounds of sauerkraut, a dozen potatoes, eight carrots, eight onions, a gallon of tomatoes, a large bowl of sour cream, three tablespoons of caraway seed, a half dozen bay leaves and a hefty dose of salt.

Jude put the meat for the soup on to boil, and cut up the vegetables, then started on the batter for *bliny*, the traditional Russian pancake that he planned to serve as the first course for dinner. He combined two pounds of butter, two quarts of milk, two pounds of flour, two pounds of sugar, two dozen eggs and two large packages of dry yeast dissolved in warm water. The image of the weary crew happily smearing sour cream on the fluffy small cakes made him smile.

Clamping his pots into place, Jude decided to take a break. He went on deck just in time to see the otter trawl net, a huge mesh basket that had been pulled behind the ship along the bottom of the ocean, being winched up the back ramp to the deck. In the bottom of the net squirmed a thousand silvery fish, which were swung over and emptied into a tank of refrigerated seawater on the lower factory deck, where men and women of the crew were preparing to process the catch.

The fish, mainly cod, sablefish and halibut, were moved out of the holding tank along a conveyor system where they were sorted, then into gutting and heading machines and finally into tanks of icy water where they were allowed to "bleed" for a half hour before being stacked in freezing rooms and stored at minus twenty degrees Fahrenheit for the remainder of the voyage. Waste fish and offal were swept into a processing tank and turned into fish meal.

The ship reeked of dead fish. The odor was in clothing, hair, skin, food. It seeped from the walls. It greeted the tired head that hit the pillow. It was in the taste of a cup of coffee. It was a miasma that permeated the ship like humidity. The only defense against the smell was self-persuasion that it didn't matter.

The *Novi Mir* was a marvel of modern seagoing automation. Inside her nearly three-hundred-foot length was ingenious machinery capable of processing and freezing fifty tons of fresh fish in twenty-four hours and reducing twenty-five tons of raw waste into five tons of bagged meal in the same period. But the trawler was running at only a fraction of its capacity because, as the fishing crew constantly grumbled, they were operating in an area of the Bering Sea normally avoided because of sparse catches. The reason they were there was not stupidity, but the tangle of electronic gear in the masts high above the ship, directed at Elmendorf Air Force Base near Anchorage.

The *Novi Mir* doubled as a spy ship. The crew knew it; the Americans knew it. Neither liked it. The crew wanted to fish; the Americans wanted to keep their secrets.

Jude walked down the iron ladder to the factory deck and moved among the men and women working on the assembly line. They ignored him while scurrying among the tireless machines, which seemed to have human qualities as they hummed and coughed and efficiently ripped open and eviscerated fish, or neatly chopped their heads off and sent them on to the next machine. Most of the workers were women, but from the back it was difficult to tell. Their short-cropped hair, broad backs and thick arms were functional for their work, but Jude felt sad for them and the femininity they were denied by a system that said being a woman was a distant second to being a worker. These women were mostly peasants from small villages, who had no marriage prospects and no career alternatives to what they were now doing. They were made to think of themselves as tools of the state, therefore no effort was expended toward grooming, diet or sensuality of any kind. The only attention they received from men was when a male crew member became amorous and figured out a way to breach the security system that separated the quarters of the two sexes. Jude looked at the women and thought of a beehive, and of them as worker bees.

Moving along the line, he came to the familiar figure of Gurko, slouched in a swivel chair next to the conveyor belt that took the finished fish to the freezing compartment. Gurko had thrown a leg over the arm of the chair and was smoking a long Cuban cigar and picking his nose as he stared appraisingly at the women tending the machinery.

Jude slapped him on the back and said in a friendly voice raised above the machinery din, "What're you doing here? I thought they kept your type locked up in cages in the engine room."

Gurko removed the spongy cigar end from his mouth and half turned to Jude. "The guy who normally does this is sick so I took it just to get the overtime credit."

Jude looked at the relaxed machinist and said, "This is work? What is it you're supposed to be doing?"

Gurko again removed the cigar but didn't take his eyes off the women. "I'm inspecting," he answered loudly. Noticing Jude's quizzical glance toward the women, Gurko said, "Not those whales—" he gestured toward the conveyor belt "—the fish. I'm inspecting the fish."

"What for, to make sure they're dead?" Jude shouted.

Gurko got out of the chair, ignoring the fish that continued to roll by, and motioned for Jude to follow him to a quiet area away from the machinery. "This is a British-built system and they put in that inspector station so the fish that had blood spots or had been chewed up by the machines could be separated from the rest and priced lower. But since we don't worry about things like that— When was the last time you heard of a Russian taking a can of fish back to the store for a refund? Well, anyway, you just sort of sit there and think dirty thoughts about them." He gestured toward the women.

"But," Jude said, "if we don't really inspect the fish, why bother?"

Gurko looked at him as though Jude were an idiot. "Because the system calls for it," he explained patiently.

"Not exactly inspiring work," Jude said.

"Oh, but it's better than what I did a few years back," Gurko said.

"What was that?"

"Jacking off monkeys," Gurko said.

"Huh?"

"Yeah, I was a research lab tech at the university in Minsk. They were doing some crazy experiment in genetics with monkey sperm. So my job was to put a tiny little condom on a spider monkey and then give him a small electrical charge in the balls with a bare wire to make him ejaculate. Never failed. Easy work, and everyone thought it was great except maybe the monkeys. Then one day, this guy in the lab says to me, 'How many monkeys did you jack off today?' All of a sudden, it dawned on me that that was what I was doing— jacking off monkeys. I hadn't thought of it in just that way before. Shit, I said to myself, how am I going to explain this someday to my grandchildren? I went down that very day and joined the fishing service. I was glad to get out of that before the monkeys got to like it—and me."

They started to share a laugh but it vanished from both their faces when they saw an approaching shadow and turned to see Florinsky standing before them.

"Hello, Comrade," Gurko muttered.

"I've been looking for you, Comrade Markov," Florinsky said to Jude. "The galley must be pretty confining for a man of your wide travels." Before Jude could answer, Florinsky turned to Gurko. "Your inspection duties don't seem to be too taxing, Comrade. Why don't you help that man?" He pointed to a sailor in hip boots with a huge squeegee pushing bloody fish entrails into a drain.

Gurko retreated with a chagrined look on his face, and Florinsky turned back to Jude. "I've been curious about the ship you were on before, Comrade, the—"

"*Zvezda*, Comrade," Jude said.

"Yes, *Zvezda*," Florinsky continued. "How long did you serve with Captain—"

"Kokoutsov. Captain Dmitry Kokoutsov, Comrade."

"Yes, Kokoutsov. How long were you with him, Comrade Markov?"

"Two years and four months," Jude answered.

"Was *Zvezda* a fine ship, Comrade Markov?"

"Very, Comrade. The crew enjoyed serving on her."

"Tell me about this fine ship. What was her length?"

"Seventy-five point five meters, Comrade."

"Her gross tonnage?"

"One thousand five hundred eighty four."

"Crew size?" Florinsky was now barking out questions.

"Fifty-seven."

"Engine?"

"Twenty-three hundred horsepower, Comrade."

"Number of burners on the galley stove?"

Jude blanched. "Uh, number of burners on the galley stove. Uh, there were—uh, eight burners on the galley stove. Yes, eight."

Florinsky grinned triumphantly. "I find it amazing that a cook would know the horsepower of a ship's engines and be uncertain about the number of burners on the stove he used many hours each day."

Jude forced a laugh. "Well, you know about the shoemaker's kids. I was just thinking about the rest of the ship, the engine and crew and all. I just drew a blank. Stupid, I guess."

Florinsky gave him an appraising look. "No, I don't think stupid . . ."

"Well—" Jude began, but Florinsky had turned his back and walked away.

"Shit, shit, shit, shit!" Jude swore at himself under his breath. "How many burners . . . *shit!*"

THE CREW ATE IN TWO SHIFTS, and Jude and his helpers had barely cleaned up from the first group when the next tramped in. Half the group was from belowdecks, mainly from the engine room, and half was from the fishing crew. Splitting them up in this fashion allowed both operations to continue functioning during mealtime.

Leading the pack, as usual, were Gurko and Kruglov. The crews generally were quiet and spoke only to those closest to them, not knowing who might be listening. Gurko, however, didn't seem to care. And while Kruglov, who was known as the silent lover type, said little, his open enjoyment of Gurko's outrageous candor made him something of a partner in crime. Both were very popular with the rest of the crew, who delighted in seeing them thumb their noses at the authority the others held in fear.

As soon as the crew was seated, men on one side and women on the other, Jude set out the *shchi* and *bliny* along with large bowls of sour cream, black bread and steaming tea.

"God, this is wonderful!" Gurko exclaimed when he tasted the soup. "Derevenko has outdone himself. I salute master chef Derevenko." Gurko looked sideways at Jude, who was steaming at losing credit to the drunken cook, who at that moment was snoring in the storeroom behind the galley. Gurko shook his finger at the pouting Jude. "Shame, shame, Comrade Markov. You should know there is no room for arrogant pride in a socialist society. Nevertheless," he said, turning to his messmates, "I give you Comrade Petr Markov, greatest chef of all the Russias." Jude bowed deeply in acknowledgment of the applause.

Just as quickly as the crew applauded him, they turned their backs and tore into the meal. Gurko, between slurps of the thick soup, said loudly, "I heard a story today that shocked me. I tell you, friends, I've never been so upset." The response from his audience was loud groans, but Gurko persisted. "No, no, it's true. Listen to this. It came from Moscow. I heard it on the shortwave. It seems that in Moscow a certain fruit and vegetable store had just received a shipment of oranges from Uzbekistan. Now, since it was midwinter, you can understand that a large group of people flocked to the store and queued up to make sure they got some of the delicious oranges. After an hour, the manager came out and said, 'It's true, comrades, that we have oranges, but not enough for everyone. Therefore, all Jews must leave the line.'

"Well, a large group left the line. An hour later, the manager came out again and said, 'Comrades, we have oranges, but not enough. All non-party members must leave the line.' And the line shrank again. An hour later, the manager again came out and said, 'Comrades, it's true we have oranges, but not enough. Therefore, all those who have not served in the Red Army must leave the line.' This time, the line got very small. And an hour later, the manager came out again and said, 'Comrades, we have oranges, but only a few. Everyone who was not wounded in the Great War must leave the line.' Then, about three hours later, he came out and said to the two freezing old men still left, 'Sorry, Comrades, but no oranges today.' As they started to leave, one old man turned to the other and said, 'Leave it to those damned Jews to come out ahead every time.'"

When the howls of laughter died down, Gurko said, "Did you hear about the argument the Soviets and Americans had over who owned the moon? Well, to settle the debate, the Russians sent up a crew of cosmonauts with a million gallons of red paint to cover the moon so everyone would know who owned it. The Americans then gave their astronauts a thousand gallons of white paint. One astronaut asked, 'What are we supposed to do with this now that the entire moon is painted red?' The boss told him, 'Just paint Budweiser across the middle.'"

The laughter that followed stopped like a pulled plug and everyone's head swiveled to the entrance. There stood Florinsky glaring at the entire room. Only a couple of nervous laughs interrupted the silence as he stood writing in a notebook. When he finished, he turned and left, leaving thirty tired, hungry crew members listlessly spooning their soup, not even missing their lost appetites.

JUDE STOOD OUTSIDE the cabin door that was labeled Kyril Florinsky, Political Officer, and fingered the strange note that requested he come here so late at night. He knocked and waited until the command "Come in" left him no choice but to open the door.

Florinsky's cabin was only about eight feet by ten feet but looked like a small shrine to Communism. Above the bunk were pictures of Marx and Lenin. Spread out the length of the opposite wall was a red and gold Soviet hammer and sickle flag. Scattered elsewhere along the walls were signed photos of various party dignitaries, large and small.

Florinsky was seated at a small desk turned sideways to Jude. He didn't stand when Jude entered but merely turned ninety degrees and stared. "Sit down," he ordered in a cold voice.

Jude sat a few feet away in a straight-backed chair and waited.

"Who are you?" Florinsky demanded.

"Who am I?" Jude asked. "I don't understand. I'm Petr Markov, cook."

Florinsky didn't answer immediately but merely gave a slight smile and stared at Jude. "Possibly. Perhaps you're Petr Markov, cook, as you say, and perhaps you're someone else."

Jude concentrated on trying not to swallow, afraid that his bobbing Adam's apple would betray his anxiety. "Who else might I be, Comrade?"

"I haven't decided," Florinsky said slowly. "But I intend to find out. I have asked the captain to radio Moscow to determine your true identity. We should know within a few days."

"If that's the case, Comrade, why are you asking me these questions?"

"Because if you're a deserter or a spy, it would be very much to my credit to find it out with no assistance from Moscow."

Jude slapped his hands against his sides in despair. "I just don't understand why a loyal Russian fisherman should be made to go through this. I am innocent of everything except not remembering how many burners were on an old stove I once used."

"Maybe you are, maybe you are," Florinsky said. "But I have to follow my—*did Armstead send you?*" he interrupted himself, shouting the question like a machine gun spitting out bullets.

"No." As soon as the word was out Jude could have bitten off his tongue. He tried to cover up. "Who is Armstead? I don't know what you're talking about."

"Hah!" Florinsky shouted in triumph. "I tricked you again. The answer was out of your mouth before you realized it would hang you. Of course you know who Armstead is. Every CIA agent knows his boss. Right? CIA? Admit it."

Jude buried his face in his hands the way he imagined a frightened sailor would. "Please, I just said 'no' because I had no idea who you were talking about. This is a nightmare."

"But a dream come true for me." Florinsky laughed. "I'd bet St. Basil's Cathedral that you're a spy." He reached into the desk and pulled out a small automatic pistol and a pair of handcuffs. Jude could tell by the way he handled the pistol and how he checked twice to make sure the safety was off that he was unfamiliar with handguns. Florinsky awkwardly separated the handcuffs and commanded Jude to turn around.

Jude obeyed and put his hands behind his back. Glancing in a wall mirror on the door of the small lavatory, he could see what Florinsky was doing. Inexpert as he was at his task, Florinsky gloated as he fumbled with the handcuffs. "Don't feel too bad, Mr. Whoever you are. The most experienced agent has trouble keeping all his lies straight in the face of expert questioning.'' Florinsky snapped on one of the hand-cuffs but managed to get the other tangled. Cursing under his breath, and unaware Jude was watching him, he tucked the gun under his armpit to free the other hand to straighten the handcuff.

Jude didn't hesitate. He jerked his cuffed wrist free and took a large step forward. Almost simultaneously, he pivoted on his right foot and swung the manacled left hand all the way around his body. The loose handcuff whistled in its arc until it collided with a dull thud against the head of Florinsky.

Florinsky went down and the gun flew away from him. Stunned, moaning and bleeding from a deep cut on his temple, Florinsky started to crawl toward the pistol lying a few feet away. Before he could get close, Jude was on him. Using the dangling handcuff as a garrote, he squeezed the slim chain against Florinsky's neck and steadily increased the pressure.

Florinsky's eyes bulged and he managed a hoarse, weak cry before the chain closed off his windpipe. His hands tugged feebly at the chain but the weight of Jude's body and his superior strength made that futile. Florinsky's life was being squeezed out of him like toothpaste from a tube. Jude knew it would take just one more push to crush the larynx. He prepared to destroy the man's throat like a farm wife with a cooking chicken, but just as his muscles bunched for the effort, he heard cheering from a crowd high above him and he smelled the bitter almond scent of cyanide. Jude looked more closely at the battered face before him and no longer saw an enemy. He saw a man who wanted to live, a man who had reasons to live, a man whose blood now ran over Jude's fingers. Jude started shaking and let go of the man's throat as he frantically wiped the blood from his hands onto Florinsky's clothing. He could no longer stand to touch his victim, nor even to look at him.

Whimpering, Jude frantically unlocked the handcuff on his wrist and threw it away from him. He pulled open the door and ran down the empty corridor, not stopping until he reached the door of the crew's quarters. He walked as quietly and quickly as he could to his bunk and threw himself face-down on the pillow, drowning his sobs and harsh breathing in the soft material. The nightmare in the stadium played itself back in his mind, but with sounds magnified to where he thought his head would burst and the color of blood such a bright red he felt the heat of it on his brain. *"Murderer."* The word echoed and reechoed until Jude could do nothing but surrender to it. His exhausted body went limp and he almost surrendered to a sleep that promised to lift all his burdens.

As the spell started to pass, Jude pushed the haunting images out of his mind and concentrated hard to comprehend what had happened. With a frightened start, he remembered Florinsky lying half-dead on his cabin floor and realized that if Florinsky lived, he, Jude, would die. He had to go back and finish it. Silently cursing whatever it was that had made him lose his nerve, Jude tiptoed out of the crew's quarters and walked as quickly as he could back to Florinsky's cabin, hoping the man had not recovered and that he could finish the job without being observed.

No one was around as Jude paused and looked both ways. He slowly pushed in the door and looked around the still-lighted room. Florinsky was not there. Frantically and irrationally, Jude looked in the tiny lavatory. He pulled the covers back on the bed and looked under it. He looked in the closet. Florinsky was not there. He looked for the gun. It was not there.

With his heart sinking in fear, Jude ran out of the cabin and back to his berth. In silence he lay down on the bunk and rummaged around until he found a hairbrush with a large plastic handle. He fumbled with the handle in the dark until he managed to rip it apart and remove a slim metal cylinder. Holding the destroyed brush and the cylinder, he padded softly to the toilet where he carefully placed the remnants of the brush beneath some wastepaper in the bin and softly closed a stall door behind him. He unscrewed the cylinder and let the contents drop into his hand. It was nothing more than a capsule, the kind that contained cold medication or allergy relief. This capsule, though, contained the antidote for Jude's blunders.

Cyanide.

Jude replaced the capsule in the cylinder and dropped his pants. Carefully he inserted the suppository, rebuckled his pants, washed his hands and returned to his bunk.

Jude lay on the hard mattress and stared at the ceiling knowing that the means of his self-destruction was carried in his own body. He closed his eyes and thought of his life while he waited for them to come for him.

HER NAME WAS MATHILDE KARSAVINA and she was an ugly woman. She was too heavy—not heavy like a fat woman, but in a mannish way. Her shoulders were too wide, her wrists too thick, and her ankles were almost as thick as her calves. Her teeth were crooked, her hair dark, stringy and thin, and one eye was slightly out of alignment. For most of her twenty-four years she had lived as a Chuvash farm girl working six days a week in the rye and potato fields of her native central Russia, chatting away in her native Turkic tongue with co-workers who valued her strong back and pleasant disposition, and ignoring the occasional cruel boy who whistled sarcastically or called her a cow.

She had been appreciated for her qualities, and assured that, when her time came and all the pretty girls were chosen, a local man with a practical eye would speak for her and she would give him many children, hard work and unwavering loyalty. It was a world she was made for and one into which she fit comfortably.

All that changed the day the recruiter came. He was a self-assured, educated man from Moscow, and he spoke to them of service to the motherland, to the party, and of adventure in distant lands and on strange seas. He asked that the boldest and most dedicated of them volunteer for the fishing service. They all had cheered and the music saluted when Mathilde stepped forward.

That was five years ago. During those years she had learned much. She had learned to gut fish; she had learned to fight off sickness in constant freezing, wet cold; she had learned to turn her back to cruel, crude men to whom no person had dignity, and no woman had value beyond their assessment of her sexuality. And from those men she had learned she was ugly. At first she resisted their insulting advances, but then she gave up and let them use her like a brood sow. She was lonely and wanted to be touched. Whenever they beckoned, she found a hidden place and flopped for them. She tolerated their bad breath, their dirty bodies, their crude manners for reasons she didn't understand. It was simply that she was ugly and they, at least, wanted her.

All but one. He used her in the same way as the others at first, but then he began to talk to her, to ask her about herself, her values and her feelings. Often he didn't even make love to her, but just sat and told her nice things about herself. He would caress her and make her feel like a woman. He was kind and intelligent and she cared for him. He didn't give his name, and she was too shy to ask her shipmates. But names weren't important. It was enough that he was not what he appeared to be; he was much finer.

It was late and they were sitting in a large supply closet next to Florinsky's cabin. It was where he had wanted to take her that night, and she was again telling him about life in the pleasant, warm sun of her homeland, when a loud crash in Florinsky's cabin jolted them. He immediately took his arm from around her shoulder and put his ear to the wall while at the same time signaling her to be quiet. In a few moments, a door slammed and they heard steps running down the corridor. He turned to her and said, "I must go. Please stay here for one hour, then go quietly back to your bunk. Never, under any circumstances, tell anyone what you heard here tonight. Promise?"

She shook her head fearfully and watched as he slipped out the door.

JUDE OPENED HIS EYES in alarm to see the red-faced mate shaking his bunk. "Come on, come on. Get up on deck," the man commanded. Jude's heart sank with the belief that he had been discovered and they had come for him. It was to his confusion as well as relief when the mate advanced to the next bunk and repeated his command. Jude looked around the crew's quarters and saw that everyone who had been sleeping was now climbing out of bed and getting dressed amid a cacophony of grumbling and questions. He put on his foul-weather clothes and joined the rest as they ascended to the deck. There they lined up in a shivering, crooked line and waited for the captain.

After a few minutes, Captain Mitrovich strode down from the bridge and approached the waiting crew. "Comrades," he shouted above the sounds of the engines and the sea, "we've had a very bad accident aboard, and I've called you together to inform you of it and also to learn what I can about what caused it." He searched their faces, then continued. "You all know Comrade Kyril Florinsky, our esteemed political officer. Well, I'm sorry to tell you that Comrade Florinsky and a cannery worker named Mathilde Karsavina were killed late last night when they fell through a hatch to the factory deck. They fell onto the knives of the gutting machines, so there was no chance of surviving." Mitrovich stopped and let the curious buzzing among his audience run its course. "Now then, what I need to know is whether any of you heard any noises or are aware of anything else that might shed some light on this sad occurrence."

Jude's knees almost collapsed, so relieved was he to hear of Florinsky's death. It meant he could live, at least for a while longer. But then, he was snapped back to alertness by the sound of his name.

Mitrovich clasped his hands behind his back and paced back and forth before the crew. "Cook Markov has told me he saw Comrade Florinsky and the woman on deck late last night. They appeared to be trying to avoid him, so Comrade Markov said he did not intrude. Markov said that before he returned belowdecks, he saw the two of them lift the hatch from the cannery hold. My preliminary opinion is that they were seeking some . . . privacy." The captain lingered on the word for the obvious implication to sink in. "That would tend to support the rather logical conclusion that Comrade Florinsky and his companion were killed accidentally by falling through an open hatchway, probably when the ship rolled. Can anyone add anything else?" Mitrovich paused. "Well, then, you are dismissed. Markov, I'd like some more details. Please come to my cabin."

Jude had not said a word to the captain and his head swam in confusion as he waded through the crew members who were milling about chuckling over the death of the hated Florinsky and speculating good-naturedly about his sex life. He reached the captain's cabin and knocked. "Come in," Mitrovich said in a tired voice. Seeing Jude, he heaved a deep sigh, and said, as soon as the door was closed, "Thanks for not looking too surprised when I used your name out there. It was all I could think of. But why did you have to kill him on my ship? No one who knew the prick can believe that bullshit about an accident with the woman. Christ, the only way the man could get a hard-on was by reading the *Communist Manifesto*." He shook his head. "They looked like they'd been through a meat grinder. I just hope I can sell it to Moscow."

Jude was stunned. "But, Captain, I didn't kill him. We had a fight in his cabin, but he was alive when I left him. I assumed you did it when he asked you to send that radio message."

"I had no intention of sending that message," Mitrovich said, then he moaned deeply. "Good God, someone else on this ship did it. That's all I need, another fucking spy to trip over. They're going to hang me yet. Thank God we'll be in Vladivostok in a few days. I hope when we dock I never see you or another spy again."

"You don't have to worry about me," Jude said. "I have a forged priority air travel pass. I plan to disappear into the woodwork."

"But who did it?" Mitrovich almost begged for an answer.

"I don't know, but if you see him, tell him he saved my life," Jude said.

CHAPTER EIGHT

THE SILVER STREAKS OF DAYBREAK were thrusting over the horizon, giving dull illumination to the towers of the nearby Leningradskaya Hotel and Yaroslavl railway station like a backlit stage while the Moscow skyline stood in the wings patiently awaiting its own light.

The greenhouses of the Botanical Gardens of Moscow State University glimmered like chandeliers as they reflected the early light. A large complex of ornate glass buildings, the gardens were an outpost of summer warmth and greenery amid the grim visual tedium of winter-bound Moscow. The exotic plants from faraway places were especially loved by those who yearned to see the warm, colorful world beyond the Soviet borders, but whose passports provided no visas for such visions.

Vladimir Ruzsky sniffed at the steamy air of the tropical plants section as if it were a delicate perfume on a woman passing by. The pungent odor of decay sprang up like a mist as the hunched old man moved his stiff body slowly along the soft black humus. He massaged the gnarled hands, which were a lingering punishment for thirty years in a wet coal mine, and felt the comforting hot air creep into his arthritic joints like a medicinal balm. He stopped and ran his fingers over the glistening purple petal of a giant orchid. He was in a dreamworld, a place far from the cruel little village in the frozen north of Russia that for fifty-two years had been a canker on his spirit, and where he had not dared dream because dreams take anchor in hope, and his life had mocked hope like a teasing child. After raising a son, who was killed in a mine accident, and a daughter, who went to work in Siberia and had never been heard from since, after tolerating a fat wife with a big mouth he despised for most of his life and all of their marriage, he finally was too lame to work the mines and was given permission to move to the city and take a night watchman's job at the Botanical Gardens. It had become the only oasis among the sand dunes of his life.

He moved among the plants like a parish priest. He had gotten to know their names, their smells; he could sense their moods. In the dim light of early dawn, the resplendent whites, yellows, reds and purples of tillandsia, pineapple and orchids, and the rich green fronds of broad ferns wove a soft tapestry that comforted Ruzsky with the evidence that life is not always gray and black.

Ruzsky stepped around the roots of a balsa and pushed aside the vine of a climbing liana in order to reach an unfamiliar plant newly arrived from South America. He ran the back of his hand gently along the bright orange flower. It felt like a baby's skin. "I'm going to have to learn your name, pretty one," he cooed. "And if it isn't good enough for such a beauty, I'll give you a new one." He carefully examined the wilt of the plant, caused by transplant shock. "Don't worry, you'll be okay. Just rest and get lots to eat. If you don't get better, I'll make sure the gardener looks after you."

The ground sprinkler system went on, making a small frog jump abruptly over Ruzsky's shoe. "Ah, drink, drink, drink. That's all the bunch of you do. Eighty inches a year. If all this was vodka instead of water, I'd be happy along with you." Ruzsky walked over to the gauges that were his responsibility to check several times each shift, to make certain that the temperature was between seventy and ninety degrees Fahrenheit, and that the timers controlling the sprinklers and sunlamps were functioning.

His work completed, he was still reluctant to leave his tropical paradise and decided to rest for a few minutes. He noticed a pile of fertilizer bags stacked tightly in the center of the room. Irritated that the gardeners would leave such a mess in his favorite room, he kicked one of the bags, then sat down on them. The bags had a strange odor, but he had long since closed his mind to the unpronounceable concoctions that invaded this place. Too bad I'm not in charge here, he mumbled to himself. Those loafers wouldn't be so damned messy. You'd see a little respect for a room like this.

He leaned back on his elbows on one of the soft bags and turned his mind loose. He had seen jungle movies and the scenes leaped out of those cinematic memories. It was easy for Ruzsky to imagine various Tarzanesque plots, casting himself as the hero in hair-raising escape situations, fighting cannibals and lions, and winning frightened damsels. His daydreams allowed no room for coal mines, ice and cold, overweight wives or arthritis. It was a scenario created to his specifications. He smiled and closed his eyes because, even sitting on a fertilizer bag, Ruzsky could create one fine world.

The sunlamps went on in the room, turning night into day in an instant, according to the whim of automatic timers. The bright lights didn't faze the old man, deeply absorbed in his peaceful fantasies. There was no way for him to know that death had just awakened and was standing at his side.

High above the tropical plants, several huge four-thousand-watt quartz floods were positioned to provide the plants with the light they needed but could not otherwise get in a place nature did not intend them to be. A string had been tied around the bulb of one of the lights, and hung down forty feet where it was attached to a small blue balloon suspended a few inches above a pie tin filled with white crystals and broken glass.

The balloon was filled with brake fluid, and the pie tin with chlorine, two everyday products as innocent as salt and pepper. A person can hold brake fluid in one hand and chlorine in the other and nothing will happen except his fingers will get dirty. But clap those hands together, and the sudden mixture will act like a match and gasoline—causing a raging fire.

As the lamp slowly became hotter, a wisp of smoke arose from the string, and then it broke. The balloon fell into the pie tin with a soft splash and was punctured by the glass. Instantly, a hot flame leaped upward and ignited a thin strip of grayish-white magnesium lying in the dish and trailing off along the floor, where it had absorbed water from the sprinklers, thus greatly magnifying its already potent combustibility. Like a berserk snake, the blinding-white glare of the magnesium raced across the floor in the direction of Vladimir Ruzsky.

The night watchman had lazily opened his eyes at the soft sound and strange scent of the balloon bursting into flame. Bewildered, he turned in time to see a small flame racing along the floor toward him with a glare so bright only a devil could have ignited it. His mind was still uncomprehending when, like a pursued mouse, the light ran beneath the pile of fertilizer bags on which he sat.

By then, it no longer mattered.

The homemade magnesium fuse headed for the middle of the stack where a single small stick of dynamite, two inches in diameter by sixteen inches in length, was stuffed between the bags along with several boxes of steel ball bearings. The six fifty-pound bags of common ammonium nitrate fertilizer had been slit at the top and a quart of diesel fuel had been poured into each. The fuel had been soaking into the fertilizer for several hours, forming the chemical reaction necessary for the purpose. The flame of the magnesium strip reached the fusing of a blasting cap and continued to the head of the cap, a small silver cylinder containing a few grains of a touchy explosive called PETN, enough to ignite the dynamite.

The blast of a single stick of dynamite will certainly get the attention of a bystander, but what occurred when that relatively small explosion ignited the soaked fertilizer was the difference between a match and a torch. The effect of the chain reaction magnified the strength of the dynamite several hundredfold. The greenhouse became a hell of red, orange and black fury. The solid mass of the explosive instantly changed to gases that expanded violently, leaping outward at a speed of four miles per second, and by so doing turned chemistry into death.

The explosion shook the ground for several blocks and broke windows for a half mile. At that hour, the enormous fireball was seen by only a few persons, though it was visible for miles. Vladimir Ruzsky was not among them.

The body of the night watchman ceased to exist. The blast burned his clothes to fine-grain ashes and turned his heavy watchman's clock into a lump of useless iron. His flesh melted like cellophane in a furnace and his bones became charred sticks with the marrow burned out of them. His skeleton was blown into fragments. A child would find the top of his skull three days later and kick it along his path to school for a few yards like a misshapen rock.

Just as the bomb went off, a hapless gardener drove up to the building and parked just a few feet from the explosion on the other side of a glass wall. Unlike Ruzsky's, the gardener's remains could be found for burial, much to the squeamishness of those who had to scrape his black incinerated body out of the molten metal his old Zaporozhet automobile had become. The heat from the blast ignited the air inside the car, making the upholstery, the plastic and the rubber all burst into flame. The most combustible thing in the car—human flesh—had burned first and most fiercely.

The car came apart like a matchbox. The steering wheel ended up in a fir tree a hundred yards distant; one of the doors was thrown a half block and buried itself deep in a snowbank as the white-hot metal burned a path through the snow like a razor through paper.

The thousands of ball bearings thrown upward like bullets hit the large windows like an army of vandals. Tons of glass came crashing down on the sensitive plants, and the frigid wind followed like a hungry brother-in-law. Hundreds of plants on the side of the blast were instantly destroyed by the waves of heat. Thousands of others that escaped immediate destruction were already beginning to wilt in the cold.

Seconds after the blast died down and ball bearings fell on the neighborhood like hail on tin, an eerie quietude returned to the scene, and the only movement to mark the holocaust was fire lazily devouring the car and branches of nearby trees. Lights in nearby buildings flicked on one by one, like stunned witnesses to a disaster, yellow eyes gazing in unblinking astonishment.

IVAN KOLCHAK STOOD with hands on hips and surveyed the pandemonium with disgust. The state militia, which was charged with day-to-day law enforcement, was obviously ill suited to deal with terrorist bombings. Kolchak was convinced Soviet police were soft compared to their more embattled counterparts in such places as New York and London. They did not have to deal with the myriad problems found in a Western society because they were not hamstrung by protective laws that artful criminals use for self-protection. Consequently, because of the fear the KGB caused in potential lawbreakers, it sometimes seemed all the militia had to worry about were drunks, wife-beaters and traffic accidents. When they had to handle an incident like this, their incompetence showed. Orders were being shouted, and then countermanded in a louder voice. Like ants at a picnic, cars were rushing to the scene and departing with full sirens and flashing lights. Flashbulbs were going off as if it were opening night at the Bolshoi, and officers were approaching the burned-out car to peer inside, almost as though they were children being challenged on a dare.

After inspecting the interior of the gardens and seeing the night watchman's detached shoe with shoelaces still neatly tied, but containing the severed foot, the only trace of the man, Kolchak walked over to a group of arguing militia officers and stood outside their tight circle with hands in his overcoat pockets until one of them recognized him. The militiaman who turned and recognized Kolchak tried to disguise his hatred for the KGB official, but Kolchak was not fooled. That's fine, he thought, let the bumbling country constables stew in envy of their betters.

"If I may make a suggestion, Comrade Colonel," Kolchak tactfully said, "I would order that tow truck away until the crime laboratory gives a release."

"They can examine this junk in the garage, Comrade," the officer answered.

"If that car is moved and it results in the obliteration of evidence, that would cause great unhappiness," Kolchak countered calmly.

The militia colonel knew he had lost already, but grumbled to save face. "Well, why don't they get on with it? I need to get this mess cleaned up so they can start repairing that goddamn overgrown flowerpot." He gestured angrily toward the shattered Botanical Gardens.

"There are a lot of other things that can be done in the meantime," Kolchak said.

"Of course," the colonel huffed. "The KGB is not the only organization that knows what it's doing. My people are already combing the neighborhood. If anyone saw or heard anything, we'll know about it before the day is over, you can count on that."

Kolchak smiled. The colonel interpreted it as a sign of approval, but it had meaning for Kolchak alone. He was smiling at the futility of all the activity. Unless this were the act of a mad bomber with a pathological hatred of flowers, those who staged the explosion would not be hard to find. It had to be a message—a meaningless one unless the messenger identified himself. There was no other logical explanation. The night watchman was a nobody and the gardener's arrival could not have been predicted closely enough. They were unfortunate bystanders, not targets. No, the purpose of the bomb was to get attention. And it had succeeded: it had his.

The group of policemen was broken apart by the frantic director of the Botanical Gardens, a man in his mid-sixties with long, disheveled white hair and steamed glasses. He was without coat or gloves in the subzero cold, but didn't seem to notice. He jumped around as though he could restore his ruined greenhouse by exercise alone.

"Help me, Comrades, help me. My poor plants will die unless we get them covered." He wrung his hands and groaned at the smoking shambles before him. Kolchak looked at the man impassively, with little respect for his devotion to the dying plants. Kolchak considered an attachment to something with no utilitarian value, such as most of these plants, to be a weakness, and he had no sympathy for this old man who couldn't control himself in front of strangers.

The director started to sob because he knew the battle was lost, that his plants were already dying. "What can I do?" he whined to the heavens.

Kolchak saw one of his assistants holding a radio microphone in his hand and beckoning him from the car, but as he turned to leave, he answered the director, "If you hurry, maybe you can make boutonnieres." A listening militiaman gave a snorting laugh, and Kolchak looked at him with the requisite frown before releasing the flicker of a smile and walking away.

"Kolchak," he said abruptly into the microphone.

"Good morning, Comrade Kolchak," the soothing voice of his secretary answered. "I have a message from security at the Bureau of Emigration. They found a letter at their door this morning when they opened. They said to tell you it was from a group called the Sicarii that claimed to have set off the bomb." She pronounced it *sic*-a-ree.

"Well, what the hell is that?" Kolchak demanded.

"They don't know, Comrade. They opened the letter just a few minutes ago. They called immediately. The only thing the letter said other than about the bombing was Exodus 9:1."

"Must be some kind of code," Kolchak said.

"It's from the Bible, Comrade, the Old Testament. There was a copy in the library. I had them look it up."

"Well, what does it say?"

"It says, 'Then the Lord said unto Moses, go in unto Pharaoh, and tell him, Thus saith the Lord God of the Hebrews, Let my people go, that they may serve me.'"

THE TIDY LITTLE MAN with the owlish glasses and shiny suit didn't seem uncomfortable or frightened to be in the office of a high-ranking KGB official, he just seemed out of place. Dmitry Nesterov and he sat in awkward silence, not knowing how to make small talk, as though they were from different planets. They were rescued by Ivan Kolchak, coming through the door.

"Kolchak, glad you're here," his superior said and motioned toward the other man. "This is Comrade Professor Vasilevich from the university. He's our expert from the classics department."

The professor stood and Kolchak shook his hand. "Hello, Comrade. How did your research go?"

The professor resumed his seat and opened a worn briefcase almost the size of a suitcase. "You've picked a fascinating subject. I assume you have some familiarity with the history of the Mideast."

Both men looked at him blankly.

"Ah, how about the history of the Roman empire?"

Nesterov and Kolchak looked at each other, then Nesterov said, "Professor, why don't you just go right into the subject? Tell us about the Sicarii."

"Yes, of course. Well, in the first place, it's not '*sic*-a-ree,' as you pronounce it, the correct form is 'sa-car-ee-*eye*,' with the accent on the last syllable. It's Latin, second declension noun, the plural form of sicarius."

Kolchak stifled a laugh when he saw the look on Nesterov's face at being corrected like a schoolboy.

"Go on," Nesterov growled.

"The Sicarii were a splinter band of Zealots in Palestine at the time of the Great Revolt against Rome, from 63 A.D. to 70 A.D. They were from Galilee, much nastier than the Jerusalem Zealots."

"You mean they actually went to war against the entire Roman empire?" Kolchak asked.

The professor sighed. "Were you not taught this? My, my, I sometimes fear for our standard of education...."

Nesterov grinned at Kolchak, who was glaring at the professor, and said, "Since we can't remedy the failures of Comrade Kolchak's education in one sitting, Professor, why don't you tell us?"

"These Jews believed that God would protect them from their enemies as long as they kept the laws and struggled in their righteous cause. There were some messianic pretensions of their founder, Menahem, which probably helped convince them of their invulnerability."

"Why would any people believe such a stupid thing?" Nesterov asked.

The professor smiled patiently at Nesterov as he would at a student. "You must understand, one man's madness is another man's bravery. To know why people act as they do, we must examine their beliefs and their values. In the case of the Jews, the driving force of their history has been a deep-seated love of homeland—'Next year in Jerusalem,' they say. To the Sicarii, the hope of that homeland being free of the Romans was strong enough to persuade them it could be done."

"Crazy," Kolchak said.

"One of the higher forms of craziness, then," the professor said. "Really, gentlemen, history is replete with examples of what the objective observer would call foolhardy courage. But these things are not done objectively, they are the result of some grand passion, some event or belief that compels individuals or nations to go far beyond what normal people are capable of or would even consider. Strong people make history by defying it. The English poet, John Dryden, called the Jews, 'A headstrong, moody, murmuring race.' I think that fits from a historical standpoint."

"What happened to these Sicarii?" Nesterov asked.

"They died."

"Everyone does that, Professor, especially after two thousand years."

"Not the way these people died, Comrade Nesterov. Did you ever hear of Masada?"

"Kindly stop giving me quizzes. I'm not one of your students," Nesterov said.

"Forgive me, gentlemen. The classroom is my work, I guess I tend to carry it with me." He coughed in embarrassment. "As I was saying, the Sicarii died after a Roman siege in 73 A.D. at a place called Masada. It was a fortress atop a steep mountain in the Palestine desert on the edge of the Dead Sea, totally inaccessible except by a winding, narrow path called the Snake Trail."

"A small trail should be easy to defend. How did the Romans reach them?" Kolchak asked.

"They built an earthen ramp. A quarter of a mile high it was," the professor said. "Stupendous feat of engineering. Anyway, the night before the final assault was to be mounted, knowing they were overwhelmingly outnumbered, the

Jews—the Sicarii and their wives and children—committed mass suicide. But not really suicide—something infinitely more noble. The men first killed their families and then one another. Nine hundred and sixty died that night rather than submit to Rome.''

"What proof is there of all this? The Jews are clever at fairy tales," Kolchak said.

The professor pushed his glasses back on his nose and rummaged around in his briefcase. "Here it is," he murmured to himself. He pulled out a tattered book, leafed through it and then turned to the waiting men. "This is the record of Josephus Flavius, an eminent historian of the period. He was a Jew who turned traitor and threw in his lot with the Romans. Not the most laudable man, perhaps, but nevertheless, his record of the times is considered quite accurate. I read to you from the speech made by Eleazar ben Yair, the commander of the Sicarii on Masada. The scene is the night before the Romans attack and the Jews are preparing to die:

"'Since we, long ago, my generous friends, resolved never to be servants to the Romans, nor to any other than to God himself, the time is now come that obliges us to make that resolution true.... We were the very first that revolted from them, and now we are the last that fight against them; and I cannot but esteem it as a favor that God hath granted us, that it is still in our power to die bravely, and in a state of freedom.... Let our wives die before they are abused, and our children before they have tasted of slavery; and after we have slain them, let us bestow that glorious benefit upon one another mutually, and preserve ourselves in freedom, as an excellent funeral monument for us.'"

The professor closed the book and looked at his silent audience. "These men, I submit, would be welcome in the Red Army."

Kolchak broke the silence. "Tell me, Professor, from what you know of these ancient Jewish warriors, if a modern group were to name themselves Sicarii, what do you think we could expect from them?"

The professor closed the book and absently chewed on the stem of his glasses. "Well," he finally said, "that's out of my specialty, but if they were to take the name Sicarii, I would think their values would be freedom at any cost, devotion to their ideals to the very end and a willingness to die for goals that other men might not understand. I should think they would try to live up to the name they adopted."

"By the way, you never told us what the name means," Kolchak said.

"I didn't?" The professor gave a blank look. "Why, Sicarii means 'the assassins.'"

CHAPTER NINE

THE ROOM WAS DARK, lit only by tiny dancing candles on mounds of melted wax, giving off a soft glow that made the murmuring men huddled together seem undefined and mystical.

It was only the shabby kitchen of a tiny log house in a grimy industrial area of suburban Moscow, but to the ten men crowded close to a rickety, paint-chipped table meant for half their number, like bankers around a rich man, it was a *shtibl*, a house of prayer. The men were in uniform, but it was no uniform prescribed for an army, or even for streetcar conductors. It was a uniform that declared their apartness. And though the room was hot and steamy from too many bodies, no one even loosened a collar.

Each had a beard—some full, some scraggly, some black, some red and some gray. Each wore a black hat, mostly old homburgs, but some with narrow brims and some with wide brims and rounded tops. Except for tieless white shirts, and in the case of a fat man leaning back in his chair with the fringed edges of his *tallit katan* ritual undershirt sticking out, black was all that showed.

The fat man leaned forward and began softly humming a slow tune. One by one, the other men picked up the wordless song and joined their voices. As the tempo quickened and the volume rose, the men started to weave back and forth rhythmically and softly pound the table with their fists. One man jumped up and whirled around; another joined him and together they circled the small room in an awkward but enthusiastic dance. At the head of the table, an old man bounced in his chair in time to the a cappella music and waved his arms like the conductor of a silent symphony.

From the doorway of the parlor, two young men dressed in blue jeans and bright sweaters and with close-cropped hair watched, one in astonishment, the other with a pained expression of embarrassment.

The bearded men in black were Hasidic Jews, and they were different. Born in eighteenth-century eastern Europe in the mind of a rabbi who assumed the name Baal Shem Tov, which means Master of the Good Name, they were an Orthodox sect that believed their faith should be rescued from the dry, spiritless interpreters of the law. They strove to bring their religion back to the people, to the common Jews who for generation after generation have labored in fields, shops and markets, and have endured the pogroms and the endless barbed reminders they were Christ killers. Traditionally, these Jews knew little Hebrew; they had not studied in yeshivas with learned rabbis. All they had was faith, a sense of destiny and a language called Yiddish, a mongrel tongue coupling Hebrew and bastardized vocabularies lifted from whatever countries the Diaspora scattered them to.

The early Hasidim recognized the same truth as other dynamic religious leaders: the man in the hut does not relate to the cathedral. The Hasidim started conducting services in Yiddish, the language of the people. They said, in effect, act toward God as though you knew him. Sing, dance, be happy. Don't conceal the joy of your faith from the source of it. The Hasidim taught their converts to stand apart from the world, to declare by their dress that God chose them and they chose God.

They did not bend easily to modern convention. Hasidic women shaved their heads at marriage and dressed with meticulous modesty to ward off the lust of other men. Shorn but strong-willed women sometimes wore wigs that made them more attractive than their natural hair, but women weren't

easily convinced that God preferred them homely. Women
also had to purify themselves at a *mikveh* ritual bath each
month following menstruation. Being a female Hasid was not
without its challenges.

The Hasidim paid the price. They became the target of
every mean kid who could reach a handy rock in the gutter,
and of every government that wanted to shift blame for its own
incompetence onto *them*. Their faith compelled them to operate outside "normal" society, and they learned the grim
lesson of the prey: eyes that glitter in the dark at the edge of
the forest are fixed on the fringe of the herd.

After the revolution, the Communists saw the Hasidic Jews
as obstacles to the homogeneous goals of the new order.
"Russification" became the code word that meant distinc-
tiveness was a threat to the state. Consequently, the Hasidim
with their full beards, black apparel and long curly *payes*
flowing past their ears, became symbols of religious obstina-
cy. Their decision to be distinctive resulted in harassment as
extreme as imprisonment in labor camps and as vexing as job
opportunities lost and ridicule on the streets.

It was late on the *shabbes* and the small congregation was
celebrating the *Seludeh shelishit*, the third meal of the day.
They had to meet in the kitchen of this ramshackle house because the Soviets had a law that stipulated no religious service could be held with fewer than twenty worshipers,
presumably to frustrate plotters of one kind or another. Such
a law made this small band into criminals, and the joy they
felt was muted out of fear of discovery. Little Russian was
heard. They talked and prayed in Yiddish and Hebrew. They
spoke to one another as they would to God.

At the head of the table sat the old man. He was the rebbe,
the Hasidic version of a rabbi, except he was venerated far
beyond most rabbis. He was not only the leader, he was God's
man. His gray beard was tangled and his eyes were rheumy
below the tattered homburg pushed back on his head. His

hands trembled slightly, but the infirmity was ignored by his followers; they admired his spirit, not his flesh. The rebbe nodded to a man on his right, his *gabbai* who assisted in the service, and who silently poured brandy from a very old decanter into the glass of every man. When he finished, a man at the far end of the table waited to catch the eye of the rebbe, then raised his glass and toasted his health. *"Lehaim."*

After the others repeated *"Lehaim,"* and sipped the brandy, the rebbe nodded and raised his own glass. *"Lehaim tovim ulesholem,"* he said, wishing them a good and peaceful life.

The food piled before the rebbe was more plentiful than the meager portions before the others: herring, sour cream, pickled cabbage and egg bread called *challah*. He slowly took a tiny taste of each and then divided the food into portions and passed them to his table mates. They accepted them gratefully, wanting to share the food touched by the great Rebbe Israel Rabinowitz, a *tsaddik*, righteous and wise, a man God could trust.

Rebbe Rabinowitz let his dim eyes roam sadly over the room. He was not dismayed that only nine faithful shared his food. God in his wisdom had decreed that the faith is healthiest in times of hardship. The rebbe would prefer one man who would stand for Israel in a drought to a thousand who would appear only to pick the fruit. The rebbe didn't grieve for the *Yiden*, his fellow Jews. He grieved for his son standing in the next room and desecrating the *shabbes* with a smirk on his face and the bright clothes of a whoremonger on his back, sharing his scorn with a disbeliever, a Ukrainian, one of those to whom, through the centuries, Jew-baiting has been a game when they sought amusement, and Jew-killing a catharsis when they were angry or frightened.

Rabinowitz had lived his long life among the people of the Soviet Union, and as a Jew, he knew them for who they were: Babylonians, Philistines, Romans, Germans, Russians,

Ukrainians. The words change, but history is not fooled. Their name is oppressor, and they are the instrument of God to test his people.

Rebbe Rabinowitz had no more fear of the Russians than David did of Goliath. In city and village, through war and pogrom, drought and famine, he had lived simply and studied Torah and Talmud, seeking only for wisdom and God's will. But now he was afraid; he feared for the soul of his son, the one who rightfully should follow him as rebbe, just as he had followed his own father.

He felt old. He needed his son. His son could tell the *shabbes* stories after he was gone.

"Children of Israel," the rebbe said softly, and the men looked up expectantly from their food. "Do you know of the Rebbe Moshe Titlebaum? He was a holy and humble man, a student of the scriptures. When the Nazis took him to Auschwitz, he got off the train and saw his people being herded like beasts and whipped like slaves. A clever man, the rebbe knew then what was to happen. This was no relocation camp, but a place of death.

"While the Nazi guards prodded the Jews into lines pointed toward the crematoriums, the good rebbe put his hand on the shoulder of a KAPO, one of the Jewish prisoners who stayed alive day to day by leading their own people to the ovens. 'I know where I am about to go, but this must not be destroyed,' said the rebbe, taking out a small Bible and putting it into the hands of the KAPO. 'This Bible belonged to Haim ben Moses Atar, a wise and good rebbe. It is two hundred years old. The truth must survive even if man does not.'

"The KAPO pulled back from the book as if it were a serpent. 'It is forbidden to have such a thing,' he said, looking around to see if the Nazis were watching. 'We're searched constantly. If they found that on me, I would be put into the ovens today with the rest of you.'

"'I tell you this,' the rebbe said, 'put this Bible in your pocket. It will not be found, and you will leave this place alive.'

"Well, brothers, the KAPO trusted the rebbe and hid the book." Rebbe Rabinowitz paused and examined the faces of those at the table. "And it was God's will that the KAPO should go through every search without the Bible being discovered, though it was kept in one of his pockets. He alone among the KAPOs lived, and he turned the ancient book over to those who treasure it to this day."

Except for a muffled cough and the scraping of a chair, there was silence in the small room as the men thought, then one of the youngest asked, "Rebbe, why is it that God chose to save a KAPO, one who stayed alive on the grief of his people, yet allowed a great man like Rebbe Titlebaum to die?"

"To confound men like us who hear the story," the rebbe answered. "In our confusion, we must then rely on our faith that God is just and merciful and has a plan for his children. He looks into our hearts. The pebble of goodness we see in a man we scorn, God sees as a mountain."

A man at the end of the table cleared his throat and said, "He who gives us teeth will give us bread."

"A wise man hears one word and understands two," the rebbe said and then lapsed into a thoughtful silence as his *gabai* started to softly sing:

"'Sound the great shofar for our freedom;
lift up the banner to bring our exiles together,
and assemble us from the four corners of the earth.
Blessed art thou, O Lord, who gatherest the despised of
thy people Israel.'"

The other men hummed along and got to their feet. They placed hands on one another's shoulders and started a slow, rhythmic dance.

The two young men—one short and blond with a flat, fleshy nose and close-set blue eyes, the other slim and tall with unruly red hair pushed across a broad, freckled forehead and a needle-point nose bent slightly off center—watched impassively from the doorway as the rebbe spoke to his tablemates.

The two sat close together in the tiny parlor, talking softly but intently, stopping only when the blonde, whose name was Nicholas Mikhailovitch, a member of the Ukrainian Freedom Movement, would stare at the men at the table when a gesture or sound caught his attention. The red-haired man paid no attention to the Hasidic worshipers; he had heard it all before. He was David Rabinowitz, son of the rebbe.

"What language is that he's talking?" Nicholas asked David.

"Yiddish," he was told.

"Sounds like gibberish to me," the blonde answered. "Back home in Kiev, they used to talk about the Zids having a crazy language, but I never heard it before."

David looked at his companion with open curiosity, and thought, by the habits of generations, we—Ukrainian and Jew—should be enemies. Except for the Nazis, your people have persecuted mine more than any other of history's bullies. But because we share a greater enemy in our Communist rulers, we're forced into this awkward alliance. What a strange world when what we call friendship is based on the lesser of two hatreds.

David noticed Nicholas looking at him expectantly, and said, "Don't worry about it. We've got more important things than an old-fashioned language to talk about."

"I drove by the university Botanical Gardens this morning. Boy, what a mess!" Nicholas chuckled at the memory. "There was glass over everything. People were running around in the snow like Jews at a widow's auction trying to put those weird-looking plants into pots—" Nicholas stopped and glanced sheepishly at David. "Sorry." He licked his lips nervously. "Anyway, you could tell the plants were already dead. I'll bet the KGB is really pissed. How'd you manage to pull that off?"

David tried to suppress a response, but a coy smile slipped out. "Pull what off? Oh, you mean the explosion at the gardens. I read about it in the newspaper. Sounds like an expert job."

"Don't congratulate yourself too much," Nicholas teased, "Blowing up a glass house can't be too tough."

David hardened his voice. "Siberia prisons are full of big-mouth braggarts. If I were responsible for such a thing, I wouldn't admit it—not even to you."

Nicholas dropped his eyes like a chastened boy. "Any-way—" he started.

"Anyway," David interrupted, "let's drop it." He glanced around reflexively and lowered his voice. "I need guns. Several automatic weapons, about six, small but nasty. Think you can help?"

Nicholas and David had met as engineering students at Moscow State University. After two years of friendship they had cautiously probed each other to gradually discover their mutual hatred of the Communist regime.

For centuries, the Ukraine and Russia lived side by side in eastern Europe with the larger Russia dominating like a neighborhood bully. Even when Russia forced their country into the Soviet Union after the Communist Revolution, Ukrainians preserved their dream of independence and, to pass the time, cultivated Russia-hating to an art form. At the time of the German invasion of 1941, when the Nazis were trying to rip out the heart of the Soviet Union as an Aztec high priest would of a human sacrifice, Ukrainians lined the streets to welcome the "liberators."

Hating well done.

For years, a deadly struggle was waged between the Soviet secret police and Ukrainian rebels. The rebels made little headway toward their freedom, but neither were they wiped out despite the ardent efforts of their enemies. They now number only a few small bands of plotters, driven underground by constant harassment and informers bought by KGB rubles.

Nicholas learned his Russia-hating from his father, who learned it from his own father, who learned it from his father before him. Nicholas planned to pass it on to his own son someday.

"It sounds like you need Uzis, you know, those tiny Israeli submachine guns. Do you have any sources?" Nicholas asked.

David shook his head. "Not yet, but we're working on it. In the meantime, I'm counting on you."

Nicholas shook his head. "They're expensive. Tough to smuggle in. I figure about a thousand rubles apiece."

"I'll get the money—somehow," David said.

Nicholas studied his friend as though to gauge his resolve. "I'll do the best I can to get the guns, but we've got a little project of our own going on. You wouldn't believe—"

"Don't tell me," David said quickly. "The less each of us knows about the other, the less the KGB can learn by torture. Remember that, Nicholas. The more ignorant you are, the more sincere you'll sound when they touch the electric wire to your balls."

Nicholas tightened his legs together playfully and laughed. "Talk like that takes the fun out of it."

David rose and Nicholas followed him to his feet and reached for his heavy coat. "I'll see you in class, David. *Chort!* (Damn!) I've got to spend the night studying chemistry. I wish I could breeze through it like you. Maybe in a few days I'll know something about those Uzis."

David shook his friend's hand. "Do us both a favor, don't come here on Saturday anymore." He gestured toward the men in the kitchen. "The KGB frowns on this. If they sud-

denly pay us a visit and discover you here, you might find it
a bit tough to pass for a Hasid.''

Nicholas glanced at the worshipers and gave a mock gri-
mace. ''*Chort!* And just when I was getting the feel of it.''

REBBE RABINOWITZ WATCHED the candles flicker weakly.
They had been very large when lighted the previous evening
before the Sabbath prohibition from doing such work took
effect, but like his life, ceaseless labor had worn them down.

The dying candles said it was time. He held up his hand,
which immediately stopped the singing and dancing. *''Gut
shabbes,''* he pronounced, and turned on the overhead light,
which signaled the end of the Sabbath. At the benediction,
the worshipers struggled into their long black *kapotas*, shook
each other's hands and headed for the door. The last act for
each was to reverently reach for the hand of the rebbe and wish
him *''gut voch,''* a good week. Rebbe Rabinowitz watched his
flock depart, then turned to David who, with a long leg flung
over the arm of the ratty easy chair, was studying an advanced inorganic chemistry text, the one that had given him
the idea for the fertilizer bomb.

''David, son, why do you blaspheme the *shabbes* by bringing a disrespectful goy to our house during services? Especially a Ukrainian...''

David looked up from his book. ''I knew you were going to
start with that. The Ukrainians are the only ones opposing the
Communists. And if they do that, they're on my side. I'm not
forgetting the past, but Nicholas isn't responsible for what his
people did to Jews aeons ago.''

''Aeons ago, is it?'' the rebbe said in astonishment. ''Was
Babi Yar aeons ago? It was less than half a century. Yesterday.
One hundred thousand of your fellow Jews died there. Taken
to an open pit on the edge of the city and machine-gunned
down—if they were lucky. The ones who did not die immediately were buried alive.''

"That was the Germans."

"The Germans, while the Ukrainians you love so much egged them on. For many years, Babi Yar had no monument telling the story of how so many innocents died. It was nothing more than dust and weeds lying in neglect outside Kiev, a dusty field telling its story to the wind. When they finally put up a statue a few years ago, there was no mention of the Jews. It was as though we weren't even there." The rebbe turned his face toward heaven in exasperation. "Even with their monuments, they insult us."

"Father—"

"Don't interrupt," the rebbe scolded. "Let me tell you more about these wonderful Ukrainians. As a youth I lived among them; more than once I heard the cry, *'Bei Zhidov! Beat the Jews.'* I've told you they wanted to ignore the dead at Babi Yar, but that doesn't mean your friends don't like monuments. Oh, no. The so-called liberator of the Ukraine, Bogdan Chmielnitzki, is honored everywhere you look in Kiev. And this is the man who in the year 1648 of the Christian calendar started the worst pogrom ever. Thousands of innocent Jewish women and children were murdered...." He shook his head in wonder. "And they honor the man."

"In fairness, Father, I don't think they honor him for that."

The rebbe shook his head in exasperation. "When are you going to learn, my son? Forget this plotting and scheming with outsiders. The trust a Jew puts in goyim is like snow in March. Just be a good Jew and shut the rest of this out. Let the Ukrainians and the Russians kill each other off. The only thing that unites them is hatred of Jews. Stay out of the middle. Study Torah and Talmud, observe the law of God and wait for his justice."

David slammed his book shut. "That's what you can't understand," he stormed. "Your idea of a good Jew is ghetto mentality. The Israelis have shown that a good Jew is one that fights, not one that lets the world use him as toilet paper.''

The rebbe raised his own voice. ''Thank God your dead mother cannot hear this. You were meant to be a rebbe, and a good rebbe pursues something more important than whatever this thing is you've got yourself mixed up with. Let others squabble with the government.''

''I was meant to be myself. I was meant to be an Israeli, and that's what I'll be if we can force the Russians to let us go,'' David said.

The rebbe clamped his hands over his ears. ''No more of this. My prayers are that you'll see the folly of such talk.''

''Bullshit! If prayer did any good, they'd be hiring men to do it twenty-four hours a day.''

The old man shook his head sadly. ''A true Jew would not say such things.''

David closed his eyes in exasperation. ''Father, don't force me into a mold. You're a traditional Jew, I'm a historical Jew. There's a difference.''

''You can't slice bread that thin, son.''

David softened his voice and tried to be persuasive. ''You grew up in a time when Jews had no hope, when contentment meant no pogroms. It's different today. Our hope is Israel, Zionism come to life in our time. My Judaism is the steel of the ancient warriors of our history, the Maccabees and the Zealots. Today's Maccabees live in a modern world and use modern weapons to spit in the eye of their enemies, just as the Sicarii did against the Romans.

''Yours is the Judaism of primitive religion, of wearing ridiculous costumes and praying to some long-bearded god invented when superstitious farmers thought he'd be good for crops and frightening enemies.''

The rebbe moved sadly toward the door, then turned and spoke slowly in Yiddish to his son: *"Az Got vil shtrofn an amho'orets, leygter im a loshn-koydesh vort in moyl arayn."*

"Chort! Damn it, Father, you know I don't know your ghetto language that well. What're you saying?"

"It's an old proverb: The Lord, when he wants to punish an ignoramus, inspires him to mouth some piece of learning."

CHAPTER TEN

THE YOUNG OFFICER STOOD in the middle of the *izba*, a single-room cabin and cautiously looked around as though on reconnaissance. It was a peasant's meager home in a poor village of a dozen huts and a dozen pigsties on the steppes of southern Ukraine. The town was occupied by humans but controlled by pigs. They ran at will, rooting and wallowing in porcine bliss. Their droppings mixed with the mud of the village square like kneaded batter, rising back to the surface as a sweet-sour odor that hung over the ground like fog. The villagers endured this, knowing their revenge would come with the autumn butchering time. No one else cared. The place was known to the tax collectors, but to no mapmakers because the rock-strewn dirt path that led to it did not merit being called a road. It had a name, but no one who did not live there knew it. The village was Russia, 1921, unknown and uncounted.

The only light in the cabin was from a small rain-streaked window and the iron stove where the coals flared into flame from the constant gusts that swept down the endless plains from the Arctic. The gaps in the mud chinking between the uneven birch logs forming the hut's walls and the straw thatching on the roof welcomed the icy wind as a fat lady does pastry.

The icons of long-dead saints peering down stonily from their frames on the walls were the spirits of the young officer's enemies, representing the musty stirrings of an oppressive past that he in his revolutionary fervor was determined to eradicate. Though he fought the superstition he had come to hate in the Russian peasant's psyche, he was made uncomfortable by the unblinking two-dimensional eyes painted on the dark panels that surrounded him from their position above the rough split-log furniture.

The smell of cooked cabbage, onions and sour milk stained the air, and the pungency of people living too close together for generation after fetid generation was like the smell of damp clothing left to mildew in a pile. He shuddered with a chill from a gust of wind, or perhaps it was from the hopeless life these people led that seemed a miasma rising from the hard-packed earthen floor. But a crude wooden cradle and a baby's playthings lying in a corner refuted the despair. Despite all, life stubbornly surges forward, like a mule straining against harness.

He heard a shout and went to the window. He could see some of his soldiers stumbling and slipping in the rain-slick mud and waving bottles of homemade liquor, willingly surrendered by townsmen who were intent on preserving wives and meager possessions, not vodka. The soldiers were themselves ignorant peasants and laborers who had grabbed the rifles the Bolshevik revolutionaries had thrust into their hands with ringing slogans and glittering promises. Having already settled old grudges by shooting landlords and bosses, they would have been happy to drop the rifles and return to their own shabby homes. But they found to their dismay that it was easier to get into an army than out. So here they were in this anonymous village, chasing enemies of the people but happy to find only peasants' vodka.

The officer turned back to the room, toward the reason he was there.

She stood next to the fireplace. The only motion in the room was the slight rise and fall of her breast. The flickering red light of the fire made her blue eyes glitter as inscrutably as a cat's. She was young, perhaps eighteen, but carried herself with the self-assurance of a woman who knows men and doesn't fear them. She pushed a wisp of blond hair away from her face with a plump hand and slowly moved toward him as the dim light reflected off the high cheekbones of her round Slavic face. She was dressed in a Ukrainian festival outfit of red and blue, covered with beadwork and lace fringing. The skirt was full and rustled as she moved. He knew it was clothing worn only at weddings and feast days. That she considered this a special occasion flattered him.

She reached out slowly and fingered the red star on his tunic and the insignia that identified him as a people's commissar as though they were religious relics. He felt the sweat of tension trickle down the collar of his scratchy wool uniform.

"What is the feeling of being a people's commissar, Nikki?" she asked in a cooing voice while letting her fingers linger on his chest. "I've never known a great man before. This village only has pig farmers."

He swallowed self-consciously, hoping his bobbing Adam's apple wouldn't betray his nervousness. "I'm just acting commissar," he said almost apologetically. He was of an age when the seriousness of life was very romantic. "I have sworn to protect young women like yourself from counterrevolutionaries." His youth shielded him from knowing that the likes of this girl seldom needed protection from anyone. As the ebb and flow of history swirled around these remote villages lost in Russia's vastness, such girls belonged to the conqueror of the moment—Tartars, Cossacks, Germans, Czarists, Communists—whoever showed up with sword or gun. Every other day, she was scorned as the village whore; today, she was a heroine. She gleefully made herself spoils of war so that the married women would be left alone. Not that Nikita would have forced himself on any woman he had come to deliver from despotism, but he was willing to observe the tradition.

She was one of the first of the many women he would come to know who found power an irresistible magnet. He was short, round and with a face like a potato, but the power he steadily accumulated through his long career was an aphrodisiac to ambitious, beautiful women. He and the women fed off each other, though neither was ever sated.

He again looked nervously around the dark cabin, which belonged to him for the day, a courtesy extended to such an honored guest as this young commander of the ragtag Bolshevik column that had come to this nameless village in pursuit of the White Army soldiers who were fighting the revolution. When you're a defenseless village, you're nice to everyone, especially those who appear to be winning. He was ill at ease knowing that the villagers stood outside glancing furtively at the cabin, knowing the intentions of the man inside. He had not yet become hardened to the curiosity of his subordinates.

"You haven't told me your name," he said.

"Maria," she whispered into his ear, leaning forward to make sure her breasts pushed against him.

He started to ask her why she was attracted to him but decided not to to risk the answer. Instead, he ran his hand over the embroidered bodice of her festival costume. The material was stiff with beadwork, but he could still feel the soft weight of her breasts beneath. She sighed theatrically as she closed her eyes and leaned back against the mattress. The bed was made atop bricks built out from the stove, a common method of construction to ward off the bitter cold of winter, and he could feel its warmth blend into her body.

Going slowly so he didn't fumble, he began to undo the buttons of her clothing. Her blouse slipped easily down her shoulders, past the line where the sun had not roughened and darkened the skin, revealing the ghostly whiteness of her. He touched her large breasts gently, watching them quiver in response. She sucked in her breath sharply as he touched his lips to an erect red nipple. He reached beneath the billowy dress and slid her underpants off. She, in turn, reached for him and began to knowledgeably knead his erection.

Without removing his eyes from her as she lifted her skirt and spread her legs in waiting, he stood up and started to unbutton his pants. All fears of clumsiness, all thoughts of inquisitive villagers had been crowded from his mind. All that mattered now was the dark slash that beckoned between her round thighs. As he removed his clothes, he felt a kinship to the girl, beyond sexual allure. This was a revolutionary act, and they were comrades in it. He threw his pants in a heap and climbed between her legs as she parted them farther to receive him. The urgency of his erection and the inexperience of his youth concealed from him the knowledge of sexual pace, the sense of building to a mutual climax that later years and a hundred unsatisfied girls like this would bring. She efficiently grasped his penis and guided it. He felt the yielding softness and warm moistness and closed his eyes in anticipation.

The pounding on the plank door almost broke its hinges and made him pull back in shock from the girl. The shouting that followed caused his erection to wilt like a weed in the August sun. "Police! Open up! We demand you turn over the criminal Khrushchev."

In panic, he grabbed his clothes and looked frantically for an escape route. The only door was the one being pounded upon. The girl started to weep in fear as he whispered, "Tell them I'm not here," squeezed into a small broom closet and pulled the squeaking door closed behind him. He held his breath and hoped his pursuers could not hear his thumping heart. Feeling self-pity at the helplessness of his situation, he closed his eyes and waited....

He lost track of time, but the pounding had stopped. He strained his hearing, but there was only silence. Suddenly, he heard loud laughter and tried to make himself smaller in a corner of his cramped hiding place.

The laughter trailed away and a man called out in a cheerful voice, "Come out, Nikita Sergeyevich. You're safe. Come out and wash your pants."

Warily, he climbed from the closet and looked around. He could see nothing except a man standing in the faint light of a window laughing at him. The man was small with the hunched knotty body of an arthritic chimney sweep. He was dressed in coarse gray prison clothing. His skin was like wrinkled wax paper and his gray hair and stubby beard looked hacked at rather than groomed. His rotting, gapped teeth were like brown nails in his mouth. One eye was covered by the milky film of an untreated cataract. He was a man who hadn't grown old, but who had been made old.

Nikita turned away in disgust and happened to look in a cracked mirror. He was no longer a young officer in the Red Army. He was an old man, bent over and gnarled with a head shaped like an egg and skin like a potato. He looked at the backs of his hands and saw age spots like splotches of tobacco spit. He turned back to the room and strained his eyes against the dark. It, too, had changed. The peasant's cabin had disappeared, as had the girl. He was now in his Moscow room overlooking the factory. But the man in prison clothing was still there, chuckling at him. The old man's mind whirled, but only for an instant. Time and reality had become burdensome to him in recent years, and he found it was easier to accept strange things, even when life swirled around him like a Siberian snowstorm.

Satisfied they were alone and in no immediate danger, the old man asked, "Who are you?"

"Me?" The man pointed a finger at himself to underscore the question. "Nobody cares anymore who I am. If the world has forgotten my name, why should I remember it?" He paused, then smiled brightly. "Call me *Fantazer*, the Dreamer. That was my crime."

The old man glared at him suspiciously. "There were no police here, were there? You were the one pounding. If that's your idea of a joke, no wonder you were in prison. *Yob*, but I thought the end had come."

Fantazer laughed again.

The old man grabbed a rickety wooden stool. "Keep laughing, *vnebrayni*, and I'll break this stool over your ugly head, you bastard. You better play your pranks on your own kind, not Nikita S. Khrushchev."

Fantazer stopped laughing, but the warmth stayed in his voice. "If it's true that the police weren't here, then I suggest you laugh heartily. There are those who have heard knocking when no humor was intended."

The old man's anger still simmered. "In the old days, you could have gotten shot for such a fool trick."

Fantazer laughed. "I don't think a bad joke should be a capital offense."

The old man frowned. "In a graveyard, you don't laugh about the dead. Back then, we were all nervous."

"When was then?"

"When else? When the Georgian jackal had us under his heel." He spat harshly on the floor. "Iosif Vissarionovich Dzhugashvili, that was how he was christened. A good name for a goatherd. In 1913 he changed it to Stalin because it meant man of steel—a stupid comic-opera thing to do." He muttered to himself, "Twisted steel is more like it."

"Stalin's face was everywhere—pictures, statues—but the man remained a mystery," Fantazer said.

"That's like not having cholera and wondering what you've missed," the old man scoffed. "Be grateful for the mystery."

"They say that in Georgia he's treated like a saint, even a third of a century after his death."

"Hah! Georgians would put a day-old dog turd on a pedestal if it were theirs."

"What *is* the truth of the man?" Fantazer asked.

The old man rubbed his hands together briskly as a happy memory revisited him. "You should have been there—February 25, 1956, I remember the date better than my birthday—when I told the Twentieth Party Congress just what that devil really did to his people. For the four hours I spoke it was as quiet as the graves of his victims. I told them about the millions—millions!—of good Soviets who were shot, tortured and imprisoned at his insane whim."

"Those were party insiders listening to you, didn't they know all this?"

"Knowing it is one thing, *hearing* it is another. There I was, the leader of all the Soviets standing straight in front of their eyes and telling them it was okay to begin breathing again, that they could go to bed that night with confidence they would not wake up staring at the truncheon of a secret police thug."

The old man shuffled to the small window and gazed into the faint light remaining above the factory smokestack. "If the Soviet people remember me for anything," he said, almost in a whisper, "I would like it to be that I exorcised Stalin's ghost."

"What was he like, this leader of yours?" Fantazer asked.

The old man glanced up suspiciously, not knowing how the remark was intended. "The leader of us all." He returned to the question and weighed his answer. "Suspicious. Humorless. Cruel. Greedy, he wouldn't share ice in winter. In his youth, he was a seminary student, did you know that? He never shook the clammy grip of religion from his mind. God should have claimed him; they were of equal service to our country."

Fantazer sat on one of the hard-backed wooden chairs near the table. "It was difficult for our people to suddenly be told the Volga flows north."

"Meaning?"

"For a half century, all they heard was that Papa Stalin was the steady hand that propped them up, the vigilant eye that watched over them. People want to believe such things. They want to ignore the assassinations and the purges and believe they, a great people, are led by a great man. That belief helped us all through the Great Patriotic War against the Nazis."

"*Yob!* Fuck," the old man snarled. "Let me tell you about your great wartime leader. The night before the Germans invaded, a deserter came over to our side and described their invasion plan, Operation Barbarossa—laid the whole thing out right there on our map table. We rushed the news to Stalin. There were enough hours left for us to alert our troops. Surely this great leader would take defensive steps, we thought."

The old man pushed his face into that of Fantazer and crashed his fist on the table. "He ignored it! The *vnebrayni* ignored a warning that could have saved thousands of our troops who died in their bedrolls. The war cost us twenty million dead. While the Germans were slaughtering their millions, Stalin was killing his, by executing most of the competent officers of the army. An army without its officers is a defenseless mob waiting to be slaughtered. His paranoia was the best ally the Germans had."

The old man lowered his voice and said, grudgingly, "I'll give him one thing: he made suckers out of Roosevelt and Churchill. They ate out of his hand like starving mongrels. In 1945, we were a starving nation, crippled like a fox in a trap; we were at the capitalists' mercy. We really expected them to invade us. Instead, that old devil Stalin stole all of Eastern Europe right out of their hands." He chuckled at the memory of the coup.

"Nikita Sergeyevich, you talk like an admirer."

"You don't have to love a rat to say his teeth are sharp. But an admirer, hardly! Just as soon as I consolidated power after he died, I threw out his entire crew of thugs, especially that crown prince of butchers, Beria, the head of the secret police.''

"Actually, you had him executed."

"Unfortunately, only once.'' Indignation entered the old man's voice. "When I think of what that *svin'ya* Beria did, the pig..."

"He was only following the orders of Stalin, was he not?''

"That's no excuse," the old man snapped. "I remember the pathetic wretches we released from the prison camps. People who had given up on life because they thought life had given up on them. There were these three old women, they shared a hut in Siberia for twenty years. When we released them and tried to send them back to their homes, they wouldn't go unless they could continue to live together. That was the only way they knew how to live. When the bureaucrats said no, the women appealed to me. I told them that if the bureaucrats continued to oppose them, I'd send the bureaucrats to Siberia for twenty years.''

"But you didn't, did you? I mean, those in the criminal system who made Stalin's crimes operational were never punished.''

"My purpose was to empty the prisons, not refill them," the old man said. "Hah! Attaching blame was like switching on a kitchen light to capture cockroaches. In an instant, they're down cracks. You wouldn't believe how many cracks there are in the bureaucracy.''

Fantazer shook his head in wonder. "To have to ease so much pain, so much grief. What a burden! And that, after surviving three decades with a twentieth-century Ivan the Terrible.''

The old man closed his eyes and shuddered. "It was a nightmare that wouldn't end. A lifetime in a spider's web. All that kept me going was my love for the Soviet people.'' He began pacing the small room in agitation, his stiff bowed legs dragging his feet slowly along the floor, leaving a scratchy trail in the thick dust. "Stalin had this apartment in the Kremlin. It was only about four rooms, but the dining room was larger than most houses. The doors were reinforced steel. When he wanted tea, he would slip a note through a slot to a servant. A very cheerful place! I and a few others—Bulganin, Voroshilov, Kaganovich, Malenkov—had to be on call to attend his dinners, which usually happened about midnight. We'd sit there and drink and listen to him talk about his boyhood in Georgia, or about all the enemies and conspirators he imagined. Each of us would hold his breath hoping those beady black eyes wouldn't turn toward him when the accusations were on Stalin's mind. We would sit there by the hour, drinking brandy and vodka, not daring to get drunk, watching Stalin sitting there smiling, waiting to trap us into some statement he could twist into a reason for killing us."

"Strange, but I don't think I've ever seen a picture of him smiling," Fantazer said.

"I used the wrong word. When a wolf shows his teeth, he's not smiling."

The old man tired of pacing and sat heavily on the edge of the bed. "The thing that drove us all to the brink of madness was not knowing what to expect. More than once, I got a phone call at four or five in the morning, and when I answered, there would only be breathing on the line. Just breathing, then nothing."

"It was him?"

"It was his direct line. It would make my blood turn to ice, but, of course, that was the idea: play with the mouse. I've seen men do things he ordered, and do them so well they could hardly wait to report their success, and then be executed for their trouble. Can you imagine living like that? It was like facing terminal cancer every day of my life." The old man lay back against the pillow but continued talking. "The man had no pity on those in his grasp; he enjoyed making us—especially me—look like monkeys, especially when important foreign guests were present. Things like putting ripe tomatoes on your chair at dinner. Sounds like a child's trick, I know, but believe me, this was no child's game, this was life and death.''

The old man pushed himself up on one elbow and stared at Fantazer as though debating whether to continue. ''I remember,'' he started slowly, ''we had a large dinner for an important Western trade delegation—Italians, I think they were. About halfway through the dinner, Stalin turned to me and started to laugh. When I saw him looking at me and I heard that sound—that dry, humorless cackle—I started to sweat. He—he—'' The old man's voice quavered and he paused to let his emotions settle. ''He said, 'Nikita, show them how a Cossack dances.' He ordered the band to play music and he gestured for me to go to the center of the room and dance in front of those drunken capitalists.''

''Did you?'' Fantazer asked.

The old man brushed aside a tear as he relived the humiliation. ''I'd rather dance than die. But as I stood there and jumped around like a monkey, I swore that someday I'd see him rot in hell.''

''If everyone was drunk, was it so bad?''

The old man acted betrayed that his listener didn't understand. ''*I* wasn't drunk,'' he said, and then, with a look of frustration, shouted in a cracking voice, *''And I can't dance!''*

Fantazer smiled sympathetically. ''Stalin seemed to regard you as a court jester, if you'll pardon the expression.''

The old man leaped to his feet with surprising agility and stood before Fantazer's table, his face flushed with anger. He pounded his fist on the table and spoke through clenched teeth, emphasizing every syllable. *''But I survived.''*

His anger left as quickly as it came. He straightened up and appeared to relax. ''I remember the night we moved his body—October 30, 1962, a beautiful night. This was after 'de-Stalinization,' as some called it, after I had exposed him to the world as the monster-murderer who killed or imprisoned fifteen million of his countrymen. It was very late and as quiet as a devil's prayer. Not a sound interfered with the wonderful noise of those shovels scraping the earth. We moved his carcass from its place of honor next to Lenin in Red Square and dumped it into a hole near the Kremlin wall. And all the time that was going on, the unhooking of the embalming pumps that kept his body preserved, the dumping of his remains into a plain wooden coffin, I kept humming the song he made me dance to that night. And I remember thinking: Hate doesn't conquer by storming, but by a long siege.''

Fantazer slowly rubbed his hands on the thighs of his gray prison flannels, and said, ''Just think of it, one man causing all that misery. I pity you, Nikita Sergeyevich, to serve under such conditions. Especially when you were head of the party in the Ukraine during many of those years.''

''I was responsible for many progressive reforms there, especially in agriculture,'' the old man said proudly.

''How many of those persecuted were from the Ukraine? One million? Two million? Three?''

''That was none of my doing,'' the old man replied. ''Those orders came directly from Moscow.''

''But signed by you,'' Fantazer said mildly.

The old man's face turned red, and he shouted, ''Signed by me, yes, but not my responsibility. My signature was a formality, they would have just gotten someone else to do it. I know what you're trying to say, you sneaky *vnebrayni*, that I was responsible. Well, it won't stick. I was just a functionary.''

''I've read that you called the people you deported to Siberia—Poles, Jews, intellectuals—'social aliens.' Were those your words?'' Fantazer asked.

The old man started to bluster, then forced himself to calm down. He was a man who had survived a thousand inquisitions. ''That doesn't sound like me. It could have been a phrase placed over my signature in Moscow. No, I don't remember saying that.''

Fantazer reached into his pants pocket and removed a rumpled, yellowing sheet of paper and a pair of bent spectacles with one cracked lens. He put on the glasses, smoothed the paper and studied it for a moment. ''Listen to this: 'The successful, triumphant crushing of the Fascist agents—all those contemptible Trotskyites and bourgeois nationalists—we owe to the personal efforts of our leader above all, to our great Stalin.''' He removed the glasses and carefully put them back in his pocket. ''What do you think of that?'' he asked the old man matter-of-factly.

The old man snorted. ''The sycophantic whining of some toady.''

Fantazer didn't take his eyes off him but tapped the paper he still held. ''This was a speech before the Eighteenth Party Congress in Moscow in the year 1938.'' He paused. ''It was delivered by Nikita S. Khrushchev.''

The old man was stunned and worked his mouth as if he were a fish out of water. ''You—you're trying to twist things and make them seem different than they were. I knew in those days that someone had to stay sane in the party, to reconstruct the country after Stalin and his madness died. That speech was a harmless little compromise, that's all.'' The old man's anger pushed him on. ''You little people who never did anything seem to think everyone around Stalin in those days should have told him to his face that he was a crazy old murderer. I remember, a few years after his death, I was giving a speech and someone sent up an unsigned note asking why I hadn't spoken up during Stalin's time. I read it aloud and then asked the audience, 'Where is the person who wrote this note?' I said it in a very gruff voice. You could have heard a frog fart it was so quiet. So I said, 'That's where I was, too.'

''Look,'' the old man almost pleaded with Fantazer. ''Those were difficult times. The revolution was still young, and strong measures were called for. Stalin took them to excess, but you have to understand the way it was. Even in my regime, those who needed to be were imprisoned; I don't apologize for that. But you have to understand what a man like myself was up against. Stalin was smart and ruthless. One of the last official acts of the great Lenin before he died was to warn the party about Stalin, but even that could not stop him from taking control of the country like a puppet master.''

Fantazer was still holding the paper and shook it gently at the old man. "During all those times you were having dinner with Stalin, did it not occur to you that one pistol shot would have prevented millions of deaths? Weren't you ever tempted to act boldly for the innocent of your country?''

"Of course," the old man said, "I thought of it a thousand times, but that would have been suicide.''

"No, that would have been patriotism.''

The old man picked up a tin cup and threw it weakly at Fantazer, missing the man by so much he didn't bother to duck. "Goddamn you!" the old man shouted. "You're so sanctimonious, you forget I released millions of prisoners Stalin sent to Siberia. Look at you, you're wearing prison clothes. I let you out, didn't I?''

"No.''

"What do you mean, no?" the old man demanded.

"You put me in.''

THE OLD MAN MUMBLED like a drugged man, but Nicholas Mikhailovitch persisted in gently shaking his shoulder. "Wake up, Chairman Khrushchev. Good news! An American. He just arrived in the country. He's going to take you out.''

CHAPTER ELEVEN

THE CRUSTED, SOOTY SNOW CRUNCHED under Jude's feet like eggshells, and the fur-hatted Muscovites, their rush-hour pace hastened by the Arctic wind from the Barents Sea north of Murmansk, swirled by him like a stream around a rock. The bus from Shermetyevo Airport had dropped him on Leningradsky Prospekt, where he blended into the pedestrian traffic.

When he reached Mayakovsky Square and saw the Central Puppet Theater on his left, he headed for a brown masonry building fronted by two round pillars with plaster flaking like day-old makeup off a streetwalker. The structure huddled anonymously between two newer, larger, glass and steel buildings like the runt of a litter. This was the Kirovskaya Hotel. In its seventy years it had served many purposes, but it had finally come to rest in the role that it seemed intended for: a resting place for tired workers. Like its counterparts the world over, it offered a cheap bed, clean linen and no room for pretenses. Those who stopped there had no illusions about final destinations.

Jude pushed gently on the heavy glass door, and then harder as it refused to budge. With a clatter the door yielded to his shove and he found himself two steps into the lobby with the clerk and lobby loungers staring at him expectantly. Feeling like a noisy intruder, he walked to the front desk, acclimatizing himself to the funeral-parlor mustiness and the lumpy sofas with mechanics and construction workers leaning back and peering at him with disinterest through clouds of cigarette smoke. Tired men going through life like actors through one more rehearsal.

The clerk was fat, middle-aged and the look on his face said he hoped something more interesting than Jude would walk through the door.

"*Zdrav'st-vuytye*, hello, Comrade," Jude greeted him.

The clerk nodded silently, waiting, but with no anticipation.

"A friend made a reservation for me. The name is Markov, Petr." Jude handed the man his forged internal passport and seaman's papers.

The clerk glanced at the documents, made the required notes, then filed them in a drawer and handed Jude a key. "Third floor, to the right. Five rubles a day, no women, no loud music." His duty done, the clerk turned away as though Jude no longer existed.

Jude entered the room and switched on the ceiling light. The room was small, barely large enough to hold the single bed and old-fashioned wardrobe. One glance told him it was as clean as the Ritz. A sign said the bathroom was down the hall to the right. When he turned to put his worn cardboard suitcase on the bed, he burned his leg on a hot steam radiator. Jude put his things away and lay on the squeaky bed with arms folded behind his head. He studied the faded wallpaper pattern until he had counted every horizontal fleur-de-lis and multiplied the total by the number of vertical lines. He then turned to the small window and watched the frost crystals that accompanied the cold of twilight as they slowly covered the glass and turned his view into milky opaqueness. Jude took the day's issue of *Izvestia* from his coat pocket and settled down to wait. . . .

For three days Jude stayed in the tiny room, leaving only to eat at the canteen around the corner and to buy newspapers. This was the part of the job that was so difficult. Waiting. A seemingly effortless task requiring only the doing of nothing. But he knew that many good agents, feeling themselves in an exposed position, cracked on the tyranny of the ticking clock and made rash moves because they didn't have the nerves for waiting. He reminded himself of that repeatedly on the hard bed in the Kirovskaya. Whenever he became edgy contemplating all the things that could have gone wrong, whenever he had an urge to disappear into the Moscow night to avoid imaginary enemies closing in, he told himself—wait. Wait. Wait.

By early evening of the third day, it was obvious that whoever was to contact him was either in no position to do so or was biding time for some reason. Knowing then that his contact seemed to require no immediacy, he decided to wander a little farther from the room, as though to say: I've waited on you, now you wait on me.

Instead of heading for his usual quick cafeteria meal, Jude started walking. Hands in pockets, fur hat pulled low over his ears, Jude strolled for many blocks along the streets of Moscow as the rapidly falling darkness seemed to shoo pedestrians away until he was nearly alone on the broad concrete avenues. Perhaps it was the subconscious urging of his loneliness, but as he crossed the long bridge over the ice-laden Moskva River, the bright lights of an approaching busy street pulled him into its flow like the vortex of a whirlpool.

His step quickened as he joined the hurrying crowds, which seemed fueled by the white steam that came out of their mouths like exhaust. The crowd flow took him to the front of the prestigious Ukraina Hotel. He stopped to take his bearings and suddenly felt hungry. Stepping into the crowded lobby, he was attracted by the warm chatter and the busy clink of dishes. He walked over to the entrance of the Ukraina Restaurant and peered inside. It was obviously a quality place, one that he yearned for after weeks of shipboard and cafeteria fare, but one that an ordinary seaman would visit only on special occasions. He glanced down at his baggy, threadbare

suit and heavy seaman's coat and hesitated. He was about to
walk away when he was crowded aside by a group of laughing
men dressed much like himself. As the group waited for a table, he learned from their loud conversation that they were
machinists celebrating a bonus for superior production at
their foundry. The presence of similarly dressed men was all
the nudging Jude required and he joined the line.

He was led to a small table in a corner, next to an older man
and young woman. Jude studied the extensive menu like a
saint reading scripture. He settled on *vareniki*, a Ukrainian
specialty of tiny dumplings filled with shredded meat and
vegetables. He also ordered *so smetanoy*, cucumber salad with
sour cream, and *tetra*, a medium-dry white Georgian wine.

The couple at the next table were speaking English. It was
obvious to Jude that the man was from the South, perhaps
Texas or Oklahoma, judging by his broad twang and the big
white Stetson lying atop the table, the lizard-skin cowboy
boots poking out from beneath the white tablecloth and his
bright red Western shirt with pearl buttons. He was about
sixty with a gray brush cut and a blue-veined red nose that said
the vodka he was drinking was not plowing fresh ground.

The woman spoke with a Russian accent and was much
younger, about thirty, with raven-black hair and swarthy skin.
Her eyes were like two olives floating in tiny gold-flecked
pools. She had prominent cheekbones and a tiny, narrow
beaked nose. Her figure was full and soft, about five years of
good eating short of pudgy. The lines of her face broke readi-
ly into a smile, like the creases of folded paper.

The man was loud and Jude could tell the woman was
looking for ways to wean the vodka away from him and quiet
his voice. Jude cut into his *vareniki* and listened but was careful not to look in their direction or react to what was said.

"Let me tell you something else about Arkansas, Missy,"
the man trumpeted. "It's the only state that could support
itself with no help from the outside. Yes, ma'am, that's true.

Know what the motto is? *Regnat populus.* 'The people rule.'"
He laughed conspiratorially. "With a little help from us leg-
islators." He gave an exaggerated wink. "Know what I
mean?"

"It must be a very nice place," the woman agreed.

The man became serious and tightened his mouth in resolve. "You should come visit." He gave thought to his own
suggestion. "Yep, it's settled. I'll even pay your way." He
laughed good-naturedly. "Can't you see those old boys at
Rotary when I introduce you? I'll say, 'You boys said I should
bring back a souvenir, well, meet Miss Tamara Cannon, my
Russian guide.'"

She smiled. "It's Khanum, Mr. Bigelow. Thank you for the
thought, but such a trip would be very expensive—"

He waved his hand to dismiss the statement. "Missy, when
I'm not the biggest pair of boots in the legislature, I happen
to be the biggest Chevy dealer in Little Rock. Forget it. Just-
you-for-get-it. It's all settled."

The woman laughed and held up her hand. "Wait a minute, Mr. Bigelow. I can't go running off to Arkansas. I have
my job. Besides, technically, you can't call me a Russian
guide. I'm Uzbekian."

The man's brow knitted in confusion, and it was apparent
to Jude that the woman was trying to sidetrack his attention.

"Well, honey, if you ain't Russian, what are you? This ain't
the Little Rock Holiday Inn we're at."

"Russia is only one of the republics of the Soviet Union,
Mr. Bigelow, although by far the largest. Uzbek, in the south,
is another. Near the Afghanistan border. That's where I'm
from."

He leaned forward and lowered his voice. "Honey, that's
fine with me." He glanced around for eavesdroppers. "What
I'm talking about is getting you out of this country. Once you
made it to Arkansas, they'd play hell getting you back he—"

"Please, Mr. Bigelow. Please understand that I don't want to leave. I'm quite happy here."

He looked around as though searching for spies and winked. "I understand."

Jude could see the woman was struggling quietly to maintain her good humor. "No, I don't think you do. I'm sure Arkansas is a wonderful place to you, but I feel the same way about my country."

In the volatile way of many drinkers, he started to turn argumentative. "Hell, you can't even speak your mind here without ending up in some goddamn Siberian salt mine. What kind of country is that?"

"Mr. Bigelow, do you know which country has the highest percentage of citizens behind bars? Your country, the United States of America."

"Yeah, but those are real criminals."

"Why are they criminals, Mr. Bigelow? Is it because of racism, the class system, inadequate social welfare, lack of opportunity?"

The man was stunned by the argument. "Lack of opportunity? Why, I'll have you know that America is *the* land of opportunity. That's official; that's what it's called."

"Can you get a young black in Harlem to believe that? Mr. Bigelow, what is the unemployment rate in Arkansas?"

His mouth worked soundlessly as he searched for a figure. "Maybe eight percent," he finally mumbled.

"In the Soviet Union it's less than one-half of one percent. In Los Angeles there are thirty thousand homeless people living on the streets in whatever shelter they can find, many of them mentally ill— I read that in *Newsweek* magazine. In Moscow, you would have to look hard to find a fraction of that number. Maybe some who can't find hotel rooms, but that's all. I don't say these things to argue with you, Mr. Bigelow; after all, you are a guest." She gave his hand a friendly pat. "I'm trying to make the point that understanding begins with appreciation. And as your Soviet friend, I would like you to appreciate my country."

The man took another sip of vodka, almost in slow motion, and started to nod sleepily.

The woman reached over and shook his shoulder. "Mr. Bigelow . . . Mr. Bigelow. You must go to bed. We have a lot of things to see tomorrow. Go on now, Mr. Bigelow."

Bigelow stumbled to his feet and looked around to get his bearings. He started for the door, and turned back to the woman. "Will you come with me?" he slurred.

"No, thank you. I'll stay here and finish my brandy. Good night."

Embarrassed at the rebuff, Bigelow tried to joke. "I can't leave you here with all these Commies."

"Mr. Bigelow, *I* am a Communist. Good night."

Bigelow mumbled something and stumbled in the direction of the door and the elevators. The woman sighed with relief and leaned back in her chair.

With Bigelow gone, it was now just the two of them, growing aware of each other at adjoining tables in a quiet corner of the dining room; Jude finishing dinner, Tamara sipping brandy. Each was intrigued by the other. Their eyes sparred like cautious boxers feeling for an opening, unwilling to make the aggressor's commitment. Finally, Jude slowly lifted his wineglass in her direction. *"Na zdorov'e,"* he toasted, "to your health." She inclined her head with a smile and raised her own glass.

"Excuse me, but do you mind if I keep you company while we finish our drinks?" He gestured to the chair opposite her.

She smiled and nodded slightly.

After introductions, Jude looked across the table and said, "Do you mind if I bore you with some poetry about yourself?"

"If it's flattering, I promise not to be bored," she said with a laugh.

Jude stared at the ceiling as though deep in thought. "Your eyes are like two black colts frisking in a field of golden wheat." He paused theatrically then squinted at her. "Shakespeare?"

She laughed. "No."

"Pushkin?"

"No."

"Me?"

"Yes, I do believe I recognize your celebrated touch." She raised her brandy glass. "*Zdorov'e*. Salute to great poets."

He clinked glasses with her. "And to what inspires them."

"Seriously," he said, "those eyes and that lovely olive complexion aren't the product of Moscow. Your name's Turkic. Where are you from?"

"Samarkand, in Uzbekistan."

"How do you like Moscow?"

"Cold." She twirled her brandy snifter slowly, watching the amber liquid roll around the glass. "Where are you from, Comrade Markov?"

"Moscow originally, but I haven't lived here for years. No family left. I'm a cook on a fishing boat. That's why I wanted a decent meal tonight." He gestured vaguely to the restaurant that surrounded them. "I'm tired of my own cooking."

"How exciting," she said, "you get to see the world."

"If you call the Bering Sea in December the world. I've never seen your home, Central Asia."

Tamara smiled fondly. "It's wonderful. Romantic. The crossroads of the ancient world. Alexander the Great, Omar Khayyam, the Golden Horde, Genghis Khan, Tamerlane. They were all in Samarkand, and in some ways, they're still there." She looked into his eyes, not romantically, but to convey something she felt deeply. "To go out among the ancient desert ruins on a quiet night and see the sand dunes— *barkhan*, we call them—and the twisted *saksaul* trees outlined against the moon, and hear nothing except the bark of a stray jackal..."

"I know," he said quietly, "you can feel it, but you can't tell it."

She nodded slowly. "I can tell you have a place like that."

"Everyone does," he said.

A waiter snapped the mood by pouring more brandy in Tamara's glass. Jude asked, "I hope I'm not prying, but what language were you speaking with your dinner partner?"

"Oh, he's an American. I've been assigned to conduct him around the city. Something of a big shot over there, I suppose."

"I don't know what he said," Jude said, putting a bit of indignation in his voice, "but he sure sounded obnoxious. Probably a typical capitalist."

Tamara shrugged. "Oh, he's really a rather nice man, just homesick, confused by all the things he doesn't understand, and probably a little threatened. For years he's read in the American press that we're bloodthirsty monsters. Like most people, he makes loud splashes when his feet don't touch the bottom of the pool."

"Is that what you do," Jude asked, "guide tourists?"

"I speak five languages—Uzbek, Russian, Turkish, English and French," she said. "Intourist finds me useful."

I'll bet the KGB does, too, Jude thought but just nodded to show he was impressed.

They talked for two hours about the little things that two people who find each other appealing manage to find interesting. Jude had to invent most of what he said, but he was amazed to discover how much of his own experience fit into a Russian setting. Talking with Tamara, he felt Russian.

As the lights dimmed and the waiter hovered with the bill, Jude picked it up and was careful to adopt the dismayed look likely of a fishing boat cook when confronted by such a check in an expensive restaurant.

Tamara noticed his look and took it from his hand. "Let me have this," she said. "I'm on an expense account."

"Are you sure?" he asked.

"Quite sure." She seemed to be pondering something, then said, "I've got an idea: since you've never been to Samarkand, why don't you come to my apartment for dinner tomorrow night? I'll fix Uzbek dishes."

Jude hesitated. The professional voice in his mind said, don't get involved; another voice, a personal one, said, there's no danger if you're careful.

Mistaking his hesitation for shyness, Tamara wrote her address on the back of a business card and pushed it toward him. "Eight o'clock," she said.

Jude looked at the card, then slowly reached out and picked it up.

JUDE FELT LIKE A TEENAGER on his way to pick up a date for the prom. He had bought a liter of *pertsovka*, vodka flavored with hot pepper, as a house gift and swung the gaily wrapped bottle nonchalantly as he briskly walked along the banks of the gray river, following the directions Tamara had given. He came to the landmark she had described—the tall onion-bulb towers of the Novodevichye Convent Museum, one of the many old churches secularized by the state—and started checking street numbers for her apartment building.

He happened to glance backward and saw a man in a gray felt hat staring at him. As soon as Jude made eye contact, the man shifted his gaze to the contents of a shop window. He was middle-aged and had an unshaved face that reminded Jude of a squirrel. He was dressed as a workman and carried a lunch pail. He didn't look at Jude again.

Okay, be cool, Jude told himself. Just because some squirrel-face happens to look at you doesn't mean he's following. Don't spoil the night by being paranoid. He chased the caution from his thoughts and resumed the hunt for Tamara's address.

It was a walk-up on the third floor and he took several deep breaths before he rang the buzzer.

"Come in," her voice immediately sang out.

He opened the door and stepped into a room dimly lit by candles. Shadows danced on one wall on which was hung a portrait of Lenin. A framed needlepoint picture of the Soviet hammer and sickle was next to it. On the opposite wall, almost in counterpoint, was a large painting of three bearded Moslem men in traditional dress, being served fruit by a veiled woman. The window was covered by damask drapes and the hardwood floor by an oval Persian carpet. Jude turned his head toward the tiny kitchen in response to a soft melody played on an instrument he couldn't identify. In a moment, the doorway was filled by a silhouette swaying slowly to the music. Tamara was playing a wistful song on a mouth harp, and as she moved close to him, he could smell jasmine perfume. She finished the song and threw out her arms. "Ta-dah! Welcome to 'Samarkand of the North,' or 'The Return of the Dreaded Tartar.' Anyway, this is my little outpost of Uzbekistan."

Jude studied the woman before him. She was dressed in Uzbek native costume. Her long hair was braided and brought forward over her shoulders. Perched atop her head was a square white hat with an orange-and-brown embroidered design. She wore a yellow shift and blousy silk pajama bottoms with a red and green floral pattern. On her feet were tiny black slippers.

"Charming," Jude said. "Absolutely charming." He took the musical instrument from her hand and examined it. It was a small iron frame in the shape of a horseshoe with an elastic metal strip, which she had held between her teeth and made to vibrate with her fingers. "Why, this is only a Jew's harp.

But I've never heard one that sounded so good. What were
you playing?''

"Lesson number one," she said, "Jew's harp is incorrect,
although it's a common mistake. The proper Western name
is *Jaw's* harp. But in my country, where it originated, it's
called a *changawuz*, and every woman and girl can play it. The
song I played was a musical poem called an epos, named
Shahsenem and Garib." She took the harp from him and held
his hand in hers. "End of music lesson. Let me show you the
menu."

She led him into the tiny kitchen, which, together with the
main room and small bathroom, was the extent of her apartment. The kitchen was alive with the smell of fiery sauces as
she uncovered the pots and pans one by one.

"This is *muntyi*, dumplings filled with meat. In this other
pan is *maniar* soup. It has meat, egg and noodles." She stirred
the soup. "And spice and more spice." She turned to the
small table. "And this is our salad, *takhor*, which includes
chicken, cucumbers, olives, apples, peaches and plums in
syrup." She picked up a long loaf of homemade bread and
poked it at him like a sword. "This is *obi non*." She waved her
arms outward. "Well, that's the kitchen tour. Ready to experiment?"

"Is a capitalist greedy?" he asked rhetorically.

They ate by candlelight sitting on silk, tasseled pillows with
the haunting strings of *ganuns* and *changs* quivering in the in-
censed air of the room. The stereo record of the native in-
struments reminded him of dulcimers and zithers.

They ate in silence except for an occasional moan of pleasure as Jude enjoyed the cuisine and wines. When they finished, he made a move to collect the plates, but she firmly
pushed him back against the pillows and removed their dishes
to the kitchen herself. She returned with two small glasses in
one hand and a bottle in the other.

"Now," she announced, "if you think you're man enough, I'll introduce you to *aleatiko*." She poured two small glasses of the liqueur, handed him one. With wordless smiles they touched glasses and drank.

"Ah!" Jude breathed deeply and softly patted his chest. "My respects to all *aleatiko* makers in Samarkand. I admire men who take their work seriously. Whew!"

She laughed and refilled their glasses. They leaned against the pillows, shoulders touching.

Jude waved his glass slowly around the room, encompassing the native art and the portrait of Lenin. "You've done beautifully with this. If I ever make it to Samarkand, I'll tell them it's my second trip. It's interesting—" he spoke slowly, he had to be careful with this "—how you've combined the old with the new in the room; the feeling of Central Asia, with the philosophy of Russia." He gestured toward the Lenin portrait.

"Comrade Lenin isn't Russian." She used the present tense. "He's Soviet. Communism belongs to all the peoples and races of the Soviet Union. Those who don't know better think of a place like Uzbekistan as so backward it couldn't possibly shed its old ways to become socialist."

Jude started to protest, but she interrupted him. "No, no, it's all right. Truthfully, if Uzbekistan were not Communist, I'd probably be running around in a veil, with six children pestering me while my Moslem husband self-righteously treated me somewhat better than a donkey, but definitely below the rank of a camel. As it is, I'm a modern woman with an excellent education living a challenging life in one of the great capitals of the world. And it's the same back home. Where once you saw camel caravans, now you see mechanized cotton farms. The fact is, Jude, the people from my part of the Soviet Union have gained even more from Communism than you in the north."

"Then you have party membership?" he asked.

"With pride. How about you?"

He shrugged. "I've thought about it, but I'm only a fishing boat cook...."

She turned to him with her hands in an imploring position in front of her. "But don't you see? That's what Communism is, it's a way for the cook—for the tourist guide, the scientist, the great and the small—all to be of equal rank in a proletarian society." Her voice became resolute. "I definitely think you should apply."

He nodded thoughtfully. "You may be right. Let me think on it."

By unspoken agreement, they leaned back against the cushions and quietly surrendered to the mood. The music transported Jude from the stress and fear of the icy prison that Moscow had become for him, to the soft breezes and moonlit palm trees of a far-off land that let a man sleep peacefully and was filled with dark-eyed women who smelled of desert flowers and whose voices tinkled when they laughed.

When he reached over to cup Tamara's face between his hands, it seemed natural, almost required if the music and the mood were to be obeyed.

"You are a sweet, sweet woman," he said, hoping to convey through his voice what he felt at that moment in his heart. The woman was a near-stranger, but her humor, beauty, graciousness needed little time to gain appreciation.

She smiled, her red lips parting like curtains to reveal glistening white teeth. The need to get nearer was compelling to Jude. His face felt flushed and inched closer to hers. His lips parted in anticipation of touching hers. He could feel her heartbeat beneath the soft silk of her breast. Her breath quickened. She reached to embrace him....

The silk peeled off her body like gauze. Her bronze skin seemed to shimmer in the teasing candlelight. He slid an arm beneath her soft buttocks and lifted to slip one of the cushions beneath her. They would make love right there, where they had eaten, and talked, and come to want each other.

He touched her and she was moist and soft and yielding. He ached for her but wanted to delay, to make the feeling last and last.

"Tamara," he whispered, "I barely know you, so I can't say that I love you; but I can say that I love this feeling you've given me. I love your mind, your laugh, your skin, your touch. Those things at this moment make all other desires seem petty."

She said nothing, only gently pulled him down to her and they made love while the music of Samarkand serenaded approvingly.

Afterward, they drank red wine and dressed each other with the reluctance of lovers who regret the passage of time and surrender to it grudgingly.

The realities returned to Jude's mind like a puppy scratching at a door. It was time to leave, because being on the streets too late in Moscow was certain to attract police attention. It was also time to acknowledge that the affair with Tamara must end. An evening was one thing, but he could not allow the relationship to deepen.

He picked up his coat and headed for the door, dreading what he was about to say. Tamara held his heavy coat while he slipped his arms into it. She then held his lapels loosely and looked sweetly into his face. "When will you be back?" she asked.

Jude looked away. He felt like a user. "I don't think I'll be able to see you again."

Tamara's eyes widened with surprise. "You're joking."

"Tamara," he began to explain, "it's been a wonderful evening, can we just leave it at that?"

She shook her head. "No. We can't just leave it at that. I may be vain as any woman, but I know when two people share something wonderful. We did. We shared something wonderful. If I thought you just wanted to fuck me and then move on, and I went along with it, I'd say, 'Fine, it's been fun.' But it wasn't that way, and I want to know why.'' She studied his nervous features. "Are you married?"

"No." He shook his head vigorously. He was thinking fast, but he hated lying to this woman. "Look, I'll be going back to sea very soon, and I couldn't bear leaving you. I'm afraid of becoming too close." He tipped her chin up so their eyes met. "Tamara, look at me. You are beautiful and wonderful."

She sighed and patted his arm, then turned away so he couldn't see the tears. "Goodbye, Comrade."

WALKING HUNCHED AGAINST THE COLD along the deserted late-night Moscow street, Jude felt as if he had touched white silk with muddy hands. Tamara had trusted him and he made her feel like a tramp. He repeated to himself all the things he had whispered to her, things he had meant, and now he knew she would dump his words like a leftover breakfast. Goddamn this filthy business, he raged to himself.

Despite his bout with self-pity, Jude kept glancing around him, ever-alert for the unordinary, for the first warning of danger. Vehicle traffic was light, and the sidewalks were deserted. But as Jude walked, he became aware of a figure about a block behind that seemed to be moving at the same pace and in the same direction. When Jude slowed or speeded up, the figure did the same; when Jude changed direction, so did that person. It's either an amateur tail or a strange coincidence, he said to himself.

With each test Jude improvised, he became more certain he was being followed. The tension rose in him like steam in a boiler. If it was the KGB, he would be surrounded and easily cut off. But wouldn't the KGB be more professional at tailing? He had to find out.

Jude turned a corner and selected a dark alleyway a short distance down the block. He ducked into it and waited. Within two minutes, he heard footsteps approaching; they were hesitant, the steps of a stalker who has lost his prey.

Standing just inside the alley, Jude held his breath as the steps grew louder. He picked up a short stick from the ground and held it in his sweating right hand. When the approaching shadow filled the entire sidewalk, Jude reached out and grabbed the figure by the arm and shoved the stick into his back.

"Don't move," he said threateningly. "This is a pistol in your back. Come into the alley—slowly."

The man gasped with surprise and fear and Jude knew his ruse had worked. Not that he had doubted it wouldn't. When a hard object is jammed into one's back from a dark alley, and it's proclaimed to be a gun, one tends to believe it. And if the "pursuit" were only a coincidence, he could show the rattled citizen the stick and apologize, complaining about the rising amount of street crime.

Jude made his captive face the alley wall and spoke over the man's shoulder. "Why were you following me?" he demanded.

The man began to recover from the shock. Jude could see in the dim light that it was the squirrel-faced man he had spotted earlier in the evening. Jude cursed himself, like a chef who burned a sauce.

"Are you Markov?" the man asked.

"Which Markov?"

"Petr."

"And if I am?"

"I'm your contact."

"Go on," Jude said.

"The message is, be at the Pushkin Fine Arts Museum at 2:00 p.m. on Friday, three days from now. Go to Hall 30 and look for a man with a bright red scarf. Ask him if there are any Van Dyck works on display.''

"And?''

"That's all I know.''

Jude released the man and instructed him to walk in the opposite direction. Just as the man turned away, Jude said, "Oh, one more thing. If you're going to follow people, learn to do it better. People have been known to resent it.''

ACROSS THE STREET in a darkened van with engine idling, two men sat quietly staring out of a camouflaged window with infrared binoculars. One man turned to his partner, and said, "Did you see that?''

The other nodded and reached for the radio microphone.

CHAPTER TWELVE

THE SQUEAK OF HIS BIG LEATHER CHAIR was the only noise in the room, but it grated on Ivan Kolchak's nerves as he leaned back to contemplate the scant notes he had just taken.

In front of his desk, the subordinates sat expectantly. One was his assistant, Kyril Petrovich, a patient, impassive man wise to the moods and expectations of his boss. The other was the leader of the unit detailed to follow one of the Ukrainian nationalist suspects. Kolchak had forgotten his name in the ten minutes since hearing it.

Kolchak didn't want to be there. Xenia was becoming even more fanatic in her religion and he had a hangover. These two men were not part of his misery, but they were handy. He felt like spreading it around.

He glared at the agent who had reported the surveillance. "Come on, damn it. You're telling me your unit tailed this Ukrainian—" he looked down at his paper for the name "—Vladimir Bukovsky, for six days, and all you uncovered was a brief rendezvous with another man late last night on a quiet residential street. That's shit. He could have been asking the other fellow for a match, the time, or even a blow job. Do you really think that would stand up in court?"

Petrovich smiled thinly. "A KGB court?"

Despite himself, Kolchak snickered. "Watch it," he growled, but the dry humor made him feel a little more human.

The agent glanced nervously between the two men. "Uh, Comrade Kolchak, with all respect, sir, they held a prolonged conversation in a dark alley. The, uh, circumstances were such that it was definitely incriminating. Definitely."

"Do both of you believe this Bukovsky is an enemy of the state?"

They nodded in unison.

"Is it time to pick him up?"

They nodded more vigorously.

Kolchak said what he had known he would say all along after he had finished playing devil's advocate. "Okay, grab him. Kyril, you take care of the paperwork." Kolchak picked up a fuzzy, dark photo taken during the surveillance. "Now, this other fellow, the one who talked to the Ukrainian in the alley, what do you know about him?"

The agent scooted forward on his chair, looked at Petrovich as though for permission and said, "Our backup team followed him. He's staying at the Kirovskaya Hotel. It's a small place for workers. He's registered as a seaman by the name of Petr Markov."

"And?" Kolchak asked. He knew there would be more.

"And his papers are phony. Both his internal passport and his maritime registration are forgeries."

"Grab him, too," Kolchak said, standing up to add immediacy to the order. Both men rose with him, but Kolchak indicated for Petrovich to stay. The other man hesitated, then left the room, relieved to escape his boss's bad temper.

Kolchak and his assistant resumed their seats. "Kyril, what have you heard about the Zids, these Sicarii who claim they blew up the Botanical Gardens?"

Petrovich shook his head. "Not a thing. They've been quiet, and none of our regular sources seems to know anything. I'd guess they're amateurs. It's the professionals who leave tracks." He shifted in his chair. "One thing, though. Our people in the States close to the Defenders of Zion say they've heard the word 'Sicarii,' but very hush-hush. They haven't been able to find out anything else, though. Not much help."

Kolchak shrugged. "We've started with less. It eventually pieces together. Keep trying."

Kolchak picked up the blurred photo on his desk. "Who do you suppose this is?" he asked in a musing voice.

Petrovich didn't know if the question was rhetorical or directed at him, but he answered anyway. "He might be a foreigner. Counterfeiting passable Soviet documents is damned tough. It almost requires the resources of a government to pull off. We may be looking at the CIA here. Or maybe British MI."

Kolchak stared at the photo in silence.

NICHOLAS MIKHAILOVITCH FROWNED and stared at the floor while the older man who had just rushed in paced a circle around his chair.

"Everything's going to hell," Leonid Deniken said, waving his hands as he walked. "And now, they've got Bukovsky, too."

"Tell me again, how did it happen?" Nicholas said.

"Just this afternoon. An hour ago. One of our people was on his way to visit him and saw the KGB drag him out of the house. They grabbed the American agent, Markov, two days ago, and now one of our key men." He paused and rubbed two fingers over his eyes. "And one of my dear friends."

"Do we know they captured the American?" Nicholas asked.

"Our contact at his hotel said he was last seen running down the street with half the Moscow KGB bureau on his tail. How many people win footraces with the KGB?"

"Just how much did Bukovsky know?" Nicholas asked.

"He knows about Khrushchev—not where he's hiding, but once the KGB gets the scent, they'll find that out. *Yob!*" He struck his fist into his palm. "That about finishes us. All the years we've kept that old man hidden . . . now, just when we almost have him out of the country—this!''

"Maybe Bukovsky won't break," Nicholas said.

Deniken looked at him with derision. "Are you serious? They always break."

Nicholas rubbed his lower lip in deep thought. "They got Bukovsky an hour ago; we're supposed to meet the American in two hours at the Pushkin museum."

"You forget, Bukovsky was the one who arranged the rendezvous. They'll squeeze that out of him like toothpaste."

"Even the KGB goons can't work that fast," Nicholas said.

"I doubt if the American is free, or even alive," Deniken said glumly.

"If he got away, he has no usable identification, no place to go, no one to fall back on. I think we owe him the benefit of those doubts," Nicholas said.

"We'd be fools to show up at that museum," Deniken said.

"We were fools to get into this business," Nicholas said. "Anyway, the contact—if there is to be one—will be made by a new man who just got into town. He'll have to decide if meeting the American is worth the risk."

JUDE PULLED HIS HEAVY COAT tightly around him as a gust of night wind funneled down the man-made canyons of city streets and attacked pedestrians like a mugger. He reached for the door of the Kirovskaya like a pilgrim for sanctuary. Inside the warm lobby, he gave an involuntary shudder of gratitude and rubbed his hands together briskly. All the worn chairs in the overheated room were occupied. Several men were watching the news on television, others were reading or talking quietly, and a few were dozing with heads nodding like chickens pecking.

Jude started toward the front desk, but one look at the clerk made him stop abruptly. The fat man who normally gave list-less disregard to everything inedible around him stood rigidly at the counter with sweat on his brow and wide-open eyes that kept glancing from Jude to a knot of four men standing by the stairway, who seemed to be trying hard not to look at Jude.

The sensors of Jude's training started a siren in his brain. Suddenly, he looked at his watch and snapped his fingers in disgust as though he had forgotten something. Shaking his head, he turned and retreated toward the door, gaining a precious few feet. The moment he touched the knob, the waiting men sprang into action. Jude flung the door open and raced down the street, pushing startled pedestrians out of the way, and ignoring the curses they flung at his back like stones.

Jude took a quick look back and saw three heavy men about a half block behind, open coats flapping as they chugged along. He knew that meant one had stayed behind to call for reinforcements. He darted down a dark side street, but the three stayed on his tail.

The cold night air burned his lungs, but Jude was glad of it. He knew the same pain was also being felt by his pursuers, and they lacked his motivation to withstand pain: he was running for his life. After two more blocks, he glanced back and saw that one of the men had dropped out and a second was lagging fifty yards behind the third, who stayed a tenacious half-block behind Jude.

After three more blocks, Jude felt his legs turning to rubber, and his breath grated harshly in his throbbing lungs. He knew he could not run much farther, and that his antagonists were tightening a net around him. He was in a hare-and-hounds situation, and he had to do something to avoid ending up as a scrap of bloody fur.

Passing a construction site, he slowed enough to pick up a crowbar lying on a pile of lumber. In the distance he could see the lights of the Ukraina Hotel and the dark line of the Moskva River. He stopped to let his tortured lungs gulp at the freezing air. The sweat was beginning to harden on his face.

He stole a look back. There were now seven or eight men about a hundred yards behind, and they were running with the ease of freshness. On the nearest side street, he could see a patrol car with flashing blue lights, coming fast. Ahead, on the river bridge, a knot of men under the lights were shouting and pointing at him. Without thinking, Jude followed his instincts and took the path that sloped downward toward the darkness of the riverbank.

A man in the uniform of the militia stepped out of the shadows just ahead. As Jude approached, the officer went into a tackling crouch and prepared to spring. Jude swung the crowbar with full force just as the man launched himself, and connected solidly with the top of his head. The sound was the thunk of a pumpkin hit by a bat. The man's cap went flying in a shower of blood and brains. Jude knew he had killed him, but there was no time for feelings. His numb fingers dropped the bloody crowbar with a clatter. He could hear footsteps and shouting approaching from three directions. Ahead was the river and he edged toward it, looking around frantically as the trap narrowed.

He stood on the bank of the river and, like a winded stag, watched them converge on him, their flashlights mocking his attempts to elude them. Several were leaning over the dead militiaman, and they shouted curses at him above the din. The circle of threatening shadows closed.

He turned to the river in desperation. The water reached noisily for the bank with black fingers. Steam rose from its surface as if from a witch's caldron. Jagged blocks of dirty ice bounced against each other and careened downstream.

The river had been frozen, then partially thawed in a warm spell, and was now quickly overcoming the action of the current and refreezing as the thermometer plunged. As Jude stood on the bank, the water temperature was nineteen degrees Fahrenheit.

Jude looked back at his pursuers. Angry hands were reaching out to grab him.

It wasn't a decision, more an impulse born of desperation. Jude turned and hurled himself into the river, disappearing with a heavy splash that his astonished pursuers shrank from as if it were hot flames.

The freezing water hit Jude's system like a charge of electricity. His eyes rolled back with the shock, his breath caught in his throat, and paralysis seized his body like a steel trap. The pain burned and he screamed in his mind to make it go away. He rolled to the surface and fought instinctively for survival. His heavy clothes were soaked and were like an anvil on his back pushing him below the surface. The thin film of ice on the water cut his hands like a sharp knife as he desperately splashed to stay afloat while the river swept him along. Just before he went under, Jude managed to grab hold of a large chunk of ice that swept past his head.

A man could live in that water eight minutes, and Jude had already been in for two. His temperature had dropped three and one-half degrees. The classic symptoms were in effect: confusion, shock, shivering.

As he was swept downstream, holding on to the ice as if it were a life preserver, time was like a gyroscope gone berserk. A minute could pass for an hour. He was aware of nothing except the knowledge he was rushing toward death. His mind chose that moment to flash before him a memory from his childhood of a playmate's body being removed from a pond several days after drowning. Jude had glimpsed the grisly sight before he was shooed away and the body covered. He now saw himself being removed from the Moskva River in the spring, bloated, fish-eaten and the color of a carp's belly. He sobbed at the thought.

Jude had now been in the water for four minutes. He was halfway to death. His temperature had dropped to ninety-one degrees. His chances of survival were now only fifty percent, even if he got out immediately. His shivering became violent; his heart beat irregularly.

Jude started to feel warmer, almost euphoric. He now was past five minutes and his body dipped to ninety degrees. A feeling of peace came over him, and he wanted to stay in the warm water and rest.

Jude's mind fought a desperate battle against the seductress. To relax and accept the peace that came with surrender was death, he told himself. He shook his head and stretched his facial muscles to force himself awake. He sensed he had to leave the water quickly if he were to live.

As he fought the lassitude, he forced himself to examine the situation.

His first problem was to leave the water. The second was to find a place to get warm and hide. His only chance to evade capture was if the Russians assumed he died and looked for a body the next morning instead of a live fugitive that night. He hoped they would be wrong.

He strained his eyes to search the bank and recognized the towers of Novoedevichye Convent over on the left, silhouetted against the city lights. The old monument reminded him that the only person in Moscow who might take him in lived a short distance from those towers—Tamara Khanum. But he had been swept toward midstream and he didn't know if he had the strength to work his way to the bank.

With great reluctance, Jude released his block of ice and started floundering his way in that direction. The only thing that kept him from sinking was the ice. He went from block to block, splashing in desperation and gagging as he swallowed great gulps of the polluted industrial waste of the river.

He had been in the water six minutes. His temperature was eighty-nine degrees. At eighty-six degrees he would lose consciousness. He had stopped shivering and his motor responses had slowed drastically. Hallucinations were at the edges of his mind, clamoring to get in. The will to survive was like a wet bar of soap he was trying to hold on to.

Jude felt himself floating away from his body. All feeling had left him, and the only way he knew he was still struggling was by watching the flailing of his arms. The image of himself as a mushy corpse floating to the surface in the spring made him whimper with determination to keep going.

So deadened were his feelings that while he was crawling along the mud of the bank, he thought he was still in midstream. All actions seemed in slow motion to his benumbed brain, as if he were struggling in quicksand. He dimly realized he was out of the water when he could look down and see his mud-caked legs. With a stiff-legged plod, he pushed himself toward the street, carrying the weight of several gallons of river water in his clothes, which was rapidly turning to ice on his face, hair and hands.

The coat of ice protected him by forming a thermal barrier against the freezing wind. As he stumbled down the street, shivering began again and his temperature climbed back to ninety-one degrees. He tried to remember Tamara's address, but his mind wouldn't respond. He concentrated so intensely he felt his brain would start bleeding. It all came down to that: remember or die.

TAMARA WAS WORKING HARD at watching television. But the more she concentrated on the documentary about tractor production in the Crimea on the small black and white set, the more the image of Jude appeared in her mind and set off anew the attacks of self-pity that had dogged her since the night he snubbed her. She had felt like a fool ever since she had offered herself to the likable Petr Markov, been used and then experienced the dull blade of rejection sawing through her ego. She repeatedly told herself that he was nothing to her, only a slight acquaintance with whom she had shared some passion. But the heart doesn't easily fall for lies. She cared—

foolishly—but she cared. She vowed never again to be so vulnerable.

A frantic knocking on the door erased her musings and she walked quickly to it and spoke through the wood. "Who is it?"

"Petr. Let—me—in."

She opened the door a crack, then flung it wide in horror. Standing before her was a cadaverous apparition identifiable only by the speaking of his own name. He was covered with a coating of ice like a glazed doughnut. His lips were blue and he cupped his porcelain-white hands like claws. He shivered uncontrollably as his body fought vainly to escape the grip of hypothermia. The words that came through his violently chattering teeth were muffled and forced, as though spoken through a wall of cotton.

She pulled him into the room and immediately attacked his frozen clothing, forcing the stiff material off his body as if it were wire. She then pulled him into the bathroom and under a hot shower.

Jude stood under the pelting water and savored the sweet pain of the thawing needles as steam enveloped him like a fog. He tried to evaluate his situation, but his mind refused to respond. All he could focus on was what was immediately before him—the life-restoring heat of the shower. He had never known such fatigue. His knees felt they were supporting the ceiling, and kept buckling under the burden.

He finally could stand no longer and stumbled out of the shower without turning off the water or drying himself. When Tamara saw him she grabbed a towel and started rubbing his red skin. He started shivering again and climbed beneath the covers of her bed like a frightened gopher seeking its hole. Tamara gathered all the blankets she had and piled them on him, but the shivering did not stop.

"I'm going to call a doctor," she said.

"No, no-o-o-o," he said, his voice sounding like a run-down gramophone. "I'm o-kay. Sleee-e-p."

THE SUN WAS STREAMING through the windows when Jude awoke and lay quietly blinking his eyes, trying to orient himself. He had no idea where he was and fought down the beginnings of panic as he labored to reconstruct the most recent hours of his life.

The answer was provided for him by a movement at the extreme of his peripheral vision. Startled, Jude jumped and twisted in bed to confront Tamara, who was sitting a few feet away in a robe, glaring at him with lips compressed into a red pencil line. Her body was rigid with anger.

The sight of Tamara was the piece that put the puzzle together for Jude, and he began to recall the events that had brought him here. His pile of clothes in a corner with the dried mud still caked on them reminded him of the freezing river, and he shuddered at the memory.

"How long have I slept?" he asked.

"About fourteen hours."

"What's wrong?"

"Can't you guess?" she said, rubbing at the tears of humiliaton that suddenly spilled down her face.

Jude had no energy for guessing. He stared at her dumbly.

"There was an announcement on the news this morning. They warned people in this area to be on the alert for a man who would have come out of the river last night. They said . . . they said . . ." She paused to let her quavering voice settle. "He is an enemy of the state."

"And you think that's me?" Jude said.

"Oh, don't play me for a fool," she shouted. "Of course that's you. How many people go swimming in freezing rivers?"

"There is an explanation, believe me."

Tamara brushed aside his words. She stood up, went to the window and stared out, trying to compose herself. "You come in here, make me fall—make me care for you, then with no warning you tell me you'll never see me again, then you show up almost frozen to death for me to nurse you, then I find out you're some kind of criminal or spy." She wheeled around and glared at him. "Just how much do you think you can play with my feelings? You're nothing but a user."

Jude winced. That was one word he had hoped she would not call him. He started to answer, but he knew it would be futile to try to explain the unexplainable. The weight of his deceit toward her was heavy on his conscience, and he didn't want to add to the burden with more lies.

"What are you going to do?"

"You may think I'm just a dumb Tartar that you can twist to your purposes, but I'll show you that you can't fuck me and then think you can turn me into a traitor." She took two steps toward the door.

"What are you going to do?" he repeated.

"What do you think, *vebdyadok*, I'm going to turn you in. You're going to pay, bastard."

Jude tried to jump out of bed, but he became tangled in the blankets, and by the time he made it halfway to the door, it slammed shut and he could hear her running down the hall. He leaned against the door, glad he hadn't caught her. He had caused enough pain for this woman.

Jude hurriedly grabbed his clothes, knocked off as much mud as possible and put them on. The pants were damp, the shoes and coat still wet, but they'd just have to dry on his body. He went into the kitchen and found a loaf of bread, some cold meat and jam. He threw the food into a paper bag and looked for her purse, which he found in the bathroom. He removed sixty rubles from it and stuffed the money into his pocket. In a matter of moments he was out the door, down the rear service entrance and mingling with the Thursday morning crowd.

Tamara ran barefoot in her dressing robe to the corner office of the state bakery, and with flashing, red-rimmed eyes and disheveled hair, begged to use the telephone for an emergency call. Then, while clerks and customers looked on, she asked the operator for the KGB. The phone was answered on the second ring. Tamara opened her mouth but no words came out. She stared at the phone, which spoke to the air: "*Da? Da? Zdrav'st-vuytye?* Yes? Yes? Hello?" Tamara collapsed on the counter with gasping sobs, and an old woman bundled into men's clothing and oversize boots lumbered over, put an arm around her and hung up the phone.

THE KGB DISPATCHER SLAMMED the phone down with an aggravated mutter.

"What's the matter?" asked a companion, filing papers nearby.

"Oh, just a family fight or lovers' quarrel. Some sobbing female. They call to complain and then change their minds. I don't know why they call us; we can't solve everything. Pain in the ass. Never amounts to anything, though."

THE HANDCUFFS ON Vladimir Bukovsky's wrists bit into flesh as he shrank back against the rear-seat cushions of the Chaika squad car when the statue of Felix Dzerzhinsky in the middle of the square came into view. The thirty-six-foot monument to the man who headed Lenin's dreaded Cheka— the Extraordinary Commission for Struggle with Counterrevolution and Sabotage—meant the car was headed for the notorious Lubyanka, headquarters of the KGB, the grandson of Cheka. The mustard-colored building, sitting on a small hill, looked like an insurance office with its white curtains and brass fittings, but in his sixty years, Bukovsky had heard the stories of prisoners disappearing forever behind its walls, of screams ripping through quiet nights.

The car pulled into an underground garage at the back of the building, and Bukovsky was pushed along a corridor until he was taken through a green metal door into a dark room with bare concrete walls. The room was lit by one small yellow bulb and contained only a single wooden chair on which he was pushed down and then left alone.

Despite the chill of the room, clammy sweat rolled down Bukovsky's face and his hands shook, even when he clasped them tightly together. He tried to relax by taking deep, slow breaths, and thinking of things other than his arrest and the ordeal certain to come. He knew he was probably being observed from some secret compartment. He concentrated on his hatred of Russians. The hatred had been passed down in his family from generation to generation, like the shoe repair trade he practiced. He thought of Stalin's bloody purges that devastated his family and people, of horror stories of starvation and Communist brutality at the time of farm collectivization in the twenties and thirties. He recalled the war against the Germans, and the Red Army political commissar he had shot in the back during a battle. Bukovsky had much hate to dwell upon, but it didn't keep his hands from shaking as he waited for his persecutors. He was a pigeon that knew a hawk was circling above.

Bukovsky thought of the American he had contacted on the streets two nights before. Had he also been arrested? Maybe he was a double agent, who had netted Bukovsky like a fish. The apprehension raced through his mind like fire through a dry field.

Bukovsky shook his head angrily and tried to control his thoughts, because he knew that the purpose of leaving him alone in such a room was to soften him for interrogation. Like seasoning a chicken before boiling it.

The door flew open and slammed against the wall, making Bukovsky jump like a released spring. Into the room walked three men, two uniformed guards and a man who at one glance made Bukovsky's heart shrivel. He was of medium height and unremarkable appearance except for a walleyed condition caused by an opaque cornea of his left eye. His hair was pure white, which belied his age, obviously early thirties. But most noticeable was a cigarette that dangled from his lips as though it had been stuck there and forgotten.

"Greetings, Comrade Bukovsky. I'm pleased you could join us. They call me Papirosa." True to his name, he removed a pack of Turkish cigarettes from his pocket and offered it to Bukovsky. The prisoner, even though he didn't smoke, nervously took one, lighted it with shaking hands and coughed deeply at the first drag.

Papirosa leaned forward and stared into Bukovsky's face. The ash of his cigarette seemed as long as the cigarette itself, and Bukovsky couldn't take his eyes off it. Why didn't it fall?

"Do you know why you're here?" Papirosa asked, the cigarette waving like a baton as he spoke.

Bukovsky stared at him.

"Because you are a traitor to your country," Papirosa taunted.

"The only way I could be a traitor would be to not oppose Russian pigs like yourself. No good Ukrainian would call me anything but a patriot."

Papirosa smiled as though enjoying a private joke. "I'm not going to argue with you. I'm not even going to torture you, because you have no information we don't have already." He smiled broadly at the guards and then at Bukovsky, as though looking for praise.

Bukovsky had vowed to keep silent, but the desire to live compelled him to ask one question.

"Then what are you going to do with me?"

Papirosa's grin disappeared and he blew a stream of smoke into his captive's face. "We're going to execute you."

Bukovsky shrugged. "I knew you would eventually shoot me."

Papirosa smiled mysteriously. "We're not going to shoot you. That's for common criminals. We're going to execute you in a way deserving of traitors." He patted Bukovsky on the shoulder. "You're going to die by snake bite."

His victim looked at him uncomprehendingly. Papirosa continued. "Do you know what a black mamba is?" Bukovsky's numb stare revealed nothing. "Well, you'll like the one you're going to meet." Papirosa laughed and the ash quivered on his cigarette. "He's just a lovable, overgrown worm. And he takes a lot of pride in his work."

At a short gesture from Papirosa, the two guards grabbed Bukovsky by the arms and tried to drag him out of the room. Bukovsky came to life and fought with the desperation of the doomed. He kicked at the guards and twisted his body like the snake he was destined to meet. The guards swore and fumbled with the struggling man. As quickly as they could free his hand from the lighting fixture, he would brace his leg against the doorjamb.

Bukovsky suddenly felt a pain in his ankle that made his whole leg throb with agony. The guards released him and he collapsed to the concrete floor, writhing in pain. Papirosa leaned over, twisting his face so the smoke didn't curl into his eyes. He patted a heavy nightstick that he had used to hit Bukovsky in the ankle.

"Didn't feel very good, did it? If you don't go quietly, I'll break your kneecap with this and we'll carry you. But, easy or hard, you're going."

Without a word, Bukovsky got to his feet and limped out of the room with the guards loosely holding his arms and followed by Papirosa. They walked a few feet to a plain wooden door with a wire-mesh screen across the top half and a sign reading Handball Court. The guards opened the door and roughly shoved Bukovsky inside.

Bukovsky picked himself up and looked around. The large room was bare and had a hardwood floor and a twenty-foot ceiling. All it contained was a brown box on the floor next to the door and a rope hanging from the ceiling.

The door opened slightly and a hand reached in and lifted the lid of the box and then quickly slammed the door. Bukovsky's head swiveled at the noise and what he saw transfixed him in horror.

Slowly lifting his small head from the box in tentative curiosity was dendroaspis polylepis, the dreaded black mamba of southern Africa. Stretched to its full length, the slim dark brown reptile was eleven feet long. Its head was narrow and rather harmless looking. Unlike the more fearsome-looking rattlesnake, its fangs were not long and frightening, but no longer than a quarter of an inch up under its nose. But the venom they injected was almost always fatal unless treated with an antivenin, which sometimes worked and sometimes didn't. The mamba was a cousin of the cobra and the coral snake, and even more deadly than either.

The snake looked at Bukovsky in its expressionless way, but it was alarmed. It had been confined in a small box and now was in a foreign place in the presence of a creature that it assumed could do it harm. Given a choice, the mamba would have turned and disappeared into the bush. But there was no cover here, only the threatening presence of the other creature.

If the mamba were to strike Bukovsky, it would inject up to two hundred milligrams of venom—ten times a fatal dose. The poison would attack his respiratory and cardiac systems. Within fifteen minutes his eyelids would droop and he would have difficulty in speaking and swallowing. He might become giddy and start drooling. But soon he would be gasping and his heartbeat would become irregular. How soon death would occur would depend upon his system. The only thing certain would be its inevitability.

Although the mamba was not particularly ominous or ugly looking, the frightening thing about it was its speed. When people see a deadly snake from a distance, about the only comfort they can gain from the situation is the knowledge they can escape. The mamba, however, is perhaps the fastest of all snakes. Rising to a height of several feet, it can outdistance a man.

The snake didn't go directly for Bukovsky. First it tested the extent of its imprisonment. It was only when it realized there was no escape that it turned toward the man.

A chill enveloped Bukovsky like a cold wind, when he saw the snake rise to a four-foot height and dart around the room. The speed of it completely unnerved him. His only hope was the rope. He grabbed it and strained to haul himself up hand over hand until he hung ten feet above the floor and half that distance above the snake.

Bukovsky had been on the rope less than three minutes when the pain started. It began in his shoulders as a dull ache, but quickly became a raging fire spreading through his biceps and forearms. Cramps seized his muscles and his arms began to tremble, then to shake violently. His hands started to go numb and lose the ability to grip. Sweat ran down his brow and stung his eyes, but still he could see the dark creature darting beneath him, waiting.

Bukovsky began to hate the snake. It seemed to be teasing him with that obscene speed and nonstop motion. He had done nothing to it, and yet it wanted to kill him. He prayed, even though the words of his childhood prayers were a dim and imprecise memory. His body was losing patience. He was asking more than it had to give. He vomited. His bladder released, spreading a dark stain across the front of his pants.

Bukovsky had hung on the rope for an eternity. His worn, sixty-year-old body could sustain the strain no longer. Still, he couldn't surrender. His life was in his fingers. The desperation to survive rose out of his guts like lava from a volcano and gave him strength greater than he had ever known. It prolonged his life a full ninety seconds.

A terrible cramp seized Bukovsky's body and a roaring red ocean flooded his brain. His mind shorted out like a blown fuse. His eyes rolled upward, unseeing. His fingers relaxed, unfeeling. Bukovsky slid down the rope and into a heap beside the startled mamba.

The snake struck Bukovsky in the neck, holding on to pump the lethal contents of its glands into his body. Finally, the snake released him and resumed a darting vigil around its prison, looking for more enemies.

Papirosa watched the death drama through the wire screen with a choreographer's satisfaction. "Okay," he said to the guards, "secure the snake and let's go have a word with our guest."

A guard wearing heavy gloves rushed into the room and grabbed the snake behind the head while it bit at him. He dropped it back into the box and closed the cover.

Papirosa strolled over to Bukovsky, who was lying in a heap where he had fallen. "You held onto that rope like a fucking monkey. I thought we were watching the Olympics." There was no movement, so he prodded Bukovsky with his toe. "Hey! The snake's put away; you're not dead yet."

There was the sudden odor of human feces. Papirosa sniffed the air, then announced, "Hey, boys, this *vebdyadok* shit his pants. *Bog!* You'd think he'd have more pride." He prodded again. "Open your eyes, goddammit." Still no movement. Suspicious, Papirosa leaned down for a closer look, then felt the man's pulse and looked under his eyelid. "*Yob!* This guy's dead!"

KOLCHAK WAS ABOUT AS HAPPY as a dancer with a sore toe. He stared at Papirosa across his desk. "Take that goddamn cigarette out of your mouth."

Papirosa looked down through the haze of smoke as though surprised he had a cigarette in his mouth. He stubbed it out as if he were killing his child.

"Now explain to me how in hell the prisoner died before you got any information out of him," Kolchak demanded.

Papirosa scrunched around in his chair nervously. He seemed almost naked without his cigarette. "Well, boss, you know how we're always looking for ways to be more effective. I was talking to a fellow I know who works at the zoo. He was telling me they had an extra black mamba—that's a snake from Africa—"

"I know what it is," Kolchak snapped.

"So I got an idea how we can use the fucking snake in interrogation. The idea is, let the damned snake bite the prisoner and then tell him you'll give him the antivenin only if he talks. Otherwise, he dies. Don't you think that's great?"

"What if the antivenin doesn't work or if he's allergic to it?" Kolchak asked.

Papirosa clapped his hands. "That's the fucking beauty of it! I had the herpetologist—the snake guy—tie off the duct between the venom gland and the fangs. That snake couldn't poison a cockroach, but the prisoner, he doesn't know that. He thinks he's going to die if he doesn't talk. See, we're getting the scare value out of the snake without any real danger."

"I see only one problem," Kolchak said.

"What's that?"

"The prisoner died."

Papirosa frowned. "Yeah. Well, we didn't know he had a heart condition. His old ticker turned into an alarm clock."

Kolchak shook his head in disgust. "You mean you submitted a sixty-year-old man to that treatment without a thorough physical? For God's sake, man, what did you expect to happen?"

Papirosa reached for a cigarette, then glanced at Kolchak and put the pack away. "Well, I can't think of everything." His lip dropped into a pout. "It seems that whenever I come up with an original idea, you pick it apart."

Kolchak threw up his hands, then dropped them on the desk with a loud slap. "I give up. You know what your problem is, Papirosa? You're a butcher when the situation calls for a surgeon." He let that sink in for a moment, then said, "Do you know that round stone platform near St. Basil's in Red Square, the one they call *Lobnoye Mesto*, the Place of the Skull?"

Papirosa nodded. "Yeah, where the czars used to execute people."

"Much more than that," Kolchak said. "They specialized in torture. Human misery elevated to a science. The favorite gimmick was to pour molten lead down the throats of counterfeiters. A specialty of Ivan the Terrible was to take people who irritated him and brand them with hot irons. Those found guilty of sacrilege were torn to pieces with iron hooks. Thieves had their heels broken, then were forced to get up and walk. They say Peter the Great put to death two hundred mutinous soldiers in one day, and then quit only because it got dark. He chopped off five heads himself. The bodies were left in the square for five months." Kolchak paused and pointed an instructive finger at the enraptured Papirosa. "My point in telling you this is that I think you were born too late. You would have gone right to the top in that environment."

Papirosa hesitated, not knowing if he had just been complimented or insulted. "I do my best." He fingered his white hair. "Look, Comrade. Do you know how I got this? Job pressures."

Kolchak frowned. "You're too intense. The objective is to extract information, not inflict pain. Done correctly, the job requires a—" Kolchak searched for the right word "—a certain sensitivity. Look, this isn't the old days. The KGB is concerned with staff morale, and you don't help when word gets around about such things as that damned snake. It makes us seem crude. And then there's image."

"What's image?" Papirosa asked.

"Forget it," Kolchak said. "Thinking about that would destroy your mind—or mine." Kolchak stood and ushered Papirosa to the door.

"I'll try, I really will," Papirosa said.

"I know you're ambitious, Papirosa," Kolchak said, "but if you want to get ahead in this business, then think surgeon, not butcher. So give that snake back to the zoo." He turned away, then stopped. "Oh, one other thing. Some of the fellows are complaining about you tying up their handball court. Find someplace else to work."

Kolchak nodded dismissal to Papirosa and signaled his assistant, Kyril Petrovich, to enter, but then he noticed Papirosa wanted to say something else. "Yes?" Kolchak said.

Papirosa got close and Kolchak bent slightly to hear. "Boss, what do you think those bodies looked like after five months?"

"Go back to work, Papirosa."

Closing the door to his office, Kolchak slammed his fist into his palm in disgust. "*Kamn*, Kyril, we *had* that Ukrainian." He squeezed his hands in front of him. "Then that idiot Papirosa got cute and we didn't get a thing out of him."

"Papirosa is dedicated," Petrovich said. "It's a thankless job."

"What's new with the sailor who jumped into the river?"

Petrovich had anticipated the question and opened the file he had brought with him. "No sign. We searched along the banks downstream as far as he could have gone. We sent out a public warning the next morning. Nothing. It's probably a safe bet that the man's dead, frozen at the bottom of the river."

"But it's a bet we're not going to make," Kolchak said. "I want every agent and policeman in the Moscow area given a full description and orders to stop anyone remotely resembling that man." Kolchak stood up and went to the window where he gazed intently at the back of the Dzerzhinsky statue with a mantle of snow on its shoulders. "The big question now is, who do you think he was—or is?"

"We traced him back to Vladivostok through his Aeroflot reservation. We discovered he joined the crew of a fishing boat that put into Alaska by claiming to be laid over because of sickness. The captain of the boat—a man named Mitrovich—told our people the man's papers seemed in order. Said he kept to himself, couldn't tell us much else. There had been a strange accident on the boat, the *Novi Mir*. The political officer, name of Florinsky, was found dead at the bottom of a hold. But that was ruled an accident."

"Do you believe him—the captain, I mean?"

Petrovich shrugged. "We'll watch him."

Kolchak paced the room with hands clasped behind his back. "So we have a probable American agent who may be— or may not be—at the bottom of the Moskva River." He turned to Petrovich. "I want you to make contact with our agent in Mexico. The one with the Ukrainian connection, who alerted us about the American infiltrator a few weeks ago. See what else might fit into this puzzle. Also, check for similarities between this sailor, Markov, and an American agent named Miller. Jude Miller."

Picking up on his boss's tone of dismissal, Petrovich started for the door.

"Oh, Kyril, anything new on our bombing Jews, the Sicarii?"

The assistant shook his head. "Same answer as before—nothing, but we'll get them. We always get amateurs."

"I hope we do, before the crazy Zids blow up the Kremlin."

CHAPTER THIRTEEN

JUDE SAT ON THE BENCH outside a museum and ate the food taken from Tamara's kitchen. He chewed slowly as his head turned from side to side and he stamped his feet against the cold. He could have passed for a curious workingman on holiday, trying to take in all the sights. But Jude was not looking for statues, he was looking for danger.

Jude felt naked. Walking the streets of Moscow with no identification, pursued by a determined KGB with all the resources of a powerful government, he was without protection and almost without hope. But he kept hoping; he kept walking.

All that day, when he would see a militiaman strolling toward him, he would move with casual speed to another place. His time was spent looking for groups of people to lose himself in. He strolled through museums, gawking at exhibits with one eye while watching for police with the other. He mingled with the crowd at a bicycle race. He twice sat through a poor movie about Catherine the Great in a small theater near the university. Now, as he finished the food, the cold and dark of evening had descended on the city and the crowds were leaving the streets like autumn leaves before the wind.

This was the time of greatest danger. Moscow at night becomes a deserted city. The people lack money for nightlife and are discouraged by a prudish government from pursuing diversions available in the West.

Jude wandered the streets as long as he dared, but finally, he stood alone on an empty street where the only other face was of the writer Nikolay Gogol. Looking past the statue fronting Gogol Street, Jude didn't realize and wouldn't have cared that he stood exactly where Napoléon positioned his cannon to assault the Kremlin gates in 1812. He was looking for safety, and neither the trivia of history nor the smiling statue of the great writer offered it.

Jude couldn't go to a hotel because his description and the fake Petr Markov identification would already have been circulated to everyone in the city. It had been retained by the Kirovskaya when he checked in, in accordance with Soviet law. His refuge for the night would have to be on the streets. Survival now depended upon showing the resourcefulness of a common hobo.

Across the street and down the block he saw the lights of the Praga Restaurant, one of the largest in Moscow. It occupied the entire corner and housed seven separate restaurants inside. As Jude neared the large building, which resembled a converted movie theater, the sounds of laughter and the busy clinking of kitchen work filtered through the windows, but for him the only appeal was the darkness of the rear work area where Dumpsters and boxes offered the concealment of a shadowy, stunted forest.

Just as he neared the safety of the alley behind the restaurant, Jude caught the reflection of a blue light bouncing off the wall. Wheeling in fright, he almost ran into a militiaman, who was standing like a bear in silhouette and shining a flashlight in his face.

Jude stood dumbstruck, squinting into the beam. The militiaman's voice rumbled from the distance beyond the flashlight. "Why do you think we paint crosswalks on streets, Comrade?" he lectured. "I'm tired of picking up the bloody remains of idiots who run across streets in traffic. I could give you a citation for that, don't you know?"

Jude started to protest that the streets were empty of traffic, but knew no cop in the world would listen to that kind of logic. Instead, he measured where the militiaman's groin was and wondered whether his kick could penetrate the heavy over-coat with sufficient force. But he also knew the militiaman's partner was alertly watching in the squad car, which was stopped at the curb, flashing its blue light.

The officer then spoke the words that could doom Jude.

"Let me see your papers."

Jude became dramatic out of desperation. "*Chort*, officer, I'm late and the wife is threatening to kill me anyway. You give me a ticket I can't afford and it'll be like a death warrant. Besides—" he started to hop on one leg and then the other "—I've got to take a piss before my eyeballs turn yellow. I was headed for that alley when you stopped me." He gestured with his head toward the back of the restaurant.

Jude could sense the officer debating. He held his breath while the man decided whether to give him a ticket or let him go. A minor thing to the officer: life and death to Jude.

Finally, the militiaman chuckled. "Take your leak and get on home. But cross streets where you're supposed to."

"*Spasibo*, thank you" Jude mumbled and scurried into the alley. He suddenly had a genuine need to relieve himself.

The area behind the restaurant was cluttered with three giant Dumpsters. Two were labeled Garbage and one had a sign attached that said Tin Cans. Jude had to stay concealed and he had to get out of the cold, so he found a large sheet of cardboard and carefully opened the creaky lid to the tin can Dumpster. If he had to sleep in one of these things, he would rather have a can thrown in on him than someone's uneaten gravy.

Snuggled under his cardboard in the darkness of the Dumpster, Jude was bombarded by an occasional can, but they became fewer and fewer as he listened to the restaurant gradually grow quiet. Soon, he gave way to the silence and drifted into a shallow sleep.

Many visitors knocked on the door of his mind that night as he rolled himself into a shivering ball inside the Dumpster. Molly, with her rosy cheeks crinkled by a happy laugh, appeared to him, bringing the smell of pine sap and forest dew with her. Lana, the dark one with the sexy aura and suspicious manner, offered herself to Jude. But just as he started to thrash about in desire in his cardboard nest, she gave way to Armstead. The officious old man glared at Jude and beckoned to someone. A man walked close to Armstead, who put his arm around the newcomer and began dabbing at his face with a handkerchief. "See what you did to this poor man, you murderer?" Armstead accused Jude.

The man standing next to Armstead was the militiaman killed by Jude near the river the previous night. The top of his head was bashed in where Jude had connected with the crowbar, and the front of his blue and gray uniform was splattered with blood and brains. He glared accusingly at Jude while Armstead tried to wipe the blood away.

"But I was only trying to get away. I was following your orders," Jude protested to Armstead.

"You know I don't condone murder," Armstead replied. "This poor policeman is your victim, just like the one in the soccer stadium."

"No, no," Jude mumbled in his sleep, but Armstead's accusation triggered the onset of the old dream, and Jude was again reluctantly dragged down to the bowels of the stadium to witness the same cyanide killing he had seen a hundred times before.

Jude was jarred awake by the sound of a powerful motor straining. The Dumpster gave a sharp jolt and he realized with a panicky jolt that he was about to be emptied into the crushing jaws of a garbage truck.

With a frenzied shout, Jude pushed against the lid of the Dumpster and his head popped up like that of a gopher out of his hole. One of the men giving hand directions to the driver saw him and signaled the truck to stop. With a jarring bounce, the Dumpster settled back to the ground and Jude scrambled out and hit the ground running. He heard one man shout, "Is it a hungry bear?" Another answered, "No, it leaps like a grasshopper." He could hear the workers roaring with laughter as he sprinted down the street, but he had concerns that made ridicule mean nothing.

Jude was not out of danger. He had several hours before his 2:00 p.m. rendezvous with the Ukrainians at the Pushkin Museum, and every step he took could attract the attention of the police. At a public bathroom he cleaned up as best he could, then headed for a canteen where he had a simple breakfast. He had gotten used to the odor of the Dumpster, so he couldn't smell himself, but the stares and upturned noses of those who gave him a wide berth in line told him he was conspicuously malodorous, a smelly bum, an easy mark for any cop in the world looking for someone to hassle.

Jude kept on the move. He visited a succession of public toilets, staying in the closed booths as long as he dared, then moving on to the next one. He mingled in the crowds at railway stations and stood in line at a bread store for more than an hour—anything to avoid the conspicuousness of being alone in public. He even gave thought to dashing for the American embassy, where he would have safe asylum, but he knew he would get no closer than a couple of blocks. The KGB kept the building staked out so thoroughly that a bat couldn't get through on a dark night.

After what seemed like an eternity of evasion, it was time to head for the museum. He timed his arrival so that he walked out of the nearby Kropotkinskaya metro station at ten minutes before two. Walking casually, he calculated he would arrive at the rendezvous about two minutes after the hour. In his condition, he didn't want to loiter around the pristine corridors. Bums and Botticelli didn't seem a natural combination.

Jude's steps echoed hollowly through the wide marbled corridors, taking him past exhibits of ancient Egypt and

Babylon, and through centuries of magnificent tapestries, paintings and sculpture. Eventually a sign indicated Hall 30, and he walked by without entering, trying to sense a trap. Satisfied that the gallery was empty, he strolled in like the curious workman on holiday he hoped he passed for, and began to admire the seventeenth-century Dutch art of the Rembrandt era.

Jude wandered through the hall for almost fifteen minutes with no sign of his contact. He felt like sitting down and weeping in the terrible despair of abandonment. Hope had become a song with no tune; Jude resigned himself to falling into the hands of his enemies.

He knew that hanging around the gallery too long, especially given his appearance, would eventually bring curious museum guards to his side, so in a defeated shuffle he headed for the door that would return him to the cold of the streets.

Just before he reached the exit, he saw a short man enter the hall at the far end, holding a program that he immediately began studying. Jude almost shouted for joy to see a dark red scarf around the man's neck. But only a couple of inches of cloth showed; perhaps it was only a coincidence. After a quick glance around, and with foot-dragging trepidation, Jude went up to the newcomer and said, "*Pozhaluista*, please, could you tell me where the Van Dycks are located?"

The stranger turned around at the sound of the voice, and Jude was thunderstruck. "Boris Gurko," he mouthed in an astonished whisper, his lips forming the sounds in pantomime.

Gurko ignored Jude's surprise and made a show of leafing through the pages of his program in pursuit of an answer to the question. He whispered through his teeth: "Meet me at the bus stop across the street in twenty minutes." Then he stopped turning the pages and said in a strong voice, "Van Dyck is in the next hall with the Flemish painters." He pointed the direction, then turned away and ignored Jude in favor of the artwork. Jude went to the next hall and spent several minutes studying the Flemish masters, just in case the conversation had been overheard. He then sauntered out of the museum in a roundabout way and headed for the bus stop, his head still buzzing with questions about the surprise appearance of Gurko, the comedic crew member from the *Novi Mir*.

Gurko was standing on the edge of a small knot of people waiting for the next bus. Jude casually sidled up to him but was pointedly ignored. Suddenly, Gurko dropped the newspaper he was carrying, and simultaneously he and Jude stooped for it. When both were reaching for the paper, Gurko whispered, "Follow me, but not too close." The two straightened and Jude handed the newspaper back to him. *"Spasibo,"* Gurko said, nodding his thanks, then drifted away.

When they boarded the bus, Gurko sat in front and Jude took a seat near the middle. A woman sat next to him, then sniffed the air, gave him a dirty look and decided to stand. After a forty-five minute stop-and-start ride to the northeast part of the city, Gurko stood up well in advance of the next stop to alert Jude, who got off several passengers behind.

Gurko walked for about a dozen blocks, stopping here and there to stare into shop windows, acting like a man in no hurry. Jude followed at a distance of a block, wondering impatiently where it was going to end.

Finally, Gurko disappeared into a narrow alley. Jude slowed as he reached the entrance, then with a quick glance around, ducked into it also. The alley was empty, but a small door creaked open and Jude heard a voice whisper, "This way. Quick."

Jude ducked inside to find himself in a small dark room about eight feet square. It contained only a small, rough plank table, a couple of shelves on which stood a few chipped dishes and boxes of food, and a narrow single bed with dirty blankets wadded on top. A small grimy light bulb burned at the end of a wire hanging from the low ceiling.

With a wide smile Gurko extended his hand and squeezed Jude's firmly. "Glad to see you again."

"I had about given up hope back at the museum," Jude said. "*Bog*, damn, was I surprised to see you."

"Sorry about being late," Gurko said. "I had to make sure we weren't followed. One of our key men—the one who contacted you—was taken by the KGB today. So I didn't know what to expect."

"You mean you kept the rendezvous even after it might have been compromised?" Jude shook his head. "Well, my thanks to you, but you took a hell of a chance."

Gurko shrugged. "I sometimes do stupid things, but we couldn't leave you drifting in Moscow with no identification and the police looking for you. And, I confess, I couldn't resist seeing the look on your face when you recognized me."

Jude laughed. "I almost said to myself, 'Jude, you've gone too far this time. This is one trick too many.' How in hell did you get here from the *Novi Mir*? For that matter, what were you doing on the ship?"

"I'm one of the Ukrainian guerrillas you were told about. When the CIA decided to plant you in a fishing boat, they just timed it with the arrival of my ship in Alaska. Just a matter of schedule juggling."

"Then you knew that the dancer in that nightclub was an agent."

Gurko nodded. "Don't you remember who suggested that particular club?"

"And it was you who threw Florinsky down the hold to save me. I thought it might be Kruglov."

"Why do you think I was always around Kruglov? He *looked* the part: big and handsome, very imposing. That's all he was, a good-looking fellow without a brain in his head, but I seemed inconspicuous in his shadow," Gurko said.

Jude's lips grew tight. "Why did you also kill the woman?"

"Because she was with me when I heard you and Florinsky fighting in his cabin. You're not bothered by that, are you?"

"I wondered why it was necessary for her to die. She was an innocent bystander."

Gurko looked at him strangely. "She was a bystander, yes, but anyone who has information—even accidental—that might put me before a firing squad isn't innocent. Hey, my friend, one misstep in this business, and you become a trophy on some KGB wall. When it's my ass on the line, the trigger finger gets itchy." He laughed to divert the conversation. "I never thought I'd meet a CIA sentimentalist."

Jude shrugged with embarrassment. "Forget it." He, too, wanted to change the subject. "Things don't look good, do they?"

"In this business, they never do," Gurko said. "But the present situation does seem especially uncomfortable. We've got to make a few adjustments in the face of some unpleasant facts." Gurko spread his fingers and touched them one by one with his thumb. "One, the KGB undoubtedly knows a foreign agent—you—is in the country; two, they've captured one of our top men, who knows we've got Khrushchev."

"And three?" Jude asked.

"We don't need a three, they can screw us with those two."

Jude sat on a creaking, dust-covered chair. "My problem is having no identification. I either have to have new papers or be taken in."

"Taken in?" Gurko asked.

"Take refuge in the American embassy. They'd have to send a car with diplomatic personnel out to sneak me in, but once I was inside, the Russians couldn't touch me. I'd just have to stay there, playing pool and getting fat, until they arranged a trade."

"A trade?" This was all foreign to Gurko.

"Yeah, one of theirs for me. We let one go, they let me go."

Gurko furrowed his brow. "But if you get taken in, as you put it, that means we wouldn't get Khrushchev out of the country. We'd be beaten."

"Look, the mission has been badly compromised. The KGB knows about me, perhaps even my name, and they'll probably find out about Khrushchev from the man they captured. What chance do we have?"

"A better chance than if we quit," Gurko said.

"Look, I'm just reviewing alternatives," Jude said, trying to conceal his irritation with the unrealistic stubbornness of amateurs. "Washington calls the shots, anyway."

Gurko nodded. "I'll send a message today."

"Another thing, you've got to move that old man, fast."

"We're working on that, too. One of our men knows of some people who might take him for safekeeping." Gurko's voice trailed off and he pounded his fist softly on the table as the dust rose in a small puff. "They've *got* to help us." He paused to force the anxiety out of his voice, then turned to Jude. "You'll be safe here until we get things decided. I'll be back. Any questions."

"Just one," Jude said, and laughed. "I haven't seen you pick your nose yet."

Gurko shook his head with embarrassment. "What a disgusting habit, but it served its purpose. Have you ever seen a man who picked his nose that you took seriously? It's an easy way to play the buffoon." He walked to the door and opened it, then turned back to Jude. "Be careful." He shoved his finger in his nose theatrically, laughed and was gone.

Jude watched Gurko disappear and thought, I'll be safe as long as you're free. *You* be careful.

THE CLOCK ON THE POLISHED OAK MANTEL was a French-made Heure Lavigne, and it cost the American taxpayers more than eleven thousand dollars. It was set in a gleaming pink marble case, and the Roman numerals on its face were eighteen-karat gold. Its chimes sounded like miniature bells perfectly cast. It was an instrument that Herbert Armstead had chosen as worthy of his importance. Now he sat in his office and listened to the chimes while an assistant patiently waited in a nearby armchair.

"So, it seems Mr. Jude Miller has gotten himself in something of a bind," Armstead said.

The assistant, not knowing if an answer was expected, said, "Yes, sir. We'd better pull him, and fast."

Armstead formed a steeple with his fingers and gave a calculating look toward the man. "So you think we should turn tail and run, just pack it in?"

The assistant sensed the need to equivocate. "Well, possibly alter our strategy, sir. After all, the Russians seem to have thoroughly infiltrated the Ukrainians. There's no security there. The next thing we can expect is for Miller to be grabbed. All the danger signs are there."

Armstead looked at the man with contempt. Gutless bureaucrat; doesn't care for anything except covering his own ass; doesn't realize the stakes involved; doesn't know that a Khrushchev defection could be a psychological blow that would cripple the Russians in the eyes of the world. Armstead hated the assistant. He was a man of about thirty-five, a product of the best schools, with all the advantages, except the man had no vision, no commitment. Would it be into such hands that his duties as director would be passed when... when...

"You don't seem to comprehend the importance of this mission. I'm going to keep it going, keep the ball in the air, as I believe it's fashionable to say among midlevel bureaucrats. The importance of this far outweighs Jude Miller, you, or even me." He slammed an open palm on the mahogany top. "I want you to get alternative identification in Miller's hands. Fast. And keep me posted."

The assistant's eyes flashed for an instant but quickly hooded over in obsequiousness. "Yes, sir." He quickly got up and left the room.

Armstead swiveled his chair around to face the ticking clock. The melodious chimes sounded like muffled bells tolling. He studied its face and tried once again to understand the meaning of time.

BASIL'S EYES FLUTTERED with drowsiness under the hot Mexican sun that streamed through the open kitchen window. In the three years since the stroke had wrapped its coils around his life, he had done nothing but sit in the sun and remember. His body, once strong and deadly, had become a disgusting, shriveled foreign object that he sat around and watched slowly dying. The only thing alive in his locust's shell of a body were images of a young Ukrainian firebrand who knew all the songs and all the girls, who loved the wind off the broad steppes and hated the shifty-eyed Communist bureaucrats who came with the shackles of their narrow laws to tie up the lives of the people. Friends and old loyalties glimmered in his reminiscences like rhinestones in the dust. After all, he remembered danger and death shared. Basil's memories were sweet, but poor change for the coin of his ruined life.

The scuffling of feet on the tile floor chased the pictures from his mind as Inez Gonzales and her son came in and sat down at the kitchen table. Inez was the housekeeper-mistress of his patron, Giorgi Harbuziak, a man from the old days who took care of Basil like a protective quail hen, and who was loved fiercely in return. He went by the name of Antonio Bustamonte in Mexico, but Basil hated the name, just as he hated everything in this country because it wasn't the Ukraine.

Harbuziak was a leader of the Ukrainian Freedom Movement, but Basil knew he wasn't suited to the task. Harbuziak was too trusting, too easily distracted from the determination of his Kremlin enemies to rid the earth—in whatever corner they had to reach—of the threat of Ukrainian nationalism. Harbuziak was a songbird ignoring the circling hawks, and this middle-aged Mexican woman, with her black hair tied in a matronly bun and her peasant ways, had the sharpest talons of all.

Inez was a revolutionary. She was not some idealistic student who finds truth in the pages of a book, somewhere between Marx and Dostoyevski, and then, consumed with outrage against overgenerous middle-class parents who don't understand, takes to the streets with placard in hand, hurling slogans like tiny barbless arrows that fall harmlessly to the ground off the thickness of a bemused public. Inez's revolt smoldered in dark-eyed fury at the injustices of thirty years of dirt, disease and futureless days. Slogans were not her tools; she commanded few words. Placards were useless; no one would read them. Her weapons were patience and hatred. She would not forget and she would not stop. And she had a secret: she had learned that life is cheap.

Inez poured a cup of coffee for her son, Esteban, and smiled at him fondly and possessively. Esteban was her revenge. For her father shot down like a rabbit by the *federales* while organizing starving Indian laborers, for her grandfather, killed by soldiers of the gringo Pershing fighting alongside Pancho Villa—Esteban would balance the shed blood. For the life of squalid poverty she had been forced to endure, Esteban would choke vengeance out of the fat necks of the capitalists. Esteban, though everyone dismissed him as a witless braggart and lazy, unteachable student, was a leader of the Communist youth movement at the university in Mexico City. He was skinny and pimply, and dressed like an ill-bred pimp with cheap imitation-gold necklaces and green high-heeled shoes. Inez didn't even know which field hand of her youth was his father, but all she saw was a knight riding to avenge the wrongs of her life.

It was to Esteban that Inez passed all the information she wheedled out of Harbuziak in bedroom whispers or eavesdropped on while he incautiously talked on the telephone as she cleaned house around him wearing her ignorant-peasant look. Thanks to her sharp ears, Moscow had learned that an American agent was en route. And, as she often grumbled to herself, if those two *cabrónes* she sent to kill him had had enough *cojones* to finish the job, that same agent never would have left Mexico alive.

Esteban blew softly on the hot coffee. "*Madre*, they want more information about the American agent."

Inez shrugged. "I told what I know, what I heard, son. Do they want me to make something up, *hijo*?"

Esteban glanced sideways at the paralyzed man strapped into the wheelchair across the room like a carelessly dropped sack. "The *viejo* makes me nervous."

Inez waved her hand in dismissal. "I've told you before, you don't have to worry about old Basil. His mind is gone. He can't talk. He can barely move. How could such a man hurt us?"

"I just don't like him being there. Cripples are bad luck. Anyway, *Mamá*, they told me to ask you for anything else you might have heard, even if it doesn't seem important."

Inez knitted her brow in concentration. "Nothing. I've heard Antonio mention the name Khrushchev several times, but it was nothing."

"Who is this Khrushchev?"

She waved her hand impatiently. "You're the student. He's always talking about some old Russian. If it had to do with anything, I'd tell you. Don't waste your time on *caca*."

"Anything else, anything at all?" Esteban did not want to go back to Mexico City with no information to show for the trip. "I better leave before your foreigner boyfriend returns.

For some reason, Moscow considers this pretty important."
He said the name of the city as though he could pick up the
phone and call it. "If you think of anything else, get word to
me."

"*Chico*, don't play the big shot with me," she scolded
gently. "I changed your diapers and wiped your runny nose."
Inez escorted her son to the door and kissed him goodbye,
then returned to the kitchen. She picked up the breakfast
dishes and stacked them on the counter. Inez brushed past
the crippled man sitting next to the sink as though he were
part of the furniture. "*Idiota*," she said absently, "what
would you think of all this if your brain worked? Here is this
Mexican peon woman who everyone thinks is just another
barnyard animal to use as they see fit, and she's tricking your
beloved Bustamonte to get information that will destroy what
he believes in."

At such moments Basil prayed for death to release him from
the humiliation of helplessness, from the pain of seeing a man
he loved put in danger by the sneakiness of this woman. Basil
was a soldier in his mind, if no longer in his body. And to a
soldier two things are important above all: loyalty to comrades and destroying enemies. Basil was incapable of both,
and his impotence was like nails driven into his soul.

Inez reached into a cupboard for the soap and began running dishwater. She turned on a small radio on a ledge next
to the sink and started to hum softly as a popular tune joined
in with a tinny clatter.

Basil sat and waited for the day to pass, waiting for her to
put him to bed with a tirade of insults that he dreaded more
than a beating. Little did she know that the gnarled, drooling wretch she belittled used to be a lion, a lion whose roar
reached from the Baltic to the Crimea. Being a cripple was a
burden that ached like Atlas's shoulders, but the worst was
getting no respect for having ever been anything else, for being
treated as if he had always been an invalid, a worthless pile of

guts and gristle and fat and vacant eyes and dead tongue, dia-
pered like a baby and scolded like a brat.

As Basil sat and wrung what comfort he could from his
melancholia, something came alive in his mind, just a glim-
mer of an idea, but he still recognized the signs and seized
upon the idea like a hungry wolf with a scent. He watched her
at the sink washing dishes . . . the water . . . the radio.

His eyes glittered—the idea just might work!

Basil was no longer a man-baby, he was once more a human to be feared, a man capable of working his will. He
shifted his left hand awkwardly to the toggle switch that controlled his wheelchair. The battery gave a low whine and he
moved to the edge of the sink.

"What do you want, *tonto*?" Inez demanded crossly.
"Leave me alone while I work."

Basil knew he would have only one chance. If he failed she
would kill him, perhaps suffocate him with a pillow while he
lay helpless, as she often threatened to do. He concentrated
with all his might on moving his left arm. It was like lifting a
heavy iron bar with his fingers. The arm lifted slowly, but it
wavered in the air. His atrophied muscles strained and jerked
with awkward spastic movements. Finally, with an effort that
almost toppled him from the wheelchair, the arm came to rest
on the shelf next to the radio. All Basil had to do now was give
the radio a small shove. But the timing had to be perfect,
anything less would accomplish nothing.

Inez's thoughts were on finding a suitable wife for Esteban, as she scrubbed the dishes clean and hummed along absently with the radio. As the water became tepid, she reached
for the steel faucet handle and turned it sharply, holding it
down as hot water flowed into the sink.

Basil knew it had to be now. Gathering all his energy, he
gritted his teeth and pushed his arm forward against the radio, shoving it into the dishwater with a splash. Basil's mo-

mentum threw him out of the wheelchair, tipping it over with a wheel-spinning crash.

Inez heard the splash and the clatter, but it was too late. The two hundred milliamperes of electricity released by the radio into the water immediately sought the nearest ground, the metal water pipes. It was Inez's misfortune that water is a poor conductor of electricity and salt is a good one. The current instantly rejected the water for the blood in Inez's body with its high saline content. It surged through the water and up Inez's arm and through her body en route to the metal faucet it was seeking.

Inez's heart was hit by a stunning shock and immediately went into fibrillation, making rapid, irregular contractions of muscle fibers that permitted no blood to flow through it. The shock also hit her larger muscles, which, operating on their own electrical impulses from the brain, seized up and fastened her grip to the deadly faucet as though with glue.

Inez's frozen body refused to push oxygen from the lungs to the brain, so she was literally drowning in electricity. Her rigid body was serving as a live wire connecting the current from the radio to the metal ground.

For almost four minutes she was held fast by the electricity. Her eyes bulged and her tongue thrust out, but the merciless current refused to release her. Finally, she died; her muscles relaxed and she slowly slid down the edge of the sink and collapsed on top of Basil.

The death smell of her was strong in Basil's nostrils as he lay awkwardly beneath her body. He knew he wouldn't be freed for several hours, until Antonio returned, but there was no sadness in him, because he knew he could still do a man's work.

IVAN KOLCHAK LEANED against one of the Bolshoi Theater's columns and watched people mingle during the intermission of *Prince Igor*. Even on a rare night at the ballet, he was still the policeman, always watching, as though a suspect might show up between acts. Kolchak knew he should just try to relax and forget his work, but it wasn't easy to suspend the kind of intensity that drove him, even at the theater.

Just as he pushed away from the column and started back to his seat, he felt a jarring in his back and was almost knocked off balance. He automatically went into a defensive posture and whirled to see what had hit him.

He came face-to-face with a woman struggling to maintain her balance. He instinctively reached out and she grabbed his arm, then pulled close to stabilize herself, leaving her face inches from his. Her eyes were brown with green flecks, and her black hair formed a wreath around her valentine-shaped face. Her perfume gave off the hint of honeysuckle and reminded him of a summer day. She was in her early thirties, with the strong, full Slavic figure that Russian men are conditioned to believe is suited for good sex and heavy work.

Her eyes were wide with shock at the collision, but the look turned to dismay as she started to brush the back of Kolchak's suit jacket. "Oh, I spilled my drink on your beautiful coat. I hope it isn't ruined."

Kolchak felt the cola seeping through to his skin and took the coat off in irritation to inspect the wide stain.

"I am so, so sorry." The woman's voice cracked, and he could see tears forming in the brown eyes.

"Forget it," he grumbled.

"No, no. The least I can do is pay for the cleaning."

Kolchak wavered. Why shouldn't she pay?

The woman was fumbling in her purse when the lights blinked to signal the next act and people started streaming back to their seats. "Oh, I don't want to make you miss the ballet, too," she said. Her eyes brightened, and she smiled with a flash of even white teeth. "I have an idea. Let's meet right here after the performance and I'll pay you for the coat and buy you a cup of coffee, as well."

"That's not necessary."

"Oh, but it is," she insisted. "Please, if I want to do penance for my clumsiness, don't try to stop me."

Kolchak permitted a guarded smile. She was pretty. "Very well."

After the final curtain, Kolchak waited in the lobby until the woman appeared, walking with a pronounced limp.

He wasn't sure if she had hurt herself in the collision or if she had a handicap that he hadn't noticed earlier, so he said nothing.

"Do you know what happened?" she asked rhetorically. "I broke the heel on my shoe when I ran into you. *Bog*, that bump is becoming a major calamity. Oh well, shall we go? There's a small place nearby. Do you mind if I hold on to your arm? Otherwise I might capsize like a two-wheeled wagon. By the way, my name is Svetlana Martinova. What's yours?"

With the woman clinging firmly to his arm, so close that her warmth touched him and caused a quiver of excitement, Kolchak led the way to the small café.

Inside, they sat at a small table while the woman inspected her shoe. Shaking her head, she sighed and said, "Maybe I can fix it. Shoes are *so* expensive. But that'll teach me to watch where I'm going."

They talked about the ballet, about the Russian winter, about all the unimportant things a man and woman discuss as they seek to know whether they want to remain strangers, become friends, or perhaps lovers. Svetlana told him she was a clerk for the state agricultural production board, that her home was originally in Kursk, and that she was widowed a year ago when her husband fell while working on a Lena River dam in Siberia.

Kolchak told her he was on the verge of a divorce and had two children, and that he was a policeman—an ordinary detective assigned to routine and boring cases.

Her mouth opened into an O of feigned fright. "Oh, can I be arrested for bumping a policeman?"

"It's not a crime—yet." Kolchak allowed a slight smile.

They ordered more coffee and didn't notice it grow cold as they chatted. The words meant little, but the message exchanged by the eyes and the smiles told them there were more important things than words.

Kolchak drove her home to an old apartment house, where she said she had a small room. Knowing the way single clerical workers with little income and no influence could be expected to live in Moscow, Kolchak envisioned a room about ten feet by fifteen, equipped with a pull-down bed and a cheap hot plate in a corner, a wooden chair or two, perhaps a small black and white television, and a single rod for her few clothes. He realized she probably saved a little here and there for weeks to afford her ballet ticket. He felt sorry for her; he felt angry on behalf of all Russians who worked so hard and had so little.

The squeal of the car brakes broke off their conversation as he pulled up in front of the gloomy old building she had directed him to. She grabbed his suit coat and opened the car door.

"Where are you taking my coat?" he asked in surprise.

"I'm going to clean it so when you come for dinner Wednesday night it'll be good as new."

He laughed. "Well, I have to go where my coat goes. I'll come on one condition." He paused and she gazed at him expectantly. "I'll come if I can bring the food and wine."

She started to protest slightly, but he put the car into gear and called out, "About eight o'clock."

Kolchak gunned the car down the street with a wide smile that gradually faded as he neared his own home and the waiting Xenia.

CHAPTER FOURTEEN

THE TWO HUNDRED THOUSAND JEWS of Moscow walk through life leaning into strong winds. Although the constitution of the Soviet Union guarantees freedom of religion, such a reassurance is good only for gallows humor. Like their two million coreligionists throughout the country, the best that Moscow Jews can hope for is living day-to-day without government harassment.

The Communist government does not like religion, and it claims to abhor all faiths equally, but somehow it manages to dislike Jews more efficiently. Possibly, it's historical habit. Perhaps Cossacks who learned to savor terror by reading it on the faces of Jewish children during centuries of pogroms somehow programmed the taste into the national psyche. Maybe Jews were simply not meant to live in Russia, a question many Jews ponder as intently as the Talmud.

The old Jews guard the faith. Whether from looking backward at centuries of tradition or forward to the approach of death, the old men are the ones who march on their brittle legs past the scowling militiamen each Sabbath, past the white pillars of Moscow's solitary synagogue and into the sanctuary for prayer. The old women are the ones who wait patiently in the synagogue yard each week for the kosher butcher to deliver his meat.

Young Jews tend to do what youth usually does—scoff. Most are too preoccupied with tomorrow to worry about the eternal. They joke about the bearded old men and point out derisively that the appointment of the rabbi must be state-approved and that he also serves on the government's anti-

Zionism committee, which is rather like a condemned man tying hangman's knots. They have no pity for the compromises of their fathers. They chafe at the barriers thrown in the paths of all Jews, practicing or not. They blame God, the Russians and luck. They sometimes curse the day they were born to be Jews.

Persecution, no matter what form it takes, is vastly underrated: it usually works because most people don't have the strength to withstand it. Accordingly, the Jews of Moscow often seem a weak, dispirited lot. But history has been confronted by this belief before and has shown a lingering patience with the Jews. No matter how the tapestry of their faith is frayed and dirtied, a few strong threads hold fast.

There will always be enough Jews to exasperate their enemies. To quote God, they are a stiff-necked people.

THE CLATTER OF DISHES and the chatter of young people made a din like payday in a barracks. David Rabinowitz leaned over the small table in the student canteen at Moscow State University and quickly glanced over both shoulders. As if on cue, his tablemates, Abraham Aleichem, Yakov Zamir and Ludmila Brassova, leaned forward to meet him.

The four were members of the Sicarii; in fact, they were the only members. In appearance, they were unexceptional: early twenties, sloppily dressed in their best Western imitation blue jeans and baggy sweaters, seemingly caring only for parties, rock music and exams. Ludmila was studying to become a physician; Yakov was unemployed because he stubbornly refused to shave the beard that in employment lines made him stand out like—well, like a Jew in an employment line. David was almost finished with chemical engineering. Abraham was an apprentice pressman in a state-run publishing house. When among academic people he self-consciously kept his hands closed to conceal ink-stained fingernails.

Except for David, none was from a strong religious background. But each, if asked, would have said quickly and defiantly that he was a Jew. They regarded the ancient precepts of Judaism as primitive nonsense and tribal folklore, but they were willing to risk their lives defending the rights of their people.

Their enemies—and possibly their friends—would call these four fanatics. In their view, Jews were in Russia only by historical happenstance. Even after hundreds of years, their people were merely passing through. Russia was only a modern-day Rome, to be tolerated for a time and then rebelled against. Israel, which they had never seen, was home, the sought-after dream.

They were not discouraged by being only four. As David, their leader, told them, all great movements begin as tiny cells in which a handful of dedicated individuals set the course that great numbers later follow. Besides, until they knew better what they were doing—and they had no delusions about their amateur skills as terrorists—they would be safer by themselves. They tried to stay out of the sight of authorities by avoiding dissident groups and public demonstrations against Soviet Jewish policies. Carrying signs in Red Square, they knew, would put them in KGB files, if not jail.

They strove to grow as political terrorists. They established a liaison with the Defenders of Zion in the United States through friendly intermediaries in the Soviet Union, and that contact, plus David's friendship with Nicholas Mikhailovitch of the Ukrainian Freedom Movement, gave them the support they needed.

David's face broke into a secretive little smile. "Good things are going to happen," he said, "I can feel it."

"There's got to be a reason for your smiling like a weasel walking out of a henhouse," Abraham said.

David squeezed Abraham's shoulder to show his pleasure. "A man I know, a friend of our struggle, has put me in touch with a fellow who deserted the army instead of being shipped back to Afghanistan. And listen to this: Do you know what this soldier took with him?'' His eyes shifted from one perplexed listener to another. He didn't expect a guess, but wanted the suspense to build. ''He stole an antitank rocket.'' Seeing no change in their expressions, David said, ''Don't you know what that means? We can blow the hell out of whatever we want and be long gone before the KGB's ears stop ringing.''

Ludmila broke the silence. ''From the look on your face, I can guess you already have a use for it.''

David grinned conspiratorially. ''When I tell you what we're going to blow up with that baby, you'll faint. We're going to hit the damned Russians like a big rock in the head. We're going to get their attention.'' He nodded assent to his own thoughts. ''Oh, yes, we're definitely going to get their attention.''

The others exchanged glances. ''So what's the plan?'' Abraham asked.

David shook his head. ''*Nyet.* For everyone's protection, the target must be kept secret until the last minute.'' He squared his shoulders proudly. ''But trust me, when you find out, you'd be willing to buy a ticket to watch.''

Ludmila frowned doubtfully, then looked at her watch and started to pick up a stack of books at her elbow. ''I have a class in ten minutes.''

David put a restraining hand on her arm. ''One more thing. The Ukrainians want us to take some hot property off their hands, a *very* important person they're hiding from the KGB.''

''The KGB must be getting closer or the Ukrainians wouldn't be trying to unload someone on us,'' Yakov said.

''Correct,'' David said, ''but don't forget, the Ukrainian Freedom Movement has been around a long time, long enough for the secret police to infiltrate it pretty well. We're the great unknowns to the KGB.''

"So far," said Yakov.

"Who is this person?" Ludmila asked.

David wagged his finger playfully at her. "Remember the rules. You'll know when you need to."

Abraham interrupted. "What's in it for us if we take him— or her? Will it help us get more Jews out of the country?"

David shrugged. "Who knows? When you have something of value, you never know what it can be traded for. But here's something to think of: if we take this person off their hands, it'll make the CIA aware of us. We'll have identity as a legitimate insurgency force, and with identity comes money, weapons and expert advice, all the things we need."

Yakov shook his head doubtfully. "I don't know, David. When we're talking about the CIA and those folks, we're talking about really slick operators. Are we ready for that?"

David gave a snort. "When they find out what I'm demanding in return, they'll know we mean business." David glanced at his watch and looked at each of his followers. "Anything else?"

Yakov said, "I was able to buy an English version of the latest Le Carré spy novel at Dom Knigi (House of Books) on Kalinin Prospekt."

"Good," David said. "He's got some terrific ideas. Pass it around when you finish." He started to rise. "See you all at my house Thursday night."

HERBERT ARMSTEAD SLAMMED his fist on the desk, making the expensive china ashtray jump precariously toward the edge. "Who in hell do these crazy Moscow Jews—" he looked down at the paper in his hand "—these Sicarii, think they're dealing with? The answer is no. Absolutely not! There will be no killings. Saud Habib is an untouchable."

His assistant sat quietly in the side chair and let his boss's wrath wind down. "Well, sir, let's look at it from their viewpoint. Whether Khrushchev lives or dies is of no consequence to them. They want a quid pro quo, a tit for tat. The Ukrainians approached them to take Khrushchev off their hands because the KGB is closing in. What's in it for the Jews? They have their own program, to pressure the Russians to allow emigration to Israel. Whether we grant their demand or not, we have to recognize it as legitimate from their viewpoint."

Armstead glared at the man. "Don't lecture me. I know perfectly well what their rationale is. But I'll be damned if I'll permit the assassination of a man who has trusted this government for his safety. I don't care what the stakes are, Habib has our promise of protection. We gave our word."

The assistant started to leave. "I'll let them know your decision, sir."

"Wait a minute," Armstead said. "Don't presume you can read my mind. Are you sure they won't settle for anything else?"

"We tried, sir. They specifically said they wouldn't hide Khrushchev until the Defenders of Zion signal them that Habib is dead."

Armstead snorted. "So the Defenders are advising them, eh? Just like them to suggest something crazy like this." He grew thoughtful. "These Sicarii sound like very tough-minded people," he said. "See what you can find out about them. Anyone who can make the CIA sweat should be on our side."

"We have to give them a response, Mr. Armstead. You've got to decide."

Armstead waited until he was alone, then closed his eyes to think. He longed for the days of his youth when decisions were either right or wrong, when morality was as easily interpreted as a vacation postcard. But now, in his old age, when the supports that held his life together had grown brittle and weak, he had to decide between the welfare of his country and his own conscience. Should he stand by the promises of sanctuary to the man the Jews wanted assassinated, or should he preserve the life of the ex-premier of an enemy nation?

Armstead grew tired of the dilemma, and the disease that was daily growing stronger, by sucking the power from his brain, drove the thoughts from his mind. He stared straight ahead, aware only of the ticking of the clock. Later, he would pull himself together and deal with the question, but first he needed to rest, to drift for a while on billowy clouds of nothingness.

SVETLANA REACHED ACROSS THE PILLOW and straightened a lock of Kolchak's sandy brown hair that had become plastered to his forehead by sweat during their lovemaking. "You have pretty hair," she said.

Kolchak reached for her hand and kissed the palm. "I would like to stay here next to you for a whole week," he said. He pulled her down on top of him, watched the softness of her breasts spread out on his chest and ran his hand down the outside of her soft thighs. "Make that a month," he said.

"I'm afraid my boss wouldn't be very understanding of that," she said. "Would you settle for the night?"

"Darling, I would like nothing more. Unfortunately, I have to be getting back to the office." He gently lifted her aside and reached for his clothes, which were in a pile at the side of the bed.

"Oh, Ivan," she said, forming the words with a pout on her lips, "surely there are enough policemen in Moscow to handle the criminals tonight. Please stay here. I'll fix something nice."

When he first met Svetlana at the ballet and their lobby collision led to her room for dinner and then bed, Kolchak had been determined to pass himself off as an ordinary policeman, but his pride and the desire to impress this woman he very quickly was growing attached to led him to drop broad hints that he was more than just an ordinary policeman. When he considered that the two of them had been together only a week, he was amazed, and a little intimidated, at how quickly they had grown close. It was almost as though she had been waiting for him to come into her life. If the stale years with Xenia were as dull and cold as a Siberia winter, as he often thought, one week with Svetlana had been like a holiday in a sunny Black Sea dacha.

He watched the outline of Svetlana's hips and buttocks beneath her robe as she moved to the tiny kitchen alcove to prepare coffee. He felt himself growing erect again and debated whether to take her back to bed or continue getting dressed. One glance at his watch pushed him to the latter, and he reached reluctantly for a shoe. As he spread the laces, he wondered why he had never met anyone like Svetlana before. Had he been too busy to look around? Was he too preoccupied with work, to the detriment of his own happiness? Or was there simply no one else like Svetlana? He dismissed the thought; no point in worrying about yesterday. The important thing was that she was here for him to have at this moment in his life.

"Police work must be *so* fascinating," she called across the room. "Are you a specialist in anything, like safecracking or murder?"

He laughed. "You make it sound like I'm the criminal. But no, nothing like that. I operate on a higher level."

"Oh? That sounds so mysterious. You must tell me the lurid details some dark and rainy night, then I'll get scared and jump right into your arms. Do you want one or two lumps?"

Svetlana brought two cups of coffee over and sat beside him on the bed. She crossed her legs and handed him a cup and nuzzled his neck at the same time. "You're a wonderful lover, Ivan. Did anyone ever tell you that?"

"You just did," he answered with slight embarrassment. He wasn't used to such blunt talk about sex, but he had to remember, she *was* a widow. His eyes kept straying to her legs, which had become uncovered when the robe slipped away.

She glanced down at the lump in his lap and grinned. "What's this?" she said and reached over to gently knead his erection. "Can I have it?"

He looked hurriedly at his watch. "I've got five minutes," he said, while pushing her back gently against the pillows, then reached to undo his pants. "This'll have to be quick, but we'll make up for it tomorrow." She giggled and spread for him to enter her. She didn't let her own passion rise, knowing there was no time for her slower-paced climax to arrive. Instead, she helped him, and in minutes his desire exploded into a shuddering gasp and he collapsed on top of her. He rolled over. "I'm sorry. I hope you don't think that was selfish. Tomorrow, we'll have more time."

She hugged him fondly. "You gave me more than any woman could hope for earlier. I'm glad to make you happy."

Kolchak hurriedly sipped his coffee and finished dressing. She watched with open affection from a chair across the room.

"Do you know what I dream about?" she asked. "I like to imagine taking care of you, cooking your meals, washing your clothes, listening to you sleep next to me at night without knowing you're going to leave and go home in the small hours, just when I most need your closeness." She gave a short, embarrassed laugh. "I'm sorry for being so silly. We've known each other such a very short time, but sometimes when I think of how you suffer when that—when that *woman*—mistreats you so badly. . ."

He put his topcoat over one arm, walked over to Svetlana and reached down and caressed her cheek. "I feel the same way, *lubimets*." He hesitated as though uncertain whether to speak. "I've known something had to be done about Xenia for a long time. I think maybe that time is now here."

She put her hand over his and squeezed in alarm. "Ivan, not on account of me!"

"No, *vozliublenyin*, sweetheart, it's something that had to happen sooner or later, anyway."

IBN SAUD HABIB SAT DOWN heavily on a large granite rock and held his heaving chest, hoping he could squeeze the pain out of his laboring lungs. His legs trembled with fatigue and, despite the cold wind of early spring, sweat poured off his head and carried stinging salt into his eyes. Habib removed the unfamiliar burden of the day pack and wiggled his toes, which were too tightly encased in the heavy hiking boots. He gazed forlornly at the rocky path that seemed to slant straight upward into the dense pine trees. He had been on the trail a little more than an hour, and had already learned that gravity meant business, that every step that took him higher came at the expense of pain in his legs that felt like hot needles, like acupuncture from a sewing machine.

"No pain, no gain, they say," a voice said laughingly behind him.

Habib turned and glared at his companion. "I was a fool to let you talk me into this."

The other man smiled slightly in sympathy. "Hiking isn't easy for anyone at first, but you'll get used to it." He stood in the middle of the trail like one of the towering trees that surrounded them, breathing easily and barely sweating, as though to mock Habib's laborings. The backpack—twice the size of Habib's—seemed to rest lightly on his shoulders.

The man Habib knew only as Tom was one of three bodyguards provided by the CIA. Although Habib was probably twenty years older than Tom, he felt almost a child's dependency on the man whose professional reason for living was to keep Habib alive. Habib was grateful for the protection but hated the dependency. I'm like a helpless child, he often thought with disgust, just as we Arabs were for so many years with the Europeans. These men hold my life in their hands like children with a toy. Looking down past his silver-flecked black beard, he examined his paunchy little body and then compared it with the toned, hard bulk of the young guardian hovering above him. Why doesn't he sit? Habib wondered crossly. Is he just trying to mock my weakness? Despite his anger at the sensed condescension, Habib felt a certain pride at being protected by such a man.

"It's only about another hour and a half to the top," Tom coaxed.

"I'm thinking right now of all those people who said I needed more exercise," Habib said. "I don't see a damned one of them right here on this little shelf of a trail hanging in the sky about a sneeze from eternity." Habib shuddered as he looked down over the edge of the trail into the valley about eight hundred feet below. "Look at those cars on that road! They're like insects." Habib abruptly started back down the trail, happy to suddenly be on the side of gravity.

Tom let him walk a few feet, then said, "I never thought Arabs were quitters."

Habib turned around with a look of disgust. "Climbing some crazy mountain is not the same as shooting a Jew. That, at least, is a service to mankind. This is ridiculous!" He looked around again and threw up his arms in disgust.

Ibn Saud Habib was fully aware that the man to whom he spoke was a member of the CIA and an ally of Israel, but he didn't care. The CIA had agreed to give him protection for life so he felt free to speak his mind.

Until two years ago, Habib had been one of the most feared terrorist leaders in the Mideast. As leader of the action front of the Palestinian Liberation Organization, he was in charge of implementing terrorist plots against the state and people of Israel. It was he who instructed idealistic young Palestinians and sent them down the roads of the Mideast that led to Israeli school buses and crowded shopping centers, where a

sudden scream of dedication to Allah followed by a hand grenade or burst from an AK-47 led to the carnage that made
grisly photo layouts in newsmagazines, accompanied by a
smiling head shot of Ibn Saud Habib proclaiming the vengeance and doctrines of the PLO.

Now, because he had lost an internal power struggle in the
PLO, he was a fugitive from both the Israeli secret service—
the Mossad—and death squads of his former compatriots in
the PLO. He became caught in a no-man's land; he stood naked between two enemies. With the possibility of prompt and
painful demise awaiting him around every corner, behind
every knock on the door, with every glance from a stranger,
Habib had no choice but to seek the safety of an intelligence
service that would exchange protection for the vast knowledge in his possession. That need took him to the CIA, who
made the bargain, but the action further inflamed his enemies, who redoubled efforts to kill him.

Habib had settled down to a quiet life of suburban opu-
lence in a forested estate not far from San Francisco, with his
family, pets and bodyguards. It wasn't as interesting as plotting a car bomb explosion, but it was comfortable and safe, a
fine retirement for a gentleman terrorist.

So why was he in this place, sweating and aching? A few
days before, his bodyguards had begun pushing him to get
more exercise. Tom had told him of this trip and urged him
to come along. For some reason, perhaps boredom, perhaps
a desire to see the country, Habib had agreed. Now, as he
rubbed his aching legs, he could only think: Why, why did I
do this?

The wind picked up and sent a chill through Habib as his
upper torso started to cool and the sweat began to turn
clammy. He shuddered and briskly rubbed his arms.

"We better keep going before we cool off. It gets damned
cold up this high when that wind bites you," Tom said.

Habib turned to his companion and whined: "Let's go back, please. I've seen enough."

"Seen enough? Mr. Habib, do you realize we're within an easy stroll of the top of Yosemite Falls, one of the most stupendous sights on earth? Why, if I stopped now, you'd never forgive me."

Habib started to protest, but Tom held up his hand for silence. "Listen," he said softly. Both men concentrated on the quiet. In a moment they heard a soft, faint rumbling, like a train approaching from around a bend. "That's the falls," Tom said, "let's go." Without giving Habib a chance to protest further, he cheerfully urged him along the trail.

Within a few minutes, Habib forgot his misery as they neared the falls. The sound gradually increased until it filled their ears like an ocean tipped on end. It became the roar of nature, drunk on the high spirits of spring.

Habib turned a corner and was hit facefirst with a howling wind and freezing spray that forced him to stumble backward in surprise. There, about a hundred yards away, was Yosemite Falls. They had come upon it about halfway to the summit, so the falling water started far above them and disappeared into the distant rocks below.

Habib stood staring with mouth wide open. "That must be all the water in the world," he gasped in astonishment.

"A reasonable portion of it, I guess." Tom chuckled. "I don't suppose they have anything like this in the Sahara?"

Habib was hypnotized by the closeness of such thunderous, wild power.

Tom put his arm around the shoulder of the smaller man and pointed to the falls. "What you see is runoff from the high country snowmelt of the Sierra Nevada. Down below, it joins the Merced River, then goes through California, and finally to the ocean."

Habib felt a surge of excitement. "Let's keep going, I want to see the top."

"Hey, what happened to the guy who wanted to quit?" Tom laughed.

They clambered up the steep trail for another hour until there was nothing more to climb, and far below the stupendous expanse of granite and greenery of Yosemite Valley spread out to the horizon. The scent of pine sap hung in the air like pungent perfume, and chipmunks nearby chattered their angry little threats. Habib felt electrified by the beauty before him. It was as though the world had turned a page and started a chapter he didn't realize had been written.

"This is wonderful, Tom. Are there other places like this?"

"Not many like this. I'm glad you think the hike was worth it."

Habib took a deep breath, letting his chest swell with pride. "I guess a lot of people couldn't make it, huh?"

They strolled along the cliff until they came to the small river that became the falls. It was only about twenty yards wide but the cold snow water ran deep and furious, tumbling over sharp granite rocks in a desperate rush to the precipice.

Habib peered in awed silence as the water disappeared over the edge with a roar. "How far down is it?"

"About a half mile."

"By Allah, if a man fell over that . . ."

Tom nodded judiciously. "He wouldn't make it a tenth of the way down alive. He'd bounce off rocks like a Ping-Pong ball. Finally, he'd end up in a pool at the bottom, and they wouldn't be able to fish out what was left of him until the water went down, about September. It happens every year." He nudged the soft soil with his foot. "This bank is water-soaked and slick as glass. Get too close, and—you're gone."

Habib gave a little shudder and moved farther away from the edge of the torrent. He glanced at Tom, who was looking around, as though searching for someone.

"What are you looking for, Tom?"

"Other people—looks like we've got the place all to ourselves. Too early for tourists." Tom gave Habib a queer look that made the Arab suddenly become quiet. "Mr. Habib, did I ever tell you that I'm a Jew?"

Habib was stunned and didn't know how to react. He gave a weak smile, hoping Tom would burst into laughter and let the nasty little joke die. "I'm glad you're with the CIA, then, and responsible for my safety."

"Un-huh," Tom said softly, then stared at Habib for long seconds.

Habib looked at Tom's face and gave a nervous giggle.

"You know, Mr. Habib, I used to hate to pick up the newspapers and read about all those children blown apart by Palestinian cowards who could only fight from ambush, twisted men who told themselves God demanded the slaughter of the helpless and innocent. Man, I used to want to get my hands on those killers."

Habib could tell by the way Tom spoke that he had planned and rehearsed his speech. He saw the black hatred creep into the man's eyes, and turned to run but stumbled on the soft ground. In a second, he felt an iron grip violently seize his arm and twist it behind his back until he screamed with pain. He suddenly knew what was about to happen and he vomited with fright. Weakly, he blubbered over his shoulder to the man who gripped him like a squirming fish, "But you promised to protect me!"

"We lied," Tom said simply. He threw Habib into the current and watched him bounce along the rapids like a fisherman's bobber until he disappeared over the lip of the falls.

For several minutes, Tom stood and looked at the spot where Habib had gone over, as though debating something with himself. Finally, he picked up his pack and headed back down the trail to civilization, where he could find a telephone and start the word on its circuitous path to Moscow that one end of the bargain had been kept.

JUDE WAS STARTLED by the brusque knock on the door. In the three days he had spent in the shack, not one human sound other than traffic and the shouts of children playing down the block had penetrated the walls. His only companions were the Greek goddesses dancing in the shadows of the oil lamp and the snare drum patterns of the early spring rain beating on the tin roof.

He jumped up from the lumpy bed and shook the dust of daydreams from his mind. He moved quickly to the door and asked in a low voice, "Who is it?"

"Gurko," came the clipped reply.

Jude swung the creaking door open and Gurko burst through, then reached back and helped a bundled-up old man waddle into the room. Without speaking to Jude, Gurko hustled the old man over to the bed, helped him remove his outer coat and left him sitting there like a bewildered Buddha. Only then did he notice Jude.

"Is that him?" Jude asked, motioning with his head toward the old man.

"That's him," Gurko said, glancing back and nodding. "Nikita Sergeyevich Khrushchev, ex-premier of all the Russias, inheritor of the czars." He turned back to Jude. "Many things are happening, my friend, most of them bad. The KGB is drilling more holes in the Ukrainian Freedom Movement than a blind dentist in a bad tooth. Everyone's on the run."

"Why?"

Gurko shrugged. "Infiltration. Leaks. They're too good, and we're not good enough. You can't go year after year with the KGB trying to destroy you and think they're not going to have some success."

"What'll happen to the fight for Ukrainian freedom?" Jude asked.

"The KGB can kill Boris Gurko—" he drew his finger across his throat "—but it can't kill what my father planted here." He tapped his heart. "The dream will go on. We'll just burrow underground and resurface another time, another place. This crazy idea of the Ukrainians didn't start yesterday, you know. We always muddle through. As we say, you don't have to teach a freezing man how to shiver.''

"More pertinent at the moment," Jude asked, "what happens to me?"

Gurko pointed to the old man. "There he is. That's what you came for."

Irritation crept into Jude's voice. "We're not aboard the *Novi Mir*, Gurko, be serious. What am I supposed to do with him?"

Gurko smiled kindly. "Relax, friend, I know you've had a long wait in this little palace, but we have it all worked out. Some friends, Jews who have their own quarrels with the Kremlin, are going to hide you until the two of you can be slipped out of the country. You're going to be contacted by one of your own people soon. Until then, I hope you like gefilte fish," he grimaced at the thought of the traditional Jewish fish cakes. "Tuesday afternoon, three days from now, you and the old man will be met in front of Detsky Mir, Children's World, on Marx Prospekt. Be standing ten feet to the right of the main entrance at two o'clock exactly. It's one of the busiest stores in Moscow, you'll blend right in."

"And if no one shows?"

Gurko shrugged. "You're supposed to be met there, that's all I can tell you." Gurko reached into his pocket. "Here are his papers and your new ones, too." He handed over the packet. "You're a schoolteacher from Smolensk by the name of Viktor Serov. You teach English, fancy that. Khrushchev is your grandfather. We gave him the name Nikita Serov—afraid he might get confused by a new first name."

"Where do I meet my *treff*?"

Gurko looked bewildered. "Who?"

Jude gave an embarrassed smile. "Sorry, trade talk. It's a German term meaning contact."

Gurko shrugged. "All I know is what I've told you. I guess they don't want to tell us Ukrainians too much. Can't say I blame them, the way things are going."

Gurko put on his coat and moved to the door. He extended his hand to Jude. "If I had a glass of vodka right now, I'd say, *na zdorov'e* to you and confusion to the KGB." Gurko held up an imaginary glass and proclaimed, "Bottoms up today, bottoms up tomorrow, and all that is left are tears and sorrow." He tipped his head and threw down the fantasy toast, then tossed the glass against the wall where the two of them watched it explode soundlessly.

"You've been damned handy to have around. Be careful," Jude said, grabbing Gurko's hand and letting the shake linger.

"Fear has big eyes," Gurko said with a sad smile. "By the way, the next time you decide to take a ride on a fishing boat, I suggest you try Lake Michigan." Then he was out the door.

Jude watched him go, then walked over to the old man. He studied him critically. He had a wispy white beard and thick glasses. The rolls of fat around his middle gave him the shape of an eggplant and made him look even shorter than he was. A dirty homburg concealed the trademark bald head. "My name is Miller, Mr. Chairman, Jude Miller." When the old man didn't respond, he raised his voice. "My name is Jude Miller. Can I get you anything?"

The old man's eyes came alive. "Yes, Comrade, you can get me out of here."

IVAN KOLCHAK LAUGHED HEARTILY as his children, Andrey and Mathilde, shrieked their delight at the antics on the ice. The Moscow Ice Ballet was performing a comedy skit of *Little Red Riding Hood*, and the children clapped in accompaniment to the bouncy music as the skaters in their flamboyant costumes swished around the rink in the Palace of Sport at Lenin Stadium.

Earlier, Xenia had been pleased that her husband was finally showing interest in the children, but out of a sense of duty she had argued mildly against letting them attend the ice ballet on a school night. But he had subtly enticed the children into the discussion and their pleading sealed the case. After promising repeatedly not to be late and to come straight home, the three of them set off for the stadium.

As soon as the Kolchaks turned the corner leading to the subway, two burly men got out of a van and entered the door the small family had just exited. Their destination was the apartment where Xenia was alone.

If there were a musk that accompanied secret police, those two would have been skunks. As they walked up the stairs, the neighbors, with that sixth sense people develop in closed societies, peeked out of their doors and then hurriedly shut them, deciding they weren't going to see anything.

Xenia answered the knock, expecting perhaps to see a neighbor requesting a cup of flour. Instead, two men stood before her in an unmistakably "official" posture that immediately made her nervous.

"What is it, Comrades? Can I help you?"

"Xenia Kolchak?" one of the men asked, flashing a badge.

"Y-es."

"May we come in?" The question was superfluous, since both had moved themselves inside the door and one was already pushing it shut with his foot.

"What do you want? My husband will be home in—"

"We came to see you, Mrs. Kolchak. I'm sorry, but you'll have to come with us for a little while."

"Where to? My children, my husband, they need—"

"You'll probably be home before them. This is just routine."

Xenia started to whimper. "Please, I don't want to go anyplace. I haven't done anything."

"No one has accused you of anything, have they? Look, Mrs. Kolchak, you don't want to make a scene that'll embarrass your family, do you? Just get your coat and let's get this over with."

An accommodating person, Xenia took great pride in never being a bother to anyone. These men seemed nice enough; she didn't want to disturb the neighbors, and anyway, Ivan would straighten all this out when he got home.

"Just a minute," she said, her lower lip quivering, "I'll get my coat and leave a note for my husband. You think I'll be home in time to put my children to bed?"

THE CHILDREN STOOD AND CHEERED as the entire cast skated out under the spotlights and took final bows as the houselights dimmed. Mathilde was still clapping when the lights went back on and the crowd started shuffling toward the exits.

"Let's stop for a soda," Kolchak said to the children when they finally reached the night air.

Mathilde, trying to act like a responsible eight-year-old, said, "Mommy told us to come straight home."

Andrey, jumping at the chance to take his father's side, patronizingly scolded his little sister. "Mathilde, be quiet. You know you want one."

Once seated inside the brightly lit sweet shop, Kolchak let them order what they wanted, then said, "Children, I have to tell you something and I want you to take it like grownups." He looked at each in turn. "Okay, Mathilde? Okay, Andrey?"

The children nodded and squared their shoulders, preparing to show their father how adult they could be.

"When we get home, Mommy won't be there. She had to go to the hospital."

The children stared uncomprehendingly. "But she didn't say anything about it before we left," Andrey said.

"That's because she didn't want to spoil tonight's fun. She asked me to tell you to behave until she gets back and that she loves you."

"How long will she be gone?" Mathilde asked.

"A while."

"Who's going to take care of us?" Andrey asked.

Kolchak fidgeted with a sugar bowl on the table. "Uh, well, I've got to work every day and most nights, and we wouldn't want you by yourselves all that time, would we? So, I've got a nice surprise for you: you're going to live at a Young Pioneers' camp. You'll stay in big rooms with other boys and girls your age; you'll swim in the summertime, ski in the winter, study hard and learn how to be good Young Communists." He looked at the children to gauge their reactions. "I'll take you there myself tomorrow," he added quickly as though to ease it by them.

Mathilde started to blubber. "I don't want to go live in any old camp. I want my mommy."

Kolchak patted her on the arm. "You promised you'd be a big girl, now don't disappoint me. Mommy would be sad if she knew you were acting like this."

The child screwed up her courage and her older brother gave her a handkerchief to blow her nose as he tried to conceal the tears welling up in his own eyes. Their father stood up awkwardly and said, "I'll be right back. Order another treat if you like."

Kolchak walked over to a public phone, checked a number on a slip of paper and dialed. The phone rang only once before a gruff voice answered. Kolchak glanced involuntarily at the children before speaking. "This is Kolchak. How did it go?" He listened and nodded with satisfaction, then hung up. He dialed another number from memory. The phone rang several times before a woman's sleepy voice answered.

"Hello, Svetlana, this is Ivan. Is Friday still your day off?... Good, we can move your things into my place that day.... No problems, went without a hitch.... I know, I'm looking forward to it, too ... I love you. Good night."

THE MASKED AND GOWNED SURGEON was poised at the head of the anesthetized patient on the operating table. Below him, a shaved head was encased in the open frame of a boxlike, calibrated vise. Several wires were attached to the head and connected to high-tech monitoring machines.

The surgeon gripped the gleaming scalpel and made a long incision along marked lines across the skull. As a nurse sponged away the blood, he peeled back the scalp and layers of tiny muscles below until the bloody flap was lifted to expose an ivorylike skull. Another nurse handed him an electric drill, which appeared to be a hybrid between a dentist's instrument and an everyday carpenter's tool. Without hesitating, he touched the sharp bit to the skull. A shrill whine erupted and was soon joined by the acrid smell of burning bone as the drill bored through the skull. After several holes had been made and cylindrical "bone buttons" removed to expose the brain, the surgeon began inserting thin needlelike wires, the tips of which were made to get hot enough to destroy flesh. In a few minutes about two dozen of these electrodes were implanted deep in the brain, and an assistant turned on the electricity. The smell of burning brain tissue wafted from the operating table like food boiling in a dry pot, as parts suspected by the psychiatrists of causing mental illness were burned out.

Working inside the human brain is like cutting a rare diamond—one slip can be disastrous. The slightest nick of a blood vessel can cause unstoppable hemorrhaging; the misplacement of an electrode by a fraction of a millimeter can alter and damage a personality or intelligence forever.

After two hours the tired surgeon, Dr. Basil Mashkov, headed for the sink to wash while his assistants finished up. Hovering at his side was a psychiatric intern, whose eyes behind thick glasses watched the surgeon as a priest would the Pope.

"Comrade Doctor, what will be the anticipated postoperative behavior of the patient?"

Mashkov shrugged. He had performed dozens of such operations and no two of them had the same results. "Generally, the patient becomes listless and submissive. Creativity, imagination and the power to make decisions will be greatly reduced. The idea, in a sense, is to return the patient to childhood so thought processes can be straightened out. What we're trying to do is burn away those minute portions of the brain that store the emotional responses we want to weed out."

The intern was writing furiously. "How precise are the results?"

Mashkov dried his hands and removed the blood-splattered gown to reveal a tailored silk shirt covering his middle-age bulge and a hand-painted tie pulled open at the collar. "The brain is the least known organ of the body, and we're trying to eliminate small—*very* small—sections of it. And don't forget, brain cells don't regenerate. Once they're gone, that's it. But to answer your question, we don't very often create a Frankenstein's monster. Once in a while, though, the effect will be unpredicted: wildly aggressive behavior, even epilepsy. As I said, they become children, and sometimes act like it, but we have drugs to balance that out, too. In most cases, psychosurgery is successful and the offending behavior is eliminated. You must remember, Comrade, that no scientific advance is without cost, but what we're doing here will eventually benefit mankind."

"Is this the best way we've found to treat this kind of schizophrenia?" the intern asked.

Mashkov pondered the question. "Religious delusion is one of the oldest problems of psychiatry. Through the years— I should say centuries—medicine has been handcuffed in treating it because of the political power of churches. Priests like to keep people enslaved in superstition to enhance their own status. Here in the Soviet Union, though, we're in the vanguard of modern treatment because the witch doctors of organized religion have no control over science. That allows us to take an enlightened approach to religious fanaticism and properly treat it as a sickness, just like alcoholism."

Mashkov crossed his arms and faced the intern, absorbed by his own lecture. "As you get more into the study, you'll be amazed at some of the religious delusions these patients have: angels ... demons ... eternal life in a heaven presumably located somewhere in the sky ... dead men rising from the grave ... the magical healing of incurable diseases ... they come here believing all that nonsense. It's our job to try and help them."

"What will be the postoperative therapy for this patient," the intern asked, reading the name on the chart lying nearby, "this Xenia Kolchak?"

Mashkov slipped on a camel hair jacket and straightened his tie in front of a mirror. "She'll be placed in a reeducation group. We'll eliminate all possible negative influences, including family contact. It'll take years, but who knows, we just might eventually make her into a useful citizen."

The intern closed his notebook. "Comrade Doctor, this has been a most instructive experience. I thank you."

Mashkov smiled and shook the proffered hand. "My pleasure; anytime."

CHAPTER FIFTEEN

EVEN ATHEISTS LOOK beyond the grave.

The government of the Soviet Union, which over the years has denuded its great old churches and turned them into museums, has created its own monument to mysticism on a scale to rival the tombs of the pharaohs. It is Lenin's Tomb, located just outside the Kremlin walls in Moscow, and it is a shrine before which Russians doff hats and bend knees.

The lines start forming before daybreak—every daybreak—at the entrance to the huge bunkerlike red and black granite mass. Whether rain, snow or freezing cold, the little people of Russia, smelling collectively like a week-old laundry basket, stand placidly in slow-moving queues for a momentary glimpse of the remains of the Saint Paul of their revolution. After slowly shuffling forward for hours, they finally reach the squat stone monolith and walk down a long flight of echoing stone steps to emerge into the room of the dead. There, in an otherwise dark chamber, displayed under glass in the glow of strong yellow light like a prize diamond in a jewelry store, lie the remains of Vladimir Ilyich Ulyanov, the great Lenin, the messiah of socialism. He is dressed in a plain business suit and his hands are crossed serenely. His sandy-colored beard is trim and pointed. His skin is bright and alive looking. He seems deep in a contented sleep.

If it is he.

Since Lenin's death in 1924, considerable evidence has accumulated that the body lying on the massive catafalque is nothing more than a wax and plastic doll of a kind found in Madame Tussaud's museum. After he died of a stroke (or

Stalin's poison, as some speculate) Lenin's body was handled somewhat like a butchered chicken's. His brain was sliced into twenty thousand pieces for microscopic evaluation, and he was autopsied for an entire day. The blood vessels that normally carry embalming fluid were collapsed by the autopsy, so the only way to preserve the remains was a form of what amounts to pickling. Several times during the early years, the body was removed from public display so the experts could have another go at patching it up. Finally, there emerged the present cadaver, looking younger and, as several who had known him said, with more hair than he had twenty years before his death.

Whatever it is lying under that glass, to believing Russians it is as holy a relic as any icon their ancestors bowed before in onion-domed churches. Many of the older peasants can be seen impulsively crossing themselves as they pass the bier, then they glance nervously at the frowning guards, ashamed and afraid after such a religious outburst. Most emerge at the other end with a bewildered look, not quite certain what to make of the wonder they have seen, like Aztecs first viewing Cortez.

Whether the body of a man or a mannequin, to the Soviet state Lenin's body is the Shroud of Turin and all the relics of the saints. To a government as horrified by religion as an anorexic by chocolate, it is the one indulgence allowed.

THE STREET REPAIRMAN NUDGED his companion, and both stared as the attractive young woman with long blond hair and huge rhinestone glasses walked up and faced them with a nervous smile.

"*Pozhaluista*, could you help me, please? My car won't start." She pointed to a small dark green Lada parked behind the yellow work truck with Department of Streets stenciled on the side.

It was two o'clock in the morning, it was cold, and the pile of gravel the men had been shoveling stubbornly refused to get smaller, so the two workmen didn't have to be urged twice to help such a pretty girl. They dropped their tools and scowled at each other as they jostled for a position at her side. Diplomatically, she moved to stand between them, and the three of them marched toward the offending automobile.

"What seems to be the problem?" one of the workers said as he rubbed the fender as though for therapeutic effect. The woman's answer was lost as a movement in the shadows of a nearby building caught their attention. They wheeled to face two men advancing on them. The newcomers moved with the litheness of youth, but with the stiffness of tension. Both were bearded and wore dark glasses and hats pulled low. Each pointed a big black pistol at the workers.

"For you, this is the problem," David Rabinowitz said, gesturing with the pistol toward the worker who had spoken.

The workers looked at each other in confusion, then at the pistols pointed at them. Finally it occurred to them to raise their hands and they did so awkwardly. David ordered them into the back seat of the car, which had been stolen only hours before. Then the three kidnappers split up; the second man drove the truck and the woman was at the wheel of the car while David kept his pistol leveled at the captive workmen from the seat beside her.

"What are you going to do with us?" one of the prisoners asked in a quavering voice.

"Just behave yourselves and you won't get hurt," David answered from behind the beard. "We want your truck, not you."

The maintenance truck followed the car as they wound through the streets of Moscow, but to the driver, Yitzchak Hurwitz, the vehicle seemed like an army truck, and the tension that crackled like electric current on the night air seemed like Afghanistan. . . .

Yitzchak Hurwitz was a twenty-three-year-old plumber from Odessa. In earlier years he was a peaceable, nonreligious Jew, who, had he not been saddled with the Hebrew name that means Isaac, would have very happily forgotten his heritage. Even tonight, given his choice, he would prefer to be asleep in his family's apartment, with the gentle winds of the Black Sea washing over him and troubled by nothing more complex than a stopped-up toilet awaiting him the next day. But fate in the form of the Red Army had intervened, and a year ago Yitzchak found himself conscripted into an infantry battalion and scouring the deep valleys and steep towering peaks of the Afghanistan Hindu Kush, trying to locate and kill Pathan tribesmen who were trying to locate and kill him. The rebels called themselves *mujahideen*, meaning those who fight a holy war, and in his dreams he often visualized them squatting around the fires of hidden mountain camps in smelly robes and dirty turbans, devising new ways to kill the infidel invaders, of whom Yitzchak was involuntarily one. It occurred to Yitzchak very early, and seemed a distinct disadvantage, that the *mujahideen* wanted to kill him more than he did them. That, plus their ability to seem always to be shooting down on him from a higher peak, severely dampened his zeal.

He was transferred to a helicopter commando unit, which meant he then flew in a Mi-24 Hind gunship. The assignment was more comfortable than climbing spiny mountains, but also made him and his compatriots pay nervous attention to scuttlebutt about how many American Stinger hand-held antiaircraft rockets had been smuggled to the rebels.

Yitzchak could have weathered those normal and reasonable fears and served out his year's tour of duty by staying drunk on vodka whenever possible and passing time by trading horror stories of what the rebels did to Russian prisoners, but the systematic, ruthless way his superiors waged war on defenseless Afghan women and children sickened and shamed

him to be even an unwilling part of it. He began to realize that
the Soviet method of combatting the Islamic traditions so in-
imical to Communism was to destroy the country, not only
its ability to fight, but if necessary, every human being who
by birth, tradition or patriotism had any reservations about
Soviet rule. It was a strategy of fire and sword not new to that
country. Genghis Khan had been one of their earlier visitors.

One day his unit landed in a small Pathan village for a routine mop-up after a strike force had hit it, but there was nothing to mop up. No dogs barked; no babies cried. Only silence.
He stood bewildered in the empty marketplace for several
minutes, ready to dive for cover at the sign of danger, but the
only activity was with a group of his mates, who had pried a
large rock away from the entrance to a cave and stood around
it gesturing and talking in low voices.

Yitzchak walked over and edged his way to the front of the
group. The only thing he later recalled hearing was one soldier saying in awed tones, "There must be a hundred." He
wondered at the time why several soldiers were vomiting,
whether the meal they had eaten before leaving base had been
tainted.

The sight hit him like something from the brush of an angry Goya, except no painting ever had live flies noisily crawling over human faces. Before him, huddled together at the
back of the shallow cave, were mounds of corpses fused together by the melted fats of their charred bodies and by the
horror of a monstrous death that drove them into one another's arms. "Liquid fire," he heard a hushed voice behind him
say. Yitzchak stared and wanted to scream on behalf of all
those who could no longer scream. He closed his eyes and demanded of God that the terrible scene should disappear. But
the odor of death that flowed out of the cave like heat waves
told him that this day belonged to Satan, not to God. His only
protest was vomit and tears, and a vow of hatred for those who
could burn living humans like garbage.

From that day forward, Yitzchak did not fire his rifle. A month later, when he drew a week's liberty, he flew to Moscow and immediately burned his uniform, then went to the synagogue to pray. He had to ask the old men in the pews how to do it because he knew nothing of being a Jew, but he remembered from the bedtime Bible stories of his childhood that the God of Israel was a vengeful God. In his hatred, Yitzchak meant to see if it were true.

THE TINY CARAVAN DROVE for several minutes and then pulled into a dark alley that led to a freight area. Before them loomed the rear of the massive two-story Victorian architecture of G.U.M. Department Store, one of the largest in the world, the steel ribs supporting its plate-glass bulk stretching almost a half-mile parallel to and facing Red Square.

They killed the lights and rolled to a stop. Yitzchak eased out of the truck and ran over to the car. After giving the pistol to Ludmila to guard the two workmen, David slipped out of the car, and he and Yitzchak crouched and whispered to each other.

"When does the night watchman come by?" Yitzchak asked.

David looked at the luminescent dial on his watch. "It should be in about eight minutes. We're right on schedule. Let's wait over there." He pointed to a dark recess next to a door. Together, the two scrambled softly up some steps and disappeared into the shadows to wait.

The elderly night watchman whistled a folk tune from his Cossack youth and prepared to punch the clock at the loading dock station when a movement caught the edge of his vision. Before he could react, a strong hand had gone over his mouth and another twisted his arm behind his back. The night watchman felt himself being slammed against the concrete wall and the breath left him like air from a bellows. Two bearded faces with glaring dark eyes thrust close to his face, and harshly whispered voices made demands on his muddled mind.

"Is there another night watchman?"

The old man shook his head. "No—not at this hour."

"Are any of the cleaning crew inside?"

"They—they've all gone home."

David nodded. The watchman had confirmed what he had been told. He shoved the old man ahead and told Yitzchak to summon Ludmila and the two workmen. They waited at the freight entry door, while David went back to the car, opened the trunk and removed a coil of rope, a bundle of clothing and a bulky suitcase. Together, they followed the night watchman as he shakily unlocked the door and the six of them walked into the cathedrallike store. David noticed a door labeled Tooale't, and steered the group through it. Inside, he told the captives to lie flat on the cold lavatory floor and then had Yitzchak tie and gag them. Afterward, he gave a sharp tug on each knot and made sure the gags didn't impede breathing.

David, Ludmila and Yitzchak stepped outside the toilet and climbed into baggy workmen's coveralls and the men removed their beards and glasses. David tugged a cloth cap low over his eyes and turned to Ludmila, who was still struggling with the unfamiliar clothing. "You stay here and watch them. We can't risk one of them wriggling free. We'll pick you up on the way out. And get rid of that yellow whore's wig before we leave. You don't see too many of those on street repair crews."

David and Yitzchak walked along the broad aisle that branched off into myriad shops offering goods from all corners of the country and the world. Hours from now, these aisles would be crowded with pushing, sweating women grasping their shopping bags and elbowing to get closer to the merchandise, which was never in quite sufficient supply. But now, the freshly mopped floors were touched only by their soft sneakered feet and the empty corridors were silent as an Inca ruin.

David motioned for Yitzchak to follow and turned into a small shop that offered East German luggage. They wended their way to the rear and found a large window. David looked out onto the broad, empty cobbled expanse of Red Square and, 150 yards to the west, the spires of the Kremlin towers rising in jagged silhouette against the night sky. He located the dominance of the Spasskaya, the clock tower along the wall, and slowly moved his vision fifteen degrees to the right to the dark huddled bulk of Lenin's Tomb. Silently, he pointed it out to Yitzchak, who nodded and started to undo the latches of the suitcase.

Yitzchak removed a device that looked like a dismantled telescope. He lifted the parts and started to assemble them in darkness with the certainty of a musician putting a clarinet together. In less than a minute he held up for David's inspection a black tube about a yard long with a pistol grip at one end and an opening at the other that flared out like an old-style blunderbuss. On top was an electronic gadget that resembled a camera.

Yitzchak gently bounced the device on his hands like an infant and smiled in appreciation, like a jeweler with a fine watch. He set it down and picked up a slim cigar-shaped missile with bomb fins at the rear. "This is the rocket," he announced to David proudly, then he picked up a cardboard cylinder and began screwing it to the rear of the missile. "This is the propellant. I attach it to the rocket, and now I connect the whole thing to the launcher," he said to David like a math teacher explaining pi, then he inserted the rocket into the muzzle, being careful, as he explained, to mate a notch in the muzzle with a small projection on the rocket so that the firing pin of the launcher would strike an explosive cap and ignite the charge. "Just like an old percussion rifle," he said. Yitzchak removed the nose cone from the rocket, extracted the safety pin and gingerly laid the weapon aside. "There," he said, scrutinizing what he had assembled, "this baby is ready to get ugly."

"Does it have a name?" David asked as though about a person.

"The technical name is RPG-7D, but I call it *Drakon Suka*, Dragon Bitch; it's a portable short-range antitank rocket launcher. The best in the world."

David gestured across the square at Lenin's Tomb. "Will you be able to hit the target with any accuracy?"

Yitzchak looked down the length of David's arm at the mausoleum. "No problem. I have night sight." He glanced at David as though to apologize for imprecision. "I mean an NSP-2 infrared image intensifier."

"Oh," David said meekly.

David turned to the window and tried to open it. He swore softly when it refused to budge. "*Chort*, this thing won't open. I'll have to cut it out." He removed a glass cutter from his pocket and began to awkwardly cut into the pane in a large circle with the unfamiliar tool. When he had completed the cut he stood back and studied the glass. "They tell me if you do this right the window should fall backward into your hands when you tap the glass just above where you make the etch." He reached up, sharply rapped the uncut part of the window and put his arms out to catch the glass. Instead, the pane fell outward and tumbled to the sidewalk below, where it fell flat and exploded like a grenade. David jumped backward and his hands flew to his mouth as if he had just dropped a baby on its head. He looked around in shock as though seeking a way to erase the shattering noise that reverberated around Red Square like a rifle shot.

The guards who stood at rigid attention on either side of the tomb entrance clearly heard the breaking glass but were helpless to do anything about it. A soldier did not leave the most honored post in the Red Army to investigate a mere burglary. They restiffened their already rigid backs and stared straight ahead into the night.

A militiaman was strolling beneath the bulb domes of St. Basil's Cathedral at the far end of Red Square, when he, too, was startled by the noise. Locating it immediately as coming from the department store and assuming it was a break-in, he loosened his pistol in its holster and began running the quarter-mile that would put him in two minutes at the freight entrance where the car and truck were parked.

Hairline cracks formed at the corners of David's nerve. As with all amateurs in such enterprises, his confidence depended on things going exactly according to plan. He tugged at Yitzchak's arm. "Let's get out of here. We can hit another target later. *Come on!*"

But Yitzchak hadn't dressed up his baby not to see her dance. He pushed David out of the way and lifted the launcher to his shoulder. "This'll be quick. Just shut up and get ready to move. And, *bog*, don't stand directly behind the launcher." He switched on the sight and pressed his eye to the rubber viewer. The entire tomb swam into view in a sea of infrared. He clicked it into 2.5 magnification, which made the great bronze doors with the name Lenin etched in purple above them and framed by two honor guards standing like brown statues, fill the scope like a family portrait. He gently moved the cross hairs until they were lined up exactly on the center of the doors. "Now, very gently, don't jerk," he softly lectured himself, held his breath, then eased pressure on the trigger until a loud whoosh and blinding light filled the room.

The projectile leaped from the launcher muzzle at a velocity of three hundred meters per second. At a distance of ten meters knifelike fins sprang out to stabilize flight and the rocket motor kicked in to enhance the acceleration. The white ball took one-half a second to cover the distance to the tomb and smashed flush on the center of the doors. On impact, the nose was crushed against an inner skin to activate an electrical fuse, which ignited the grenade and unleashed a force capable of penetrating a foot of solid steel.

The concussion broke a hundred windows in the buildings surrounding Red Square and within the walls of the Kremlin itself. The guards were thrown aside like paper in a strong wind to lie many yards away like smoking piles of old clothes. The great doors caved in like a paper sack and the force of the explosion pushed its way deep into the stone corridors below. The glass case holding the body of Lenin shuddered and shifted off its catafalque, and great cracks appeared on the surface like those in a smashed windshield. The folded hands of Lenin were torn from their serene pose and were transformed into the empty claws of a dead man. Glass dust sprinkled down on the face that once glared defiance at the world.

For long moments only a canopy of smoke stirred in the great square, but then the calm was broken by a forest of lights and confused shouts within the Kremlin walls. Outside, only the militiaman's feet rang on the cobblestones as he neared the department store.

Yitzchak threw aside the used-up launcher and he and David sprinted madly down the corridor. There they were met by Ludmila, who threw aside her wig as she ran. In seconds, they pushed through the heavy doors of the freight entrance and into the cold early-morning air. They sprinted for the truck and jumped in like gophers diving for a hole. David pumped the acclerator in frustration as the grinding starter tore at their frazzled nerves.

"You've flooded the damned thing!" Ludmila cried as her hands fluttered on the dashboard, drumming out a frantic rhythm of fear.

Yitzchak reached over and switched off the ignition. "Let it sit for a minute. You don't have any choice."

They sat in the cab like prisoners in a windowed cage, watching the sirens and flashing lights converge on them like a tightening net. After a minute that seemed eternal, Yitzchak said, "Okay, try it now." David held his breath and gingerly turned the key as though it were made of brittle glass. The motor sputtered, then roared to life, drowning out the audible sighs of the three in the cab. David slammed the engine into gear, raced it loudly just to make sure, and the truck lurched forward toward the alley leading to Kuibyshev Street.

Just as David started to shift to second gear, the militiaman emerged directly in front of them, raised his pistol with both hands and shouted, *"Prival! Halt!"*

David, faced with a person blocking his vehicle, instinctively hit the brake, but then gritted his teeth and gunned the motor, bearing directly down on the policeman.

Before he was thrown aside with a muffled thump by the grill of the truck, the militiaman managed to squeeze off one shot that drilled a neat hole through the windshield on the passenger side.

David steered the truck into the wide avenue, flicked on the headlights and headed east, away from Red Square, as the rushing squad cars barreled past on the way to the scene of the explosion, in far too much of a hurry to worry about a street maintenance truck seemingly wandering from one pothole to the next.

David let his breath out slowly and concentrated on steadying his shaky hands, while he tried to think of a joke that would cover his earlier loss of nerve with a patina of bravado. With a broad smile of success, he turned to Ludmila, who was seated in the middle, only to notice her face squeezed together in grief and uttering a low wail that was almost inaudible. Her hands were splotched with something dark and held in front of her as though the strange substance would infect her if it spread.

David was confused, but the sense of tragedy was very apparent, so with a sinking heart he turned to Yitzchak on the other side for reassurance. What he saw in the darkness made his brain freeze in horror and his hands turn white as he gripped the steering wheel as though it were the anchor of sanity. Yitzchak was slumped against the far door with his eyes half-closed. A round black hole in his forehead gave a cyclops effect and spurted blood like a pump. A noxious odor filled the closed cab and overwhelmed the sweet smell of blood as the dead man's sphincter muscle relaxed.

David rolled down the window and took deep gulps of the cold air, not to clear the odor from the cab, but to free his brain of the shock of death, a death that he knew would not have happened except for him and the plan he had created. In that moment, David learned the commander's lesson, that to take people's lives into one's hands is to stand alone with the responsibility when the grip slips and those lives are shattered like old crystal. He learned that when the fierceness of the battle wanes, it leaves behind on the battlefield unmoving heaps in the morning fog whose only statement is silent accusation.

And he couldn't even bury his friend.

CHAPTER SIXTEEN

IVAN KOLCHAK SLAMMED the telephone down and raked his fingers through his hair. "Kyril, get in here," he bellowed through the closed office door. The speed with which the door opened and his assistant, Kyril Petrovich, entered told Kolchak with perverse satisfaction that his assistant was hovering just outside, expecting such a summons.

As soon as Petrovich was seated in the hard wooden chair directly in front of the desk, Kolchak glared at him and pointed to the phone. "Do you know who that was? That was the deputy secretary of the presidium wanting to know what's been done about the bombing of Lenin's Tomb. He was kind enough to remind me it's been several days since it happened. Do you know what I told him? I told him that I was doing everything possible. *I*. Did you notice the first person singular pronoun? *I* took the blame for not having a single lead to the worst crime committed in this country since the time of the czar. All we have is the dead body of a Zid army deserter left in a stolen truck, a used rocket launcher and three babbling hostages who were too damned scared to piss their pants, let alone observe anything about the criminals who grabbed them."

Petrovich hunched down in the chair and gazed at the floor, though he wanted to stare Kolchak square in the face and tell him to go to hell, that only an incompetent blames his assistant for his own shortcomings.

"Let's go over this one more time," Kolchak said like a teacher talking to the class idiot. "Have they found any fingerprints at the scene?"

Petrovich shrugged. "About a thousand—it's a store."

"How about in the truck or the stolen car."

"Wiped clean."

"Well, obvious—" Kolchak was interrupted by his secretary, who put her head inside the office and told him a man on the phone claimed knowledge of the bombing. Kolchak picked up the receiver and frantically signaled Petrovich to prepare to trace the call.

"This is Kolchak," he said with police crispness, but only after suppressing the excitement he felt.

"My name is Moses. I am the one who desecrated the tomb of your beloved Lenin," David said in a deep, slow voice meant to convey seriousness. Kolchak started to speak, but David cut him off. "I know you're trying to trace this, *Mr.* Kolchak," he said sarcastically, "but I'm calling from a public phone in central Moscow and will hang up in exactly one minute, so don't waste your time."

"What are you after?" Kolchak asked.

"Jews. I want them released from this God-forsaken country."

"Do you think you'll get your wish by blowing up public monuments?"

"Yes. I demand that the Soviet government allow one hundred thousand Jews to emigrate to Israel every year, and that such a program be announced publicly."

"I can't grant your wish," Kolchak said.

"It's not a wish. You can convey my demands to your masters, and then you can tell them how difficult it is to catch someone like me."

"Difficult, but we'll do it; and do you know how we'll start, my sneaky saboteur friend? We'll arrest every suspicious Jew in Moscow. I want to see how arrogant you sound when your Zid friends—and maybe yourself—are enjoying the Siberian climate. Who the hell do you think you're dealing with, anyway?"

"You don't frighten the Sicarii."

"You say that now," Kolchak said in a cold voice.

"Jews are used to being persecuted," David said. "Better men than those in the Kremlin and their toadies such as you have tried. Right now, I'm trying to decide on the next target. Would you like a hint? . . . No, I think I'll make it a surprise." He chuckled softly.

Kolchak became enraged at the laugh. "I know you Jews are big on funerals. What kind of burial would you like for your friend, the cowardly deserter Hurwitz? Let me tell you about the funeral I've got planned. I'm going to have his body thrown into the swamp where the bugs and fish will eat his flesh as it rots and falls off. And that's what I'll do for you when I catch you."

"Let my people go."

Kolchak stared at the buzzing receiver and swore at the man who was no longer at the other end.

Petrovich made a quick call and silently scribbled notes. He walked over and handed the paper to his boss. "It's like he said, a public phone on one of the busiest streets in the city." He frowned over his bifocals at Kolchak. "You shouldn't have lost your temper, we might have kept him on the line longer." As soon as the words left his lips he realized his mistake, but it was too late.

Kolchak sputtered at the impertinence. "Listen, Petrovich, I've been after you to do something ever since these damned Sicarii, or whatever they call themselves, started this business, and all you ever said was that you're working on it. Well, I'm telling you we're going to start seeing some results fast or I'll find someone who *can* do the job. Now, I want you to get me a list of all the smart-ass, so-called dissident Jews in this city and alert the militia to get ready to start picking them up. Do you think you can handle that, or would you like to try insulting your superior again?"

Petrovich started to leave, but stopped short when he remembered the file in his hand. He held it up and said, "By the way, Comrade Kolchak, you wanted a check on the American agent, Jude Miller. Well, the lab says he's the same as the man who met the Ukrainian in the alley."

"For all we know, he was drowned in the Moskva River."

"For all we know he wasn't," Petrovich countered.

"How did the lab find out they're the same person?" Kolchak asked.

"By the nose."

"The nose? What the hell are you talking about? Petrovich, I'm in no mood..."

"Let me explain," Petrovich said hastily. He took two blown-up photographs out of the file and held one aloft. "This is our only photo of Jude Miller. It was taken several years ago in West Berlin." The picture was a yellowed black and white of a man standing at a side angle with a tall steel and glass building in the background a couple of blocks away. Petrovich then held up the other photograph. "This is the picture taken a few nights ago of the man talking to the Ukrainian traitor, Vladimir Bukovsky, the one we arrested." The photograph, taken from a considerable distance, showed two men in a very dim silhouette not far from a streetlight. He removed another picture from the file, one enlarged several times and so grainy it was barely discernible as a man's profile. "Here is a blowup of the man we want to identify in the second photo."

"Get to the point, Kyril. I've got a lot on my mind."

You have no feel for the nuances of this business, *vnebrayni*, Petrovich thought. "We identified the building in the first picture as one on Klausstrasse in Berlin. By knowing the height of the building, and scaling it according to the picture, we were able to ascertain the exact dimensions of the man standing in front of it. Likewise, in the second photo, by measuring the streetlight pole, we established the dimen-

sions of those men. By triangulating the angles of the noses
in both photos, we proved to almost a mathematical certainty
that the man in the first photo is the same as the second man
in the other photo.'' He consulted a slip of paper in the file.
''They tell me the odds are 55,000 to one that they're the
same.''

''You could have spared me all the statistical crap. I've got
other things on my mind now. Do we have his fingerprints?''

''A very old, blurry set.''

''Well, get his description out. We'll keep our eyes open.
Right now, I'm worried about those damned Jews.''

''Comrade—'' Petrovich knew if he were smart, he would
keep his mouth shut and leave quietly at that point
''—shouldn't we at least consider that this Miller might be
connected with the Sicarii?''

Kolchak heaved a condescending sigh. ''We never dismiss
any possibility, Kyril, but there is nothing whatsoever to tie
him to them. Now, be a good clerk and do as I ask.''

Petrovich inclined his head and backed out of the room.
Stupid, insensitive bureaucrat, he thought of his harried,
unshaved boss, who fidgeted nervously with a stack of papers in his hands, his mind now far from the assistant who
glared at him while he was not looking.

JUDE PACED BACK AND FORTH in the tiny room in which
Gurko had placed him and Khrushchev. He used his energy
to resist the temptations of impatience and anxiety. He knew
those reactions to be archenemies of the gone-to-ground
agent, constantly inviting a rash act or impulsive decision.
Waiting well was the professional's advantage, and he was
doing it better than ever before. Even the old nightmares no
longer visited his sleep. He was growing increasingly comfortable with the old life; it was fitting better and better, like
a new pair of shoes slowly becoming comfortable.

He stopped and looked down on his companion, the old man who was sleeping on the cot, with a mixture of awe and pity. The man had been a giant of his time, a crude, brash peasant who became one of the world's most powerful men, a face remembered from a flickering black-and-white television screen, belonging to one who made empires stop and great men listen when he spoke. But that was history; what Jude now looked at was just another snoring old man drooling like a wrinkled infant as he thrashed about, fighting forgotten and long-settled battles, events that now mattered only in his sleep.

Suddenly, Jude was jolted by surprise to look at the old man's face and see eyes alertly staring back at him. He had observed that the old man slid in and out of coherency like the prow of a ship in the troughs of a storm, but to catch even a momentary glimpse of the powerful personality that once imposed itself like a stamp on this country unnerved him slightly.

"Good evening, Comrade Chairman, did you sleep well?"

The old man cleared his throat with a hacking effort that turned his face red and made his big belly tremble. "Who are you?"

"Don't you remember? I'm the American who's going to take you out. But for the time being, I'm your grandson, Viktor Serov, a teacher from Smolensk."

"Are you a Communist?"

"Uh—no."

The old man pushed his hands backward on the cot and forced his body to stand erect, then began a slow shuffle toward the ancient toilet. "Then don't call me comrade. Comrade is what one Communist calls another. I've got to piss. That's all I seem to do anymore, piss; that and think about the other things I used to use this for." He grabbed his crotch in a theatrical gesture. The old man stood patiently over the toilet for what seemed like long minutes to Jude who said nothing, as though afraid to interrupt the slow dribbling sound. "Don't even do that worth a damn anymore," the old man grumbled as he flushed the toilet, zipped up his trousers and returned to the bed where he sat heavily and faced Jude. "So, *Amerikanski*, you're the one who's going to take me out of here."

Jude nodded.

"Did you ever meet President Kennedy?"

Jude shook his head, astonished by the question.

"Too bad; a splendid young fellow. I liked him." He pondered the thought for a moment. "We liked each other. Even when we had that little disagreement over Cuba, and then over Berlin, we got on well." He chuckled. "We used to make fun of de Gaulle's nose. I told him if a Russian had a nose that long, we'd circumcise him and put him behind a pushcart."

"What did he say to that?" Jude asked.

"He laughed, I'm sure. The young fellow had a great sense of humor, folksy, like mine. He was quite a man for the ladies, too. Once, in Vienna, when we were alone, we compared some notes, just man-to-man talk—helped break the ice. Despite his bad back and my big belly, it seems we both did pretty well." He frowned and shook his head. "Then the Americans had to shoot him—goddamn barbarians."

"Mr. Chairman, I can't help wondering, how did you ever manage to trick the entire country into thinking you were dead?"

The old man grunted derisively. "It wasn't the whole country, only a few dim-witted bureaucrats who weren't paying attention, weren't doing their jobs, as usual. As they say, while the dog panted, the hare went over the hill." He chuckled at the memory of his victory. "One day I received a letter from old Tarkonian, the man who had served as my double. It was uncanny; sometimes I thought I was looking in the mirror. The fellow was all alone and dying from a bad heart, so he asked my blessing, like I was a priest or something. Can you imagine? But it gave me an idea, just the germ of a plan, you understand. I contacted some friends from my time in the Ukraine, men whom I knew to be Ukrainian nationalists, enemies of the state, but that was information I kept to myself, sort of like squirrels hiding food for the winter. Those friends took care of Tarkonian and kept him alive until we were ready to make our move.

"My doctor, a loyal friend from the good days, taught me how to fake heart symptoms, then when Tarkonian was near death, he alerted the hospital that he was bringing me in. They just switched Tarkonian for me, and the only thing the authorities knew was that Khrushchev's doctor had brought his patient to the hospital where he promptly died. They looked at the body, saw that it looked like me, and all that remained was burying the wrong body and hiding me."

Jude shook his head. "It sounds so simple."

"Simple, eh? That must be why they call fools like those simpletons."

Jude chuckled in admiration. "I have to give—" Jude stopped and looked uneasily at the old man. He had changed: the laugh was gone and his eyes flashed fiercely at Jude but with a loss of focus. The old man squared his shoulders and swept a gnarled finger around the cabin and at the man with whom he had been laughing only seconds before. When he spoke, his words were flat and recited as though from memory.

"Comrades, yesterday I awoke in my holiday dacha on the Black Sea. I said to myself, it's October 13, 1964, the sun is warm and I can enjoy a pleasant visit with my guest, Gaston Palewski, the French Minister of State, knowing that my loyal comrades are back in Moscow making certain that the great revolution that we all bled and sweated to make a reality is safely on course. That is what I thought yesterday, and every day for more than ten years, since being entrusted with the great duties bestowed upon me. But I was wrong. While I was relaxing on my first real holiday in years, you, my trusted compatriots of the Central Committee Presidium, were meeting in this room planning to depose me, and then you had the nerve to demand I fly here to stand before you like a criminal.''

Khrushchev waved his arm around the cabin as though it were a paneled state conference room in the Kremlin. ''You took your vote and decreed that the twenty-two of you could take it upon yourselves to end the career of a man who served the revolution from the day the first shot was fired, through the Stalin terror and the Great Patriotic War, to the triumph of Sputnik. And now you would end all that by holding up your arms to vote that this man who has given so much should be thrown on the trash heap.''

Khrushchev let his eyes roam around the small room as though searching for someone. He stopped and stared toward the toilet. ''You, Comrade Brezhnev, and you Comrade Kosygin, I see your hands dripping from having stirred this soup. You want power; it's on your faces. So be it. But be honest about it, don't destroy a comrade's good name like you were castrating an animal in a barnyard.''

Khrushchev stamped his foot so hard the dust billowed from the floor and his ancient body was almost thrown off balance. ''You defame me. You say that I ruined the economy, but I won't even dignify that with an answer. The statistics show that to be a lie.

''You say that I was brash and demanding of you, that I didn't give you, the leaders of the party, the respect you deserve.'' His voice mocked a mother talking to an infant. ''Did I hurt your feelings?'' Then he thundered, ''To that I plead guilty. I confess to putting the revolution before cronyism; I confess to thinking it more important to push programs forward to help this country get out of the economic dark ages than catering to the laziness and fumbling of a bunch of old bureaucrats.'' The old man laughed sarcastically. ''I would like that 'crime' chiseled on my tombstone, because it served the people well.''

The old man's eyes continued to sweep the small room without noticing Jude, who was standing directly in front of him, mouth agape. ''Now, comrades, let's get to the heart of the matter. You claim my handling of the so-called Cuban Missile Crisis of a year and a half ago was inept. You blame me for 'losing face' in a confrontation with President Kennedy and 'backing down' to the embarrassment of the Soviet Union. That just shows how ignorant you are. This country *won* that test of wills. We forced the United States to guarantee they would never invade Cuba, thus we assured the survival of a socialist ally living right in the path of the dragon's breath. It's clear to me you wouldn't recognize a victory if you stepped in it like cowshit in a pasture.

''Now, about the backing off from Kennedy's Cuba blockade, the turning back of our ships—if you had the vision of a mole, you'd know that was just the moving of a few pawns in the chess game. It meant nothing except a few sensationalized headlines in the capitalist press. Maybe you would have preferred a nuclear war? The point is, we achieved our objective. Has it occurred to any of you that the reason Kennedy was killed might be because he displeased the capitalist bosses over his handling of that same affair?'' The old man waved his hand in dismissal. ''*Chort*, explaining the finer points of statecraft to the bunch of you is like trying to teach geometry to monkeys.''

The old man clasped his hands behind his back and Jude noticed a slump in his shoulders. ''You've had your vote, and if you want to throw out your premier like Saturday night's bathwater, then I won't stand in your way. But I'll tell you this, no matter what you do to me, even if you make me live in poverty, I'll survive. I'll go door-to-door to the peasants and they'll feed me.'' He tightened his jaw and glared at the stove. ''And that's more than they'd do for any of you.''

The old man seemed to wilt and stumbled the few steps to the cot and was asleep in seconds.

Jude walked over and gazed kindly down at the ancient statesman. "You may not know it, *Dedushka*, grandfather, but surrendering power to a vote was your finest moment. That such a thing could happen only eleven years after a dictator like Stalin is a tribute to you, you crusty old bastard."

THE LIGHT KNOCK ON THE DOOR went through Jude's nerves like an electric charge, and he moved quickly to the side of the door and whispered, "Who is it?"

"A friend. Let me in," came the reply in a vaguely familiar female voice.

Jude opened the door and let the woman slip inside. When she turned toward the faint light of the lamp, Jude gasped. It was Lana Martin, the agent who had accompanied him to Mexico.

She laughed at his surprise. "I told you I'd see you again, didn't I?" She opened her arms wide for his inspection. "Well, here I am."

Jude chuckled. "Would it be considered prying if I asked just what in hell you're doing here?"

"I'm your contact. I hope you didn't think we'd abandon you," she teased.

"In situations like this, the doubts do creep into one's mind. I hoped there'd be someone, I just didn't know she'd be so beautiful," he said sincerely as his eyes involuntarily wandered down to her full breasts poorly hidden by a tight sweater. He tried to conceal his gaze, but it was as plain as that of a bored person glancing at a wristwatch.

She recognized his stare, and their eyes locked in a sexual tension that happened upon both of them as suddenly as a truck around a sharp corner and was equally uncontrollable. The looks lingered until Lana threw back her head and her laughter rang through the room. "I'd walk through Lubyanka Prison to hear that compliment." She turned and walked a few feet to stand over the sleeping old man. "Is that him?" she asked as though viewing a museum exhibit.

"In the flesh."

She turned back to Jude. "We get asked to deliver some interesting packages, don't we?" Without waiting for an answer, she said, "Tell me, are you ready to head for your rendezvous with the Jews, the Sicarii, as they call themselves?"

He looked at his watch. "In three hours—time enough for you to tell me what's going on. Why didn't I know you'd be my contact? How'd you get into the country?"

She put a slim, well-groomed hand on his arm. "One thing at a time. I can understand your confusion. You weren't told about me because the agency wasn't sure we could trust you after your—your retirement."

"Armstead said that?" he said angrily.

"Not to me, not directly. But you can understand; we had to watch you a step at a time until we were certain." She noticed his hurt feelings and stepped forward and patted his cheek. "You did marvelously, handsome."

"What are you doing here? In Russia, I mean."

"My job was to infiltrate the KGB, to get next to the agent in charge of tracking you. He's one of their hotshots named Ivan Kolchak."

Jude nodded. "I think I've heard of him. And did you make contact?"

She averted her eyes for an instant, but long enough for Jude to sense the truth of what he did not want to know. "Yes. Comrade Kolchak has become my—confidant."

"Does he know about me?"

"Yes, he knows your name—your real name, not your cover—and he knows you're in Moscow, either alive or drowned in the Moskva River. He hasn't connected you with either the Ukrainians or the Sicarii. And he doesn't have the foggiest idea about Khrushchev. Yet."

"You say 'yet.'"

She shrugged. "He's a smart man. Time, twisting a few arms and asking intelligent questions will eventually make him a very educated man. My job is to find out when that education occurs."

"Can you be certain he doesn't know?"

"Who's certain about anything?" she asked. "He talks freely to me. I don't mean he lays his head on my shoulder and confesses—" Jude's eyes flashed and she blushed to realize her poor choice of words. "He drops little things here and there, things that would mean nothing to the average person, but to the trained ear, it's like a typed memo. For the present, you should be okay so long as you distance yourself from the Ukrainians, but that can change quicker than the weather."

Jude realized they had been standing so he offered her a chair at the small table. "When and how do I get him out of the country?" he asked, gesturing with his head toward the old man.

"Soon and quietly, I hope," she said. "Ten days from now, the two of you will take the Red Arrow sleeper from Leningrad station on Komsomolskaya Square. Your train will be met in Leningrad by one of our people. From there, you'll go by small plane to Finland. The plane will hedgehop at night to evade radar. From Finland, you're as good as home."

"You make it sound so simple."

"If it goes well, it will be."

Jude gave a short laugh. "The word 'if' gives me a headache. It's a bad-news warning, like rain to arthritis."

"If there's any trouble leaving Moscow, I'll know it and meet you at 3:00 p.m. the next day on the bench nearest the tiger cage at Durov's Corner. Do you know that little zoo for trained animals?"

He nodded. "I know it, but what if I can't make it that day?"

"Then I'll be there the next day, and the next, until . . ."

"Until you know I won't be coming," he mumbled.

"The pass-by signal will be a newspaper in my lap. If you see that, keep going, it'll mean I suspect a tail on one of us. In the meantime, the Sicarii will take care of you."

"Who exactly are they?"

"I never met them. All I know is they hate the Communists enough to help us. The word is, they check out okay. Anyway, with the Ukrainian Freedom Movement on the run, we can't be too choosy. Not everyone in Russia would be willing to have him as a houseguest." Lana gestured with her head in the direction of the cot. She suddenly reached into her handbag. "By the way, I brought you a present, something you need." She lifted her hand cupped over a black object and handed it to Jude.

He looked down on a small .25-caliber automatic and started to hand it back to her. "No thanks. I've learned that guns lead to three bad things: they make killing easy, an exercise I never found entertaining; they persuade you to stand and fight when the sensible thing is to run; and they tend to get you charged with murder in countries where the victim is usually the best friend of someone important and a fair trial is about as common as a duck in the desert."

She pushed his hand back. "Please take it for me." He shrugged and put it on the counter by the sink.

"Tell me," Jude said, "how did you get mixed up in all this? I mean, meeting me with Danton back in California, that fellow Harbuziak in Mexico, showing up at this shack like you were expected for dinner. When I least expect it, I get bumped into by you."

"You make a nice bump," she joked but with a sensuous undertone.

He smiled broadly. Even a vague sexual reference gave him a tingling feeling.

"To be serious, I know what you mean," she said. "My real name is Svetlana Martinova. In the States I go by Lana Martin. My parents lived in Novgorod, north of here, until the Second World War when they were uprooted and shuffled into Western Europe, and eventually ended up in the United States. I grew up speaking Russian at home and English in school. My parents hated Communism, so I guess that rubbed off. After college, I was recruited by the CIA and sent to 'The Farm,' Camp Peary in Virginia. After two years, I came out a guaranteed, certified Russian. I knew where to get the best deal on nylons or fresh fish in Moscow, and I could name the best players on the Dynamo soccer team. Coming here to take up with Ivan Kolchak was just like coming home. Headquarters equipped me with an identity using my old name that only the most thorough cross-checking would uncover. They even arranged a job and provided a dead husband."

"Weren't you afraid that Kolchak would check you out closely?"

"When was the last time you checked out someone you dated?" she asked bluntly. "My job was to be convincing enough so that wouldn't happen."

"Have you done this kind of assignment before, I mean, uh, like with Kolchak?" Jude asked with a trace of embarrassment in his voice.

Lana blushed and said a little too quickly, "Remember when we sat in that little café in Mexico, the one I thought had the great lobster, and you laid out your life story? Well, we're now even. Let's call it a tie."

Jude laughed softly. "Did you know that I actually suspected you of being part of the attack on me by those two Mexicans? Can you imagine that?"

Her soprano laughter blended with his. "I knew that, but there wasn't anything I could do. You wouldn't have believed me at the time. You were so suspicious." She lowered her voice. "And so cute."

Jude shifted nervously and looked at his watch. "Would you like a drink? I have almost an hour and a half before we go to meet the Sicarii."

"I'd love it—even vodka."

Jude went to the plank shelf above the stove and took down a half full bottle and two glasses. While he prepared the drinks, she talked to his back. "Do you have any idea how respected you are in the agency? I was in absolute awe of meeting the great Jude Miller. Even the trouble you got into made you seem even more larger-than-life. Everyone said you were the best—except Danton, of course. I think he's jealous. If I were going to pick a hero, it'd be you."

"That's silly," Jude said with an embarrassed laugh while he poured. He knew she was being half-humorous, but the compliment made his heart quicken with a sense of redemption. When he turned back to her, she had moved over to the corner and was sitting on his sleeping bag. "Do you sleep on this?" she asked, patting the quilted material. "It's really quite comfortable."

Jude sat down awkwardly beside her with two glasses in his hands. "Better sleep on it yourself before you make that judgment," he said.

Lana took one of the glasses and smiled at him brazenly. "Is that an invitation?" She broke up into giggles. "I can't believe I said that! I must sound like an escapee from a soap opera. 'Is that an invitation?'" She listened to her own words disbelievingly. "Tell me I didn't say that."

They rocked with laughter and the vodka in their glasses jiggled precariously. Jude looked at her dark eyes and gently bouncing breasts. He felt a sudden rage toward any other man who would touch her, especially Kolchak, the enemy. It wasn't fair; Jude wanted her, and she wanted him. It was right that they have each other. He felt himself harden and he put a hand timorously toward the soft flesh of her cheek. She leaned forward and he could smell the essence of jasmine in her perfume; it fleetingly reminded him of Tamara, but the warmth of Lana's breath chased that ghost from his mind.

Their shoulders had barely touched when a stirring from the other side of the room broke them apart.

"I've got to piss," the old man said and struggled like an overturned turtle to get to his feet.

Jude and Lana looked at each other with disappointment. "We'll meet again," she said.

A SHARP WIND CUT THROUGH Jude's heavy coat, making him hunch his shoulders for warmth, but the old man beside him seemed unaffected by the cold even though his face had turned a cheery red under the white whiskers of his disguise. Jude glanced over and it occurred to him that the old man could pass for Santa Claus, given the correct red uniform. Hell of a comedown, he thought, from premier to jolly old St. Nick.

The two were standing in front of Detsky Mir, the giant children's store, ten feet to the right of the main entrance, just as Gurko had instructed. Jude glanced at his watch. Twelve minutes past two. They had stood in the same spot, being brushed and pushed by an endless crowd of milling mothers, for almost twenty minutes, and no contact from the Sicarii had resulted.

Jude was starting to rack his brain for ideas on how to survive a blown meeting when a small black car pulled up to the curb and the driver motioned hurriedly for them to get in. After a moment's hesitation to make sure they were the ones being signaled, Jude guided the old man through the crowd and into the back seat.

The car pulled away sharply from the curb and the driver, without taking his eyes from the road, said, "I'm David. You're safe now."

"Well, I can't say I regret that," Jude said with exasperation, "but why did you have to be so damned late? *Chort*, my nerves can only take so much."

"I went around several times to make sure it was safe," David said. Before Jude could answer, David looked in the rearview mirror and Jude could see the dark eyes crinkle with amusement. "What's the matter, *Amerikanski*, losing your nerve?"

THE TWO OLD MEN MET in the center of the room and touched parchment hands warily, like unfamiliar cats meeting in an alley. Although they had lived many decades in the same country, so unalike were they that the meeting had all the familiarity of Columbus meeting the Indians. Rebbe Israel Rabinowitz had existed in a subculture that created a world of its own, and because of it he had been forced to live his life as a hare among hounds. Nikita S. Khrushchev had been a giant, who strode the middle of the street that Rabinowitz avoided. He had been a hound.

"Welcome to our home, Mr. Chairman, although I must tell you I strongly disapprove of this thing my son is involved in. But our tradition is to never turn away the man who runs from injustice, so this house becomes yours," the rebbe said, still shaking Khrushchev's hand.

"Thank you, Your Holiness," Khrushchev said, fumbling for the correct form of address.

The rebbe shook his head. "I am not a patriarch; rebbe is what I am called."

"What can we call you?" David said sarcastically to Khrushchev. "Prince, as in prince of overstuffed bureaucrats?"

Khrushchev laughed dryly. His eyes were more alert than Jude had ever seen before. He seemed to relish being among strangers for a change. "Some of those so-called agricultural experts in their fancy London-tailored suits used to wish I *was* a bureaucrat when I kicked them out of their warm Moscow offices to tromp around in pig shit with the farmers they were supposed to be serving. *Chort*, did they grumble and whine! I used to go through those parlor revolutionaries like a goose goes through corn. As for being 'overstuffed'—'' he patted his ample belly judiciously ''—well, a smart peasant never passed up a free meal or a willing woman, and I had plenty of each blocking my path.'' He grinned broadly. ''A farmer sees a fertile field, he plows it.''

Seeing no reaction from his new hosts, Khrushchev slapped his hands nervously against his stomach. ''Did you hear the story about the Cossacks on a pogrom? It seems these four Cossacks were on their ponies overlooking this Jewish village. The leader says, 'Okay, comrades, here's the plan for today's raid: Ivan, I want you to plunder; Vassily, you pillage; and Mikhail, you burn.' Well, Vladimir is toward the back of the group and he says to himself, very upset, '*Yob*, that means I have to rape again.'''

The rebbe, David and Jude exchanged embarrassed looks. Khrushchev, who was waiting for them to share his laughter, grew quiet and asked, ''Don't any of you have a sense of humor?''

The rebbe cleared his throat. ''Sir, not enough time has passed for Jews in this country to find pogroms humorous. You'll forgive us; we don't mean to be rude.''

''Rude?'' David said with astonishment. ''How could we be rude to this old Jew-baiter? Tell me, *vebdyadok*, how many Jews did you kill in the old days? How many did you rape?''

''David!'' the rebbe shouted, shock and disapproval in his voice.

Khrushchev held up his palm. ''It's all right. I've been baited by Richard Nixon and Mao Tse-tung; I can handle this puppy.'' Turning to David, he said, ''When I was your age, I was a machinist's mate in Mariupol, a small port in the Ukraine where many Jews lived. I boarded with a Jewish

family named Yenkelevich. They were kind people. I would
light the fire on cold Sabbath mornings, which their religion
wouldn't permit them to do. It was 1913 and the Black
Hundreds—they were the worst Jew-haters, your father will
remember—attacked the Jewish quarter. I was injured in the
battle, fighting alongside the Jews. My landlady bandaged my
wounds, and I'll never forget what she said to me: 'Nikita
Sergeyevich, you are a true friend of the Jews.'" He repeated the words softly, as though addressing a memory, "A
true friend of the Jews."

David laughed sarcastically. "One old man's fish story
doesn't change the fact that you made life miserable for millions of Jews when you were premier."

The rebbe had a stricken look on his face and started to interrupt.

Khrushchev stopped him with a voice that rose above the
rebbe's, a voice accustomed to holding the floor. He pointed
a stern finger at David. "The only trouble I ever gave the Jews
was the same trouble I gave anyone who refused to cooperate
with the state. We were trying to build socialism while surrounded by capitalist enemies, who lurked like hungry wea-
sels waiting outside a henhouse. The only thing I asked of any
Soviet citizen was to put his country first, and that was the
thing many Jews refused to do. They wanted to go their own
way, and if everyone in Russia had done that, the capitalists
would have had us for dinner, like a dumb, juicy lamb. By the
memory of Lenin, I swear I never lifted a finger against a man
because he was a Jew." Khrushchev looked to the rebbe in
appeal. "Speak up, holy man, did I persecute the Jews?"

The rebbe looked at David, then at Jude, then at Khrushchev. Jude had never seen a man who looked so at peace,
so unassumingly certain of the path of goodness. "In fairness, life for Jews became less threatening under Chairman
Khrushchev. The years before him, under Stalin, were a cancer on Russia's soul and a knife in many a Jew's heart." He

looked squarely at Khrushchev, who returned the look. "I believe Chairman Khrushchev tried to do good for most people and meant no evil toward Jews. Any harm that resulted was from ignorance or passion, and that's the easiest kind to forgive."

Khrushchev shook his head at a frustrating memory, "When you're a ruler, Jews drive you crazy. All I asked was for them to blend in and go along, not be so stubborn and fractious. But no, they had to be different."

"If we weren't different, we wouldn't be Jews," the rebbe said. "I sympathize with the goyim in trying to deal with us. Being Jews is not easy for us, either, but we must live as God commands."

"God has never given me advice, but I can understand the problems," Khrushchev said so uncharacteristically that the others were left looking for the sarcasm.

David slammed his fist on the arm of his chair. "When Stalin was tormenting the Jews, you were there, doing the devil's bidding," he said, pointing accusingly at Khrushchev. "The only reason I'm saving your carcass is to help free Jews like the ones the two of you persecuted."

"Stop!" The rebbe's voice thundered through the room. "You will not invite a man into this house and then abuse him. You shame me. The son of a rebbe should not behave like an ignorant lout, insulting guests in his father's home. Such conduct isn't our way."

Jude listened to the indignation of the rebbe and smiled slightly. All righhhht! he said to himself.

David stood up and, without a word, stomped out of the house.

The rebbe ignored his son's departure and swept an arm toward the kitchen. "I have cooked a chicken."

Khrushchev grinned. "When a peasant gets to eat a chicken, it's usually because one of them is sick."

CHAPTER SEVENTEEN

BORIS GURKO STARED LONGINGLY at the patch of sunlight cut into small squares by the window bars. The clang of steel doors and the steady thud of anonymous footsteps on the catwalk beyond his cell reminded him that other humans shared this desolate space, but the knowledge provided no comfort.

Gurko was imprisoned somewhere in Moscow. He had been picked up by the KGB while sitting in a restaurant on Gorky Street eating dinner. They had been quick and efficient, like good bureaucrats well practiced in their routine. Two of them grabbed Gurko by the arms and three others formed a cordon to escort him to a closed van at curbside. The other patrons pretended not to notice, seeing no reason why dinner should be spoiled by a routine secret police arrest.

Now, sitting on his cot with only a thin blanket to pad the iron ridges below, he tried to get into the game. And it was a game, he was convinced. They were letting him sit, stew, worry, and then when they thought he had been softened up enough, they would come for him. The idea that perhaps they were too busy with other prisoners and that he would have to wait his turn did not occur to him. The egocentricity that accompanies imprisonment would not allow it. Nothing in the world exists to the prisoner except his own misery.

Gurko steeled himself against the torture he was certain would soon be upon him. He thought of the ways they might try to hurt him, thought of how the pain might feel and how he could withstand it. He prepared himself as a soldier does before battle, knowing that he will soon be at the mercy of devils turned loose and that his only defense will be his wits, his only revenge a sealed-lips death.

He heard keys rattle in the lock and watched curiously until the iron door swung open and a stony-faced guard entered and motioned for Gurko to follow. He was escorted to a dark room with a hard-backed chair and a single light beating down in a circle like a spotlight. Gurko guessed the room was soundproof by the hollow sounds their footsteps made.

The guard gestured to the chair and Gurko sat down and peered into the darkness. After a few minutes, he heard a door open and close and footsteps walk slowly toward him. A face emerged into the light. It was a face that mothers describe to threaten naughty children. One eye was skewed off to the side and a milky surface was where the pupil should have been. The hair and skin were almost albino-white, and a cigarette dangled from the lips providing a diabolical smoke screen reminiscent of Dante's *Inferno*.

"My name is Papirosa. I will be your host."

Gurko sensed the presence of evil, but he persuaded himself to see it as comical. He had to fight intimidation. He forced a laugh.

Papirosa watched Gurko laugh and smiled himself. "You're amused? That's good. It's nice to have my hospitality appreciated."

"It's not your hospitality, it's your face," Gurko said. "You're even uglier than I."

Papirosa's face lost its smile. "Bravado is a wonderful thing. Do you really think you can maintain it?"

Gurko stared at his inquisitor and said nothing, but he was thinking, I will do my best for as long as I can.

Papirosa walked in a little circle just outside the lighted area of Gurko's chair, just out of sight, but his voice and footsteps assaulted Gurko's mind like an echo chamber. "What we are faced with, friend Gurko, is a difficult situation. You see, we need the information that's in your head, but we don't believe you'll share it with us honestly, even though you'll promise to do so before we're through. You could call it a credibility gap. Put yourself in our shoes and maybe you can understand the need to give you a little test to make sure you're telling the truth. Oh, I'm not talking about a truth serum or lie detector, those aren't reliable enough for our standards. I'm talking about something more basic, more— primitive. You probably won't enjoy the experience, but I hope you can sympathize with our problem."

Papirosa abruptly stepped into the light and gestured with his head. Two guards that Gurko hadn't even realized were present reached out and grabbed his arms while Papirosa wound a rope tightly around his upper body, tying him to the chair.

Papirosa surveyed his trussed-up victim critically. "Not a bad piece of work. I prefer to do the skill jobs myself— professional pride. Do you have circulation in the arms?" He felt the ropes. "Good. Now, the lights."

Gurko blinked as powerful bulbs flashed on. It was a long moment before the black and red dots before his eyes gradually cleared. He saw that the center of the room contained a small pool of water flush with the floor, about five feet deep and an equal distance in diameter. The guards fastened a winch to the legs of his chair and stood back as Papirosa again stepped forward. He gestured toward the pool. "This is my own invention. I got the idea from the dunking chairs used in the witch trials in the old days. I like history; the past has a lot to teach us. We're going to put you into the pool for long enough to get your attention." He gave a happy sigh. "Oh, yes, definitely get your attention. Then we'll lift you out and ask some questions. If we're not satisfied you're telling the truth, we'll put you back in, and so on. You get the idea. The important thing for you to remember is that if you don't convince us you're telling everything you know, the last time we won't pull you out. What you won't know is which time will be the last." Papirosa stepped back and made a short gesture to the guards who hoisted the chair and lowered it into the water.

Gurko felt the warm water as it touched his ankles, his legs, his stomach, his chest, and finally, inexorably, his face. Just before it covered his head he took a deep breath and then was completely submerged.

For the first thirty seconds, Gurko stayed calm. He sat in the pool waiting to see how long they would keep him under, not knowing what else to do, incapable of doing anything else.

Looking down into the water, Papirosa slowly counted off the seconds. "One thousand forty, one thousand forty-one..."

After one minute, Gurko began to slowly release short bursts of tiny air bubbles to relieve the gradually increasing pressure in his lungs.

"One thousand sixty-nine, one thousand seventy..."

At one minute fifteen seconds the air had been expended from his lungs and Gurko felt the pressure in his chest mounting like a heated thermometer. He clamped his lips sealed, shook his head wildly and strained against the ropes to ease the pressure, but it only tightened its hold. His rational powers fled and he no longer knew where he was. He was only aware of the pressure, not a pain exactly, more like a panic. His body was pleading desperately for something he didn't have the power to give—oxygen.

"One thousand eighty, one thousand eighty-one..."

Gurko had to escape the pressure, even if it killed him. He opened his mouth and inhaled deeply. The water flooded into his mouth and down into his lungs, but his body demanded more, so he inhaled again. There was still no oxygen, so his body again did the only thing nature equipped it for, it inhaled again. Unconsciousness flickered in his brain like a shorted-out bulb. He was about to die.

"One thousand ninety..."

One of the guards, a twenty-year-old farm boy from Siberia named Vassily, looked at Gurko struggling in the water and glanced questioningly at the placid-faced older guard and then at the leering Papirosa. Vassily had just transferred to this duty from a prison in Odessa, but he had never seen a man tortured. What he had witnessed in the past two weeks of working with Papirosa had destroyed his sleep, ruined his appetite, and given him a bitter hatred for the cruel man happily staring into the water.

"One thousand ninety-seven. Okay, haul him up," Papirosa commanded Vassily and his partner. The guards didn't know that Papirosa was conducting an experiment to see how long he could keep prisoners submerged and still revive them. It was an exercise that led to no conclusions other than satisfying his curiosity, like an overweight jogger recording his times.

Gurko was hauled dripping from the pool. His body sagged against the ropes and his head rolled on his shoulders. He was vomiting and gagging as his lungs demanded the sweet air. Papirosa pounded him on the back helpfully and said between Gurko's coughing fits, "One minute forty. Great. I see you as maybe a two-minute man. Maybe you'll get the record. Good going."

Papirosa waited for Gurko to recover, then he sat directly in front of the still-trussed man, who weakly stared back at him. "Friend Gurko, tell me all about the Ukrainian Freedom Movement. I want every name in your memory. I want the address of every meeting you've attended. I want all the dates."

Gurko tiredly raised his head and glared at Papirosa through red-rimmed eyes. *"Idi na uberasya,"* he said. "Suck my prick."

Papirosa laughed loudly with a childlike delight. "Wonderful! Wonderful!" he shouted. "Men," he called, gesturing to the guards, "come over here."

Vassily and the other guard moved close to Papirosa and Gurko. Papirosa spoke as though conducting a clinic. "If you boys are ambitious, you can learn something from this. What we are witnessing here is a classic example of psychological vulnerability. This prisoner—" he let his hand rest lightly on Gurko's head "—has been preparing for this moment by screwing up his courage to say to me what you just heard. That tells me the only thing he has remaining is a false sense of what the Spanish call machismo, which means he is defenseless. When the bluster deserts him—and I assure you it will—he'll become gelatin; anything I want him to do he will do. I might even have him suck *my* prick." He paused and gave a theatrical wince. "After we've pulled his teeth, of course."

Papirosa's grating laugh drew a lukewarm response from the second guard, but the face of Vassily, who was standing behind Papirosa, looked as if he had just heard his mother insulted.

Twice more that day Gurko was lowered into the water. Twice more he endured the panic of near-drowning. Twice more he hurled insults at Papirosa, but each time the words lacked the force and confidence of the last. He was finally dragged back to his cell with the promise of more sessions the next day.

Stretched out exhausted on the hard bunk, Gurko lay awake in wide-eyed dread as the hours passed, every minute marked in his mind, every minute narrowing the time until the water would again tease him with death. He knew that another day of the torture would break him, reduce him to a quivering, pleading tool of the man who called himself Papirosa.

The guards came for him early, barely past the time he had pushed aside uneaten the thin gruel they called breakfast. Numbly, he allowed himself to be led back into the room with the pool, where he was pushed down on the chair. The still-wet ropes were on the floor nearby, ready to be used again.

Papirosa cheerfully greeted him like a colleague. "Aha, friend Gurko! Good morning. Ready to go to work?"

Gurko buried his head in his hands and began to weep. His shoulders shook as his mind tried to cope with the fear and dread.

A look of triumph flashed across Papirosa's face. "Are you giving up? Are you ready to talk?"

Gurko nodded.

Papirosa switched on a tape recorder. "All right, then, let's start with when you first made contact with the Ukrainian Freedom Movement."

Gurko looked up at Papirosa, tears still streaming down his face, and then glanced resentfully at the guards, then back at Papirosa.

Papirosa's eyes followed Gurko's movements until a look of comprehension came over his face. With a confession at hand, he could afford to play a compassion card. "I understand. Men," he said to the guards, "why don't you step outside for a few minutes? It's embarrassing for friend Gurko to do this in front of so many people."

"But, your safety—" the second guard said.

Papirosa laughed. "My safety? I could break this little fellow like a nun's cherry. You," he said, putting his hand on Vassily's shoulder, "stand guard at the door, and you—" he indicated the second guard "—why don't you get us some coffee?"

When the door closed, Papirosa came closer and stood between Gurko and the pool. "Now, little fellow, let's—"

The force of Gurko's shoulder in his stomach drove the air from Papirosa's lungs, popping the cigarette from his mouth like a champagne cork. He collapsed into the water with a loud splash, with Gurko atop him, clawing for his throat. Water filled Papirosa's mouth and nose and he thrashed about aimlessly in panic, making him easy prey for the fury of his attacker. Gurko entwined his hands in Papirosa's white hair and pushed him under the water, then pulled him up, gagging and moaning, and began to beat his head against the tiled edge of the pool. Once, twice, three times he heard the satisfying dull thud of Papirosa's head slammed against the stone, leaving widening red smears on the white surface.

Vassily was standing in the corridor, leaning against the door, when he heard the splash and Papirosa's muffled shouts. He threw the door open and saw Gurko climbing all over Papirosa, like an angry bulldog. Vassily drew his pistol and pointed it at Gurko's back. He pulled the trigger and heard the click of the empty chamber. In the shock of what he had seen, he had forgotten that the clip was in his pocket, a standard precaution against prisoners who might grab a gun. With the fumbling movements of extreme haste, he slammed the clip into the butt of the automatic, pulled back the cocking slide and fired two bullets into Gurko's back.

As the roar of the pistol collided with the steel walls, Gurko released Papirosa's head and slid facedown into the pool. Vassily holstered the pistol and ran around to where Papirosa was propped against the side of the pool, his bloody head resting on the edge. Papirosa's eyes were closed and his breathing came in shallow spurts. Vassily looked up to make sure that no one had followed him in and that the door had closed behind him. Confirming he was alone, he roughly grabbed Papirosa by the hair and slammed his head against the tile with all his power. The sound was like that of an apple thrown against a wall. Vassily dropped Papirosa's lolling head like a piece of rotten fruit and stared at the man he had just shot to death. He whispered sadly to Gurko's body, "Poor bastard, you got the best end you could hope for," and started to pull Papirosa's body from the pool as the door burst open and guards filled the room.

IT COULD HAVE BEEN JERUSALEM around the time of Christ. It could have been Spain in the fifteenth century. It could have been the Berlin of the Third Reich. The men could have been arrogant Roman legionnaires in plumed helmets or Torquemada's priests with the fever of the Inquisition burning in their brains. They could have been Gestapo. The years pass and the uniforms change, but for the Jews of the Diaspora, one thing does not: the knock on the door.

Persecutors prefer nighttime when their targets are asleep, but they can strike anywhere, anytime: the classroom, the breakfast table, the synagogue, even the toilet.

The KGB had more than a thousand Jews to arrest quickly, a circumstance that crowded out finesse and good manners.

ANTON IGNATOV WAS UNDISTINGUISHED among thousands of students at Moscow State University, where he studied mechanical engineering. A young man of average abilities, cursed with chronic bronchitis, he kept pace with his brighter colleagues despite frequent illnesses, by working harder and blocking out all diversions. He wanted only to graduate and start a career that would allow him to repay his struggling parents, who devoted their meager resources to the dream that Anton and his sister, Irina, would achieve the education they were denied.

Anton wearily turned back the page of the text to try again to understand the problem. It was in a course named Experimental Stress Analysis, and Anton had been over the material a dozen times, two dozen, and still it wasn't clear. He sighed and started to read again.

A heavy pounding forced Anton's eyes off the page and he stared at the door, which seemed to jump against its hinges at the steady pounding. Anton's father rushed out of the single bedroom, falling against furniture as he tried to put on his glasses on the move. He approached the door and said nervously, "Who is it?"

"Militia. Open up."

As soon as Anton's father turned the key, the door flew open and three men rushed into the room. "Is the Jew Anton Ignatov here?"

Anton slowly rose from the kitchen table where he was working. "I am he. What's wrong? What have I done?"

The oldest militiaman strode over to the table and snapped handcuffs on Anton. "You are a collaborator with anti-Soviet elements."

Anton was baffled by the charge, and then he remembered signing a petition a few weeks before in front of the synagogue, for the release of political prisoners. It had been an impulsive act, one that Anton had instantly regretted. It had to be that.

"All I did was sign a petition, a harmless thing! Will you take me away for that?"

"For less than that, Jew," the senior guard taunted and gave the handcuffs a sharp tug as Anton stumbled awkwardly toward the door.

IRINA IGNATOV TRIED to take notes on the lecture, but the tears blinded her and turned the words on the lined paper into an unreadable pool of blue ink. At the end of the class, she uttered a throaty sob, slammed her books shut and headed for the door. David Rabinowitz had been watching her from across the lecture hall and moved to intercept her.

"Irina, what's the matter?" he asked, putting his arm around her and drawing her close in a protective gesture.

"The police came last night and arrested Anton. They took him away in handcuffs." The words seemed to breach the dam of her emotions, and she wilted against David and sobbed loudly. "What's happening, David? Why are they arresting so many Jews? Anton did nothing. He's so weak, he can't live through something like this. Isn't there anyone who can help?"

David said nothing, but he patted her shoulder gently and looked over her head into the distance, the knots of his jaw working angrily. With a wan smile, he told Irina that things would get better, then he turned and walked away with his head down, the captive of a deep depression that struck as suddenly as a spring storm. David was learning that to swat at a wasp is to invite the sting. Whether in a just cause or not, it is a frightening thing to cause terror and misery to hundreds of one's own people. David thought desperately of how he could accomplish his purpose yet spare the Jews of Moscow the consequences. Slowly, an idea took shape. It was a distasteful plan, but David was not in a state of mind to quibble over the fine points of morality.

THE WEEK HAD BEEN TOUGH for Ivan Kolchak. He and his men were working around the clock, sorting out and interrogating the nearly seventeen hundred Jews and other known dissidents arrested following the bombing of Lenin's Tomb. Some who had been arrested before were sent to prison in faraway places; some were interrogated and released; others were held for "deeper interrogation," which was a euphemism for torture. In addition, it seemed that every KGB superior and party bureaucrat insisted on being briefed at every turn. With soldiers guarding every public monument, Moscow was beginning to resemble a city besieged, and although the Lenin's Tomb bombing had been concealed under the pretext of the tomb's being closed for repairs, the foreign press hummed with speculation on the reason for the intensified security.

It had become increasingly apparent to Kolchak that his career was tied to success or failure in this case. The pressure of that realization, coupled with the necessary absences from Svetlana, made his temper perilously frayed, something for which his subordinates, especially the ever-handy Kyril Petrovich, constantly bore the brunt.

The intercom line rang and Kolchak picked up the receiver and growled, "Yes?"

Petrovich spoke quietly but with excitement in his voice. "It's him, Comrade Kolchak, the Jew who claims he blew up the tomb. He wants to talk to you. I'll put a trace on the call."

Kolchak grunted and waited for the call to be switched. When he heard the hum of the line coming alive, he snapped, "This is Kolchak."

"This is Moses of the Sicarii."

"So, we haven't caught you yet. That means we'll just have to arrest more Jews. How do you like it so far, Zid? A little more than you bargained for?"

"I never underestimate the power of evil, Kolchak, but we have survived your worst for hundreds of years; we'll survive this."

"What is it you want?" Kolchak demanded.

"A deal. I have an offer for you."

"Yes?" Kolchak said impatiently.

"I don't think that's the correct attitude in which to negotiate. Speak politely or we don't talk."

"What is it you want to say?" Kolchak said less harshly.

"In exchange for the release of the Jewish prisoners you arrested in the past few days, and the same emigration demand I mentioned before, I will give you Nikita Khrushchev."

Kolchak grimaced at the phone. "*Dolboyob*, what are you talking about?"

"Just as I said. Khrushchev for the Jews."

"You're crazy. Khrushchev died in 1971. He's buried in the cemetery at Novodevichye Convent. I was at the funeral myself."

"I'm telling you, I have Khrushchev, alive, and if you don't want him, the Americans do. Check it out—you know how. I assume your men have traced this call and are on the way. We'll talk again."

Kolchak stared perplexed at the dead phone. "Kyril," he bellowed, "get in here."

Petrovich was through the door in moments, shaking his head. "Same as before, public phone in a busy place. We won't catch him."

"What do you think?" Kolchak asked.

"What is there to think? It's crazy. He sounds like a nut, but given the stakes, we'll just have to do as he says and check it out."

Kolchak nodded. "Prepare to quietly exhume the grave. Quietly," he added again for emphasis. "I'll have to go upstairs—all the way to the top—to get permission. Meanwhile, I want a constant, twenty-four-hour guard on the grave, but stay out of sight. Check out anyone who shows an interest, even tourists. Considering whose grave is involved, I have a very queasy feeling, but we've got to follow through, weird as it is."

Kolchak drew a deep breath and dialed the number of his superior, Dmitry Nesterov. He always became nervous at the prospect of talking to senior government officials, and the beads of sweat popped out on his forehead despite the coolness of the room.

THEY MOVED FURTIVELY in the quiet cemetery, like superstitious grave robbers, hunched silhouettes backdropped by the spiny tentacles of leafless trees reaching toward the moonlit sky.

Although the old cemetery of Novodevichye Convent was deserted in the early-morning hours, the stern instructions of Ivan Kolchak that absolutely no one should know of their mission made the exhumation team extra cautious.

The night watchman had been sent home and even the superintendent of the museum housed in the converted convent was told only that the KGB had important work to do.

His curiosity had deferred to discretion and he hadn't asked further questions.

One man stopped and splashed the yellow beam of a flashlight onto an imposing tombstone. Silently he read the letters spread across the rough granite: NIKITA SERGEYEVICH KHRUSHCHEV. "Over here," he called softly and the team clustered around. A large mechanical shovel was backed into position and soon was carving great scoops from the black earth of the burial site. When they heard the steel blade of the shovel scrape against concrete, they pulled the machine away and four men jumped into the hole. They quickly cleared the remaining dirt, then, with strong lights beaming directly down into the hole, they heaved together until the heavy lid of the concrete liner slid off and tipped against the wall of the grave.

The concrete had cracked in several places, allowing water to seep inside and collect at the bottom. The steel casket was pitted with rust and several insects scurried out of the way of the bright lights.

"*Yob*, they sure did a cheap job on this fellow," one of the workers said.

"He was lucky they didn't just throw him into a hole, goddamned traitor," one of the others said as he placed a chisel against the metal and hammered the locks off. He was from the medical examiner's office and had exhumed scores of bodies. He turned and grinned up into the lights directed down into the grave. He knew that for the KGB observers this was a first time, and he relished the chance to make them uneasy.

"I hope you fellows have strong stomachs. After seventeen years, you never know what you're going to see when you open the lid. I've seen them where it looked like they'd just fallen asleep, and I've opened some and found only a few bones and some hair. Once, all I found were two rats." He patted the coffin top and the hollow sound was ominous in its reply. "You'll notice that water has leaked into the liner. That's bad. And the casket's pitted with rust. That means worms might have gotten inside. I'll—"

"Get on with it," said a deep, irritated voice from behind the lights.

Knowing that his little tease had lost its humor, the man slid a mask over his mouth and nose and slowly lifted the coffin lid as the rusted hinges squealed a protest.

An odor rose from the box that drove the onlookers on the surface back several steps. One man could be heard retching. Several cursed in disgust. It was the smell of death, an odor so repugnant that it sticks to the memory like neurosensory glue. It is the smell of a dead animal being picked at by crows as heat waves rise from the pavement, of garbage covered by squirming maggots, of cheese left in a hot room. It is all these smells, and more. Death is nature rendering works, and its purpose is not to make perfume.

The lights flashed into the coffin and the onlookers leaned forward to see. The red satin of the lining had faded to a watery brown. The body was obviously that of an old man but badly decomposed. The moisture in the casket had hastened the process and the body was close to becoming a skeleton. It had lost about half its bulk. The collar of the white shirt fitted loosely around the shriveled neck, as though made for a much larger man. Around the edges of the moldy black suit was an eighth of an inch of liquid with brown splotches on its surface—body fluids with fat on top. The portions of the body showing, head and hands, were part yellowish-brown bone, part grayish-green mold and part skin. The skin was the same color as the bone and resembled cracked leather. On the scalp was a small tuft of white hair. The eyes and eyelids had rotted away and two tiny plastic caps rested atop the remaining black holes. One cheek was covered with mold and the other had patches of dried skin clinging to it, but the lips had vanished leaving only grinning white teeth.

The examiner put on rubber gloves, unclasped the dead man's hands and inspected each finger in turn. Most of the fingers had become skeletonized, but two still had patches of dried skin on the tips, possibly enough to obtain finger prints. He snapped those off and placed them carefully in a box and then into a plastic bag. Next, he placed both hands firmly around the skull and twisted with all his strength. A sharp crack violated the hushed quiet and two of the observers visibly winced. The examiner put the detached skull in the bag for later dental comparisons and climbed out of the grave. The other men closed the coffin and slid the concrete lid back in place.

"Okay, men, show's over," the KGB agent in charge said. "Get this hole filled in and then bring in those landscapers. By dawn, I want this place looking as usual."

"SATISFIED?" the voice on the telephone asked Kolchak in a familiar gloating manner that infuriated him.

"Satisfied with what?" Kolchak pretended to not know what the man who called himself Moses meant.

"Don't be coy, Mr. KGB thug. You know what I mean. You found out that the body in Khrushchev's grave is some one else, didn't you?"

"Regardless of what we may or may not have found, how do I know you've got the real Khrushchev?"

"Because, *dura*, I'm telling you I do, you fool. What would be the point of lying?"

Kolchak's fist squeezed the telephone in silent rage at the insult, but he refused to give his adversary the satisfaction of knowing that. "This is what I'm prepared to offer: if you deliver the man we can positively identify as Nikita S. Khrushchev, we will release all the Jews we rounded up since the bombing of Lenin's Tomb, and we will allow them, except any who might have knowledge of state secrets, to emigrate to Israel. In addition, you, and all members of your Sicarii organization, up to one hundred, can accompany them.''

There was a deep silence at the other end as the offer was considered. ''I'll call you back in a couple of hours—from a different phone,'' David said and hung up.

When the telephone with the special number Kolchak had given David rang again two and a half hours later, Kolchak let it ring several times to avoid appearing overanxious. ''Kolchak,'' he said crisply when he finally picked it up.

''Moses. One further question: what about my demand to allow one hundred thousand Jews per year to leave for Israel?''

Kolchak cleared his throat and recited the remarks he had carefully prepared. ''That's an issue we can't settle quite so easily. It involves decisions at the highest level of government. Delicate and complicated negotiations with the Israeli government will be necessary. Then, there is the matter of establishing priority lists for those emigrating. You can see, it isn't a simple yes or no matter. I can assure you, however that the government of the Soviet Union has recognized the value of ridding the country of all those who might express their dissatisfaction the way your group has. You can anticipate your demands being looked on favorably, subject to working out a great many complex details.''

''Not good enough. How do I know you'd keep your word? Nothing happens until the government makes a public statement—a clear, unequivocal statement—that the exact number of Jews I specified will be allowed to emigrate.''

''The government of the Soviet Union does not double-cross,'' Kolchak said huffily. ''There would be no point in it, since you could then resume your rather tiresome terrorist activities.''

''Tell it to the Afghans. I have nothing more to say. You knew my demands and you refused to meet them. The next time you see Khrushchev, he'll be on television. Good-bye—''

"Wait!" Kolchak said hurriedly, then forced himself to calm down when he realized David was still on the line. "It'll take me a little time, but I'll see what I can do."

"What arrangements have you made to get us out of the country?" David said.

"Two days after you give us Khrushchev, which will allow time to make definite identification, you and your followers will phone the Swiss embassy and their officials will meet you at a place of your choosing. From there, they will escort you to Shermetyevo Airport where an Israeli plane will fly you out. The Israelis and Swiss have assured us that the entire operation will be given highest state secrecy so as not to give encouragement to other potential terrorists. If you say anything to the foreign press, all three governments will deny it."

"Okay, but I want to hear it from the Swiss ambassador himself. Tell the ambassador that I'll phone him tomorrow morning at nine. And I warn you, I'll make a tape of the conversation, so if there's any betrayal, the American press will be given proof of it."

Kolchak struggled to control his anger. "How will you deliver him?"

David gave a short laugh. "Not personally, you can count on that." Pride kept into his voice. "I've already thought this out. I'll arrange to leave him on a street corner; he's an old man, he won't go anyplace. Then I'll call you to come pick him up. How quickly can you respond?"

"We will be wherever you say in this city within two or three minutes. When can you do this?"

"A day or two. I'll have to work out the timing."

"One other thing," Kolchak said. "We also want the American agent involved in this."

Caught off guard, David was silent for a long moment. "No—I mean there's no such person."

You're lying, Kolchak said to himself. "We believe there
s. We want him, too."

"If there were such a man, I wouldn't give him to you.
Khrushchev, yes, the Jews owe him nothing, but I wouldn't
betray an innocent man to your clutches." After a pause, David added hastily, "Even if such a person existed."

"We'll wait for your call," Kolchak said and both men
hung up.

"*Malen'kii vebdyadok*, little bastard," Kolchak muttered
to Petrovich, who had been listening on an extension.
"Smart-ass punk, who does he think he's dealing with? We'll
be happy to get rid of his gang. Let the Israelis put up with
them. He may get his way for the moment, but does he really
think he's going to dictate to the Soviet government? *We* will
decide how to treat the Jews of this country, and no one else.
And our little hoodlum who calls himself Moses will be stuck
in Israel with no place to plant his bombs."

Petrovich nodded. "He tripped up on the question about
the American, Jude Miller, though. It was pretty obvious he
knows about him, that Miller didn't die in the river. At least
we now know the Americans are tied in to this Khrushchev
thing."

Kolchak shrugged. "So what if we don't catch Miller this
time? With Khrushchev out of the way, Miller's mission will
be over, which means he'll either sneak out of the country or
we'll pick him up in due course."

Petrovich shook his head. "That Jew is a hard man to bargain with."

Kolchak snorted. "They're born with that ability. The
government has made the recovery of Khrushchev absolute
top priority—can you imagine the damage that old traitor
could do to this country? Except for my orders, I'd outsmart
that Jew any day."

Petrovich looked away and clamped down on his lip to suppress a smile.

CHAPTER EIGHTEEN

REBBE RABINOWITZ AND Nikita Khrushchev glared at each other across the rickety kitchen table, with flushed faces and flashing eyes.

Khrushchev pounded on the table and his voice would have dominated an auditorium. "Tolstoy, I tell you. He understood the Russian character. Dostoyevski had too much self pity. He was too much influenced by his own troubles. They distorted his thinking."

The rebbe shook his head as though trying to be patient with a child. "You don't understand that hardship and suffering is what made Dostoyevski great, while Tolstoy, being an aristocrat, could only guess at the pain of man's struggles."

Jude, sitting at the end of the table, chuckled to see the two old men haranguing each other, because it was obvious each was enjoying himself, like a child with a new playmate. He understood that for a bright, well-read person, the cruelest fate is having no one with which to share, and for the past few days, these two lonely men had had each other.

David stood at the counter by the sink with his back turned preparing lunch. Ever since his father had chastised him for his behavior toward Khrushchev, he had been polite but quiet and aloof, an attitude that lulled Jude into disregarding him. With only two days left before Jude and Khrushchev caught the train to Leningrad, the display of David's early antagonism toward the former premier seemed of no consequence to Jude.

David interrupted the literary debate by placing in front of ude and his father large bowls of *okroshka*, a cold vegetable oup very similar to Spanish gazpacho. He returned to the counter for a dish of black bread and butter and a bowl of soup or Khrushchev.

"Aren't you going to eat?" Jude asked.

"I'm not hungry," David said, wiping his hands on the apron he wore.

The two old men attacked the soup as if today was the eve of a famine, but at the same time they kept up the discussion.

The rebbe was making a point about the influence of Rasputin on the czar's court, jabbing his spoon toward his guest's midsection, when Khrushchev suddenly turned pale and lumbered to his feet like an old walrus, overturned his empty soup bowl and headed for the bathroom. He made it about halfway, then fell against the ancient refrigerator. Struggling to a sitting position, he doubled over and vomited the soup he had just consumed onto the kitchen floor. Slipping in the mess, he pushed his way to the bathroom, where they could hear him retching violently into the toilet.

Jude sidestepped the smelly pool on the floor and went into the bathroom, where he found Khrushchev on his knees, lying against the splattered stool. Beads of sweat stood out on his forehead and he struggled for breath. Jude helped him to his feet and dropped the toilet lid for him to sit. "Are you all right?" he asked lamely.

Khrushchev nodded. "Just let me rest."

Jude went back to the kitchen where David and the rebbe were already mopping the floor. "I don't know what's wrong," he said. "It just seemed to hit him suddenly."

"At his age, we should be concerned," David said.

"What can I do? I'm no doctor," Jude said.

David thought for a moment, then snapped his fingers. "No, neither am I, but I know a man who is."

Jude and the rebbe looked at him expectantly.

"This is a man we can trust. I knew him when he was i
medical school. He's a friend and won't ask any questions.
could take Mr. Khrushchev for a checkup this afternoon an
have him back in a couple of hours. At least then you'll know
if it's safe to take him out of here. What you can't afford is fo
him to collapse on a busy street."

Jude nodded slowly as he envisioned the danger. "It migh
be a prudent step," he said. "I'll go with you."

"No!" David said hastily. "I mean, my friend doesn'
know you, and two men attract a lot less attention than three
He'll be safe with me."

Jude studied him shrewdly. "I didn't know you were tha
concerned about him."

David shrugged. "I don't have to love the man to keep m
end of the bargain, which is to help you get him out of Rus
sia."

"No deal," Jude said. "He's my responsibility and I'm no
letting him out of my sight. Where he goes, I go."

David shook his head vigorously. "I know my friend and
know the dangers. If you don't trust me to take the old ma
alone, then you can take him." He folded his arms to signify
the argument had ended.

Jude looked to the rebbe for support.

Rebbe Rabinowitz spread his arms in helplessness. "Th
important thing is that our guest receive medical help soon."

Jude knew he had lost and reluctantly nodded. "Okay, bu
hurry. I want him back as soon as possible."

Khrushchev had stopped vomiting but he was still weak
and it took all three of them to get him into a sweater and
overcoat. They had just stood him up to see if he could wall
well enough, when an impatient knock on the door mad
them all turn in that direction.

The rebbe went to the door and opened it a few inches. Jude
could hear muffled voices, and a moment later a figure pushed
by the rebbe and rushed into the room.

It was Lana. She was panting and her eyes darted around the room until they landed on Khrushchev in his coat and hat, ready for the outdoors. "Where's he going?" she demanded of no one in particular.

"He's not well. I'm taking him to the doctor," David said.

Lana glared at the young man. "Like hell you are!"

Jude moved to her side, and said, "You shouldn't be here. You're breaking cover."

Lana turned to Jude. "I had no choice. I learned that Khrushchev is going to be betrayed, turned over to the KGB." She pointed a long, accusing finger at David and let her voice ring out. "By him!"

David's eyes became wide and he took an involuntary step away from Jude and Lana. "Who told you that?"

Lana gestured with her head toward Jude. "He knows my source. And you know it's true."

The four people in the room all stared at David, whose own looks progressed from surprise to innocence, to anger, to defiance. His Mr. Hyde-like transformation confirmed Lana's charge. Everyone in the room realized there was a traitor in their midst.

Jude looked at David as if he'd just discovered a pickpocket holding his watch. His cold voice was an indictment. "There's no doctor. You were going straight to the KGB. Did you drug his food to make him sick?"

David glared back in silence.

"Answer me," Jude thundered.

"I gave him a little ipecac to make him vomit. It'll wear off soon," David said grudgingly.

Lana took a small pistol from her purse and pointed it at David. She cocked it and extended her arm. "Judas," she hissed.

Jude looked at David, then at the rebbe standing silently off to the side. He gently took Lana's arm and forced it down.

"We should kill him, now," she protested.

"No, not for his sake, but for his father's." Jude looked sympathetically in the rebbe's direction.

The rebbe had been stunned by Lana's accusation and his mind did not immediately focus on the situation. But finally he looked at David as though they were alone. His voice was flat and barely above a whisper, but the stricken look on his blanched face compelled the others to listen in silence. "First you abandoned your faith and now you have abandoned honor. You would betray a man after promising him sanctuary?" he asked incredulously. "You would deliver him who trusts you into the hands of his enemies, to a certain death? Are *you* the result of the love your good mother and I shared? We hoped we were bringing forth a lion of God, and instead we hatched a snake."

The rebbe's voice rose and his face became flushed. "You are a disgrace, an abomination in the sight of God." The rebbe was now shouting; his face was turning purple and his eyes bulged. His blood pressure soared to 200/120 and turned his blood vessels into mountain streams choked by spring flooding.

"You are *herem*, banished. 'A fugitive and a vagabond shalt thou be in the earth.' I turn my face—"

The rebbe, betrayed once by his son, was now betrayed by his own body. His aging blood vessels, choked by plaque and cholesterol like boulders lying in a narrow road, could not handle the pressure caused by his anger. A tiny piece of fatty plaque broke from the wall of a blood vessel in his neck and raced unimpeded toward the left side of the brain. It lodged at the edge of the frontal lobe, just behind the eyebrows. The effect was to seal off all oxygen from a substantial portion of the brain.

A bewildered look came over the rebbe's face and his speech became a slur. The right side of his body stiffened into paralysis and he slowly pitched to the floor, the victim of a massive stroke.

For a moment, everyone stood looking at the fallen old man, too stunned to move, knowing something dreadful had happened. Then David, with a cry of despair, rushed over, fell to his knees and cradled his father's head in his arms.

Lana started to move toward them, but Jude caught her arm and shook his head. Together, they watched the son try with his sobs to restore to the father what his disobedience had taken.

"Let's go," Jude said.

"We can't leave that turncoat here," Lana protested.

"He doesn't know about the train to Leningrad," Jude whispered. "He can't do us any more harm." He looked at the pair on the floor. "He's going to be needed here."

Jude called an ambulance for the rebbe, then went over to Khrushchev and found that he was weak but recovering quickly from his sickness. He took the old man by the arm and Lana followed them out the door.

"Where will you go?" Lana asked as they walked down the street.

"Our papers are in order, so we'll get a hotel room until we leave for Leningrad. We can catch a bus just down the street."

"Remember the contact point—the tiger cage, Durov's Corner—if anything goes wrong. I'll use the discarded wrapper method for further instructions," Lana said.

They arrived at Lana's car, a late-model Zhiguli, and turned to face each other.

"Not many clerks in Moscow drive a car like this," Jude said.

She glanced at the automobile with disinterest. "It's Kolchak's. He lets me use it."

Jude's look became wistful. "I wish you weren't doing that."

She nodded. "I know, but it's got to be done."

Jude touched her arm. "I don't want to sound melodramatic, but you saved the bacon today. Thanks, from a man who doesn't want to sightsee in Siberia."

She smiled demurely. "Just another day at the office."

WITH ALL OF THE MACHINES scattered about, the intensive care room resembled an auto repair shop except for its antiseptic whiteness and the nurses scowling at the young man sitting near the bedside of his elderly father, as they walked around him to monitor the devices hooked up to their patient. They had asked him to leave, but the sadness on his face had made them stop short of insisting.

When he and the rebbe were finally alone, David stood up and walked over to sit on the edge of the bed. For the first time in his life, he was dressed in traditional Hasidic black and wore an embroidered yarmulke on the back of his head. It matched the one his father wore because both had been made by David's mother years ago. This was the first time David had worn it since his bar mitzvah. In his left hand he held a copy of the Torah and his right grasped the limp hand of the rebbe.

David searched his father's eyes hopefully, looking for a sign of recognition. There was none. "Father," he said softly. "I hope you can hear me. Khrushchev and the American are safe. They'll have no more trouble from me." He released his father's hand and his fingers worked absently on some loose threads on the blanket. "I'm not very good at this. Learning humility never seemed worthwhile to me." His jaw worked furiously and his broken voice had to start over several times. "I'm—I'm sorry, deeply, terribly sorry. I wish I had listened, but I didn't.... I'm so ashamed." He looked down at the black coat and fingered a button. "I'm going to try to become the son you deserve."

David looked again for a response, but the only movement was a blip on a computer screen that proved the old man still lived.

Sadly, David opened the book and started to read aloud, repeating the prayer of a repentant Job. He rocked gently back and forth as the words pushed their way past his sobs:

"... I have spoken what I did not understand:
things too wonderful for me which I did not know....
I have heard of Thee by the hearing of the ear;
but now my eyes see Thee.
Therefore I despise myself, and repent in dust and ashes."

KOLCHAK PICKED UP THE TELEPHONE and barked like a teased terrier. "Who do you think you're playing games with, Moses, or whatever your name is? I've had men on standby for days waiting for you to deliver Khrushchev. And nothing. They just sit there and stare at one another, scratch their asses and wonder if I've gone nuts. You trying to make me look like a fool?"

"There will be no Khrushchev," David said quietly.

Kolchak was silent for a long moment, trying to mask his disappointment. "A double-cross, eh? Well, maybe you didn't have him to begin with; maybe he's already dead. But I'll tell you this, *dolboyob*, several hundred of your precious Jews are going to pay for your smart-ass trick. And I'll tell you this, too: I'm going to catch you and personally cut your balls off. When—"

"We can still make a deal," David interrupted.

Kolchak sputtered indignantly. "A deal? A deal? I've got a deal for you, I'll—"

David spoke patiently, like a teacher trying to explain arithmetic. "If you release the Jews you're holding and let

them emigrate, just as we agreed, I'll promise you there'll b
no more bombings, no more attacks. The Sicarii will disap
pear.''

Kolchak laughed sarcastically. ''Sure, I'll believe what
ever you tell me. You'd never double-cross me, would you?''

''It'd be to your advantage: no more bombs, and you'd ge
rid of a lot of troublesome Jews.''

''I want Khrushchev,'' Kolchak enunciated firmly.

''There is no Khrushchev.''

''I don't believe you,'' Kolchak shouted. ''The American
put you up to this.''

''You've heard my offer.''

Kolchak closed his eyes and concentrated on the problem
He was certain the Sicarii no longer had Khrushchev; the ex
premier might even be dead. There were other ways tha
question could be pursued. The bigger issue at the momen
was terrorism. If the Sicarii kept up their attacks they coul
disrupt the whole pattern of Soviet civil obedience. Other fa
natics might even try to get in on the act. More personally, h
knew if he didn't come up with something positive out of this
insane mess, his career would be over. If he couldn't ge
Khrushchev, perhaps he could at least get rid of a bunch o
trouble-making Jews and buy peace from the Sicarii at the
same time. He needed a victory of some sort.

Kolchak's voice softened. ''If something could be worked
out—and I say *if*—we would have to be convinced you
wouldn't betray us. We'd need maybe a waiting period o
several months. Then, if there were no more attacks, perhaps a deal might be possible. But it would have to be cleared
at the highest levels, you understand that.''

''I understand.''

''And realize that one more bomb means that every Jew
we're holding goes straight to Siberia, and I mean *remote* Siberia.''

''That's within your power,'' David said.

"If and when we put those Jews on a plane, I want you aboard, too."

"That's not possible," David said. "I have to stay here."

"Why?"

There was silence and Kolchak heard pages turning in the background. Then David spoke: "'And the Lord spoke to Moses: "Because you sinned against me, because you did not sanctify me, you shall not go there unto the land which I give the children of Israel."'"

"Huh? What does that gibberish mean?"

"It means I have to stay here and fight for my people," David said.

"Now just a minute," Kolchak said, alarm creeping into his voice, "you said no more terrorism."

"I'll fight you with words, with truth."

"You're crazy," Kolchak said in disgust. "You have the chance to go free, but you want to stay. You must know it's only a matter of time before your luck runs out."

"Probably," David said, "but you'll find it's easier to destroy a man than an idea."

David hung up abruptly. Once again Kolchak found himself staring into a dead telephone. "Kyril," he shouted, "get in here."

Petrovich entered with hunched-shoulder subservience. "I've got it on tape, Comrade Kolchak."

"What do you make of it?" Kolchak asked.

Petrovich thought silently for a moment, then said, "I don't doubt that the Jews *did* have Khrushchev. Why else would they try to make a deal? My guess is that the Americans double-crossed them and took old Nikita for themselves. That's probably where the mysterious Jude Miller enters in."

Kolchak suddenly stirred as though he'd made an important decision. "Anyway, it's not our decision. I'm going to boot it upstairs. Make a copy of that tape and I'll personally deliver it. Let the politicians worry about it."

THE MERCEDES LIMOUSINE SLIPPED OUT of the gate of the Soviet embassy in Washington, D.C., and flowed gracefully through the early-afternoon traffic along boulevards lined by trees in leafy spring exuberance. In minutes, it reached a secret entrance to the block-long stone State Department building.

The car pulled into a secluded parking space, and a burly, grim-faced bodyguard jumped from the front passenger seat and opened the rear door for a confident-looking man expensively dressed in a homburg and a pearl-gray pin-striped suit.

The Soviet diplomat was escorted to a private elevator by a senior American official, who had been awaiting his arrival like a doorman. After a short ride that allowed time only for a chatty comment and a polite response about the cherry blossoms that had appeared along the Tidal Basin, the elevator stopped and automatically opened across from an elegant conference room. The two men stepped into the hall and were met by the secretary of state, who advanced with extended hand to greet the Soviet ambassador.

The afternoon became evening, then night, and sunlight gave way to an ornate crystal chandelier. Below the soft yellow light, the diplomats were deep in earnest, sometimes quarrelsome, negotiations, practicing statecraft like high-stakes gamblers.

The city went to sleep, but the lights shone on, just as they did in the White House a few blocks away, and in the Kremlin, half a world away.

IN A SMALL SEEDY HOTEL ROOM in the middle of Moscow, Jude Miller and Nikita Khrushchev waited for the hours to pass, not thinking that fate is intermeshed and that therefore their very small cog was turning the giant wheel of nations.

CHAPTER NINETEEN

"*MOY KLYUCH PAZHALUISTA*, my key, please," Jude said to the *dezhurnaya*, who frowned and rummaged around in a shoebox and finally found the right one. The floor lady's sourness was not due to anger or a bad mood; it was just the manner of the old women who sit in the corridors of virtually every floor of every hotel in Russia. In the event a guest is planning to sneak a woman into his room or play a radio too loudly, the management wants him to know in advance that the gray-haired obstacle sitting in the hallway like a suspicious Slavic Buddha is a no-nonsense rule-enforcer.

"*Spasibo,*" Jude said, "thank you," and he walked along the threadbare carpeting to the room he and Khrushchev had occupied for the past two nights. The Volgograd was a dark, smelly, third-rate hotel, but to Jude it was the Moscow Ritz and he felt lucky to be there. Hotel rooms in Moscow are scarce, a characteristic they share with bread, bacon and every other desirable commodity. Only after trying two others when they left the Sicarii safe house did they manage to find this one, and then it was because the desk clerk seemed to take pity on the tired old man at Jude's elbow.

Jude unlocked the door and entered to find Khrushchev eagerly awaiting his breakfast. As Jude unwrapped the black bread and sausage, he noticed with relief that the old man was still bright and alert. The bad spells where he seemed to imagine himself in another time and place had not affected him since they left the room where Gurko hid them.

The old man's gutsy; the action seems to pump him up, Jude said to himself.

"Good morning," Jude called out cheerily. "Well, Mr. Chairman, today's the big day. We leave for Leningrad in a few hours. After Leningrad, it's Finland, then the U.S.A."

"There is a saying, *Amerikanski*: 'Overfeed on hope and you'll sicken on disappointment.'"

"There's another saying, Mr. Chairman: 'When Madame Fortune comes calling, offer her a chair.'"

Khrushchev grinned. "When do we leave?"

Jude checked his watch. "In about two hours."

"Let's leave now," Khrushchev said.

"Why?"

"I want to visit my grave."

Jude stared blankly. "But why? You're not in it. I mean, it's not really your grave."

"It's the only monument to me in all of Russia. How many men get to see how they're remembered while they're still alive?"

Jude did silent battle with his professional judgment. This wasn't the time for frivolous side excursions, but there was something very appealing about the idea of watching this man who made history stand before his only marker to it.

Jude frowned. "We can only stay a few minutes, okay?"

"It'll give you something to tell your grandchildren," Khrushchev said as he prepared to bite into the sandwich Jude handed him.

"If my unborn grandchildren are watching, they're probably despairing of their birth right now."

THE NOVODEVICHYE CONVENT (New Convent for Young Ladies), with its high white walls, twelve battlementlike towers and a red and white bell tower rising like a tiered two-hundred-foot wedding cake, has decorated a wide area of the Moskva River's east bank since 1524, when it was built as an eight-acre fortress and religious center.

It was right outside the walls of this convent that Peter the Great hanged three hundred Streltsy guardsmen who supported his sister and adversary, Princess Sophia. Her Highness, who was confined inside, may have had the first ringside seat in Russia. In case that didn't get her attention, Peter had the severed hand of her principal supporter, Prince Khovansky, nailed to her door.

Something about the fairy-castle complex seemed to irritate Napoléon. On the last day of his occupation of Moscow in 1812, he ordered the convent blown up. Only a courageous nun named Sara saved it by extinguishing all the fuses.

To Jude, the place had a different significance, something much more personal. It was on this bank, not far from the convent walls, that he had dragged himself out of the freezing water of the Moskva. In the distance, he could see the top of Tamara's apartment house. For a moment, his thoughts drifted to the scent of jasmine and raven-black hair, but he pushed her from his mind. Tamara was in the past, recent but untouchable, a memory destined to fade and then disappear.

Jude and Khrushchev made their way under the towering walls, through the gate and down the gravel path of one of the world's most illustrious cemeteries, where many of the exalted of Russian arts and letters lay beneath markers bereft of religious symbolism. Stone angels weren't welcome in this graveyard, to play their soundless trumpets celebrating victory over death. Standing alone in a quiet corner was a stately white sculpture of Stalin's wife, Nadezhda Aliluyeva Stalina, who shot herself rather than live under the gaze of a madman. This was *the* place to be fashionably dead.

"You picked some pretty good company," Jude joked as they passed by the grave of the composer Sergey Prokofiev.

"Ha!" Khrushchev complained. "I should have been buried at the Kremlin wall."

Khrushchev stopped and Jude turned back to him, then followed the old man's gaze to a large black and white granite memorial. Sculpted on top was the unmistakable round head with slightly porcine features of the man standing next to him. Even though Khrushchev now had a long beard and a hat pulled low, Jude could not resist glancing back and forth, from tombstone to man. At the base of the monument was the inscription: NIKITA SERGEYEVICH KHRUSHCHEV, 1894–1971. Below that were several bunches of dying flowers left by anonymous visitors who fondly remembered their colorful premier of two decades ago.

They stared in silence. Jude felt his mind bend to the warp of time as the man who would never occupy the soil underneath stared for the last time at the stone testament to his life.

"This tombstone was carved by a friend of mine." Khrushchev paused to pull the name from his memory. "Ernst Neizvestny. That's right, the artist Ernst Neizvestny, at the request of my son." He let his voice trail off as a man in a black leather jacket slowly came near, studiously examining each tombstone and then walking on. Jude and Khrushchev maintained silence until they heard the crunch of gravel fade into the distance.

"My doctor attended the funeral," Khrushchev continued. "He was the only one there except my wife, who knew I was still alive. He told me my Nina Petrovna performed beautifully, tears and all. First time I knew I married an actress."

"How about your children?" Jude asked.

Khrushchev smiled. "Sergey and Rada. They were never told. Life is difficult enough without having to know something like that. My children believed they watched their father being buried right there." He pointed at the mound. "It's just as well."

Jude looked up and saw Leather Jacket studying a tombstone about fifty yards away. There was something ominous about the man, and the danger antenna in his brain began to hum.

"The funeral was at noon on a gray, drizzly September day," Khrushchev recited, recalling from memory the description passed on to him. "They hadn't even allowed an obituary to be published, but somehow the people found out. By early morning, a big crowd gathered outside those locked gates we passed through." He pointed back toward the convent entrance. "My enemies in power had a sign put up that said, Cleaning Day, Cemetery Closed. They also posted police all the way around to discourage the crowd. Still, the people waited, looking through those iron gates, not making a sound. If there's anything Russians can do, it's wait with patience. There's no one on earth like them." Khrushchev stopped and wiped at one eye.

"Not one member of the Central Committee bothered to come—but they sent a wreath," he added sarcastically. "It made no difference to me if they weren't there, the phony bastards. What mattered was that several political prisoners I set free were present. I can see those gaunt, broken-spirited victims in my mind as I stand here talking. I freed them from prison, but their faces were never free from the marks of it." He shook his head sadly as distant, blurred faces marched before his memory.

"Those ex-prisoners somehow got special passes—can you imagine having to get a pass for a funeral?" He shook his head in disgust. "Like sticking someone in the ground was a damned state secret."

Khrushchev raised his voice to speech-giving level while Jude tried to quiet him. "I'm more honored by the bared head of a single honest Russian than by the sanctimonious prattle of a thousand bureaucrats."

He lowered his voice again to Jude's relief. "Someone held an umbrella over my face while people filed by. I was wearing a black suit and tie and a white shirt. The coffin was lined with red satin.

"My son gave a short oration. I remember the words just as they were repeated to me: 'I won't talk about the great statesman.... I won't evaluate the contributions my father made. History will do that. The only thing I can say is that he left no one indifferent. There are people who love him and people who hate him, but no one can pass him by without turning to look.... A man has gone from us who had the right to be called a man.' "

Khrushchev let a sigh escape like a heavy burden. "Such a son." He picked up and fingered one of the wilted flowers. "Such a people."

Jude was becoming increasingly nervous. Leather Jacket was still lurking about. "Let's go, Mr. Chairman. We have to catch our train." He gently pulled Khrushchev away.

The old man slowly followed him toward the exit, casting backward glances at the grave. Jude saw that Leather Jacket was walking on another path at an angle and pace that would intersect with theirs at the gate. He watched and kept walking, hoping it was only a coincidence. Tied to the old man, he was slowed as effectively as with a ball and chain.

Leather Jacket walked toward them casually, not seeming to pay to them any more attention than to the other tourists wandering about. Jude had just about decided he was unnecessarily jittery when the man abruptly wheeled and pushed his face into Jude's like a schoolyard bully. His thin nose, slicked-down hair and angry black eyes made him look like a hungry bird.

"Your papers," he demanded, flashing KGB identification before Jude's eyes.

"What's wrong, Comrade?" Jude asked in a shaken voice, the way he imagined a schoolteacher would react. He jerked his head backward, away from the man's face, mainly because the smell of garlic on his breath hit Jude like an ocean wave.

"No questions. Papers," the man demanded.

Jude removed his identity documents from a pocket and handed them over without comment.

"Viktor Serov, schoolteacher," the man read aloud. "What are you doing in this cemetery, schoolteacher?"

"Why, sight-seeing among all the famous graves, Comrade."

Leather Jacket turned to Khrushchev. "And who are you, old-timer? Are you a tourist, also? Your papers?"

Khrushchev was fumbling for his own forged papers when the KGB agent stepped closer and studied his face. He reached up and lifted Khrushchev's hat and then stared at the beard, trying to imagine it not there. Suddenly his eyes widened, and he said, "Why, you're *him*!"

Jude witnessed the recognition and saw the KGB man's hand leap for the inside of his coat. Jude knew what was in there, and for a sliver of a second he felt gratitude toward Lana. He reached inside his own coat pocket and felt the handle of the small automatic she had insisted he take. He thumbed off the safety as it came out and lifted it to the center of Leather Jacket's chest, not six inches away. In the corner of his eye he saw the other man's pistol clear the flap of his coat.

Jude felt his hand jump and the noise and bitter smell of gunpowder told him he had fired. The shocked look on his adversary's face and the shuddering of his body just before he slumped to the ground confirmed Jude had shot straight. The bystanders stared at the spreading pool of blood beside the man's body. Before anyone could react, Jude grabbed Khrushchev by the arm and hurried him past the gate, waving his pistol as frightened witnesses scattered like startled pigeons.

Jude knew it was only a matter of minutes before the area had more police than tombstones. He had to get the two of them far away, fast. At just that moment, a taxi drove up to drop off a fare. Before it could pull back out into traffic, Jude ran around to the driver's side and pointed the gun directly in the man's face. "Get out," he demanded.

The driver, eyes wide and mouth agape, let his foot slip on the clutch and the car jolted ahead and died. He started to remove the keys from habit, but Jude commanded, "Leave those in there. Get out! Hurry!" The driver jumped out and scurried around to the other side as Jude directed, never taking his eyes off the pistol.

"Help him in," Jude shouted, gesturing toward Khrushchev.

The driver, frozen with fear, just looked at him.

"Help him in!" Jude screamed.

The driver scurried to push Khrushchev into the taxi as though he were trying to plug a leaky dam. Jude jumped in the driver's seat and pulled away in a screech of tires as sirens wailed in the distance and bystanders converged at the convent gates to stare at the disappearing taxi.

"Goddammit," Jude muttered at the sound of grinding metal as he levered through the gears of the unfamiliar vehicle. He pushed the accelerator to the floor and glanced nervously in the rearview mirror. Satisfied there was as yet no pursuit, he drummed his fingers on the steering wheel in consternation while he drove, and breathed deeply to gain control of his nerves. He looked over at Khrushchev sitting placidly in the passenger seat. "What's the matter," he said in irritation, "don't you understand the mess we're in?"

"I understand a foolish and stubborn old man almost got us killed."

"The 'almost' isn't over yet," Jude said as he maneuvered the taxi around slower vehicles.

Khrushchev reached over and patted Jude's knee. "I have faith in you, *Amerikanski*."

The sweat popped out on Jude's face and soaked his shirt as he tried to think and drive at the same time. He struggled to fight back the beginnings of panic, which welled in his throat like nausea when he thought about what had happened.

They were in deep trouble. When Leather Jacket recognized Khrushchev so easily, it had told Jude that the KGB knew the ex-premier was still alive and were looking for him. That was why the grave was staked out. They would turn the city upside down now that they also knew Khrushchev was in Moscow. Jude shivered as he considered the odds against them. He twisted the wheel sharply to avoid a woman on a bicycle. "Steady, be a pro," he lectured himself as he straightened the car.

Jude first tried to sort out what they could *not* do. One, they couldn't stay in this taxi; in minutes, every policeman in the city would have its license number. Two, they couldn't take the Leningrad train; again, thousands of pairs of official eyes would converge on every airport and train station looking for them, and they weren't exactly inconspicuous. Three, no hotel in the city would be safe, since every desk clerk would be on the alert. As he discarded options like lint off cotton, Jude decided the only thing to do at the moment was ditch the taxi and get off the street—fast.

The taxi careened to make a sharp left onto Smolensky Boulevard and Jude slowed as he saw several patrol cars rushing to the convent, not realizing their prey was passing them in the opposite direction.

In the distance, Jude could see the tall spire of the Gothic-style Foreign Ministry building and knew he was approaching busy Smolenskaya Square.

He quickly scanned the square for a traffic officer, and seeing none, pulled into a no-parking zone with a squeal of brakes. He rushed around the cab and helped Khrushchev out of the seat. As fast as he could coax the puffing old man, they made their way down the stairs of the Smolenskaya metro station, hugging the right-hand rail so younger commuters could stream past.

The Moscow metro has long been the pride of Soviet Russia. Officialdom loves to boast of the absolutely safe, antiseptically clean corridors and giant chandeliers hanging from decorated ceilings, and to contrast them with the New York subway where a passenger risks hepatitis from the rest rooms and instant, terminal anemia from muggers' knives.

Jude wasn't interested in aesthetics, he was too concerned about looking for police and dreading the moment the net would collapse around them and drag him off to a lifetime in a cold, brutal prison.

When the train came, Jude ran interference for Khrushchev, who inched his way aboard to hard looks from impatient passengers stalled behind them. When the old man finally sat down heavily with Jude beside him, he grumbled, "Ill-mannered bastards. There was a time they would wait an hour in the rain just to get a glimpse of me."

At the first stop, a young officer in the blue and gray of the militia came aboard and slowly walked down the aisle. Alert sky-blue eyes in an unsmiling round Slavic face swept the car like lasers.

Jude held his breath, hoping the officer would walk on past. But when he came to where they sat, he stopped. Jude didn't dare look, but he could feel the heavy presence of the man. Without saying a word, the militiaman sat on the seat across the narrow aisle from Khrushchev and turned toward them. Although he kept a calm face, Jude was frantically trying to think of a way out. He was trapped behind the unyielding bulk of Khrushchev as effectively as in a locked room.

The militiaman stared at Jude then Khrushchev. Then he spoke. "*Zdras*, hi, where are you from, *Dedushka*?"

Jude almost sang with joy to realize this militiaman hadn't been alerted to the manhunt yet, but instead he leaned forward and said quickly, "We're from Smolensk. I'm a schoolteacher and this is my grandfather."

The officer smiled, showing a great display of crooked teeth. "I hope you enjoy your visit." He leaned forward to speak to Jude. "Your grandfather reminds me of my own. He's in Riga, in Latvia. Have you ever been there?"

Jude shook his head. "No, but I hear the beaches on the Baltic are wonderful in the summer."

The officer nodded as though confirming a great truth. "Very wonderful."

Khrushchev turned to the officer and growled, "Why don't you do something about the crime in the streets? In the old days, a person could walk out to buy a newspaper without fear of being murdered."

Jude thought he was going to faint. What they did not need at the moment was an argument with a militia officer.

The officer smiled. "It's true. We're trying, but I'm afraid American rock and roll is turning teenagers into criminals. Jungle music has no place in a socialist society."

Jude smiled weakly. "You'll have to pardon my grandfather, he sometimes speaks bluntly."

The militiaman laughed. "Don't all grandfathers? Mine makes my ears burn on far less important matters." He stood and took a step toward the door. "This is where I get off. *Dosvedanya*, see you later."

Jude turned to Khrushchev. "Why did you have to do that? I almost had a heart attack."

The old man smiled. "I was just acting like a grandfather."

The train slowed and Jude looked up to see they were entering the station at Dzerzhinsky Square. Knowing it was a major transfer point, he decided to get off and switch to a smaller metro line that would take them to an isolated suburban station that might not be patrolled.

Jude and Khrushchev stepped off the train into the bustling station and Jude immediately recognized trouble. Policemen were everywhere. There were several at each exit, checking the papers of everyone who entered or left. More dangerous at the moment were the teams of uniformed men combing the crowds inside the station, stopping any old man who even remotely resembled the description of Khrushchev.

Jude quickly took stock. He figured the government couldn't afford to let so many know Khrushchev was still alive, so the only thing these policemen could know was that they were looking for a heavy-set old man in the company of a younger one. Jude thought of splitting up, but he realized Khrushchev couldn't manage on his own. Suddenly, he got an idea and pulled Khrushchev into a corner and whispered in his ear.

He outlined the plan and Khrushchev was willing to give it a try. The old man went to a nearby bench and lay down. Jude walked over to a newspaper kiosk and urgently asked the clerk to call an ambulance. The woman immediately picked up the telephone and dialed an emergency number.

For several minutes Jude stood by the old man like a solicitous grandson and looked impatiently around the area, hoping desperately that the next police sweep would not happen before the medics arrived.

He peered anxiously in one direction, then the other. He saw two uniformed KGB men working their way through the commuter throngs, checking the papers of every old man in range, detaining the few accompanied by younger men. From the other direction he saw two ambulance attendants dressed in white hurrying along with a wheeled gurney between them.

Jude's head swung back and forth between the KGB and the medics. Who would reach them first? His stomach churned and threatened to erupt in vomit.

Jude was counting on the single-mindedness of policemen on a chase—they weren't looking for a sick man—and the tendency of all people not to interfere with medics rushing to a hospital. But the plan wouldn't mean anything if the KGB got to them first.

The medics approached the kiosk and began talking to the clerk. Jude rushed over and said excitedly, "Over here. Hurry."

The medics moved to the bench where Khrushchev lay. "What seems to be the matter?" said the one who seemed to be the leader as he attached a blood pressure cuff to the old man's arm.

"I don't know. He became dizzy and short of breath. He's very old, more than ninety," Jude said. He glanced over his shoulder and saw the uniformed men talking to an old man only about ten yards away.

The medic nodded. "Can't be too careful at that age. We better take him in."

As they lifted their patient onto the gurney, one of the KGB men noticed the crowd and started to walk over. Jude's knees went weak and his head swiveled as he looked for an escape route. The KGB man tapped the medic on the shoulder and said, "What's the problem here?"

The chief attendant was arranging Khrushchev's feet and didn't look up. "No problem, Comrade. But if we don't get this man to the hospital, there might be one." Without giving the KGB man a chance to reply, he started moving the gurney toward the exit, leaving an indecisive and confused KGB man behind. Jude uttered a silent prayer of thanks that there was at least one man in Moscow who didn't cower before a uniform.

He followed at a distance until they were out of sight of the KGB officers, then he quickly caught up and said to the chief medic, "My grandfather doesn't seem in immediate danger, and I've got to arrange our lodging. Tell me where you're taking him and I'll follow in a few minutes."

As the medic began writing down the name of the hospital, Jude couldn't resist saying, "That was great how you handled that cop back there."

The medic gave a thin smile. "It's like handling a chimpanzee. A chimp is mean and can tear you apart unless you convince him you're in control." He tore off the paper and handed it to Jude. "Chimps like to wear uniforms."

The medics continued wheeling Khrushchev toward the exit and Jude watched them mix into the crowd. He would know in a few moments if his desperate plan would work.

The attendants pushed their patient up to the nearest exit as those lined up to be checked peeled back to let them through. Jude waited tensely and watched from a distance. To his vast relief, the chief medic spoke a few words to one of the militiamen, who nodded in return and motioned them on.

Jude, unencumbered by the old man, had no difficulty clearing the checkpoint. He walked out into the sunshine, where he stopped and sucked in the sweet air of freedom. He looked in the distance, past the traffic of the square and the statue of that original terror cop, Felix Dzerzhinsky, and stared at the KGB Lubyanka headquarters just beyond. He grinned and gave a big wink to the innocent-looking building.

Jude waited an hour, then called the hospital, and after being transferred twice, finally spoke to the nurse in charge. She told him his grandfather seemed fine except for the normal problems of advanced old age, but that the doctor recommended keeping him under observation for a few days.

"Is he in a private room?" Jude asked.

"Why, no, he certainly isn't that sick," the nurse said.

"That could be a problem," Jude said.

"What do you mean?"

"My grandfather is in Moscow on important matters. He'll need a private room to conduct his affairs."

"We're not in the hotel business."

"What a shame," Jude said sadly. "To come all the way here on vital party business, and then—"

"Party business, did you say?" There was a long pause, then the nurse said, "We do have an empty private room.... I'm sure we can arrange it."

"Thank you so much, Comrade. Tell my grandfather I'll be up to see him soon."

JUDE GOT OFF THE METRO at Kolkhoznaya Square and walked the short distance to Durov's Corner. He once more felt in control. He had visited Khrushchev in his private hospital room that morning and had found him alert and healthily cantankerous. Jude himself had experienced no problems getting a hotel room. The breath of the KGB didn't seem quite so hot on his neck now.

Durov's Corner is a small zoo in central Moscow known for the incredible feats the trainers somehow induce the animals to perform. Jude slipped into its usual milling, festive crowd and wandered around the animal cages, waiting for Lana to arrive.

Ten minutes later, he glanced over to the tiger area and saw her sitting on a bench eating a candy bar. The newspaper that would have given a warning was nowhere in sight. Gradually, Jude worked his way in her direction, making sure he stopped at every cage in between. Finally, he stood near her bench and watched the tigers. He put his hand in his coat pocket and closed his fist around a crumpled-up candy wrapper. He turned to Lana at the far end of the bench and politely gestured toward the end nearest him. She nodded that the seat was not taken, and he sat down. To any passerby, both would seem intent only on resting their feet and watching the tigers, two strangers innocently sharing a bench.

After a couple of minutes, Lana finished her candy bar, wadded up the wrapper and carelessly dropped it on the

ground near Jude's feet. She got up and walked away without giving him a glance.

Jude waited a few moments, then looked down, shook his
head in disapproval and picked up the discarded paper in the
same hand that held his own wrapper. He switched them in
his palm, stood, threw his in a nearby trash container and
sauntered away in the opposite direction.

In the distance, by the bear cage, a woman stood fixing her
makeup in a small hand mirror. But though she patted pow-
der on her face, her eyes were looking over the mirror at what
was happening by the tiger cage. She watched Lana leave and
Jude pick up the litter and depart himself. Smiling with success, she took a small walkie-talkie out of her purse and spoke
into it.

As soon as Jude left Durov's Corner, he ducked into a
nearby hotel lobby and read the message on Lana's wrapper.

Something's happened! Go to 128 Petrovsky Prospekt,
apartment 14B. *Immediately!*

CHAPTER TWENTY

JUDE STARED UP at the tall building with the faded and chipped green paint, looked around to make certain he wasn't followed, then entered 128 Petrovsky Prospekt.

It was one of those mass-produced apartment buildings thrown up in the 1960s when the Soviet Union was even more desperate for housing than now. The ill-fitting main door had to be wrenched open, and everywhere concrete and plaster seemed to be crumbling, leaving a fine chalky dust over floors and windows. The smell of cooked cabbage seemed to ooze from the walls like sweat. The sounds of crowded family life formed a pulsing compression: the crying of babies, the scolding of harried mothers, the shouting of playing children filled the air like traffic on a busy street.

Jude punched the button of an elevator and watched the door creak open and then close behind him. With the trepidation of a man having entered a groaning mine shaft, Jude rode the rumbling canister to the fourteenth floor.

After a cautious look up and down the deserted corridor, Jude moved to the door labeled 14B. He listened intently. Nothing. He knocked softly and waited. After about a minute, the door slowly swung open and Jude stepped inside. His eyes quickly swept the single room. It was empty. Jude turned around, knowing that whoever opened the door was behind him.

''Bang!'' said a voice, followed by a harsh laugh, and Jude saw a finger pointed at him with a thumb cocked like a pistol. ''You're slipping, Miller. You could be dead right now.''

Jude looked with astonishment at the burly figure and sneering face of Richard Danton. "When my own people send me to an address, I don't expect to be ambushed," he said.

"Sit down," Danton said, but there was no hospitality in his tone.

Jude remained standing. "What are you doing here?"

Danton poured a glass of vodka for himself from a bottle on a nearby table and motioned for Jude to help himself. Jude ignored the invitation. "What am I doing here?" Danton repeated Jude's question. "Maybe I've turned and gone over to the other side. Maybe there are some KGB agents in the bathroom waiting to grab you. It worries you, seeing me, doesn't it?" Danton leered at Jude, enjoying the power of his advantage.

Jude sighed impatiently. "Come on, asshole, tell me what this is all about. What do you want?"

Danton snarled. "Clean your mouth up when you talk to your betters, boy. I'm working for the State Department now. I'm a diplomat. Assistant press attaché." He pronounced the last word with an exaggerated but clumsy French accent. "I have a nice car, shop at the best stores and—get this—I have diplomatic immunity. I don't have to look over my shoulder anymore or wonder about strange noises in the night. No cops, no KGB can bother me."

"What you mean is, you're a CIA plant inside the embassy. But that still doesn't tell me what you're doing here."

"As usual, it's my job to save your ass. I get tired of bailing you out, Miller."

"Cut the crap," Jude said calmly. "If you've got instructions for me, then let's get on with it."

"Okay," Danton said, glaring, "do you have Khrushchev?"

"Yes."

"Is he safe?"

"Yes."

"Where?"

"He's safe."

Danton ignored the rebuff; he was enjoying himself too much. "Well, wherever he is, keep him hidden for a while longer. At least until we can work a deal with the Russians."

Jude cocked his head as though he hadn't heard correctly. "A deal with the Russians?"

Danton leaned back in the chair, crossed his legs and grinned. He relished knowing something the man he hated did not. "Very big things are happening. That old man you're hiding just might get traded." He chuckled. "Like a football player. One washed-up premier for a high draft choice."

Jude's voice dripped with exasperation. "Just what in hell are you talking about?"

"The State Department is talking with the Russians. They're playing chess and your Khrushchev is a pawn." Danton acted as though he knew more than he actually did. "But all that concerns you is that when the deal is made, you and Lana get safe passage out of the country. The only problem is, these things take time. Meanwhile, the KGB is still trying to find the old bastard. If they do, they can tell us to stick the deal up our asses. That's why you've got to keep him hidden a while longer."

Jude sat down heavily. "There must be some mistake."

"No mistake."

"The deal was to get him out of the country. If that's changed, I want it confirmed—in writing."

Danton's face started to darken. "What do you think this is, some damned game? Being a drug-crazed hippie all those years must have softened your brain. This is classified as ears only. We're sure as hell not going to put anything in writing. You want confirmation? You just got it from me. Now, obey your orders."

"And if I don't?"

Danton's eyes widened. "If you don't? What the hell could you do, turn Khrushchev over to the KGB for spite? All I'm asking is that you keep him hidden, same as you've been doing." Danton's eyes narrowed. "I don't know what's going on in that screwy mind of yours, but if you defy your government, you'll be a dead man. We'll deny you ever existed. Personally, I'd be happy to see it."

Jude suddenly felt very weary. He lowered his head and tried to relax. Perhaps if he rested a moment this would go away. "Why, for God's sake, did you people bring me all the way over here, make me go through hell, and *then* betray that old man when you could have done that from the beginning?"

Danton became exasperated. "How the hell should I know? Miller, you're a real pain in the ass. Why don't you just do as you're told?"

Jude held up his hands as though warding off an evil spell. "Spare me your good-German drivel. I want to know why. I want some answers, or else."

Danton leaned forward and sneered. "Or else what?"

Jude's voice almost became pleading. "Richard, you know what'll happen, they'll kill him. He's an embarrassment to them alive."

"Who gives a rat's ass? What the hell does it matter what happens to an old Commie, an enemy of our country?"

Jude's emotions were on a roller coaster between anger, confusion and dismay. He glared at Danton. "I still want it from someone other than you."

"Fuck you. Do as you're told. That's an order."

"What does Armstead say about this?"

Danton laughed. "He doesn't even know about it yet. This came straight from State. We had to act fast." He said "we" as though he meant himself and the secretary of state. Danton reached into his pocket for a small folded piece of paper. "Here's the address of a safe house where you can hold him

Also, two phone numbers. One is Lana's. Connect with her and you two stay together with the old man. The other is for check-in. It's a secure line direct to a man in the embassy named Henry Geist. He'll give you instructions, whether to stay hidden or to bring Khrushchev in."

Jude glanced at the paper and stuffed it into his pocket. He knew he was losing—losing Khrushchev whom he had fought so hard to save and had been on the verge of doing so, and maybe losing his sanity. He closed his eyes, and the old image of the man dying beneath the stadium filled his mind once again. The crowd above roared and the smell of cyanide filled the air. He felt the soft flesh of his victim's throat, felt the weak thrashing of his dying struggle.... "I won't be your assassin again," he gasped in a hoarse voice.

Danton at first didn't know what he meant, then a smile crossed his face. "Oh, you mean when you killed that guy in the stadium?" He laughed. "Hell, that was a setup all the way. Armstead wanted to trump up a charge to put you on the shelf, make the Ruskies think you were kicked out so we could bring you back fresh for a job like this. What better way than a phony charge like that?"

Danton could have been a ghost the way Jude raised his head and stared at him. "You mean that man didn't have to die? That I killed him just so Armstead could play games with the KGB? Who *was* the man I killed? What had he done?"

Danton shrugged. "Who was he? Nobody. What had he done? He was handy."

Jude's anger was molten lava spilling over his indignation. "You bastards," he hissed. "You shit all over human decency and then you wipe your asses with patriotism. Killing is like fucking to you people, just another way to get your rocks off."

Danton rose with a threatening edge to his voice. "Now, just a minute, fella—"

Before Jude realized it, the automatic was in his hand
pointing straight at Danton's face. Danton backed up as if
were a snarling dog. Jude cocked the hammer and Danton'
eyes grew wider. Jude's finger tightened on the trigger in
cold rage. He wanted blood to atone for the piece of his sou
they had carved out of his life. But before he could pull th
trigger, another force worked with him and gradually calme
his fury, like the quieting of a nervous animal.

"Take it easy, Jude. I was just—"

"Shut up," Jude said. "Get your clothes off."

"What?"

"Get your clothes off."

"I'm not—"

Jude extended his gun hand and pushed it into Danton'
belly, making the front sight almost disappear in rubber
flesh. "Another killing won't matter, Richard. What's ar
other notch on the gun, right? Do as I say or I'll kill you."

Danton started stripping, as if his clothes were on fire. I
seconds, he stood in the middle of a pile of garments, wear
ing only boxer shorts.

"Those, too."

Danton's face was that of a contrite child trying to avoid
spanking, all sweetness and pleading. "Not these, too?"

The look on Jude's face and the nearness of the gun pro
vided the answer, and with a slowness born of humiliatior
Danton dropped the shorts and stood facing Jude completel
naked.

"Okay," Jude said, opening the door, "walk down th
corridor."

A look of horror crossed Danton's face, but one glance a
Jude told him there was no appeal. With enormous reluc
tance Danton shuffled down the corridor with Jude and th
gun at his back. The hallway was empty, but a door opene
and then slammed shut as a neighbor decided to let this scen
pass by.

They soon reached the end of the corridor and the only thing ahead was a heavy fire escape door, the kind that opened from the inside by a horizontal bar.

Danton turned back to Jude with a "What now?" look.

"Open it."

Danton pushed the bar and swung the steel door open as a blast of cold air rushed in.

"Outside."

Danton looked back in panic.

Jude gave a hard shove and Danton stumbled out onto the metal grating of the landing. "I could shoot you, but that would only prove I'd let you and Armstead turn me into your kind. This is better because the thing a bully fears most is ridicule." Jude looked at Danton and gave a loud, mocking laugh. "When the police come, be sure to tell them you're a diplomat." Jude took a deep breath and shouted at the top of his lungs, "Help! Help!"

The door slammed and Danton tried to pull it open. When it wouldn't budge he turned and looked around frantically. All he saw were faces staring at him from windows in the next building and a hundred children stopping their play in the yard to crane their necks upward to the strange sight fourteen floors above.

Danton made a fig leaf out of his hands to cover his penis, the tip of which had already started to turn blue in the cold and shrivel beneath his overhanging belly. From his contorted lips came a low whine of despair, like that of a dog denied a bone.

HERBERT ARMSTEAD KEPT CLIMBING over the wet rocks trying to get above the thick fog, but every time he almost made it, he slipped and fell back. Suddenly, bright lights came on and he blinked to see his worried secretary standing over him.

"Sir, sir, are you all right? You didn't answer the phone, and..."

"I—I'm perfectly fine, Miss Anderson, just taking a little nap. What is it?"

"The President is calling, sir. On the classified telephone." She unlocked a drawer and lifted out the small black telephone and quietly slipped out of the room.

Armstead took a moment to settle himself, then lifted the receiver. "Hello, Mr. President. Sorry to keep you waiting."

"Good morning, Herbert, how are you feeling?"

"Fine, sir, just fine."

"Good. Ah, Herbert, I wanted to talk to you about the Khrushchev thing."

"Excellent news there, Mr. President. We had some problems with the Jews who were supposed to be helping us, but our people got clear of that and our agent should be bringing Khrushchev out through Finland any day now."

"Well, I've got better news, Herbert." The President tried to sound cheerful, but the nervous edge in his voice made Armstead uneasy. "I don't think it'll be necessary to bring him out. What I mean to say is, we're talking with the Soviets about a trade—a very advantageous trade, I might add. If we play our cards right, we'll give them Khrushchev in return for their increasing wheat purchases and paying more per bushel. It looks set, all we need is a little more time to squeeze the last concessions out of them."

"But, Mr.—"

"And, I might add, Herbert, this wouldn't have been possible without a fine, fine effort from you and your excellent staff."

"But, Mr. President, we've practically got him out."

"Don't you see, Herbert? Your success drove them to the bargaining table. That's what the secretary of state and I were hoping for all along."

"All along, sir?"

"Beautiful, Herbert, beautiful."

"How about the man? What happens to Khrushchev?"

"Well, he *is* a Russian. I mean, what is our responsibility to a foreigner who is a traitor to his own people? Granted, the old fellow has a certain propaganda value, but not much more. The intelligence he would have to offer is more than a quarter-century old. Anyway, I believe we're more obligated to those hardworking American farmers who sweat for the free-enterprise system and who have a chance to make a decent profit out of this. After all, we have to keep our priorities straight."

Armstead closed his eyes and took a deep breath to control his anger. He reminded himself that this was the Chief Executive. He couldn't say what was in his mind, that the polls showed the President in a neck-and-neck reelection campaign, and that the grain-exporting farm states would probably make the difference. The swine was willing to trade the greatest counterintelligence coup of the century, the capstone of Armstead's career, for political expedience. Despite his caution, Armstead couldn't resist saying, "And this is an election year and the party has problems in the farm belt."

The President's voice took on a hard edge. "Politics has nothing to do with this. I'm thinking only of what's best for the country. I'll ignore that comment because I know you've been working hard. Too hard. In fact, I think we should have a talk about that sometime soon. In the meantime, State has started the wheels in motion in Moscow."

"State, Sir? You mean they're giving orders to *my* people?"

"Only to expedite things. We needed to make sure Khrushchev was kept hidden until the last *t* was crossed and the last *i* dotted." He gave a nervous laugh. "It'd be pretty tough to trade Khrushchev if they captured him, right?" The President paused awkwardly. "Well, Herbert, take care of yourself, and let's have that little chat soon. Goodbye."

Armstead sat looking at the dead receiver as if it were a snake ready to strike.

He felt the earth move and the skies collapse. The beliefs he had lived by had turned into a hollow creed mocked by hypocrites. He had served in the army of the just, was a defender of the faith, and now his defenses had crumbled, like a tall tower before the wind.

Armstead walked over to the paneled wall covered with framed photographs. He studied the pictures, glossy black-and-whites of smiling, posturing men. He saw himself shaking hands with men in out-of-date dress, smiling broadly to celebrate events dimly recalled. They were presidents from the past, lawmakers long dead and colleagues now remembered only by him. This was the visual record of his career—the chronicles of his life preserving his place among the mighty of his day. But like all archives, they recorded only what the keeper wanted preserved. And for the first time, Armstead saw clearly what was not there: the duplicity, the cruel deceptions, the using and, yes, the murders. All the things he detested, but had done and had ordered others to do, now became framed pictures in his mind—not smiling, hand-shaking men in tuxedos, but contorted faces of the dead, the deceived and the betrayed.

Herbert Armstead had told himself for years that what made him different, what made it all okay, was his commitment to the idea that his country was right, and that patriotism excused in him what he would condemn in others.

He had accepted the fact of his approaching death, that it would be preceded by his soon sinking into the idiocy of an incurable disease that would render him nothing more than a forgetful child shuffling around an old folks' home. He had prayed for a little more time so he could complete this last mission to deliver Khrushchev, a man who would prove to mankind that Communism was nothing more than a deceitful lie whispered in a struggling world's ear. And now he had been told that even his last aspiration, the capstone of his career for which he had ordered a man assassinated, was only a pawn on the board of greed, to be exchanged by a President he had admired and obeyed for a few thousand farmers' votes.

Armstead felt betrayed, and his anger was stoked by the knowledge that the real betrayer was himself. He was a sick old man who had just learned that what he had lived for was not worth dying for.

The telephone rang and he went to his desk to answer it. "Yes, what the hell do you want?" he shouted, his anger seeking an available target.

The startled voice of his secretary trembled in the receiver. "Ex-excuse me, sir, but you have a meeting in five minutes."

"Cancel it. I don't want to be disturbed."

"Yes, sir." The hurt in his secretary's voice was the reproach of good intentions wronged.

"Ah, Miss Anderson . . ."

"Yes, sir?"

"I'm sorry for the way I spoke; it's been a bad day. Please forgive me. I didn't mean it." He paused, then added softly, his voice filled with resignation, "I never meant anything wrong."

"Thank you, sir," she said in a puzzled tone and hung up.

Armstead went to his desk and sat behind the ornate antique that had once served a Bourbon king. He ran his hands over the expensive, smooth surface. He looked again at the pictures and listened to the clock. He opened a drawer and took out a heavy .45 caliber automatic given to him personally by General Douglas MacArthur. It hadn't been shot in years, but he kept it well oiled and loaded; such a weapon should never be retired.

Herbert Farleigh Armstead closed his eyes and said, "Forgive me, God, but you are not who I thought you were."

He put the gun to his temple and pulled the trigger. The roar of the weapon rang through the soundproof office for a

few seconds and then gave way to silence. Armstead's blood
ran across the polished mahogany and spilled onto the thick
carpet. But otherwise, the room returned to normal: the faces
in the photographs still smiled and the clock still ticked.

KOLCHAK LOOKED UP IRRITABLY from the report he was
studying. "Yes, Kyril, what is it?"

"I need a minute of your time, Ivan."

Kolchak was taken aback. He had never before been ad-
dressed so informally by his assistant. His eyes narrowed.
There was something different about the man's attitude,
something that prickled the back of Kolchak's neck with
foreboding. This was not the hangdog Kyril of the past. The
Petrovich standing before him was a man who no longer
avoided his gaze but looked him squarely in the eye. "What
do you want?"

Petrovich held a thick brown official envelope, bouncing it
in the palm of his other hand like a favorite weapon. "This is
a special communiqué from the Central Committee regard-
ing the Khrushchev case. I think you'll find it very interesting."

Kolchak reached across the desk. "Well, give it to me."

Petrovich pulled the envelope back. "I think not. The
shock might give you a heart attack."

"What the hell are you talking about?"

"I'll tell you what's in it. It says the government is close to
making a deal with the United States for Khrushchev to be
turned over to us. In the meantime, they want us to redouble
our efforts to capture him."

Petrovich paused and Kolchak gave no response. He knew
from experience never to react to any report until he'd heard
the last line. "Go on," Kolchak said.

"We've tied two CIA agents operating in this country to
Khrushchev. If we can follow them, they'll eventually lead
us to him." He paused. "Their names are Jude Miller and
Lana Martin."

"I knew about Miller," Kolchak said, "but not about the second one. Why was that information kept from me? It's obviously a woman."

"Yes, you should know that," Petrovich said with a big grin.

Kolchak's temper flared. "Why are you acting so strange? I want to know what the hell is going on."

"Oh, you do? All right, then, you will." Petrovich wrote the name Lana Martin on a sheet of paper in large block letters and held it up for Kolchak to see. "This is a name in English. What does it remind you of in Russian?"

Petrovich waited as Kolchak studied the paper. Gradually, a look of horror spread over his face, which Petrovich noticed with glee.

"That's right, *dolboyob*. Svetlana Martinova. Your beloved Svetlana is an American spy. A damned good one, it appears. She tricked a horny KGB boss—you—into falling for her so she could steal information. Information that may have made it impossible for us to catch Khrushchev."

Kolchak was stunned. He looked at his assistant with unfocused horror. "How did you know?" There was no bluster to the question, it was as though the dazed man was reacting reflexively with professional curiosity.

"When I heard you took up with a new woman after your wife was committed, I had her checked out. The CIA did a clever job of inventing a cover for Lana Martin, but not good enough. The past few days, I also had her tailed. She passed a message to someone at Durov's Corner just yesterday. It was probably Jude Miller. We still have her under surveillance, and I—I, you understand—will let her lead our men right to Khrushchev."

The words floated past Kolchak's uncaring brain. Khrushchev no longer mattered. "Why have you done this to me?"

"Why?" Petrovich seemed amused by the question. "Because I hate your guts. You've treated me like shit for seven years, and now I'm even. I've finally got you."

Kolchak thought desperately. "Kyril, if you'll forget what you learned, I'll make it up to you. I'll—"

"Too late. I just came from Comrade Nesterov. I showed him everything I have. He was unhappy. He was *very* unhappy." He looked at his watch. "You can expect to be arrested right here in about five minutes." He chortled and shook his head in wonder. "You say you'd make it up to me. That's hilarious. What could you do for me when I'm going to have your job and you'll be in prison—or worse?"

Kolchak slammed his fist down on the desk, both in frustration and defiance. "I've been a damned good agent. The best."

Petrovich gave a small nod. "You've got a bulldog's teeth, and you've mastered the mechanics. A lot of men have looked over their shoulders wondering if you were there. But—"

Kolchak stared and waited.

Petrovich glanced down to make sure Kolchak's tape recorder was not on. "You're a pure believer." He waved his hand around the room, encompassing the furniture, but intending more. Petrovich referred to the whole system and the Communistic state. "You believed everything they told you, and you thought it made you invincible. You forgot the hunter can become the hunted. So, when you got that throbbing hard-on for the American spy, you got sucked right in." Petrovich smiled and shook his head. "Mr. Soviet Hero got trapped, and meek little Petrovich was the trapper."

Kolchak's face turned ashen. "Are you enjoying this?"

Petrovich nodded matter-of-factly. "Yes." He got up and headed toward the door. He put his hand on the doorknob and then as an afterthought turned to face Kolchak again. "You were the coldest bastard I've ever seen. Your career was God to you. You betrayed your wife and children like it was a

Sunday afternoon trip to the zoo, and then you let some slut of a spy lead you around by the dick like a little child's toy wagon. Stupid. Sort of funny, but sort of sad."

Petrovich started to open the door, but a glance backward made him freeze. Kolchak was pointing a black 9 mm at him. After an abrupt gesture from Kolchak, he stepped back from the door with quick, tense steps. "Don't make it worse for yourself," he warned in a shaky voice.

Kolchak gave a strained laugh. "Worse for myself? The worst thing for me is to sit here like a trussed-up chicken." He grabbed his coat and shoved the pistol into a pocket, but kept it pointing through the cloth at Petrovich. "Like all sniveling schemers, you underestimate a real man. We're going for a ride, and if you so much as frown on the way out, you and I will arrive in hell together."

With Kolchak walking closely at Petrovich's elbow, the two made their way through the outer office and down to the garage, where they drove off with Petrovich behind the wheel of an unmarked radio car. Kolchak sat in silence with the gun pointing unwaveringly at his captive. His mind was filled with the knowledge that his only chance at self-justification required the capture of Khrushchev and the deaths of two American agents—and of one Russian, the man beside him.

JUDE WALKED OUT of the apartment building unnoticed by the throng of children laughing and pointing upward at the naked man trapped high on the fire escape.

He telephoned Lana to pick him up, and while he waited, his brain swam in anguish—a man cuckolded by his own government. He kept asking himself the same soul-searing question: what can redeem a man who does wrong in the name of right?

"WHAT'S YOUR PROBLEM?" Lana asked as she watched Jud climb into the passenger seat of the black Zhiguli. "You loo like a man on a falling trapeze."

Jude sullenly gave her directions to the hospital, then asked "Do you know what they've got planned for Khrushchev?"

"You mean a swap? Yeah, pretty clever, huh?"

Jude swiveled to face her with a glare. "Does that amuse you? The man will be killed because of us."

She shrugged her shoulders. "I do my job and State doe theirs."

"Wonderful. Deceit in the name of democracy," he grum bled.

"Yes," she said, "and when necessary, lying, cheating, stealing and—"

"And fucking," he said sarcastically.

Lana blushed and her voice tightened. "That's right. And fucking."

"I'm sorry," he said quickly.

Lana furtively brushed away a tear. "Here's the hospital. Why can't we just leave him here for a while?"

"Because safety depends on movement. Especially since both sides seem to be his enemy," he said bitterly.

A NURSE WENT TO LOCATE the physician in charge, and in a few minutes he walked up to Jude and Lana, who were standing outside Khrushchev's room.

"How's he doing?" Jude asked after a perfunctory greeting.

"He seems fine, he's sleeping right now. He should be able to leave tomorrow."

"I've just been talking about him to a government official," Jude said. "We're all grateful for the care he's received here."

The doctor grinned. "Well, it's a pleasure to help any citizen, especially one involved in party work."

"Speaking of that, we have a slight problem. Could he be released right now? There's an important party meeting scheduled for this evening."

The doctor frowned for a moment to underscore the importance of his decision. "Well, if he took it easy, and..."

"*Spasibo*, Doctor." Jude wrung the man's hand and reached for the doorknob of Khrushchev's room.

Within minutes, Lana was holding open the front door while Jude pushed the grumbling ex-premier in a wheelchair down the ramp and onto the street. Jude thought of discarding the wheelchair, but found they could move much faster with the deadweight of the old man being pushed before them than if they waited for him to hobble like an enfeebled crab behind them.

Both were too busy maneuvering the chair to notice a blue Zaporozhets, about a block away with two hulking silhouettes in the front seat. When Lana pulled the car away from the curb, the blue car waited a moment, then fell in behind at an inconspicuous distance.

Lana settled into the middle lane and said, "By the way, can I have my gun back? It's an old friend."

Jude handed her the small automatic, and she said, "Okay, I'm dressed for work. Point the way. Where's the safe house?"

Jude was thinking hard and pretended not to hear. Taking refuge in the safe house provided by Danton would be like flies hiding in a spider's web. He and the old man would be at the mercy of whatever machinations the two governments could agree on—herring awaiting the net. He didn't know what to do, except he knew he didn't want that kind of vulnerability. Lana repeated the question.

Jude turned to face her and took a deep breath. "There is no safe house. Danton said they didn't have time to arrange one. We're on our own."

Lana gasped. "That's incredible. We've got to have someplace to go. We can't drive around indefinitely."

Jude was quiet for a moment, then asked, "What was that you said earlier? Something about . . . yeah, you said I looked like a man on a falling trapeze. I know where we can go."

"Where?"

"The circus. Even we aren't weird enough to be noticeable there."

CHAPTER TWENTY-ONE

THE MOSCOW CIRCUS is the Disneyland of Russia. Along with the Bolshoi, it is one of the few things in that grim, struggling society of which it can be said: No one does it better. Ringling Brothers on the Moskva.

Lana pulled into the parking area off Vernadskovo Prospekt and stopped near a sign that read Moskovskii Tsirk, Moscow Circus. The three bought their tickets and entered an entrancing world of dancing bears, leering clowns and awed children with wide eyes, who were eager to absorb a realm that validated their fantasies.

KOLCHAK KEPT THE GUN pointed steadily at Petrovich's midsection and pulled the microphone to his mouth while his captive gripped the steering wheel tightly and drove slowly down the crowded central Moscow streets. "Unit 174, this is Petrovich. Do you read me? Over."

"This is 174, we read you. Over."

"Report your position, please."

"We're five cars behind subject woman and two men in black Zhiguli. Just turned onto Vernadskovo Prospekt, headed south out of the city. Speed normal. Unit 32 has dropped back. We'll keep them—wait! They're pulling into the circus parking lot. Will drop back and observe. Over."

"Standing by for report," Kolchak said. "Out." He turned to Petrovich with a thin smile. "Good surveillance, Kyril. Too bad you can't enjoy it."

"What good is this going to do you?" Petrovich said pleadingly. "It's one thing to fall for a pretty American spy—

that's only incompetence; what you're doing now is treason. Give it up, man.''

"Is that *friendly* advice, Kyril? The only chance I have is to capture Khrushchev. Besides, I've got business with that bitch.'' His jaw worked in anger. "I want to see the look on her face when she sees me.''

"What about me?'' Petrovich tried to conceal his nervousness.

"You don't count,'' Kolchak said, turning away and leaving unsaid the rest of the thought: because you're going to be dead, you conniving weasel.

Radio static interrupted them, and Kolchak pushed the microphone button, disregarding code in his eagerness. "Petrovich here. What is it, what's happening?''

The man at the other end was caught off guard by the blunt question. "Uh, this is 174. Subjects have parked and are entering circus building, two men, one in a wheelchair, and one woman. Awaiting instructions. Over.''

"174, break off surveillance and return to base, we'll handle from here. Relay same instructions to unit 32. Out.''

The voice on the radio was troubled at the unusual order. "Uh, won't you need help? We are in position to provide backup.''

"Obey orders, damn you.''

"Yes, Comrade. Out.''

LANA AND JUDE SETTLED into their seats in the floor-level section that could accommodate Khrushchev's wheelchair.

"Where do we go when the show's over?'' Lana asked in a whisper.

"I'm thinking,'' Jude said.

While Khrushchev slumbered in his chair, Lana and Jude tried to become absorbed in the show, to relax their frayed nerves, which had become stretched like piano wire. They saw people around them being transported to childhood

again, laughing at the predictable silliness of clowns, holding
their breath while acrobats teased gravity on high trapezes to
the tempo of bouncy music, and staring at jungle animals pa-
rading across the ring with the docility of home-bound bureaucrats on the metro. But for Lana and Jude, try though
they might, there was to be no circus, no escape from reality.
They were still fugitives, and their tensions couldn't be
checked at the door.

Trying to submerge herself into the show, Lana reached
across Jude to point out an elephant grasping a girl in span-
gled tights in its trunk and holding her high in the air. Jude
followed her pointing finger and was acutely aware of her
warmth as she brushed against him, of the perfume in the soft
hair that tickled his cheek. She leaned back slowly, but with
a challenging look that said she was aware of what he had felt.

A troika galloped in a wide circle around the ring with two
men in billowing green silk shirts standing atop the backs of
the three horses, while a pretty blonde in revealing tights
balanced on their shoulders. A thousand onlookers gasped in
unison as the girl seemed to teeter. She quickly regained her
balance, and the audience laughed with relief when she con-
fidently waved to them beyond the lights. Jude and Lana remained stoically silent; they weren't in a mood to be
impressed by someone else's danger.

Lana turned to Jude to say something, but the words never
left her open mouth. Jude felt her stiffen and looked at her
questioningly. Her eyes were wide with fright and her stare
was rigid like a pointing dog's.

"What's wrong?" he asked urgently. "What the hell's
wrong?"

"That man—" she gestured with a movement of her chin
"—the one by the pillar, the third from the right. That's
Kolchak."

Jude desperately sought out the man she meant, and at the
moment he located him, Kolchak, in turn, spotted them.

Though he was a hundred yards distant, his eyes burrowed deep into Lana's, trying to transfer with a single look the deep hatred he felt, the fiery malevolence of a betrayer who has become the betrayed. He held her eyes as a snake holds its prey.

Lana shuddered. "Oh, God."

Jude grabbed Lana's hand and jerked her to her feet. In the next instant he grabbed the handles of the wheelchair and roughly pushed it down the aisle as its startled occupant mumbled in sleepy protest. With Lana glancing backward they ran down the aisle, forcing startled patrons to jump out of the way, and oblivious to the angry shouts that fell at their heels like spent stones. Ahead, Jude saw a concrete wall that offered only a left turn into a well-lighted lobby packed with a solid wall of people awaiting the next show. To the right was a dark passage from which came a musty barnyard smell. Hesitating only a moment, Jude wheeled the chair in that direction and they quickly disappeared into a tunnel. After fifty yards, they emerged into a broad, dimly lit area that looked like a staging area for Noah's ark. Lions, donkeys, monkeys, elephants, bears and less exotic horses and dogs created a babel of honks, whinnies, barks and screeches that blended into a strangely melodic mixture. Moving among the animals was an equally odd assortment of humankind: businesslike trainers; girls in frilly costumes; clowns in baggy pants and garish greasepaint, strangely stripped, offstage, of their humor; and tired workers, listlessly pitching hay or manure, seeing no glamour in their labor and ignoring everything but the slow-moving clock.

As Jude pushed Khrushchev into the center of the area, with Lana at his side, both casting frequent glances behind them, a uniformed security guard standing beside a hay pile frowned and, with thumbs hooked into his belt, advanced toward them.

Jude saw the approaching guard and took the initiative. "We're relatives of the manager," he said, moving toward the man. "He told us any security guard back here could help us look around."

The guard looked perplexed. "You're not supposed—"

Jude laughed. "We were told you were conscientious fellows, but also very helpful."

"Well..." It was near the end of his shift and the guard didn't feel like any hassles with bosses. "I guess it's okay to look around. Just stay clear of the animals."

Jude smiled his thanks and turned back to the others. With all the speed he thought permissible for sightseers, he moved Lana and Khrushchev away from the heavy traffic of the main area.

"Do you see him?" Lana asked, craning her neck toward the tunnel entrance. She shuddered. "He gives me the creeps."

"No, but he knows we're somewhere in the building. We've got to figure a way out before he has about a hundred men surrounding this place. You stay here with the old man and I'll look around."

Jude disappeared among the animal pens, leaving Lana and Khrushchev huddled in the shadows. Lana squinted against the poor light and looked around. They were secluded in a dark corner of the large barnlike enclosure, shielded by the backside of a shed. Twenty feet to the right, inside a corral of high iron fencing, were two wrinkled Indian elephants lazily lifting hay into their mouths in great clumps. Fifteen feet behind them was a huge trained brown bear, restrained by a dangling chain attached to a steel collar and playing with an empty water pail like a contented child. The chain was the only thing holding the animal, and Lana looked warily at the shiny links to determine the chain's length, but it disappeared into the shadows. Maybe it's just as well I don't know, she thought.

For the first time since entering the circus, Khrushche[v]
spoke. "We're trapped in this goddamned manure pile. Th[e]
KGB will squeeze us off like a sausage." He gave a dolef[ul]
laugh. "I was born a peasant's son next to a barnyard, but [I]
never thought I'd die in one. From premier of all the Russia[s]
to an invalid surrounded by elephant shit . . ."

Lana patted his shoulder. "Don't give up. We're not dea[d]
yet."

"Who's giving up? And who do you think you're patron[-]
izing, young woman? I didn't survive Stalin to go whining int[o]
an early grave."

She started to chuckle when a movement in the shadow[s]
caught her attention. She spoke softly at the noise. "Jude[?]
Jude?"

A man stepped forward into the hazy yellow light. Eve[n]
before his face became visible, Lana knew who it was. It wa[s]
the walk, the build, but even more, it was a sensed presenc[e]
of danger. Kolchak. She started to reach into her purse, bu[t]
his harsh voice commanded, "Remove your hand or I'll blow
it off."

Lana recoiled at the hating face of Ivan Kolchak and slowly
raised her hands.

"Where's your boyfriend, the other American?"

"I don't know."

"If he's smart, he ran out on you. If he comes back here . . ."
Kolchak hefted his pistol meaningfully.

A second man stood next to Kolchak, and was also obviously covered by the gun. "This is Kyril Petrovich." Kolchak gestured with the weapon. "He's my faithful assistant,"
he added sarcastically. "He was kind enough to tell me how
you betrayed me, *lubimets*."

Lana searched her mind for the right words, but quickly
realized there were none. He had believed her once, but never
again. He was a man who had trusted love begrudgingly, and
it had mocked him.

Just seeing Lana made the anger build in Kolchak like
team. "You thought you'd never have to face me again,
didn't you, *suka*, bitch?" Rage made his breath come in uneven rasps. "Now you'll know what kind of man you double-crossed. Give me the gun you've got hidden in there—
carefully."

Slowly, Lana reached into her purse, picked up her small
automatic by the butt with two fingers and handed it over.
Kolchak put his own gun under his arm and made certain hers
was cocked by a quick slide of the barrel. He pointed it at her
and Lana felt her muscles tense and the breath catch in her
throat.

With a sudden ninety-degree movement, Kolchak turned
and pointed the gun at Petrovich, whose face turned ashen at
the sight of the small barrel mouth. "Please, Ivan."

"So, it's still 'Ivan'?"

"I mean, Comrade Kolchak."

"How smart do you feel now, Kyril?"

"Comrade, I never—"

Kolchak snickered and shot Petrovich in the forehead, then
watched the man crumple to the ground. Stunned, Lana
looked first at the dead man lying in a heap, with blood trick-
ling out of the black hole in his forehead, and then her eyes
swept the area, hoping the pop of the small gun had been
heard by someone, anyone.

"That was a personal matter," Kolchak said, as though an
explanation were expected. "He was disloyal, too." Kolchak
threw her gun down beside the body with a clatter.

"You killed your own man?" Lana was stunned and confused.

"No, you did it. I'll arrange the scene very professionally.
He will be killed by your gun; you will be killed by mine."
He lifted the heavy 9 mm and pointed it at Khrushchev. "But
first, we'll see if ghosts can die twice."

With a stiff effort, Khrushchev pushed himself erect out of
the wheelchair. "If the security of the state is entrusted to
animals like you, then it truly is time to die. But I'll be
damned if I'll be looking up to a coward when it happens."

The scorn of a man he had once revered, who for years had
seemed to personify Communism, rattled Kolchak and reminded him of how confused his life had become in so short
a time. He lowered the gun slightly and glared at Lana.
"Look what you've done to me." Suddenly his face crumpled and the words he shouted at her were torn from his throat
like jagged glass. *"I loved you!"* His eyes pleaded the need to
understand something that was beyond him. But quickly, like
a modest nude draping herself, he returned the mask of hate
to his face. He did the only thing he felt sure of: he raised the
gun....

Lana closed her eyes and Khrushchev forced a sneer on his
lips. They awaited death.

RETURNING FROM FINDING an unguarded exit, Jude almost
blundered into Kolchak's gun sights. As he stood in the
shadows watching Kolchak prepare to kill Lana and
Khrushchev, with no gun of his own, Jude's knees turned
rubbery with helplessness. Frantically, he looked around and
grabbed a rusted old pitchfork leaning nearby. He hefted it
into an awkward javelin and prayed wordlessly.

The gun thundered and Lana flinched, braced for the pain,
but feeling none. She opened her eyes expecting to see
Khrushchev dead at her feet. Instead, she saw Kolchak pulling the tines of a pitchfork out of the forearm of his gun arm
and swearing furiously. Behind her, a terrible roar of agony
filled the air. She turned and saw the huge bear, standing a
full nine feet tall, pawing at his neck, where Kolchak's stray
bullet had struck him and from which blood was flowing and
matting the coarse fur. The beast strained at his heavy chain
leash, trying to reach the humans who had inflicted his agony.

ny. All the docility of his training vanished, replaced by the natural instincts of an indomitable killer. The chain stretched taut as a guy wire, but the flailing claws of the bear could come no closer than five feet from Kolchak. Lana grabbed Khrushchev by the arm and guided him away from the furious animal.

In the next instant, Jude leaped out and hit Kolchak with a body block that knocked both men to the ground and sent the gun flying into the elephant pen, where it would have taken a death wish to retrieve it from the stamping beasts. With labored grunts the two men wrestled, grappling for an advantage. Jude smelled something sweet and felt a softness beneath him. He became dimly aware that they were fighting on top of Petrovich's body and that the sickening sweet smell came from that man's blood directly beneath Jude's face. A few feet away, a small crowd of circus people had gathered in response to the gunshot and the bear's roars, and their shrieks and cries of confusion further infuriated the bear, making him redouble his efforts against the chain.

A woman in the crowd panicked and screamed, "The bear is breaking loose!" In an instant, the onlookers scattered wildly, leaving only the fighting men, Lana and Khrushchev and the still-chained bear. In the background, the elephants chimed in with their trumpeted annoyance.

Kolchak's training wasn't wasted. Despite the pain of the pitchfork wound and the shock of Jude's collision, he managed to lock his forearm around his enemy's windpipe as they struggled on the ground. Kolchak grimaced with the effort as he squeezed with all his power.

Jude tightened his neck muscles and grabbed at Kolchak's arm, but it was like a padlocked iron bar. He managed to croak a protest, but no air could enter his lungs and he felt dizziness start to blur his senses. He slammed his elbow back into Kolchak's midsection, but the man only grunted and increased the pressure. He kicked backward, but hit nothing.

Dimly, he heard a ferocious growling somewhere near him, but his attention was occupied with fighting off the visit of death. Jude's eyes saw red and he felt himself slipping near the point of helplessness. Frantically, he reached down behind himself and groped for Kolchak's genitals. Despite Kolchak's squirming, Jude kept feeling until he located a soft mass. He gripped with all his strength and twisted. Jude used all his strength to give one last vicious twist. Kolchak surrendered his choke hold with a cry of pain and grabbed his crotch protectively. In an instant, Jude wrenched free and both men scrambled to their feet. Kolchak saw the pitchfork lying near the bear and made a daring grab for it, just beyond the furious swipes of the bellowing animal. Holding it like a pike, he advanced toward Jude, who warily circled away from the sharp points. Kolchak jabbed just as Jude jumped aside. Grinning, Kolchak faked a thrust and moved to an angle that would force Jude toward either him or the bear. Casting fearful glances behind him at the bear, Jude kept feinting, trying to keep Kolchak off balance.

Both men were gasping for breath, but Kolchak managed to say, "You're going to die...then her." Then he made a wicked thrust that almost pinned Jude against the pipe fence of the elephant enclosure.

Lana, standing nearby, finally got a chance to dart after her small pistol lying next to Petrovich's body, but Kolchak saw her in his peripheral vision and, still holding Jude at bay, kicked her in the ribs as she reached for it. With a cry, she collapsed into a protective ball. The gun went skittering toward the bear.

As Kolchak missed with another thrust and swung the pitchfork back in an arc, the bear managed to reach out and hit the end of it, snapping it in two and tearing it from Kolchak's hands. Both men jumped back from the bear and faced each other weaponless. They circled cautiously, catching their breath and making certain the other man wasn't in position

o chance the split second necessary to reach the splintered
pitchfork. They looked for openings for either a kick or a ka-
ate thrust. Neither gave a thought to fist-punching, a far too
clumsy move to attempt on an experienced adversary.

Kolchak faked with his shoulder and connected with a
round kick to the outside of Jude's knee. Jude felt a flash of
pain and the knee began to collapse, but he fought for his
balance and moved closer to the bear, hoping Kolchak would
be too cautious to follow. But Kolchak sensed the kill and
rushed forward to end the struggle. He aimed the palm of his
hand in an upward sweep at Jude's nose, intending to drive
bone splinters into his brain. Jude jerked his head enough to
catch the heavy blow on the cheek, and like a stunned boxer,
clinched with his opponent.

They were face-to-face, Kolchak trying to use his greater
bulk, Jude his agility. Kolchak managed to get his forearm
under Jude's chin and slowly force it back. Inch by inch,
Jude's head edged backward over the elephant fence until he
could hear the bones creak in his neck. Without consciously
thinking it, he knew his neck was close to breaking. The pain
made a roar in his ears and the lights of his brain began to flick.
He fought against fear and agony to maintain a clear head.
Desperation, his training told him, would only make him flail
helplessly. As unconsciousness began to close its curtain, he
hooked his thumb into Kolchak's mouth and pulled the corner of the lip downward with all his strength. Kolchak, to get
away from the excruciating pain, twisted his head sideways
and eased up on his forearm pressure.

In an instant, Jude ducked away and slipped his foot behind Kolchak's legs. With an upward shove, he tripped Kolchak backward. Falling, Kolchak flailed his arms to regain
balance, but it was too late. He fell heavily onto his back with
a loud grunt. He had no chance to move before the bear, who
could now reach him, was on him. The animal, crazy with
pain, took Kolchak's head between his paws like a small

melon. The bear's red eyes blazed with fury, and with a dee
bellow and one swipe of his curved claws, he raked the fles
from Kolchak's face like a butcher's cleaver. The bear the
clamped his jaws over Kolchak's head and bit down. Th
crunch of skull and bones sounded like dry sticks bein
stepped on.

While the bear was diverted abusing Kolchak's body, Jud
slipped close and grabbed Lana's pistol. In the worst way h
wanted to rest and catch his breath, but he saw two uni
formed security men with guns drawn approaching throug
the regathering crowd. Jude aimed the gun over their head
and fired three times. The already agitated elephants roare
in fright and the crowd screamed with one voice and scat
tered, the poorly trained security men among the most nim
ble.

In the confusion, Jude helped Lana to her feet, and sai
urgently, "Anything broken?"

She tried to move and winced. "Just bruised ribs, I think
I can make it."

Jude guided the complaining Khrushchev to his wheel
chair. "I'll push him, you take the gun."

As Jude pushed Khrushchev down the aisle, the peopl
scattered in front of them at the sight of the pistol in the han
of Lana, who hobbled alongside. Near the parking lot exi
that Jude had found earlier, he saw an electrical control bo
with thick wires protruding from it. Finding a heavy board
Jude threw it across the wires, and with a flash of sparks, th
entire building became pitch-dark. Among a cacophony o
renewed screams from hundreds of people left milling with
frightened, roaring animals, Jude led his companions to th
car.

"I CAN'T BELIEVE Kolchak had no backup," Jude said as he
drove toward the center of Moscow. "There was no one outside the circus. Was he that bad at his job?"

"No, he was good at his job. I think it was something he had to do himself—a point of honor, or some jazz like that. Who knows the mind of Macho Man? Who cares?" Lana laughed, then caught her breath after a stab of pain from her ribs. "When I saw him walking toward me out of those shadows, I thought to myself: Self, you're in deep shit."

Jude gave her a quizzical look. "That whole business charged you up, didn't it?"

"Like good sex," she said with a giggle. "Anyway, the big question now is, where to next?" She touched her side and winced. "I don't feel up to another circus just yet."

Jude turned into a smaller street. "I've been thinking. There's only one place left—David's house."

Lana's mouth dropped. "You mean the Sicarii double-crosser?"

"I'm open to ideas, but we've got a persuader." Jude touched the automatic lying on the seat between them. "This tends to encourage cooperation." He abruptly pulled off to the side. "I'm going to check in," he said, and left the engine running as he walked over to a public telephone.

The phone rang only once before a cold voice answered. "Geist."

"Miller."

"Bring him in. The trade is all set."

Jude started to answer, but the words of obedience were like glue in his throat. Instead, he said, "What? I can't hear you. The connection's bad."

"I can hear you fine. I said, bring him in."

Jude raised his voice almost to a shout. "Can you speak louder?"

Geist sighed. "Very well, call me back when you get to another phone."

Jude walked back to the car and Lana asked, "Did you reach Geist? What'd he say?"

"Nothing. Bad connection. We'll try later."

THE HEAVY, PERSISTENT KNOCKING made David quicken his step to the door. When he opened it, he recoiled in surprise. Standing before him were Khrushchev and the two American agents, one of them pointing a pistol directly at his face. "C-come in," he stammered, then stood aside while they moved through the door.

"You don't seem too happy to see us," Lana said sarcastically.

"Only surprised," David answered quietly.

Jude quickly checked through the house while Lana made Khrushchev comfortable in an easy chair. Jude returned to the living room and lowered the pistol. "We won't be here long, but while we are, you'll do exactly as we say. Understand?"

"You won't have any trouble from me," David said quietly.

Jude looked at the young man closely and sensed a difference. He seemed quieter and ten years older. There was a self-assurance, as in a man who had wrestled a demon and won. "How's your father?" Jude asked.

"He's paralyzed and can't speak. They don't give him long."

Jude dropped his eyes. "Sorry. He was—is—a good man."

David took a deep breath to get past the moment. "You can put the gun away. You have nothing more to fear from me. On my father's memory, no more tricks."

Jude nodded. "I believe you."

Lana walked over and took the gun from Jude's hand. "So I'll keep the gun, because I don't."

Jude frowned at her, but turned back to David. "We won't stay long, but first, I want you and Lana to run some errands."

"Just tell me what you want."

Jude went to the window and peered past the edge of the curtains into the gloom of evening. "Do you have vodka? I could use a drink."

"There's a full bottle in the kitchen cabinet."

Jude turned back. "You two take the car and get some medicine and tape for her ribs. Then, Lana, you call Geist, find out where we stand. Take your time and drive a round-about way back. I don't think we were followed, but use caution anyway." He looked at Khrushchev, who had fallen asleep in a chair. "Everything will be fine here."

When the old man blinked his eyes open and looked around, he saw Jude sitting quietly alone in a corner of David's empty living room. "Don't you have anything better to do, *Amerikanski*, than sit and watch an ornery old bastard sleep?"

"I just don't like to drink alone," Jude said, rising to pour the vodka into two water glasses. He handed one to Khrushchev.

"Ah, I'd love some vodka, but the damned doctors said I couldn't."

"I talked to the doctor at the hospital and he said it was fine," Jude said, pushing the glass toward him.

"Really? Well, I can't disobey the doctor, can I?" Khrushchev took the glass and examined the clear liquid critically. He swung it around to salute Jude. "One may drink or abstain, in his grave he'll be lain... Bottoms up today, bottoms up tomorrow, and all that is left are tears and sorrow."

Khrushchev threw back his head and emptied the glass, grimacing from the jolt of the powerful liquor. Jude poured a refill. They touched glasses silently. This time, the old man sipped more slowly, but the glass was soon empty until Jude filled it for a third time.

"I've been thinking, *Amerikanski*. I don't think we're going to make it." He spoke with the unconcern of a man who had lived a very long time and grown accustomed to the nearness of death, like an unwelcome companion who won't go away.

"Where's your optimism? You Russians always sound so grim, like Dostoyevski wrote your lines."

"It's just a feeling I have. This old bull has run around the pasture long enough to smell a bad wind. If it's true, I can face death, but I can't stand the idea of losing to those bastards in the Kremlin who betrayed me and the revolution. Those pretty little bureaucrats wouldn't know Marx from Mickey Mouse."

"Mickey Mouse? What would the former head of the Communist Party know about Mickey Mouse?"

Khrushchev laughed conspiratorially. "Don't you think we Russians know about that mouse? When I visited Los Angeles—I think it was in '59—I wanted to go to Disneyland, but your government wouldn't allow it. They said the crowds would be a security risk." He sighed. "I never got to see Mickey Mouse."

Jude laughed. "Just another rich, capitalist mouse."

Khrushchev's smile turned to a scowl. "Enough nonsense. Get my overcoat."

Mystified, Jude picked up the heavy old black coat draped across a chair.

"Feel the inside lining, near the bottom."

Jude ran his hand along the lining until he felt a foreign object. More finger exploration told him it was a thick sheaf of papers folded double. He faced Khrushchev with a quizzical look.

Khrushchev took another drink, and said, "What you are touching is the real truth, the untold story. I wrote it in my own hand over the past few years. That document is my vengeance. It will prove once and for all to the Soviet people that they've been betrayed."

"How?"

The old man grinned. "In due time, *Amerikanski*, in due time. But I will tell you that if the pirates running the government knew that document existed, they'd close all the borders and search every inch of this country until they found it. That's how dangerous it is to them."

"What are you going to do with it?"

"Release it to the world," Khrushchev boomed. "It'll be my legacy. And if something happens to me, I want you to do it."

"My word on it."

"This is no small matter, *Amerikanski*. I'll be called a traitor, a madman and worse. Those I've told the truth about will moan and cry and try to blacken my name, but they've already attempted that, and I don't care about them, anyway. But I don't want the common people to remember me as a traitor. They've been denied the truth so long it may not be recognizable."

Jude weighed his words. "I think, like your son said at the funeral they held for you, some will love you and some will hate you."

"Well, at my age there's no point in worrying about what I can't control." Khrushchev waved his empty glass. "All I can control right now is the level of vodka in that bottle."

Jude poured Khrushchev another glass, but left his own untouched.

"You know, *Amerikanski*, I used to be able to drink a priest and any other two drunks under the table, but maybe I've slowed some. How're you doing?"

Jude raised his nearly full glass for inspection. "Fine."

Another glass turned Khrushchev's thoughts to slurred musings. "Once in a while, I think about what I would have done different. I wasn't perfect, you know. There are a few things I'd like to undo." He paused. "Boris Pasternak. I didn't like him. He was a patronizing smart ass, so I out-

lawed his writings.'' He shook his head. ''He shouldn't hav
made me mad.'' But a moment later, in almost a whisper, h
added, ''There was nothing wrong with *Dr. Zhivago*.''

He threw his arms out in drunken abandon. ''Oh, wel
what difference does it make now? *Chort!* I used to boil ove
like a plugged kettle. My temper and big mouth made trou
ble for me my whole life. I'd say to myself, 'Now, Nikita
you've got to learn to shut your mouth.' I even tried some
times to be a gentleman, but I guess all the gentlemen lef
Russia when we kicked out the upper classes. There was n
one left to tell us how a gentleman acts.''

''It comes naturally for some people.''

Khrushchev didn't hear Jude. His eyes were fluttering and
tongue thickening. ''Killed the czar, but we wanted more . .
Destroyed it all . . . went too far. . . .''

Jude emptied what little was left of the vodka into Khru
shchev's glass. The old man tipped the glass to his lips bu
most of it ran down his cheeks. The glass slipped out of hi
hand and Jude caught it and set it on the table. Khrushchev
sagged back against the chair and his voice became a ragged
snore.

Jude walked quietly to the door and made sure it wa
locked. He came back to the chair and took a pillow from the
couch and placed it over the old man's wrists so no bruises
would show. He took a plastic bag he found in the kitchen and
slipped it over Khrushchev's head, securing it around the
neck with a large rubber band.

Within seconds, the old man's breathing vacuumed the
plastic up against his nose and mouth like a plug sealing off
all oxygen. Khrushchev didn't wake up but he thrashed about
as his body fought instinctively for air. Jude firmly held his
arms pinned as easily as a child's. It was then just a matter o
waiting.

As a minute passed, Khrushchev's struggles weakened and
then abruptly surrendered to unconsciousness. His lips